the month of March in Millers Kill. A subtle sense of humor further enhances this poignant and provocative mystery."

—*Publishers Weekly* (starred review)

"This is the author's best story yet . . . presented with the flair and polish of the finest artisan. . . . The ending is enough to make the hardest heart melt."   —*Chicago Sun-Times*

PRAISE FOR *TO DARKNESS AND TO DEATH*

"Clare Fergusson and Russ Van Alstyne make a fresh and unusual detective partnership, and I always welcome Clare's impetuous but wise take on the world around her."   —Sara Paretsky, *New York Times* bestselling author of the V. I. Warshawski novels

"The friendship of these solid, down-to-earth characters moves closer to romance, and the intrigue continues to build, revealing a riveting, well-plotted criminal adventure."

—*RT Book Reviews* (starred review)

PRAISE FOR *ALL MORTAL FLESH*

"The best yet in an already amazing series."

—Lee Child, *New York Times* bestselling author

"Spencer-Fleming does it again! Taut prose, brilliant pacing, and two of the most interesting characters around make *All Mortal Flesh* all the mystery you could desire."

—Lisa Gardner, *New York Times* bestselling author

"[A] dizzying roller coaster of a ride, with one wholly unexpected plot twist after another following in rapid succession. And just when things seem sorted out at last, the author has one last surprise in store for the reader, one that raises all sorts of questions about where the series is headed."

—*The Denver Post*

ONE WAS
A SOLDIER

~

JULIA SPENCER-FLEMING

MINOTAUR BOOKS

A THOMAS DUNNE BOOK

NEW YORK

A THOMAS DUNNE BOOK FOR MINOTAUR BOOKS.
An imprint of St. Martin's Publishing Group.

www.thomasdunnebooks.com
www.minotaurbooks.com

The Library of Congress has cataloged the hardcover edition as follows:

Spencer-Fleming, Julia.
    One was a soldier : a Clare Fergusson/Russ van Alstyne novel / Julia
Spencer-Fleming. — 1st ed.
        p. cm.
    ISBN 978-0-312-33489-5 (alk. paper)
    1. Iraq War, 2003—Veterans—Fiction.   2. Veterans—Crimes against—
Fiction.   3. Fergusson, Clare (Fictitious character)—Fiction.   4. Van Alstyne, Russ
(Fictitious character)—Fiction.   5. Women clergy—Fiction.   6. Police chiefs—
Fiction.   7. Murder—Investigation—Fiction.   8. City and town life—New York
(State)—Adirondack Mountains–Fiction.   I. Title.
    PS3619.P467064   2011
    813'.6–dc22
ISBN 978-1-250-00387-4 (trade paperback)

                                                                        2010042002

First Minotaur Books Paperback Edition: April 2012

            10   9   8   7   6   5   4   3   2   1

To the woman left holding the flag:

"Mother whose heart hung humble as a button
On the bright splendid shroud of your son,
Do not weep.
War is kind."

—*Stephen Crane*

ACKNOWLEDGMENTS

Thanks to my husband, Ross Hugo-Vidal, and to my children, Victoria, Spencer, and Virginia Hugo-Vidal. Without their love, support, and willingness to eat a lot of spaghetti-and-canned-sauce dinners, I couldn't be a writer.

Thanks to everyone at St. Martin's Press/Minotaur Books, especially Pete Wolverton and Katie Gilligan. Their keen editorial insight and well-thought-out suggestions (and suggestions, and another round of suggestions!) shaped this book.

I would not be published by Minotaur if the legendary Ruth Cavin hadn't picked my maiden manuscript out of a pile of contest submissions. She was a teacher, a drinking partner, a creative lifeline, sometimes a bit of a noodge when I was running behind, and always a pleasure to work with. She died before this book came to print, but her influence lives on in my work, and in the work of every writer who was fortunate enough to call her "my editor."

I talked with a number of veterans and service members while writing this book. Particularly, CH (LTC) Linda Leibhart, USA Reserve, planted the seeds for this story during a long conversation in a bar in Bath, New York. Senior Chief Hayley (Zeller) Hutchin, USN, generously shared her many experiences of deployment and coming home. As ever, LTC Les Smith (Ret.) and Timothy LaMar, late of the 101st Air Mobile, inspired me. I know none of you likes to hear, "Thanks for your service," so I will simply say: Thank you.

I Sing a Song of the Saints of God

I sing a song of the saints of God,
Patient and brave and true,
Who toiled and fought and lived and died
For the Lord they loved and knew.
And one was a doctor, and one was a queen,
And one was a shepherdess on the green;
They were all of them saints of God, and I mean,
God helping, to be one too.

They loved their Lord so dear, so dear,
And his love made them strong;
And they followed the right for Jesus' sake
The whole of their good lives long.
And one was a soldier, and one was a priest,
And one was slain by a fierce wild beast;
And there's not any reason, no, not the least,
Why I shouldn't be one too.

They lived not only in ages past,
There are hundreds of thousands still.
The world is bright with the joyous saints
Who love to do Jesus' will.
You can meet them in school, or in planes, or at sea,
In church, or in trains, or in shops, or at tea;
For the saints of God are just folk like me,
And I mean to be one too.

-Lesbia Scott, 1929, *The Hymnal 1982*, Church Publishing Inc.

I BELIEVE IN . . . THE COMMUNION OF SAINTS . . .

—The Apostles' Creed, The Book of Common Prayer

Sarah Dowling's first thought, peering through the wire-reinforced glass of the community center's door, was that they were an odd group. Usually returned vets had a lot to talk about with one another, even if they were embarrassed to be seen in counseling. She would have thought that in a tiny town like Millers Kill—she couldn't help it, she still saw the place as a cross between a Thomas Kinkade painting and Bedford Falls—they'd be even easier together, but none of these soldiers was speaking to each other.

The two men unracking metal chairs could have been father and son; both middling height, in khakis and button-downs, both with regulation crew cuts—the fifty-something graying, the thirty-something dark brown. The younger man kept glancing sideways at the older as if looking for clues on how to behave. He didn't pay attention to the young woman opening the chairs in a ragged circle, watching him. She was maybe midtwenties but dressed like a teen, with a little muffin top squeezed between low-rider jeans and a mini-tee. Sarah would have to include her no-romantic-relationships spiel in tonight's session.

The other woman in the group was a decade or more older than the little cutie, wearing unrelieved black that almost hid her taut physique. As Sarah watched, she stirred spoon after spoon of sugar into coffee poured from the community hall's industrial-sized coffeemaker. The last participant—Sarah frowned. A young man, maybe still a teenager. His hair had grown out, indicating he'd been out of the service for several months, at least. Well, she could have guessed that even if he had still been wearing it shaved to the skin. They didn't let double amputees out of Walter Reed until at least four months after admission. His presence here worried her. If he was having post-amputation issues, he ought to be seeing a psychologist at the VA Hospital, not hanging around an LCT's group.

3

She checked her watch, then gathered up her stack of handouts. Time to get the road on the show. She opened the office door and strode into the meeting room, the soles of her shoes squeaking on the polished wooden floor. Beyond the closed door, she could hear the faint thump and holler of the basketball game going on in the gym. On the far wall, construction-paper letters spelling out HELLO SEPTEMBER were taped over bright cutouts of apples and school buses. A preschool met here mornings. She thought of the stiflingly tasteful tenth-story office she had left behind in Silver Spring. *Free at last, free at last.*

"Hello, everyone." She gestured toward the chairs. "Why don't we get started? If we have any latecomers, they can join us in progress." She smiled and took her own advice, selecting the twelve o'clock position in the circle. The woman in black pulled two chairs out of the way to make room for the teen in the wheelchair. The rest of the gang of five followed suit, scraping and clunking the cheap chairs until they were all roughly equidistant from one another, and twice as far from her.

"I'm Sarah Dowling," she began. "I'm a licensed clinical therapist. For those of you who aren't familiar with the term, that means I've been trained in psychology and in facilitating therapy, but I am not allowed to diagnose or to prescribe medications." She stood up and handed the first stack of papers to the graying man seated to her left. "Take one and pass it along." She resumed her seat. "I've just recently relocated here from the Washington, D.C., area, so this is my first group in New York State. However, I've been doing veterans' counseling and running the on-base family mental health program for the past four years at Fort Meade."

The older man nodded in approval. *Officer,* she thought.

"Just to make sure we're all on the same page, this is not a Veterans Affairs program, although it does receive funding from VA, as well as from New York State and the National Institute of Mental Health." She leaned forward. "Participating in our group will not affect your VA benefits or treatment, nor will it be in any official record." For those in the group who would be continuing on in the service, that was often critical. Seeking out therapy was still viewed in many quarters of the military as suspect. Talking about feelings was not a high priority for the average CO.

"I apologize for scheduling the first session on Labor Day, but the community center gave me this time slot, and I didn't want to lose it." She smiled at them. "I was afraid I'd be the only person here, so believe me when I say I'm glad to meet you all. Why don't we start by introducing ourselves, and saying a little something about our service." She looked encouragingly at the older man.

He looked around the circle, knitted up his brows as if he didn't understand the reasoning behind her request, then shrugged. "Sure. If you think it's helpful." He straightened in his seat. "I'm George Stillman. The Third. I'm a doctor and a lieutenant colonel in the Army National Guard. I was with a forward surgical team outside Mosul."

"When did you get back, George?"

He smiled a little. "Please. Call me Trip. I hear George and I look around for my father."

Sarah nodded.

"Oh. I got back from my second tour of duty about two months ago."

The kid in the wheelchair looked at him oddly. "Three months ago. You were here in June."

The doctor stared at the kid for a moment, then wrinkled his face into an apologetic smile. "Sorry. We had a death in the family this summer, and I swear it's thrown my whole sense of time out of kilter." He tapped his palm. "I'd better start carrying my PalmPilot around again. My wife calls it my portable brain."

Sarah smiled reassuringly at him before gesturing to the young man. "Would you introduce yourself?"

"Yes, ma'am." *Marine,* she thought, just as he said, "I'm Lance Corporal Willem Ellis, of the 5th Marine Division." He looked down at the prosthetics strapped to his knees. "Formerly of the 5th Marine Division." He glanced back up at her, then dropped his gaze. "I was only in-country a little over two months when this happened, so I can't say I saw much traumatizing action."

"How 'bout when your mother found out you'd enlisted?" Sarah was surprised by the black-clad woman's accent, a southern Virginia drawl that sounded more out of place up here in the North Country than her own clipped urban consonants.

Willem Ellis laughed at the woman's remark. "Yeah, I guess that counts as combat. Or at least battle royal."

"And you are . . . ?"

The woman slouched in her seat. "Clare Fergusson." There was a pause. Sarah made a go-on gesture. Clare Fergusson sighed. "Major in the Guard, 142nd Aviation Support. Stationed in Ramadi, Tikrit, and Kirkuk." She took a long drink from her coffee cup. Nothing more seemed forthcoming.

"Aviation support?" Sarah said.

"She flies helicopters," the brown-haired man said. Before Sarah could ask, he went on, "I'm Eric McCrea. I'm a sergeant. Also in the Guard."

"Did you serve with Major Fergusson?"

"No." His gaze slid away from her and came to rest on the doctor. His lip curled up in what might have been a sneer. "I'm an MP."

"What were you assigned to?" the young woman demanded. "Were you on base patrol? At the Green Zone?"

His lips thinned. "I was on prisoner detail. Camp Bucca."

Sarah kept herself from reacting, but the rest of the group stared. They had all seen the pictures.

"That figures." The young woman folded her arms over her generous chest.

"That has nothing to do with it." Eric McCrea's cheeks blotched with color. "You think you know what it was like—"

Sarah held up her hands. "Stop right there." She gave both McCrea and the girl a measured look. "Let's not go jumping in the deep end before we've finished getting our toes wet." She dropped her hand, opening it to the last person in the circle. "Why don't you introduce yourself."

The brunette braced her hands on her thighs. "My name's Mary McNabb, but everybody calls me Tally." She looked at Stillman. "Sorta like you, I guess. I was formerly a specialist, formerly in the United States Army."

"Where did you serve, Tally?"

"Camp Anaconda."

That got some whistles from the rest. "Mortaritaville," Fergusson said.

"Yeah, well." McNabb ran her hands through her short hair.

Stillman snapped his fingers. "Mary McNabb. Fractured left ankle. A car dropped on you?"

McNabb laughed. "I was helping my husband fix it up for resale. I'm impressed you remember."

Sarah put her hands up again. "Wait." She looked around the circle. "Do you all know each other?"

They looked at each other. They looked at her. "Yes," they all said. "It's a very small town." Clare Fergusson's voice was dry.

Sarah stopped herself before she could ask them to explain. She'd need a clearer picture of their interrelationships eventually, but right now she wanted to focus on opening the first door to whatever issues they might have. "We'll get into that later," she said. "I'd like to start by discussing your homecomings."

MONDAY, JUNE 6   Their dispatcher, Harlene, had managed to get a red, white, and blue WELCOME HOME, ERIC banner printed up and hung from the front of the Millers Kill Police Department. It billowed and snapped in the warm wind gusting up Main Street.

"We gonna have to do the same thing for Kevin, when he gets back?" Deputy Chief Lyle MacAuley squinted in the bright morning sunshine.

The youngest officer on the MKPD had been shipped off for temporary detached duty almost a year ago, first with the Capital Area Drug Enforcement Association in Albany, then with the Special Investigation Division of the Syracuse PD, which saw more major crimes in two weeks than Millers Kill might see in a year.

"Kevin Flynn's welcome home is going to be a bump up in pay grade, if I can ram it down the aldermen's throats." Chief of Police Russ Van Alstyne shook his head. "What we really need is another officer on the force. That way, we wouldn't be overscheduling everybody. I worry that we're putting Eric back on the streets too soon. A few days ago he was eating MREs and holding down a guard post in Umm Qasr."

Lyle raised an eyebrow. "I'm impressed. The only place I could name in Iraq is Baghdad, and don't ask me to find it on a map."

"I was in that neck of the woods, remember? First Gulf War." He rubbed the back of his neck. "God, doesn't that feel like an age ago."

"It was. I think Eric was finishing up high school. Kevin was probably still in diapers."

"Hunh." And Lieutenant Clare Fergusson had been twenty-three. "They probably already have our beds reserved up at the Infirmary."

"Speak for yourself. I plan to be shot to death by the enraged father of a pair of twenty-year-old twins."

Russ laughed. Lyle gave him a sideways look. "You hear from the reverend lately?"

Russ's laugh died away. "A phone call five days ago. The 142nd is still on target to ship home in three weeks." He tried to smile. "Of course, they were on target to leave last March, too. Until their tour got extended."

"She should'a gone into the chaplain's corps instead of air support. She'd have been home by now." Lyle hooked his thumbs in his duty belt. "A year and a half's a long time."

"Oh, yeah." The longest damn eighteen months of his life, and that included a tour in Vietnam, going cold turkey on cigarettes, and quitting booze. Sitting home night after night, watching the casualty counts mount on the news—hell, giving up drinking again would have been easier. Drinking *and* smoking.

"How's she sounding?"

"Like she always sounds. Chipper. Everything's fine. She's fine. The weather's fine." Russ glanced up at the banner, the granite, the clear blue sky. "You know what the temperature was in Basra that day? A hundred and five degrees. I saw it on CNN." He pinched the bridge of his nose. "I can't decide if she's so happy flying helicopters again she's forgotten there's a war on, or if she's babying me so I don't . . ." He looked at Lyle. "You know how many helos have crashed or been shot down in Iraq since the beginning of the year? Fifteen. You wanna know how many pilots have been killed?"

"No." Lyle held up a hand. "Stop it, or you're going to make yourself crazy. Crazier," he amended. "Eric's home safe and sound, and your lady'll get here, too."

Russ touched the spot where, beneath his uniform blouse and undershirt, Clare's silver cross rested against his chest. She had given it to him for safekeeping the day she left, and he hadn't taken it off yet. He might not believe in a god, but that didn't seem to stop him from putting his faith in superstition.

"Eric." Lyle's tone was deliberately workaday. "When I spoke with him, he was hot to get back into investigation, but if you think he needs more time, I can find some desk work to keep him busy."

"What, running down addresses for check bouncers and updating the evidence lists? The last thing I want is for him to think we don't need him anymore and head off for better-paying pastures. He's our best investigator, after you."

MacAuley touched one bristly gray eyebrow and smirked.

"Don't look so smug," Russ said. "Consider the competition."

"A diamond in an ashtray is still a diamond," Lyle said with immense dignity.

Which made Russ think of his recent purchase. He hadn't told Lyle about that. He hadn't told anybody, yet. What if she turned him down? A fifty-two-year-old widower with a bum hip wasn't any great prize. His phone rang. He fished it out of his pocket. "Van Alstyne here."

"His wife says he's on his way." Harlene, who had been at the MKPD longer than Russ and Lyle combined, didn't believe in deferring to rank. "Get in here or you'll spoil the surprise."

"We're coming." He shut his phone. "Harlene says it's time to get into the squad room and hide behind a desk."

"I think she does these surprise parties as an excuse to stuff us with sweets until we can't move."

Russ thwacked Lyle on his still-flat belly. "She's got a way to go with you, then, old-timer."

Lyle tugged his uniform blouse into place. "I gotta keep my boyish figure. Just in case I find the woman of my dreams hanging around a church or something."

◆ ◆ ◆

Eric thought he might never have had a better moment, standing in the squad room, getting roasted by his brother officers. Harlene was squeezing his arm like she was testing to see if he was done, and the big boxed assortment from the Kreemy Kakes diner was on the scarred table where the chief liked to sit, and the old paint was still flaking beneath the windows, and nothing was changed. Everything was the same.

"Good Lord," Harlene said. "How many chin-ups do they make you do in the army? You feel like you could pick me up, and let me tell you, there's not many men as could do that." She slapped her ample hips.

Eric wrapped his arms around her midsection and hoisted her a few inches off the floor. She whooped. "Now, don't tell Harold," he said, re-settling her solidly on her feet, "but I did it all for you." In fact, there just hadn't been anything to do on his off-hours except sleep and pump iron. He'd heard up in the Green Zone, they had round-the-clock computers, and movies, and clubs, but in Camp Bucca, the only diversions were once-a-week access to a staticky phone line and the occasional smuggled-in bottle of hajji juice—Iraqi moonshine that was rumored to be al Qaeda's secret weapon against the occupancy.

"Jesum, Eric." MacAuley hitched himself up against one of the desks. "We oughta put you in one of them beefcake calendars."

Eric laughed. "I'll have to ask my wife first."

"Might improve the recruitment rates down to the academy." Harlene fanned herself.

"Only if you're trying to get girls and gays." Paul Urquhart laced his hands across his expansive middle, as if a beer belly were the mark of a real man. The chief frowned.

"How do you know we don't already have someone gay on the force, Paul?" Hadley Knox picked through a Kreemy Kakes box. Despite her regulation uniform and cropped hair, she looked more like a model in a commercial than a real cop. "After all, we've already got a girl." She ripped a doughnut in half and popped one piece in her mouth. "Come to think of it, I don't recall ever hearing about you going out on a date."

Urquhart straightened, quivering with outrage. "I'm divorced! I've got kids!"

Noble Entwhistle squinted, concentrating. He wasn't the fastest runner off the block, but he had a prodigious memory for people and places. "Dr. Dvorak, the ME, was divorced. He's got grown kids."

"Yeah, and now he's living with a big bearded guy." Hadley leaned toward Urquhart, her brown eyes filled with sympathy. "We're your fellow officers, Paul. You don't have to hide who you are with us."

"That's enough," the chief said.

Hadley grinned and bit into the other half of her doughnut.

Eric was laughing into his fist. It was so familiar, so normal and un-complicated. "Man, I missed this place."

"I'm glad to hear it." The chief beckoned to him and stepped away to one of the tall windows. Eric followed him farther out of earshot of the others, who were continuing with jokes at Urquhart's expense. The chief looked at him, steady, not smiling. "How are you? Really?"

Eric spread his hands. "You're ex-army, chief. You know what it's like."

"Yeah," the chief agreed, "but I don't know if what's going on over there is like Desert Storm or Vietnam."

Eric thought of the wire. The prison barracks. "It's not like either of them. I think . . ." The heat, pounding air and dust and dogs flat beneath it. Patrolling dirty streets down to the scummy harbor. "It's its own thing. It's . . ." The eyes of men, hating on him so hard that if they had had anything—sticks, stones, bottles—he would be dead. He snapped to focus again. Looked at the chief.

"It wasn't any Caribbean cruise, but I'm okay." He glanced around at the squad room. "And I gotta tell you, being back here, with all of you guys, is—" He didn't know what to do, shake his head or nod. "It feels real good."

"Good." The chief slapped him lightly on his upper arm. "Look, if at any time you're feeling stressed out, or if you feel like you need to dial back a bit—"

Eric shook his head. "That's not going to happen."

"If it does," the chief emphasized, "I want you to come to me. You don't have to give me any details. You don't have to justify yourself. Just give me the word, and we'll lighten things up for you for as long as you need it."

"That's not going to happen," Eric said again. And it wasn't. Home was stressful. Trying to deal with a wife who'd been running everything her way for a year was stressful. Discovering his son had gone from being a sweet, goofy kid to a moody irritable teen while he was away was stressful. Getting back to chasing down bad guys? That was pure gravy.

You here to arrest somebody?" The man with the fistful of helium balloons next to Russ grinned.

"Huh?" Russ's focus had been on the hangar-sized doors at the end of the armory. He couldn't decide if staring at the damn things would make the 142nd Aviation Support Battalion appear sooner or not.

The man thumbed toward Russ's brown-and-khakis. "That's not the sort of uniform you expect to see here." He squinted at the MKPD shoulder badge. "Millers Kill, huh? I'm from Gloversville. We used to play you guys at b-ball. You rode us hard for the Class E championship in '69."

"I was on that team," Russ said. "Class of '70."

"Me, too!" The man laughed. "Hair down to my nipples and a big 'Peace Now' headband I never took off. Who'd'a guessed I'd wind up here waiting for my girl to get back from war?" He bounced his balloon bouquet in the air.

"Yeah. Same here. Well. Not the long hair bit." Russ clutched the green-paper-wrapped roses he'd gotten from Yarter's. They'd looked a lot better few hours ago. How had all those petals fallen off? "The waiting for my girl part."

A harried-looking woman elbowed her way through the crowd, one little kid on her hip and a six- or seven-year-old dragging along in her grip. "There you are," she said. "You would not believe how far we had to go to reach a bathroom." She handed the little one over to the balloon man. "Go to Grandpa, now."

"Grandpa! Grandpa!" The seven-year-old pirouetted and leaped. "I think I saw the buses!"

The balloon guy—the *grandpa*—nodded toward Russ. "Turns out I played basketball against this fella in high school. He's meeting his daughter, too."

His wife smiled at Russ, amused. "You'd better stop whacking those flowers against your leg or there won't be anything left for your girl."

He could feel the tips of his ears turning pink. "It's not—I'm—" He was saved by the rumble of the buses, bumping over the slow strip into the cavernous building, a sound immediately drowned out by the roar of the waiting crowd.

Russ didn't join in. He watched the buses maneuvering into place, watched the exhaust rising to the fluorescent lights above, felt the sound and the light rising in him, lifting him off his feet, until he wouldn't have been surprised to find himself floating through the air like one of those helium balloons.

The buses parked. The doors slid open. Guardsmen started shuffling down the steps, anonymous in urban camo. Was that her? No. Not that one, either.

He suddenly couldn't stand it, couldn't stand one more minute of not seeing her; after counting off the seasons, and then the months, and then the days, and the hours, he realized all the waiting had accumulated, and he was going to be crushed beneath it.

Clare, he mouthed without speaking. A stab of pain made him look at his palm. He had driven one of the roses' thorns through the paper and into his flesh.

The dancing girl had stilled and was looking at his hand. Then she looked up at him. She had hazel eyes and a pointed nose.

"It's really hard to wait," he said.

She nodded. "My mommy says count to ten, ten times. She's a helicopter pilot."

"So's my . . . friend."

The little girl reached into her pocket and pulled out a grubby tissue. She handed it to him. "Thanks," he said, wiping up the blood.

"Pumpkin, I think I see Mommy," her grandmother said. The girl whirled and danced away. That's what their daughter would look like, he realized. His and Clare's.

Then she stepped off the bus. He almost didn't recognize her. Beneath her black beret, her hair was short, bleached lighter than he had ever seen it, and her face, all points and angles, was deeply tanned. She was looking around, scanning the crowd, her eyes alight with hope and anxiety.

The band struck up a tune, combining with squeals from children and the howls of babies to create an echoing cacophony that guaranteed she wouldn't hear him call her name if he was standing five feet away instead of fifty. Instead, he willed her to find him. *Clare. Clare. Clare.*

She paused for a second, closing her eyes, breathing in as if she could taste the far-off Adirondack air above the fog of bus exhaust and machine oil and human sweat. Then she opened her eyes and met his over the heads of the crowd.

Her mouth formed a perfect O, then curved into a heartbreaking smile. She blinked hard and raised one hand, and then she was bumped from behind by the next man in line and stumbled forward.

He watched as she lined up with the rest of the brigade and came to attention. When the last guardsman was off the bus and in formation, the band wheezed to a stop. There was a shuffle of dignitaries and brass at the front, and then the families were welcomed, and a minister gave an invocation, and the CO read a letter from the governor, and the XO gave a speech about the brigade's accomplishments in Iraq, and Russ thwacked and thwacked and thwacked the roses against his leg, until he looked down to see his well-worn service boot decorated with crimson petals.

Come on already! Come on! What jackass had decided it was a good idea to separate family members from soldiers they hadn't seen for eighteen months? When he'd come home from Vietnam, he'd just stumbled off a Pan Am flight from Hawaii. Yeah, it wasn't a hero's welcome, but at least he got to hug his mom and his sister, not stand at parade rest in front of an officer who sounded like he was running for Congress.

Finally, *finally,* the official orders terminating the brigade's deployment were read, and the CO dismissed his command, his words drowned out at the end by a howl of glee from the waiting crowd as they surged forward, mothers and fathers and wives and children, arms outstretched, too eager to wait any longer.

Russ stayed where he was as civilians swept past him. She had seen him. She had marked him. He had no doubt she would find him. Sure enough, there she was, wrestling her way through the crowd, beret stowed in her epaulet, rucksack over her shoulder, the reverse image of the woman he had last seen walking away from him beneath a gray January sky eighteen months ago. Major Clare Fergusson. She kept her eyes on him the whole while, an undeveloped smile on her face. She halted in front of him. Dropped the rucksack to the concrete floor. Looked up at him.

"Promised you I'd come back." Her faint Virginia drawl sounded out of place against the North Country Yankee burrs and flat Finger Lakes twangs all around them.

She didn't leap into his arms. They had been circumspect for so long, always standing apart, controlling their eyes and hands like nuns in a medieval abbey. They had no easy familiarity with each other's body. The two weeks they had been lovers—a year and a half ago, before she shipped out—seemed like a fever dream to him now. The small velvet box he had stuffed in his pants pocket suddenly felt like a five-pound brick.

He thrust the roses toward her. Two more ragged petals fell to the concrete floor. The bouquet looked as if a goat had been chewing on it. She bit her lip, just barely keeping a smile from breaking out. "Why, thank you, Chief Van Alstyne." She took the flowers in both hands and buried her face in what remained of them. She had tiny lines etched along the outsides of her eyes that hadn't been there when she left.

"They don't have much of a scent." He shoved his hands in his pockets, brushed the velvet box, jerked them out again. "But wait till you get to St. Alban's. You missed the lilacs, but the roses are amazing. You can smell 'em halfway across the park."

She looked up at him over the fraying flowers, her smile changing to something wistful. "I can't wait."

He stepped toward her just as she bent to reshoulder her rucksack. She let go, opening her arms in time for him to nearly knock her over as he ducked to grab the duffel for her.

"Screw this." He kicked the canvas sack to one side and took her by the shoulders. "C'mere." She folded inside his embrace as if she had always been there, and he kept his arms hard around her, his cheek resting on her too light, too short hair. Letting the reality of her, the warmth and weight and solidity of her, sink into his bones.

"Holding on," she said against his chest.

"Not letting go."

"I want to go home." She tipped her face up. "Take me home."

He smiled. "Petersburg, Virginia?"

She shook her head. "No. Millers Kill, New York."

The parking lot was throwing off heat like a griddle in the late June sun. He tossed her rucksack into his truck bed and popped the doors. He thought for a second, then slipped the velvet box from his pants to the driver's seat pocket. He jumped in, ratcheting the AC to full as soon as the engine caught. "Sorry," he said as she climbed into the ovenlike cab. "I would've kept it on for you, but I didn't want to risk running out of gas. The army doesn't seem to have changed its hurry-up-and-wait policy since I was in."

She laughed. "Don't worry. It's been so long since I've been in an air-conditioned vehicle, I've forgotten what it's like." She unbuttoned her bulky uniform blouse and stripped it off, revealing a gray T-shirt that stretched across her breasts when she twisted to drop the heavy shirt and the roses onto the narrow backseat. His throat went hot and tight. He shifted into gear and rolled out of the lot.

"Do you—" He coughed to get his voice under control. "Do you want to stop for a bite to eat? I went by the rectory yesterday with the fixings for a couple meals, but I didn't know what you'd feel like doing. What you'd want to do."

She stretched her arms toward the vents, which had begun blasting cool air, and closed her eyes. "Oh, Lord, this feels good." She smiled, still shut-eyed. "Just to be sitting here in a truck without having to wear thirty pounds of Kevlar." She ran her hands flat-palmed down her T-shirt from her collarbone to her waist, a perfectly natural gesture that nearly caused him to swerve over the centerline.

He corrected with a jerk. Which he was starting to feel like. She had just gotten in from a combat zone, for chrissakes. She still had dust on her boots. She was enjoying the first real freedom she'd had in a year and a half, and all he could do was salivate over her. *She's not a piece of meat, asshole.*

He focused on getting up the ramp and into the flow of traffic on the Northway. The only good thing about the battalion's delay and the interminable ceremony was that it put them on the road after Albany's rush hour. In his rearview mirror, the Empire Plaza towers caught the setting sun, their marble and steel surfaces almost too bright to look at.

From the corner of his eye, he saw her turn toward him, tucking one leg beneath her. "You've gotten back from more deployments than I have."

"Probably." Definitely. He'd been in more than twenty years. Funny. He'd thought that would make him more sure of himself, welcoming her home.

"What were the first things you always wanted?"

"A shower." He didn't have to think about that one. "A home-cooked meal. A bottle of whisky. Sex." He felt the tips of his ears pink up.

He felt, rather than saw, her slow smile. "Well. That's what I want. A shower, Lord, yes. A home-cooked meal. A bottle of whisky. Sex."

He took a breath.

"And I can't wait to celebrate the Eucharist again at St. Alban's."

He laughed. "I can guarantee you that's one thing I never considered when coming home."

"Multifaceted, that's me." She touched the side of his face, curved around his ear, traced his jawbone. "What sort of fixins did you put in the fridge?"

He swallowed. "Uh. A rotisserie chicken and a bag of salad."

She slid her hand down until it rested on his thigh. "Doesn't sound very home-cooked to me." Her fingers kneaded his suddenly tense muscles.

"Quick," he said. "Quick prep."

"Good." He heard the snick as her seat belt unlatched. "I've waited eighteen months for you. I think I'm about out of patience." She flipped the console out of the way and slid toward him.

"Buckle up," he said automatically, and then she wrapped her arms around his chest and shoulders and her lips were on his neck, her tongue flickering along his jaw, her teeth worrying his ear.

He braced against the wheel, arms shaking, trying not to let his head drop back and his eyes close. "Clare," he got out. "Jesus, Clare . . ." Her hands were all over him, touching him, unbuttoning his uniform blouse, tugging his T-shirt out of his pants. "What are you doing, you crazy woman?"

She kissed the corner of his mouth. "If you can't recognize it, it's been too long."

He flew through the twin bridges, barely keeping the truck in its lane.

"I got it all set up for you at the rectory." His voice was a grating whisper. "I got candles."

"I hope they're in better shape than your flowers." She pried his belt buckle apart.

He gritted his teeth. "I was shooting for romantic."

"I don't need romance," she said. "You had me at ''Scuse my French.'"

She laughed against the back of his neck, and he laughed, and he said, "God, I love you," and her hand closed around him and he groaned, laughed and groaned and shook. "Stop."

She pulled his T-shirt away from his neck and bit into his shoulder. "Do you mean that?"

"God! No." He thumped the back of his head against the headrest. "I mean yes." He flapped a hand at her in a half-assed way. "I don't want to make love with you for the first time in a year and a half in my goddamn truck."

"I missed you," she said into his skin. "Oh, my love. I missed you so much." She stroked him, once, twice, three times. He made a strangled sound in the back of his throat. Exit 14 was coming up fast. He could pull off there. Where could they go? It wasn't dark enough to park behind— he lifted his eyes to the rear view mirror and saw the whirling red-and-whites behind him.

"Oh, shit," he said. "Clare, get off me." He glanced at the speedometer. Eighty miles an hour. He jerked his foot off the gas and signaled to pull over.

Clare looked back over the edge of the seats. "Uh-oh. Is that what I think it is?"

"Sit down and buckle up." One-handed, he attempted to zip back up and refasten his belt.

"Can I help you with that?"

"I think you've helped quite enough, don't you?"

Laughing, she swung back into her seat and put on her seat belt.

"Christ." He brought the truck to a standstill and turned off the ignition before stuffing his T-shirt back into his pants. "Let's hope it's not somebody I know."

In his side mirror, he saw the state trooper get out of his car. Russ placed his hands on the steering wheel in plain sight. Clare had hers over her mouth, trying—not very successfully—to stifle her laughter.

The trooper reached Russ's window and signaled him to roll it down. Russ complied. The trooper glanced into the cab, taking in Russ's radio and switch light, the lockbox and roses in the back, and Russ's crumpled uniform blouse, hanging loose over his T-shirt.

"License and registration, please."

Russ reached for his rear pocket. "I'm retrieving my billfold," he told the statie. "Clare, will you get my registration out of the glove box?" He waited until she had gotten the slip of paper, then passed both documents through the window.

The trooper studied them. "Sir," he said, "are you a peace officer?"

Russ sighed. "Yes, I am."

"In Millers Kill?"

"That's right."

"Can I see your identification, please?"

Russ flipped open his billfold and handed it to the guy. The trooper studied the badge and ID. Looked up at Russ. "*Chief* Van Alstyne?"

Russ pinched the bridge of his nose beneath his glasses.

"That's correct, Trooper—" he peered at the man's name tag— "Richards."

Richards handed the billfold, license, and registration back to him. "Mark Durkee's in my troop. He was one of yours, right? He speaks very highly of you."

Russ couldn't think of a good response to that.

"Do you know why I stopped you, sir?"

"I was driving fifteen miles over the posted limit with an unbelted passenger in the front seat."

"Actually, sir, when I first picked you up, you were going twenty-five miles over the speed limit. I've been following you for eight miles. You didn't notice me?"

"I was . . . distracted."

Trooper Richards looked at Clare, who was doing her best good-soldier imitation. "I see."

"She's just gotten back from Iraq," Russ said inanely.

"Welcome home, ma'am." The trooper eyed Russ. "I don't need to lecture you on the importance of safe driving, do I, sir?"

"No."

"Or the importance of making sure everyone in the vehicle is properly belted?"

Russ resisted the urge to check his pants to see if anything was still hanging open. "No."

"Then I trust the next time I make you at eighty miles per hour, you'll be responding to a call." He glanced at the radio mount. "You haven't been on the radio, have you?"

"No." Russ frowned. "Why?"

"Your dispatcher's looking for coverage. A bar fight at some place named the Dew Drop Inn. She's sent one unit out, but she wants another for backup."

"I'll get on it. Thanks for the tip."

The trooper touched his hat. "You have a good night then, sir." He glanced at Clare. "Ma'am."

"Thank you, Trooper Richards. I'll try to see that he does."

The trooper's stone face twitched. "*After* you get him home, please."

"Absolutely."

Russ powered up his window as Richards got back into his car. "God." He pinched the bridge of his nose again.

"What? You got out of a ticket. If I'd been driving it would've been two hundred dollars and a point off my license."

"I'd rather get a ticket, if it meant I wasn't going to become tomorrow's coffee break hot topic. Staties are gossip hounds. They make Geraldine Bain seem like a hermit under a vow of silence." The Millers Kill postmistress was better known for passing on the latest tidbits than she was for handing out the mail. He switched on his radio and unhooked the mic. "Dispatch, this is Van Alstyne, in own vehicle. I understand you've got some trouble?"

Harlene's voice came on immediately. "Chief? What are you doing on the air? I thought you were picking up Reverend Fergusson?"

"I've got her right here. What's up?"

"Brawling at the Dew Drop Inn. Hadley's on her way, but I thought she should have some backup."

"Good call." Knox had graduated from Police Basic a year and a half ago, and she had come a long way, but he didn't like the idea of a woman alone tackling the lowlifes that frequented the Dew Drop. "Who've you got?"

"Paul's tied down with a three-car accident out past Lucher's Corners. Tourists. Eric's in the hospital with a drunk driver."

"Lyle?"

"Off fishing somewheres. I left a message for Kevin. He was planning on getting back to town today. I asked him to call me if he can assist."

"He doesn't have to report for duty until tomorrow."

"Tonight, tomorrow, what's the difference?"

He sighed. "I'm on my way."

"No!" Harlene sounded scandalized.

He looked at Clare. She nodded.

"I'm on my way. ETA thirty minutes. Let Hadley know."

"What about Reverend Fergusson?"

He looked at Clare again.

"I guess I can be patient a little longer," she said.

He keyed the mic. "Reverend Fergusson," he said, and she smiled at him, as if there were a chance in hell she'd do as he asked, "will wait in the truck. Chief out."

◆ ◆ ◆

Love makes people do some pretty dumb-ass things, Officer Hadley Knox thought. In her case, it had convinced her a self-absorbed La-La Land user would make a good husband and father. She had paid big for her mistake; crawling back to her grandfather's hometown for refuge, taking this pain-in-the-ass job to support her kids.

In the case of the shaved-head army guy in front of her, it had made taking on a small-town thug and his posse seem like a good idea. He had paid for it with a split lip and battered face.

When she arrived at the bar, he'd been getting the worst of it from a group of the Dew Drop's finest: skinny-shanked guys with ropy muscles and nicotine-stained teeth. The big black guy in camo pants looked like he could have taken on two, maybe even three of them, but five tilted the odds way out of his favor.

Hadley had waded in, rapping elbows and knees with her extendable baton, giving it her best Russ Van Alstyne impression: hard voice, big presence, short commands. A pair of construction-worker types helped her take hold of Soldier Boy and drag him back into the jukebox corner; the locals retreated behind one of the pool tables.

Now, she noticed the soldier kept looking toward a trio of girls backed against the bar. Two of them had long acrylic nails and streaked hair scraped back in Tonya Harding ponytails, but the third was a blunt-fingered natural brunette with a Dutch Boy bob. Short. Practical. Like maybe it fit under a helmet. Tears had smeared the girl's makeup, but she looked more angry than upset. "Tally, get your ass over here," a good-looking guy in a Poison T-shirt and steel-capped boots yelled; in response, the girl flipped him the bird.

The soldier lurched forward. Hadley blocked his path. "Sir, you have got to stay here." The man wiped his bloody nose on the back of his hand and stared over her shoulder. "Sir? Are you listening to me?" Hadley slapped her baton into her palm for emphasis.

The man shrugged off the hands holding him. Hadley nodded to the two guys behind him, letting them know it was okay, even though she was worried it wasn't. The air in the Dew Drop sparked with the tension of a boxing ring between rounds. "What's your name, soldier?"

"Nichols," he said. "Chief Warrant Officer Quentan Nichols."

"What are you doing here, Chief Warrant Officer Nichols?"

Finally, he focused on her. "You ask that of everybody who visits this podunk town? Or just the black folks?"

She thumbed toward the pool table. In the light cast by the hanging lamp, she could see the good ol' boys scowling and glaring at the CWO. Poison T-shirt was at the center, speaking fast and low to the guy next to him. "I want to know why that man and his buddies were trying to take you apart."

"Maybe they're down on the army." His eyes darted back to the angry brunette. This guy was a worse liar than her eleven-year-old.

She pointed the baton toward the girl. "You know her?"

Nichols jerked his attention back to Hadley. "We were talking."

"Uh-huh." She slapped the baton into her palm one more time. "Stay here."

She crossed the scarred wooden floor toward the bar, her boots sticking with every second step. She was maybe five feet away from the girl, close enough to read the IN MEMORIAM tattoo circling her arm, when she heard the thud of footsteps and the shouts and she whirled to see the locals charging Nichols. *Shit!* Dumb, sophomore mistake. She should've shut those assholes down once and for all before talking with anybody else. Somebody bumped her from behind, sending her stumbling. She staggered upright, baton at the ready, but it hadn't been aimed at her. The brunette had joined the melee, punching and kicking at the white boys like Xena, Warrior Princess, while her girlfriends screamed and wailed.

Hadley breathed in deep and bellowed, "Break it up!" One of the construction workers, a fresh-faced blond with pierced ears and impressive muscles, came in on Nichols's side. *Oh, great.* Hadley advanced toward the nearest man, baton extended, and whacked him: back of the thigh, side of the arm. He staggered away, howling, but two more roughnecks came off their bar stools in defense of the home team, causing the construction worker's buddy to wade in, airlifting another guy, who went flying into the jukebox. *Shit! Property damage.* Hadley advanced again, whacking away with her baton, trying to weigh her blows—pain, not injury, because injury could mean lawsuits—aware that she wasn't going to be able to stop them unless she reached the ringleader, aware that getting into the middle of the fight would make her utterly vulnerable.

A crack, rifle-sharp, sliced through the meaty thuds and half-voiced curses, bringing every head up for a second, like a pack of coyotes spotting a much larger wolf. "Police!" a man bellowed from the door.

Now or never. Hadley thrust herself into the crowd, driving the butt end of her baton into stomachs. Men folded, retching, around her. She reached Poison T-shirt, grappling with Nichols, and swung the baton with all her might into the small of his back. He arched upward, screaming, and Nichols lunged toward him, knocking Hadley aside, and then there was a tall, lean man blocking the way; yellow letters on a black T-shirt, cropped red hair, and Officer Kevin Flynn was twisting Nichols's arm around like a pretzel, bringing the soldier to his knees.

"Straps?" he asked, speaking loudly to be heard, and she tugged the plastic restraints off her belt and tossed them to him.

Poison T-shirt was pawing at his back. "You broke something!" She captured one wrist with her cuffs and locked the other one in place. "Didja hear me? Jesus Christ, you broke my friggin' spine!"

She pushed his shoulder, nudging the back of his knee so he'd get the message. "We will provide transportation to the hospital if you've been injured." He collapsed into a sitting position. "Sir," she tacked on.

With two cops in the room and the instigators restrained on the floor, the air went out of the balloon fast. Poison's buddies limped back to the bar and the pool table, clutching their midsections and wiping blood off their mouths. The frosted-blond gal pals tried to drag the brunette away, but she shoved them off to kneel beside Nichols. "I'm sorry," she said, low, for his ears alone. "I'm so sorry, Quentan."

"Goddamn it, Tally!" Poison T-shirt made to rise from the floor. "You were supposed to have got rid of him!"

Hadley pushed his shoulder down, harder this time. "Stay seated. You get up again before I tell you to and I'll cuff your ankles as well."

He sank back down, glaring at the brunette across the floor.

Hadley gestured to Flynn to step away, out of earshot, trying to figure out what was an appropriate way to welcome a fellow officer back after a year. A fellow officer she had dumped after a very against-the-regs one-night stand.

The earringed construction worker came up to them, grinning and wiping his hair out of his eyes. "Hey, Kev! Haven't seen you in dogs' years, man. Where you been?"

"Hey, Carter." Flynn bumped fists with the guy. "I was away on detached duty. Albany, and then Syracuse." He sounded older to Hadley. More assured. Or maybe she had forgotten his voice.

"Dude. They put you on a SWAT team or something? You look like you're ready to blow shit up."

Flynn did look like a tactical agent, with the black POLICE T-shirt and the many-pocketed pants laced inside a pair of paratrooper boots.

"Badass Officer Flynn," she said under her breath.

"Yeah. Well." Flynn's cheekbones went pink and he rubbed the back of his neck, popping a bicep and a blue Celtic armband. Hadley knew neither the muscle nor the tattoo had been there a year ago. He still looked like a reed next to Carter's bulk, but he had put on some much-needed weight while he was away. She became aware that she was staring at him.

"So." She bobbed her chin at him. "Not that I don't appreciate it, but what the hell are you doing here? I heard you weren't back on duty until tomorrow."

"Harlene called me, looking for backup for you." He glanced to where Poison was rocking back and forth on the floor. "Although it looks like you didn't really need it."

She snorted. "Right. John McClane with boobs, that's me."

Carter stared at her chest. "Who?"

"*Die Hard,*" she and Flynn said at the same time. He dropped his eyes to the floor and smiled before looking back up at Carter.

"You know this guy?" Flynn gestured toward the black soldier, who was sitting quietly, bent well forward to take the stress off his shoulders.

"Never saw him before in my life." Carter dragged his gaze away from Hadley's chest. "But I know that dipshit." He flicked a finger at Poison. "We worked together on the new resort before his ass got fired." Carter shook his head, sending his blond hair swinging. "What a tool. I figured if he was against somebody, I'm for him."

"What's his name?" Hadley asked.

"Wyler McNabb." Carter smiled winningly at her, displaying teeth as dazzling as the diamond studs in his earlobes. "What's yours?"

"Not Available." She turned toward Flynn. "Will you find out what McNabb's story is? I want to talk to her." The brunette was hunkered down next to Nichols, arguing with him, from the tone and her body language, though Hadley couldn't make out what they were saying.

Hadley slid her baton back in her duty belt and squatted next to the girl. "Ma'am, I need to talk with you." Hadley stood up. "Leave your friend for a minute, and let's go over there where we can have some privacy." She waited while the girl rose, then steered her toward the dark corner past the jukebox.

"Am I in trouble?" Up close, she was older than Hadley had guessed. Flynn's age, maybe; twenty-five or twenty-six.

"Let's try to figure out what happened before we start assigning blame. What's your name?"

"Tally. Tally McNabb." She rubbed her hand over her IN MEMORIAM tattoo. "It's really Mary, but nobody ever calls me that except my mom."

"Okay. Private McNabb?"

"Specialist. But I'm out of the army now. It's just plain Tally."

"Okay. Tally. Chief Warrant Officer Nichols there said he was talking to you before the fight started, but you two didn't just meet tonight, did you?"

Tally shook her head. "We served together."

"In Iraq?"

Tally nodded.

"Did Nichols come here looking for you?"

Tally nodded. She looked at her feet. She was wearing red and white high-tops. "He wanted to see me again."

"Uh-huh." Hadley glanced over to where Flynn had hauled McNabb off the floor and was questioning him. "Is that your brother, then?"

Tally sighed. "My husband."

Oh ho ho. "Wait here." Hadley crossed the floor, now decorated with blood spatters to go with the spilled beer, and gestured to Flynn. "Officer Flynn?"

He laid a hand on the guy's shoulder. "Sit down." McNabb did so, groaning theatrically. "I'll be right back. Don't move."

Hadley retreated a few steps to make sure the guy couldn't overhear them. Flynn closed in, towering over her. He was definitely taller than she had remembered. Either he had grown or she had been squashing him in her mind's eye. "What is it?" he said.

"What's his story?"

"He says he works construction for BWI and your girl over there's his wife. He claims the black guy came into the bar and started hassling her. When he told him to back off, the guy swung on him."

Hadley nodded. "I got a slightly different take. The one on the floor is Chief Warrant Officer Quentan Nichols. *Specialist* Tally McNabb says they served together in Iraq and that Nichols came here because he, quote, wanted to see her again."

"Ah-hah." Kevin sucked in his lower lip. "Yeah, that does put a different perspective on it. Whaddaya want to do?"

She felt a flush of pleasure. He might be eight years her junior, but he'd been on the force for five of those years, and whatever they'd had him doing in Syracuse and Albany the year he'd been gone, it was clearly more involved than manning the radar gun and making DARE presentations. She had assumed he'd be telling her what to do.

"I think we ought to book both of 'em. That'll give 'em time to cool off, and make sure the bar owner has an arrest report if he has to make an insurance claim."

Flynn nodded.

"I'm going to try to gauge how safe the wife feels. Ask her if she wants to file a restraining order."

"Against which one? The husband or the boyfriend?"

Hadley shrugged. "I dunno." She almost made a crack about one man being as bad as another, but that wasn't fair to Flynn. He was a good guy. Too damn good. She had no doubt that beneath the menacing black uniform and the pumped-up bod, he still had the heart of an Eagle Scout. An Eagle Scout who'd been a virgin until he was twenty-four. Until she had nailed him. *God.*

"Okay, look," she said, then the door opened. Another soldier, in urban camo and a black beret. This one was a woman, older, and she swung through the door with the ease and command of someone used to stepping in and taking charge.

"Military police?" Kevin said, and then, right on her heels, the chief walked in.

"No." Hadley started to smile. "It's her. She's back." She waved. "Reverend Clare!"

◆ ◆ ◆

Clare waltzed into the Dew Drop like she was going to tea with the bishop. No, scratch that. She wouldn't have been that enthusiastic about sitting down with her superior. Russ lengthened his stride, crunching across the gravel parking lot, and caught up with her inside the door.

He blinked, letting his eyes adjust to the dimness in the entryway. No fighting—at least not at the moment. Clusters of people at the pool table, the bar, half hidden in the darkness of the booths at the back.

Two perps restrained on the floor, bloodied but conscious. Hadley standing at the midpoint between 'em, talking to an officer in tacticals—Russ blinked again. It was Kevin. Twenty pounds heavier and looking like a real live grown-up. Huh. He was going to have to stop calling him "the Kid."

Clare, he saw, had scanned the scene and was sensibly holding back. Or at least she did until Hadley waved. "Reverend Clare!" Well, she did go to Clare's church. He could hardly blame her for being happy to see her pastor again.

The two women embraced, but Russ's attention was caught by the perp in the BDU pants. He had been leaning forward, taking the pressure off his cuffs, but now he sat upright, craning his neck to get a better look at Clare. His expression, beneath the blood from his nose and a cut on his temple, was wary.

Clare was hugging Kevin now, setting the kid's cheeks on fire. Russ crossed the floor. "Couldn't wait to get started, huh?" He shook Flynn's hand. "It's damn good to have you back again, Kevin." He slapped him on the shoulder, seeing, as he did so, the blue tattoo twining around his officer's arm.

Kevin's eyes followed his gaze. "It doesn't show in uniform, Chief. I made sure of that."

"Hmn." Russ turned toward Hadley. "Knox? Talk to me."

"Two guys, one gal." She indicated the sullen white guy on the floor. "Wyler McNabb, the husband. He was here with his wife, Specialist Tally McNabb." She pointed toward the black soldier. "Chief Warrant Officer Quentan Nichols, the boyfriend, who showed up apparently unexpected by either of the McNabbs."

"A warrant officer?" Clare looked up at Russ. "May I speak with him?"

"Do you recognize him?" At Knox's and Flynn's puzzled expressions, he added, "Most of the army's aviators are warrant officers."

"No . . ." Clare's expression was thoughtful.

"Then hang on a sec." He turned to Knox. "Where's the woman?"

She swiveled. "She was right here a minute ago."

"You didn't have her under restraint?"

"No. We figured—" She glanced at Flynn. "That is, I figured there were several individuals involved in the fight, but these two were the proximate cause. Since nobody else was hurt"—she laid her hand on her baton—"or hurt enough to complain to me or Officer Flynn, I thought we should book the two principals and leave it at that."

She still had a tendency to give information like she was answering a quiz at the police academy, but he had to admit, she was always thorough.

"Go see if she's in the ladies' room. Clare?" He tipped his head toward Nichols.

Clare walked over to the man and plopped cross-legged in front of him as if sitting on a dirty barroom floor were something she did every day. "Chief Nichols," she said, "I'm Clare Fergusson."

He took a long look at her insignia. "Major," he said. "I thought you were 31B for a minute there." *31B?* Russ couldn't help himself, he stepped forward. "Then I heard the officer call you Reverend, but you don't have any chaplain's cross on."

"That's my civilian job," she said. "I'm Guard. I'm sorry, I'm not familiar with 31B."

"I am." Russ reached down and hauled Nichols into a standing position. "It's the MOS for military police. Mr. Nichols isn't an aviator, are you, Mr. Nichols?"

The man shook his head. On his feet, he was several inches shorter than Russ, but he must have outweighed him by ten, twenty pounds of solid muscle. And Kevin had put him down?

"He's an MP," Russ said. Clare scrambled up off the floor.

Nichols eyed him. "You army?"

"I was. A long time ago." Russ held out his hand to Hadley. "Gimme your clip, Knox." She frowned but fished it out of her pouch. He turned back to Nichols. "Are you going to give me any more trouble if I cut you loose?"

"No, sir."

"You don't have to 'sir' me." Russ snipped the clip through the flexible restraints. "I was a CWO just like you." He glanced at Clare. "Her, you have to call ma'am, though." She made a face.

Nichols rubbed his wrists.

"You have any ID?"

Nichols reached for a pocket on the side of his BDUs. "I'm retrieving my billfold." Russ caught Clare's flashing look from the corner of his eye.

He took the leather wallet. Twenty bucks. A military police badge. A base ID for Fort Leonard Wood, in Missouri. An Illinois driver's license with a Chicago address. "You're a long way from home, Mr. Nichols." He handed the ID back. "I don't suppose you're working a case and just happened to forget to notify the local law enforcement?"

The flat, wary line of Nichols's mouth widened into an embarrassed grimace. "No."

"Didn't think so. Would you care to give your version of events?"

Nichols's gaze shifted away from Russ. "I've been trying to contact Tally—Specialist McNabb—ever since I got back stateside. She didn't answer my e-mails. Her phone wasn't working. I decided to take leave and come out here to talk to her in person."

"Did you know Specialist McNabb was married?"

Nichols kept his eyes straight ahead. "Yes, sir. Chief."

"And you didn't think that might be the reason she was ignoring you?"

"She . . . I was under the impression the marriage was broken, Chief."

Russ let his silence speak for him.

"It's not what it sounds like! She wasn't—" Nichols turned to Clare. "It's different over there."

"Yes." Clare nodded, a small, sober agreement. "It is."

Russ sighed. "So you came to the Dew Drop—how'd you find out she was here, anyway?"

"Her neighbor gave me a friend's name and address. The friend told me where I could find her."

"You flash your badge around to get that information?"

Nichols grimaced. Fresh blood welled out of the cut in his lip. "Yes." He looked at Russ. "I didn't set out to do it. It was the only way I could get the neighbor to open her door and talk to me." His mouth twisted. "I take it seeing a black man on your porch is no common occurrence here in the Great White North."

Russ opened his mouth. Closed it. "Mr. Nichols, what would you do if a civilian law enforcement officer came onto your post, used his police credentials to question a dependent, and then went to the enlisted men's club and got into a fight with somebody's significant other?"

To his credit, Nichols didn't hesitate. "Arrest him and charge him."

Russ nodded. "Wait here." He crossed toward the bar. Hadley met him halfway across the floor, coming from the opposite direction. She looked upset.

"She's not in the building anymore, Chief."

"Not anywhere?"

"I checked both restrooms. The second bartender says the door to the storage room out back wasn't locked, because he'd been hauling kegs in and out. Once you're in the storage room, you can get out through the delivery door."

Russ huffed in frustration. "Is she trying to get away from Nichols? Or from her husband?"

"Maybe from you," Hadley said. "She was hanging around the boyfriend, and she sure didn't seem afraid of her husband. He yelled something about her getting rid of Nichols, after he was in custody, but she ignored him. She only took off after you and Reverend Clare came in. Maybe she thought you were here to haul her away?"

He glanced back toward Nichols. Clare was still standing there. She was speaking to him in low tones that didn't carry. As Russ watched, she laid her hand on Nichols's arm.

He shifted his gaze toward Kevin and Wyler McNabb. The latter was still seated on the floor, still complaining loudly about his injuries. "What'd Kevin do to him?"

"*I* hit him with the baton just above his tailbone." Hadley indicated the spot on her own back. "I figured it would hurt enough to make him forget about fighting for a while, without causing any real damage." She frowned. "You don't think I did, do you? Really hurt him?"

He snorted. "No." He looked at Nichols again. The chief had settled himself back on the floor, hands open on his knees, the image of compliance. Clare was making a beeline for Russ and Hadley.

"He doesn't have any place to stay," she said without preamble. "I was thinking—"

"No."

She frowned. "You could at least hear me out."

"You're not putting him up at the rectory, Clare." He held up one hand to forestall whatever half-baked idea she was about to start in on. "Knox, get the address and phone number from the husband. Try to get some friends' or relatives' names, too."

She nodded and strode off toward the guy, one hand still resting on her baton. Clare immediately said, "We can at least help him find a local motel."

"He's going to be spending the night in the lockup."

Her mouth dropped open. "For defending himself in a bar fight? You can't do that to him."

He stared at her. "Of course I can."

She blew out an impatient breath. "You know what I mean. Out here, it's thirty days' community service or a couple hundred bucks, but when the army gets wind of it, it'll mean serious trouble."

She was right. What was a normal Friday night on the town for a twenty-year-old enlisted kid could be a career killer for a thirty-year-old CWO.

"I didn't say I was going to charge him, just that I'm going to book him." She spread her hands in a *what?* gesture.

"Look." He touched her sleeve lightly, drawing her in closer. "My primary concern right now is the woman they were fighting over. She's taken off, and I don't know if one, or both, of these guys is a threat to her. Until I can locate her and get some more information, I don't want to release either of 'em. So I'm going to send Knox out to track her down, and in the meantime, both men can cool their heels in the county jail."

"You're not going to book the husband? He started it."

"What are you, the judge and jury? I'm going to develop facts, Clare. Then I'll make a decision. That's how people who think things through do it."

She made a noise.

He smiled despite himself. "I gotta talk to the owner." He started toward the bar. She fell into step beside him. He sighed. "Now you've seen what all the fuss was about, why don't you go back to the truck and wait for me?"

"Are you kidding?" She looked around with lively interest. "I've never been in the Dew Drop Inn before."

"For a very good reason. This piss-hole is no place for a—a—"

"Officer? Lady? Priest?"

"A nice Episcopalian."

She laughed.

The owner, washing glasses behind the bar, looked up at Clare. Then at Russ. Back to Clare. Then to Russ. "Chief." His balding head dipped in a motion halfway between greeting and warning. "She with that black guy?"

"She's with me." Russ spread his hands on the bar. The odor of yeast and wood and wet soapy rag, the smell of his days as a drunk, rose up around him. For a second, he felt the deep, gut-pulling urge for a Jack Daniel's. He ignored it. "Want to tell me what you saw?"

"That black boy came in, ordered some fancy beer I ain't never heard of. Told him I got Miller's, Bud, and Matt's. He bought a Matt's and hung out at the bar until Wyler McNabb's wife came up for another Seven-and-Seven. Then they got to talking. Arguing."

"You hear anything that went on between 'em?"

The old guy was still eying Clare. Trying to figure her out. "Hell, no. After all these years with that damn jukebox playing, it's a wonder I can hear a customer order."

"Okay. Then what?"

"Wyler McNabb saw 'em. Came up, started getting in the boy's face, with his pack o' friends hanging off behind a ways. I could tell then and there it was gonna come to trouble, so I called your guys." He raised his eyebrows. "And this woman shows up." He shook his head. "Pretty goddamn embarrassing. Back in the day, I woulda run 'em all out with my baseball bat, but nowadays a man can't protect what's his for fear the lawyers'll come after him."

"Mmn. You want to press charges?"

"Naw. Wyler's a good customer. Likes to buy a whole round at a time for his buddies. If I find something broke, I'll just hit him up for the cost next time he's in."

"Okay." Russ hooked Clare's arm and drew her away. "I need to wrap things up, but—"

A pair of bikers walked up to them. One had a handkerchief where his hair used to be, and the other's gray beard was so long he had twined the end of it into braids. Screaming eagles and snapping flags covered the fronts of their leather vests. Russ tensed, but they ignored him. "Ma'am?" the bearded guy said. "That lady cop over there said you was just back from Iraq."

"That's right," Clare said warily. "I got home today."

Both men grinned. "In that case, ma'am, we'd be honored to buy you a drink."

She raised her eyebrows and looked bemused. "Why, thank you. I'd like that."

"I don't know—" Russ started, but Clare put her hand on his arm.

"I think I have time for a drink while you wrap things up, don't I, Chief Van Alstyne?" She smiled up at him in a particularly Southern way, and that was it—she was off toward the bar, looking fascinated as one of 'em rattled on about how a helicopter pilot had saved his life. As they walked away, Russ could see the regimental and service tags from Vietnam sewn on the backs of their vests. These gray and balding bikers were his contemporaries. His brothers in arms.

It didn't take him long to finish up. Kevin had driven his Aztek, so Russ had Knox transport both Nichols and McNabb in her unit—Nichols up front, as both a professional courtesy and a precaution against McNabb going after him again.

"I want all the info you have for the wife on Eric's desk," Russ told her. "He'll follow up tomorrow and get her side of the story." Knox nodded. "Tell the booking officer I want both these guys in a twenty-four-hour hold for D and D, and then he can release them."

Knox worried her lower lip. "What about McNabb's back? He's still complaining."

"Tell him we'll take him to the hospital, but first he has to have a full body cavity search." Kevin, who'd been hovering behind Knox, snorted laughter. "If he accepts on those terms, you'll know he's really hurting. If not, ignore him."

"Got it."

Russ glanced at his other junior officer. "Kevin, we'll see you at the morning briefing tomorrow." He pointed to the blue band twining around the kid's bicep. "You don't have any other surprises for me, do you? Piercings, earrings?"

Kevin grinned. "Nothing you'll see, Chief." Knox glanced toward him, the twist of her mouth suggesting a kind of unwilling curiosity.

Russ shook his head. "Get out of here, both of you." God, he was old. Old, old, old. Then he turned and saw Clare standing at the bar, laughing at something one of the bikers said, and as he watched she tilted her head back and swallowed the last of a tall glass of peat-brown liquor, her eyes closing, the long line of her throat exposed, and suddenly, in a rush of heat, he didn't feel old at all.

O ALMIGHTY GOD, WHO HAST
COMPASSED US ABOUT WITH
SO GREAT A CLOUD
OF WITNESSES . . .

—Collect for the Proper of a Saint, The Book of Common Prayer

MONDAY, SEPTEMBER 12   At their second meeting, Sarah saw that the preschoolers had taped up large autumn leaves to go with the apples and school buses. Each leaf had a name on it in bold block letters. KATELYNN. BRIANA. JOHN. SAMANTHA. TYLER.

She watched through the window as Clare Fergusson loaded up her coffee with sugar. The amount she'd drunk at the first meeting exceeded Sarah's daily limit, and they met at seven o'clock at night. That sugar . . . Sarah wondered if Fergusson was a closet drinker. A lot of alcoholics craved sugar carbohydrates to get them through until their next fix.

From her angle, she couldn't see Will Ellis's face as he watched Trip Stillman and Eric McCrea unload the folding chairs from the storage rack. He worried her. He had seemed too upbeat, too—for lack of a better phrase—too well adjusted, for his condition. He was playacting, she was sure of it, but she couldn't figure out why. He had already been medically discharged. It wasn't as if the marines were going to take him back if he had the right mental attitude.

She couldn't put her finger on Tally McNabb, either. Last week, the woman had limited her remarks about homecoming to her last duty station at Fort Drum. She hadn't touched at all on returning to Millers Kill, or her family, or transitioning to work. Well, that was going to be tonight's topic.

Sarah emerged from the office. "Hi, everyone." She took the twelve o'clock seat again and watched the group members drag and drop into position. They sat in exactly the same configuration as last week, except Tally and Trip Stillman switched places, so that she was on Sarah's left and he was on the right. "How did everyone's assignment go this past week?" She had asked them to share their feelings about homecoming with one other person in their lives.

There was a general silence. Sarah looked around at each of them. Twenty seconds passed. Forty. Fergusson fiddled with her ring, twisting it back and forth, before she reached down and picked her coffee cup off the floor. "I feel fortunate," she said. "My spiritual adviser was a marine in Korea. Fought at the Chosin Reservoir."

Sarah was about to point out that military history was all very good, but Fergusson hadn't said she had spoken about her experiences with—what the hell was a spiritual adviser? Sounded like somebody who read tea leaves. Then Will Ellis said, "Really? Do I know him?"

"He's Deacon Willard Aberforth. You've seen him during the bishop's visitation, but you probably don't remember."

"Chosin Reservoir," Will said, a light in his eyes. "Wow."

"I'll introduce you, if you like."

"I'm sorry," Sarah said. "I don't think we got into this last week. What is it you do?"

"I'm a priest," Fergusson said. "An Episcopal priest. I'm the rector of St. Alban's, here in town."

Sarah blinked. Well, that explained all the black. Over the years, she'd counseled lots of service members and dependents who were religious, of course, but she'd never had a cleric. Intellectually, she knew they must have the same sort of mental health problems as the rest of the population, but it surprised her that one would be self-aware enough to recognize she needed help—and humble enough to get it. All the preachers she had met in her girlhood and youth had been raging egoholics, far more concerned with exhortation than with introspection. Then again, the various storefront churches her parents dragged her to didn't feature any women in the pulpit. Maybe it was a gender thing.

"I'm glad I asked, because we're going to talk about work this session. How the switch from your military to civilian occupations is going. Where the bumps are, and some strategies for helping the people around you adjust to the new you."

"That sounds like a makeover article." Tally framed air quotes. "It's a new you for fall!"

Sarah pushed on. "Tally, what do you do, and how long have you done it?"

"I started as a bookkeeper at the new resort at the beginning of August. My husband works construction for them."

"My sister's at the resort. I didn't think they still had construction going on." Stillman sounded dubious.

"Naw. He's an employee of BWI Opperman, the holding company. They send him out on jobs all over the place."

Fergusson looked as if she wanted to ask a question, but she glanced over at Eric and shut her mouth.

"Trip, I know you're a doctor," Sarah said.

"Third-generation Dr. Stillman in Millers Kill." Stillman looked justifiably proud. "I have an orthopedic practice with two partners."

"Eric?"

"I'm a sergeant at the MKPD. I've been there nine years now. My duties split between investigation and regular patrol time. If we were a bigger department, I'd probably be a detective by now, but . . ." He shrugged.

Follow up on that, Sarah thought. "Will? I know you're not working at the moment, but do you have plans for after you complete your rehab?"

"I . . ." Will's sunny smile faded into a blank line. He sat without moving, like an automaton whose battery had run out. "I don't know," he finally said. "I've never been real academic, like my brothers. I liked working out. Fixing up cars. Playing my guitar." He shrugged. "Being a marine seemed like the best thing for me after I graduated."

"But most marines aren't career service," she said. McCrea frowned at her and looked pointedly at the boy's rolled-up pants legs, pinned beneath his knees. She ignored him. She wanted to push Will a little, to see if he had some sense of identity beyond that of lance corporal. Or amputee. "What did you want to do after you got out?"

There was another long pause. Then, "Coach." He was so quiet she almost didn't hear him.

"I beg your pardon?"

"Coach," he said, more loudly. "I was an Empire State champion in track and field when I was in school. I helped out with the middle school track and cross-country team, too. I liked working with kids." For a moment, he looked straight at her, as if defying her to point out the obvious. Then his gaze slid away. "I thought maybe I could get an ed degree at

Plattsburgh after my enlistment was up. Coach for middle school or high school."

No one spoke. Fergusson folded her hands and set them in her lap. Eric compressed his lips and crossed his arms over his chest. Finally, Trip Stillman leaned forward. "You know, there are double-amputee runners out there."

Sarah watched as the cheerful mask came back up. "Yeah," Will said, "but I've decided I want to be a tap dancer instead."

Everyone laughed, the relieved laughter of those who had gotten to the brink of the abyss but had avoided falling into the bottomless pit of complete and merciless honesty.

Sarah sighed. "Work," she said. "Let's talk about work."

MONDAY, JUNE 27   Trip Stillman sat across his desk from his old colleague, watching her fall apart.

"I'm just trying to get him the help he needs." Dr. Anne Vining-Ellis's voice was clogged with tears. "But it's so hard! Since he came home from Walter Reed it's been like pushing a rock uphill. On both sides! He qualifies for physical therapy, but Stratton Medical Center can only fit him in once a week. Chris hauls him down to Albany for his sessions, and the rest of the week, he just sits there. Then they suggested a therapist for his depression, but he refuses to go."

"Depression?"

"Lethargy, sleeping dysfunction, loss of appetite—you could use him as a teaching case for interns." Anne swiped at her eyes with a crumpled tissue and waved her hand. "Oh, he's trying to hide it from me, with his smiles and his jokes. I think the marines indoctrinated him with a good-little-soldier attitude." Her lip curled and cracked around the word "marines." "But he's lost interest in everything. He doesn't want to go anywhere, he doesn't want to do anything—"

"Have you prescribed anything?"

"No, of course not. Not that I haven't been tempted."

"And now he's reporting pain?"

"At the amputation site. Whenever he tries to walk on his prosthetics. I don't know if he's really having a problem or if it's an excuse to not do his exercises at home. I'll take him back down to D.C. and get him refitted if it's necessary, but what if it's not?" She blew her nose.

Trip slid the tissue box toward her. "Let me take a look at him."

"Oh, God. Thank you, Trip. I know you've done a couple of tours of duty. I'm hoping he'll listen to another soldier where he won't listen to me."

He pushed back from his desk. "I don't know if two ninety-day stints will qualify me as a fellow soldier to a marine, but I'll do what I can." He opened his office door, ushering Anne into the wide corridor that led to the waiting room. Trip had to admit, her tears and jitters shook him. Anne was the very definition of an emergency department jockey—cool under pressure, calm when everything around her fell apart, able to process rapid-fire information and turn it into a rational diagnosis and a measured treatment plan. He had consulted with her half a hundred times before she left the Washington County Hospital for Glens Falls. He had never seen her lose it. Never.

Will was slouching in his wheelchair as they entered the waiting room. He sat up immediately. He would have been a big kid before—all the Ellis boys took after their dad—and his five months post-trauma hadn't entirely wasted his natural youthful muscle, although he looked way too pale and had clearly lost weight.

"Hi, Will. I'm Dr. Stillman." They shook hands. "We've met before, haven't we? You were in Catrin's class." Trip's middle daughter was a sophomore at Smith. No wonder Anne was so overwrought. A nineteen-year-old ought to be in college, his worst problems hangovers and getting girls to go out with him.

Will nodded. His light brown hair was growing out of its baldy sour, giving him the appearance of a hedgehog. "Catrin and I were on the cross-country and track team together."

Behind Will, his mother made frantic no-no-no gestures. Talking about running was off-limits? That wasn't a good sign. "Your mom says you've been experiencing some difficulties with the prosthetics." He gestured to the hall. "Why don't you come on in and we'll take a look?"

Anne swooped behind Will and grabbed the handles of his chair just as the boy laid hold of the wheels. "I can do it, Mom." He sounded like a nice son trying not to be annoyed with his mother.

"Of course. Of course you can." Anne's voice was unnaturally perky. Trip led them down the hall, opening the door to his largest examining room. Will back-and-forthed a couple of times before getting the chair lined up with the entryway. He rolled through, Anne right behind him.

Trip made a hold-up gesture. "Will? Do you want your mother to wait while we talk?" Anne's frown almost made him miss the boy's expression. It clearly hadn't occurred to either of them that Will could see a doctor without his mother tagging along.

Will looked at Trip. Looked at his mother. "No, it's fine." He smiled weakly at Anne. "After all, she's the expert."

"Okay." Trip took his usual seat, the rolling stool tucked under the counter. He flopped open the fresh case file and clicked his pen. *Ask if P. wants alone w/o mom nearby!*

Anne hovered behind and to the side of the wheelchair.

"Why don't you tell me what's up?" Trip said.

"He's been complaining of pain—"

He held up one hand. "Let me hear it from him, Anne. You know a history isn't complete without the patient's own words."

She made a disparaging sound and clamped her lips together. Trip looked at Will. "Well?"

Will shrugged. "It's not a big deal. It hurts some when I practice standing."

His mother took a quick breath.

"I haven't been working on my mobility as much as I should," he added quickly.

"Why's that?"

Will shrugged. "The wheelchair's actually more convenient. With the crutches, my arms and hands are all tied up. It's like . . . it's like I've got four prosthetics instead of two. In the chair my upper body is completely free. And it's hard. Walking, I mean. Just a couple steps and I'm sweating." He spread his hands. "Why not use the wheels?"

Trip rolled toward him. "How about I take a look?" Will pulled his loose khakis up and unstrapped his prosthetics one at a time. Trip took them and examined their cups, running his fingers inside and pressing into the pads. They were very high quality work, suggesting made-to-measure. There shouldn't be any mechanical irritation involved. Will pulled off his socks—the close-fitting coverings that went over his stumps—and Trip cradled the amputation sites in his hands.

It was a classic traumatic transtibial amputation, neatly finished off and well healed. The left leg was a little rawer than the right. "This is the one that was an attempted tarsal resection?"

"Yes," Anne said. "They tried to save his entire tibia, but his vascular network was too compromised."

"My foot got blown off, and then they had to chop the rest of it off up to my knee," Will translated.

Trip rolled back to his bench and scribbled a note on the stump condition. "Are you experiencing pain at any other times?"

"Not in my . . . not there. I get phantom pain sometimes, especially at the end of the day, before I go to bed. Tingly, crampy sensations, like I'm getting a charley horse in my calves." Will's mouth screwed up. "In what used to be my calves. They told me I could expect that, once the real pain from the operations went away."

Trip nodded. "Phantom pain may be your brain's way of trying to create input from nerves that ought to be there, but aren't. Practicing your walking could help that, by giving your brain real nerve information to deal with." He pulled an X-ray request from a tray and jotted down the series he wanted. "I want to get a few X-rays while you're here, just to make sure you aren't developing bone spurs or stress fractures. Once we rule those out, I'd like to get you into physical therapy." He glanced up at Will. "Have you seen anyone since you were released from Walter Reed?"

Anne frowned. "I told you. He has a once-a-week appointment at the Stratton VA Medical Center."

Trip's hand involuntarily went to the scar half hidden by his hair. "Sorry. Since I got back, I've been more scatterbrained than usual. Will, I'd like you to do another two sessions each week at our PT facility. We have an excellent therapist who has a lot of experience with diabetes-related amputees. In the meantime, if you don't have a weight set at home, I suggest you get one." Trip smiled at Will. "I'm betting you were used to working out hard in the Corps. Let's get you back into that routine." He stood. "You can head over to the waiting room until the radiology tech calls you." He ripped the PT request off its pad and handed it to Will.

He walked them to the waiting room before heading over to radiology to drop off his request form. Parker Weyer, one of his partners, spotted him in the hall. "Trip. Can I have a quick consult with you?" It turned out to be a C4 fracture that wasn't responding to immobilization. Trip and Parker debated fusion versus screws and eventually decided on the former, given the age of the patient. On his way back to his office, their practice manager snagged him. One of the radiology techs was pregnant and being pulled off duty. Did the partners want to make up her absence by offering the other techs overtime? Or did they want to hire a sub for the length of her maternity leave? He took the printout of cost comparisons and promised to confer with Parker and Madeline.

His stomach rumbled like a passing freight train as he passed the reception desk. He glanced at his watch. One o'clock? Where the hell had the day gone? He opened his office door, intent on retrieving his lunch from his bottom drawer, and was startled beyond words to see Anne Vining-Ellis sitting in front of his desk.

"I just wanted to speak to you privately before you get the X-rays back," she said. "I wanted to know what you thought about counseling."

What the hell was she talking about? Why was she here, in the middle of the day, instead of at the emergency department of the Glens Falls Hospital?

"Well," he temporized, "what do you think?"

"I think he ought to be seeing someone, but he won't listen to me. There's this ridiculous prejudice against mental health treatment in the military." She looked up at him. "But you're in the army."

"The Guard," he corrected automatically. He knew that much, at least.

"Whatever. You understand the culture. Maybe he'll listen to you."

"Hmm." He crossed the carpeted floor, sat at his desk. He dropped a file he hadn't been aware he was carrying onto his blotter. His heart was pounding so hard he was amazed Anne couldn't hear it from across the desk. "I'm hardly an expert at psychology." He kept his voice steady.

Anne leaned forward. "I don't mean you should counsel him. You're going way above and beyond as it is."

He glanced at the papers atop the file. Some sort of spreadsheet. He slid it aside and flipped open the folder. There was a copy of a PT order for Willem Ellis. Beneath it, a copy of an X-ray request. Beneath that, exam notes in his own hand. *Bilateral TT amp,* he read. *Inadequate exercise. Depressed affect.*

"Let's see how he responds to physical therapy." He looked up at Anne. "That can have a dramatic effect on a patient's mood." He let his eyes drop to the notes again. *P. 19. Was X-C. Touchy issue—P? or mom?* "Especially for a young, athletic guy like your son."

The phone buzzed, thank God, thank God. He answered it. "It's Cindy," the voice on the other end said. "I've got the Ellis pictures for you, if you're ready."

"I'll be right there." He could have kissed her. Cindy. He remembered her. He could picture her brightly colored lab coat, the way she wore her hair screwed up on top of her head. Last Halloween, she baked skeleton-shaped cookies for the office.

He could remember her. Why couldn't he recall a single thing about the file in his hands? He stood up. "The X-rays are ready. Do you want to wait—" He had no idea whether Will Ellis was still around or not. He changed the question to "Where would you like to wait?"

"Why don't you meet us back in the exam room?"

Which one?

"That's fine." He let her precede him out the door and watched her walk up the hallway to the waiting room. He took the side way to radiology and ducked into the staff bathroom. Locked the door behind him. Leaned against it. Breathed in. Breathed out. He had been forgetting things since he got back from his tour of duty. His wife had said . . . she had said . . . he couldn't remember what she had said.

He lurched forward to face the mirror. He looked pale and damp in his own eyes. "Stress," he said to his reflection. "The symptoms of post-traumatic stress disorder include mood swings, sleep disorders, inability to concentrate, and short-term memory loss." Reciting the symptoms made him feel better. He was a doctor. If he could survive going without sleep for thirty hours at a pop during his residency, he could survive this.

His gaze shifted to the still-pink scar curling through his hair. It had been made by a chunk of cement, part of a makeshift clinic until it was blown to pieces by insurgents. The impact had rendered him profoundly unconscious, thank God. He had never had to witness what the explosions did to the kids and parents waiting to be seen by army doctors. He had done his time in his own Forward Response Station and been cleared for duty by his superior. These . . . memory lapses weren't related. He was suffering from—

Traumatic brain injury.

"Stress disorder," he said loudly.

There was a knock at the door. "Dr. Stillman?" One of the insurance clerks. "Are you okay?"

He closed his eyes. "Yeah." *Nobody can know about this.* "Be out in a sec." He turned on the faucet and flipped open the Ellis file. While the water ran and splashed, he read over the complete history. When he was done, he turned the faucet off and reflexively pulled three paper towels from the dispenser. He stared at them for a second before throwing them away, unused.

The corridor was empty when he emerged. He had to get the X-rays and meet the Ellises—meet them—his mind was blank for a bowel-dropping second. Then he pulled *examining room* out of the darkness. He flipped open the file and wrote it down. Notes. That would be the key.

He could deal with this. PTSD responded favorably to therapy and stress management techniques. He could prescribe himself Xanax for anxiety. He would—for a moment, his future yawned away beneath him, an endless, dark pool. He shuddered.

Parker swung around the corner, nearly bowling into him. "There you are." He thrust an X-ray folder into Trip's hands. "Cindy gave me these to give to you. Don't you have the Ellises waiting in D?"

"Huh? Oh. Yes."

"Meeting at four." Parker continued down the hallway. "Don't forget," he called over his shoulder.

Trip's hand, scrawling *D* and *MEET AT 4* on the folder, fell still. "I won't."

FRIDAY, JULY 1   Clare had thought slipping in the deliveries door of the soup kitchen and tying an apron on over her jeans and sleeveless shirt would make her entrance a little less noticeable. She was wrong. As soon as she crossed from the large food storage area into the steamy kitchen, one of her congregation spotted her. "Reverend Clare!" he yelled. "It's Reverend Clare!" A cheer went up. She resisted covering her cheeks, although she could feel them pinking up.

The volunteer crew clustered around, smiling, laughing, pelting her with questions.

"When did you get in?"

"Why didn't you tell us?"

"What are you doing here?"

"I thought we were going to have a reception!"

Clare raised her hands, laughing. "If y'all will let me get a word in edgewise—"

Velma Drassler, the head cook, wrapped her arms around Clare and squeezed her hard enough to crack ribs. "Oh, it's so good to have our rector back."

"I got in late last Friday and took the weekend off," Clare said when she had her breath back. "I've been meeting with Father Lawrence and with the vestry." That had been a surreal experience. They, too, had hugged her and thumped her back and escorted her to her old seat in the meeting room, and the whole time she'd been laughing and talking and answering questions, she'd been thinking *What is it? Why do they look so strange?* When Mrs. Marshall laid her hand on Clare's arm, frail bones and onionskin and blue veins, she realized: *They're old.* With the exception of Junior Warden Geoff Burns, every member of the vestry was over sixty. In a year and a half, Clare hadn't clapped eyes on another American older than—well, older than Russ.

Of course, she had seen Iraqis, men and women who had been sand-blasted by war and hardship and deprivation until they looked more preserved than alive. They weren't healthy and affluent, either, like her vestry; they had been poor and angry, poor and desperate, poor and screaming for help after—

"You met with the vestry . . . ?" Velma prompted.

Clare wrenched her head away from the narrowing bloodred place it was sliding toward. "Yes. Um. They had a very ambitious meet-and-greet planned for me, but I told them I just wanted to get back to work." She hadn't told them the idea of being hailed as the returning hero turned her stomach. "Instead, we agreed I'd drop in on as many of our groups and outreach programs as possible. Kind of like wading into the pool from the shallow end." She needed to start at the shallow end. Her body's clock was still set seven time zones away, and it was only thanks to the go and no-go pills she had brought back from Iraq that she opened her eyes in the morning and shut them at night. Plus, she had been having nightmares—

"Are you going to be at church on Sunday?"

Velma's question brought her back to the moment. "I'll be celebrating, yeah, but Father Lawrence will be preaching. Writing sermons is the only thing I didn't miss while I was gone."

They laughed again, and the rest of her dangerous thoughts retreated into the dark, turned away by her parishioners' good humor. She went to work in the dining room, taking the chairs off the tables, carting plastic glasses and coffee cups to the drink station; laying out cheap, disposable salt and pepper shakers at every table. She pushed open narrow casement windows and switched on every standing fan to move the sticky, over-heated air around.

At noon the doors, beneath their inscription I WAS HUNGRY, AND YOU GAVE ME FOOD, opened. One by two by four, the diners came in, some silent, some chatting with friends, some talking to companions only they could see and hear.

It had surprised her, when she'd first arrived in Millers Kill, that there could be any street people in such a small town, but Russ had shown her the derelict waterfront buildings where they sheltered. The untreated mentally ill, the hard-core alcoholic addicts, the people who would not or could not be reached.

Then there were the teens and early twenties, often passing through; sometimes a couple of Appalachian Trail hikers looking to save a buck, other times twitchy, defensive kids who looked as if they could never remember being cuddled on someone's lap.

The St. Alban's volunteers served lunch to men in mechanic's overalls and feed store caps, and to women headed to Fort Henry for the afternoon shift behind a cash register at the Kmart or the Stewart's. They served the slow-moving, dignified elderly, and occasionally the young, darting around their mothers or fathers.

Clare tried to speak with as many people as she could, even if it was as brief as a greeting and a "Lord, it sure is hot today, isn't it?" Pouring drinks, swiping spills off the tables, bringing diners seconds, she could feel her vocation reassembling around her, feel herself changing from a single recipient of God's grace into a conduit, from someone clutching with tight fingers to someone giving away with both hands. She had long thought that if Jesus were around today, he'd be feeding people at a soup kitchen instead of washing their feet.

There was a cry of distress and a flurry of motion at one of the tables farthest from the door. An older woman had knocked over her iced tea, and the two others sitting near her were trying to sop up the rapidly spreading puddle with their inadequate paper napkins. Clare strode through the dining hall, waving her large stained cloth like a martyr's relic. "Let me. I can get the whole thing with this monster."

One woman in polyester uniform pants and a tired expression suggesting she was between two shifts plunked back down into her seat as Clare attacked the spill. The younger woman stayed by the old lady's side, her hand on her shoulder. "Let me get you another drink," she said.

"Oh, thank you, Tally." Her dining companion's voice shook. "That would be nice."

Clare lifted her head. Tally? Tally McNabb had vanished last week from the Dew Drop Inn and hadn't been seen since. Russ had waited twenty-four hours, then released her husband and Warrant Officer Nichols. Nichols had left town, and when Tally failed to turn up, Russ had speculated she had gone with him. Maybe he was wrong. Maybe she had been living on the streets or bunking with friends until her husband cooled off.

How many Tallys could there be in Millers Kill?

Clare rolled the wet cloth and ice cubes into a ball and went after her. The young woman was reaching for a pebbled plastic glass. "Tally?" Clare said. "Specialist Tally McNabb?"

She spun around, staring, and Clare had an impression of brown eyes and fear and a tattoo on one arm, and then Tally hurled the iced tea straight at Clare and bolted for the door.

The plastic glass bounced off Clare's forehead.

"Ow!" Ice cubes flew into the air and chunked down onto her head and shoulders. Sweet tea drenched her shirt and runneled down her hair. She dashed liquid out of her eyes. "What the hell?" She took off after the fleeing woman, shouts of "She attacked Reverend Clare!" and "Call nine-one-one!" rising from the kitchen behind her.

Clare dodged tables, chairs, people leaping and lurching to get out of Tally's way. A grizzled man in an overcoat opened the door and staggered back as Tally rammed into him, caromed off his chest, and sprinted down the sidewalk.

Clare skidded to a stop, grabbing the man's shoulders to steady him. "You okay?" Alcohol fumes rose off him like heat shimmers off the street.

He nodded and smiled, cheerily and toothlessly. "Enjoy your lunch," Clare said and pounded after the younger woman, who now had almost a block's lead on her. Clare concentrated on closing it, lengthening her stride, shortening her arm swing, matching her breathing to the thwap-thwap-thwap of her sneakers hitting the pavement. She'd been running six, eight, ten miles a day these past months, endless, punishing loops around the base perimeter, kicking it up, kicking it and kicking it until she out-ran her mind and was nothing but a body, all sensation, no thought.

She drew closer and closer to Tally, her breath sawing in her ears, her feet thudding along with her heart. She was getting into that zone where all the noise in her head went away and she just felt: anger and excitement and the heat on her skin and the stretch and flex of her muscles. When Tally pivoted into an alley between the Goodwill and a dilapidated hobby shop, Clare didn't hesitate. She followed—right into the garbage can the girl had toppled in her path.

Clare hit the can, flipping over it, smashing shoulder-first onto the gritty asphalt. Her lungs emptied. Her eyes filled. She heard the pounding of footsteps behind her, then the thud and swish of someone leaping over her, then the footsteps receding as Tally ran back onto Mill Street. Clare swore. Pushed herself off the pavement, her shoulder burning and cramping. Wiped her forearm across her eyes to clear her tear-and-dust-clouded vision. Took a step and collapsed at the stab of pain in her right ankle. She swore again. Limped out of the alley as fast as one and a half legs could take her. Spotted Tally one block up, bent over, hands braced on her knees, her body bowed before the limits of her heart and lungs. When she saw Clare, she started upright and staggered toward the Riverside Park.

"Wait, goddammit!"

Tally ignored her. Clare cursed again then clamped her mouth shut as she realized she had brought more than a running habit back from Iraq. Limping up the sidewalk, she tried again. "I just want to talk with you!"

Even Tally's lurching half-jog was going to outstrip Clare's speed with a twisted ankle. "It's about Quentan Nichols!"

Tally paused, still not turning.

C'mon, Clare thought. *C'mon, c'mon, c'mon.*

A cruiser flew from the end of Burgoyne Street, crossed Mill, and kept right on going, over the curb, onto the sidewalk, and the door swung open and Eric McCrea was there, gun out, pointing it at Tally, bellowing, "Police! Get down on the ground!"

What the hell? Russ's officers didn't respond to assault by a plastic cup with deadly force. Tally seemed locked in place, swaying; whether from fear or exhaustion, Clare couldn't tell. She limped faster, trying to reach them, to tell McCrea that whatever he was told, there must be some mistake—when he closed on Tally and kicked across her shins, toppling her over.

"Stop!" Clare yelled, but he didn't seem to hear her. She watched, horrified, as he stomped his boot into the downed woman's back and yanked her arm up.

Tally screamed. Clare gritted her teeth and ran, feeling the tear and stab, almost light-headed with pain. "Sergeant McCrea," she shouted, putting everything she had learned about command into her voice. "Release that woman now!"

He dropped Tally's wrist. Stepped off her. Stared at Clare. "Reverend Clare." He sounded surprised. Defiant. She knelt on the sidewalk next to the moaning woman and helped her sit up.

"What the hell were you doing? If Russ—if Chief Van Alstyne had seen this . . ." She was suddenly in her kitchen on a warm night in May, watching Russ open and close his fist after he had broken his own rules and, enraged, punched a man in his custody. *If one of my officers had done that, I'd a had him on suspension by now.*

McCrea jerked his chin up. The look in his eyes reminded her of an unsocialized dog, afraid and dangerous. "We had a report you'd been assaulted at the soup kitchen. I get to the scene, this"—he waved his hand toward Tally, bent beneath Clare's arm, still gasping—"perp is fleeing, and you look like someone's knifed and rolled you? What was I supposed to think?"

"She threw a glass of iced tea on me. There was no need to—"

"I used appropriate force for someone I believed to be dangerous. If you want to report me to the chief, go ahead."

She shook her head, all her anger and adrenaline beaten down to a heartsick weariness. "I'm not looking to tattle on you, Sergeant McCrea."

Tally looked up at her, her face mottled with exertion and pain. "You're not an MP?"

Clare sighed. "No, Tally, I'm not an MP. I'm a priest." Her brain caught up with what the woman's statement implied. "You saw me last week, didn't you? At the Dew Drop." Tally nodded. "I'm serving in the Guard. That's why I was in uniform. And the reason I approached you in the soup kitchen is that the police want to make sure that you're not in danger from your husband or from Chief Nichols."

For the first time, McCrea looked at Tally as if she might be human. "That's her? McNabb's wife?"

"Yes." Clare tried to keep her voice even. "This is her."

"We've been trying to track her down since last Friday." He stepped back, well away from the two women. "Mrs. McNabb, I'd like you to come with me to the station to make a statement."

Tally got to her feet. She rubbed her shins. Tried her shoulder. "You're joking, right?"

Clare struggled to stand up. "They need your side of the story about the fight at the Dew Drop, and if you need a restraining order, they'll support your petition."

"Restraining order? Against who?"

"Against whoever's scared you enough so that you drop out of sight for a week."

"I wasn't scared. Exactly." Tally wiped a bare arm across her nose. "I just needed some time away so I could think. I couldn't deal with my husband just yet."

Clare reached out and touched the other woman, sending electric shocks of pain through her own shoulder. "Tally. Go with Sergeant Mc-Crea. I promise you, you'll be unharmed and treated fairly. You can tell Chief Van Alstyne Clare Fergusson has given you her word."

"And he's going to care . . . why?"

McCrea snorted.

Clare frowned at him. "Because the chief believes in doing the right thing."

In the end, the young woman went, sitting guarded and stiff on the other side of the cruiser from Clare, who was dropped off back at the soup kitchen. As Clare exited the police car, she saw she had left a smear of blood where her shoulder pressed against the seat. *Oh, God.*

She paused before shutting the door. "Sergeant McCrea . . ." She didn't know what to say that wouldn't sound like a threat to run to Russ if he didn't behave.

"Reverend."

Finally, she sighed. "I'll see you around." She shut the door. Limping into the soup kitchen, she was surrounded by concerned parishioners, all of whom backed away when they saw her bloody clothing and her dirt-and-tea-spattered hair. Velma Drassler looked her up and down, shaking her head. "We've got our rector back," she said, in a different tone than before.

The meal service was almost over. The other volunteers were washing and reshelving and sweeping and mopping, and Clare insisted, despite being urged to go home, on closing. She retrieved a bottle of blackberry brandy from the depths of a pantry shelf and self-medicated until she could ignore the pain in her shoulder and ankle. Then she limped to clean the bathroom.

Squirting and wiping the tile with as much energy as she could muster, trying not to look at herself in the mirror, she realized Eric McCrea had never once looked at her before she had screamed his name. She had been back far enough to have a clear view: as he drove onto the scene, as he exited the car, as he kicked and stomped Tally McNabb. *You look like someone's knifed and rolled you,* he had said. *What was I supposed to think?*

He hadn't seen her, though, hadn't seen her blood or bruises or limp, not until after he had—

She closed her eyes and bent over the sink. Ammonia and pine stung her nose. *What am I supposed to do now?* she thought. *What am I supposed to do now?*

◆ ◆ ◆

Russ caught up with her on her way home. Literally. She had locked up the soup kitchen and, with no one to witness her weakness, painfully climbed behind the wheel of her ten-year-old Jeep Cherokee. It was a high-mileage, oil-leaking beater, but she hadn't gotten any insurance money after she'd wrecked her last car, and this was what she could afford. Garaging it for a year and a half hadn't improved its performance any.

She was coasting down Depot Street, gritting her teeth every time she had to accelerate, when the cruiser swung in behind her. Its lights came on. She sighed, signaled, and rolled to the curb. Russ got out. She cranked the window down as he strode toward her. She looked up into his face, set in grim lines. "What seems to be the problem, Officer?"

"What the hell were you thinking?" His eyes were hot and hard. "You didn't know who that woman was. For all you knew, she could've had a gun. She could've been mentally ill. She could've—" He banged his fist against the edge of her door, making her jump in her seat. "God, Clare." He shook his head. "Lean forward."

"Why?"

"Eric said you scraped up your back."

"It's not that bad." She dropped her head against the edge of the steering wheel, too tired and achy to argue.

He sucked in a breath. "Oh, darlin'." He glanced at his unit. "Can you drive?"

"Of course I can drive. I was driving home when you stopped me.

Probably would have been there by now." Lord, she sounded like a five-year-old who'd missed her nap.

He gave her a look. "You were straddling the centerline, going ten miles below the speed limit."

"Oh."

"How's your ankle?"

"Eric gave you the whole report, did he?"

"Just tell me," he said patiently.

"It hurts," she admitted.

"Okay. I'm going off duty. I'm going to follow you back to the rectory. If it gets too hard to use the accelerator, pull over and I'll drive you the rest of the way home."

"Russ . . ."

"Clare . . ."

She threw in the towel. Agreed to his terms. Driving home, every square inch of her body either stinging, aching, or throbbing, she had a sudden image of Linda Van Alstyne. Pretty, petite, and picture-perfect. She was quite sure Russ's late wife had never in her life rolled through garbage. The thought made her feel even worse. Or it might have been the sprain. Pulling into the rectory drive, she stumbled out of the Jeep to discover that her ankle, swollen and purpling, now resembled an overripe eggplant.

"Stay there." Russ thunked his car door closed, crossed her drive in three steps, and scooped her up in his arms.

"I do not need to be carried into my own house."

He huffed. "Anybody ever tell you you're too damn independent for your own good?" He trudged up the steps to her kitchen door. "Unlocked?"

She still had her keys in her hand. She angled toward the door and unlatched it.

"I'm impressed." He lugged her into the kitchen, kicking the door closed behind him. "Didn't think you knew how to lock doors." He glanced at her ancient refrigerator, wheezing in the corner. "That ankle needs ice."

"I have a wrap in the freezer, but what I really want is a shower." Her hair was stiff with sweet tea, and her skin was layered in sweat and alley dirt.

Russ sniffed at her. "Good idea."

"Oh, my hero. You can just let me on down now."

Instead, he tightened his grip and backed through the kitchen's swinging doors into the living room.

"Russ, I mean it. You'll give yourself a hernia."

"You kidding? You're skin and bones. Didn't they feed you in Iraq?" He paused, panting, at the foot of her stairs, then carted her up to the second floor. He staggered into her bedroom and dropped her on the bed, collapsing beside her. He groaned.

"Was that your version of sweeping me off my feet?"

"Trying . . ." He sucked in air. ". . . romantic."

"Heart attacks aren't romantic." She curled into a sitting position, then got up on one foot, bracing herself against her bedside table.

"What do you think you're doing?"

"Going to the shower."

He rolled over. Climbed to his feet.

"You're not trying the Rhett Butler thing again."

"Just put your arm around my neck, will you? Ungrateful woman."

She followed orders and leaned against him as they crossed the hall landing. "This reminds me of when you broke your leg," she said. "Remember how you hung on to me to make it to your truck?"

"I promise you, that little episode remains fresh in my memory. I still have two pins in my ankle."

"Or the time I nearly froze my feet off up on Mount Tenant? You carried me into the rectory then, too."

He flipped down the lid and set her on the toilet. "My life's been filled with exciting incidents since I met you. I'm hoping our future together will be dull." He leaned down and looked into her eyes. "Very dull."

"I'll try to be more boring."

"Good." He turned on the shower to get the water running hot. "Don't slip on the tile and knock yourself unconscious while I'm downstairs."

"Were you always this bossy, or did I forget while I was deployed?"

"You haven't seen anything yet, darlin'."

She made a rude noise, but the truth was, she didn't feel up to any activity more strenuous than sitting upright. Her momentum had drained away, leaving her shaky and in pain. She watched his back disappearing down the stairs, felt her ankle throbbing, breathed in the first tendrils of steam from the shower. Her glance fell on her toiletries kit, balanced on the back of the sink. *Of course.* She grabbed it, unzipped it, pulled out the plastic bag of sleeping pills, the bag of antibiotics, the bag of amphetamines. Found the one she was looking for. Percocet. Prescription painkillers. She pinched one out of the plastic bag and, leaning over the sink, ran some water into the cup she kept next to her toothbrush. She tossed the pill into her throat, chased it down with the water, and, as she heard Russ's step on the stair, stuffed all the bags back into her kit. She was zipping it up when he pushed through the half-open door.

"What have you got there?"

"I had one leftover pain pill," she lied, wondering in the same instant why she was doing so. It wasn't like what she had was illegal. She'd been given those medications by a flight surgeon. Everybody got them. She pictured showing them to Russ. Pictured him saying, *Clare, what the hell do you need speed and downers for?* Pictured herself surrendering the pills. Her hand closed over the top of her kit. She slid it back into place on the sink. "Help me into the shower?"

After she had washed the stink and the sugar off, Russ wrapped the ice pack around her ankle and bandaged her shoulder. He whistled at the damage the pavement and garbage had wrought. "This looks nasty, darlin'. Let me take you to the hospital. They can give you something to make sure you don't get an infection."

"No hospital."

"Clare." He breathed through his nose. "Seeking medical attention doesn't mean you'll be diagnosed with cancer." He cupped her face in his hands. "Hmm?" Her sister, Grace, had gone to her doctor one summer day with a stomachache. Four months later she was dead. Colorectal cancer. Virulent. Fast moving.

"I'm not afraid to get treatment," she lied. "I just don't want to go now. I promise I'll get it seen to if I show any signs of infection." That would be easy. The antibiotics she had brought back with her would kill any bug up to and including flesh-eating bacteria.

He growled but helped her back into her bedroom. The pill was kicking in, and she felt more relaxed and carefree than she had at any time since she'd gotten home. Well. Any time when she wasn't having sex. She caught

Russ's hands and fell backward onto the bed. He leaned over her, one knee on the bed, one foot on the floor. "Take off your clothes," she said.

He laughed. "That's mighty ambitious for someone as banged up as you are."

"Army tough."

He kissed her lightly. "Sorry, darlin'." He stood up. "I just started my shift. Besides, my unit is smack-dab in the middle of your driveway. Might as well hang a sign out."

"I don't care."

"Yes, you do. You're not in the army now, you're in Millers Kill. If someone isn't over at the Kreemy Kakes diner right now talking about how the police chief's squad car is parked at Reverend Fergusson's place, I'll eat my shorts."

She wobbled into a seated position. "We're two single adults over the age of consent." She eyed him. "Well over."

"Ha. Remember all that stuff about setting an example for your congregation? Sex should be reserved for marriage? Practicing celibacy?"

"That was a hell of a lot easier before we started doing it."

He grinned. "I'll take that as a compliment." He pulled the covers back and rolled her into bed. "Get some rest. I'll see if I can stash my truck somewhere and sneak over tonight."

"Hypocrite," she said into her pillow.

"It's called discretion." He tugged the covers over her. Smoothed her hair away from her face. "I don't want you to get hurt, love. Not by crazy women at the soup kitchen, not by gossip."

"Tally." She tried to keep her thoughts from floating into the smooth cotton darkness. "What did she say?"

Russ made a noise. "Said she was fine. She didn't feel threatened by either her husband or Chief Nichols."

"You believe her?"

"I don't have any reason not to, other than her going to ground for a couple days. She said she just wanted some time alone to think. I had Knox take her home, to get a feel for the situation."

Her eyes had closed while he was speaking. She felt his lips on her forehead. "Later."

There was something else . . . she heard his footsteps headed for the hall. "Eric," she said.

"I'll thank him for you."

No. That's not it. Then the narcotic took her and she was gone.

MONDAY, JULY 4   There had been times in the last two years when Hadley Knox had been overwhelmed by the differences between her old life in Los Angeles and her new one in Millers Kill. Controlling traffic for the Independence Day Parade was turning out to be one of them.

She had taken her kids to a parade once in L.A., a spectacle of Disneyland-quality floats, the Golden Bears marching band, and professional dancers twirling flaming batons. In Millers Kill, half the town was marching. DAR ladies in nineteenth-century dresses and VFW men carrying cap lock rifles. A group from St. Alban's toting their THE EPISCO-PAL CHURCH WELCOMES YOU banner. The chief's mother rode past on the Adirondack Conservancy's Green Future float, and her own kids pedaled by on bikes they had spent all Saturday decorating.

There was the middle school band, and the antique and modern fire trucks, and finally the MKPD cruiser marking the end of the parade. Flynn was driving, one arm hanging out the window in a very nonregulation way, grinning and waving to the children lining the road.

He looked so young, so ridiculously hopeful and helpful, almost like a kid himself. She flashed on the night they had spent together, his eyes dark, his voice hard, saying, *Once and for all, I'm not a kid.* Her saying, *No. You're not.*

God. She shook her head to clear it. She cleared traffic and drove toward the park, wedging her cruiser into a tow zone on Main.

Wading into the crowd, she spotted the chief right off, his height a reliable beacon. He was walking beat along the grassy edge of the park, scanning from the street-side shops to the gazebo at the center of the green and back again. He stopped to greet someone, then caught sight of her and changed direction. "Knox. Hi. Talk to me."

"Everything quiet. Traffic is flowing."

He nodded. "Good."

"Did I, uh, miss anything?"

"Our assemblyman donated a new flag." He thumbed toward the flag-pole. "Reverend Fergusson"—he looked like he was trying not to smile—"gave a nice invocation." He thumbed toward the Gothic tower of St. Alban's. "She's at your church's yard sale."

She stood on tiptoe. Between the lush green foliage of the park's maples and the holiday crowd, she couldn't see a thing. "How are we doing?"

"The Presbyterians are beating you all to hell. They've got an Italian sausage stand."

"How's Reverend Clare?"

"Hurting." The chief looked exasperated. "I told her she shouldn't have come. She's on crutches, for chrissakes. Borrowed from somebody in your congregation, of course, because God forbid she go see a doctor."

Hadley spotted Anne Vining-Ellis, one of the movers and shakers of St. Alban's, crossing the road. Her youngest son trailed behind her, all pipe-cleaner legs and bangs in his eyes.

"You should ask Dr. Anne to check her out."

"Check who out?" The doctor had gotten close enough to hear them.

"Clare. I'm trying to get her to see someone about her ankle. Plus, the back of her shoulder looks awful, like it might be getting infected."

"I saw the crutches and the ACE bandage, but I didn't know she had another injury. I'll make sure to take a look before we go home."

"Thanks. I swear, she—" The chief stopped, took a breath, and gestured toward Hadley. "Do you know Officer Knox?"

"Of course I do." She smiled at Hadley. "We just ran into your kids over at the yard sale with your grandfather. Their bikes look amazing."

"Thanks. They actually did most of the decorating themselves." Hadley nodded toward Dr. Anne's boy. "Are you helping out at St. Alban's?"

"Not this time." Dr. Anne threw an arm around her son. "Colin's won the Civic Essay Award. He's here to get the scholarship check from the mayor."

Colin Ellis, who had been looking at the crowd while the adults droned on, straightened and pointed. "Mom! It's Dad and Will." He grinned. "He decided to come after all. All right. Hey! Will!"

Dr. Anne's face froze, and suddenly Hadley could see her age around her eyes. Hadley followed the older woman's gaze to see Mr. Ellis pushing a young man in a wheelchair.

A legless young man in a wheelchair. Whoa. Her stomach squeezed.

"Ah," the chief said.

The pair came to a stop in front of Dr. Anne. "You've met my husband, Chris." The doctor's voice was strange, like an imitation of herself. "And this is my son Will. Will, this is Chief Van Alstyne, Reverend Clare's . . . friend."

The chief shook the kid's hand. "I think Clare told me you had enlisted. What branch?"

"Marines."

"Uncle Sam's Misguided Children. Where were you serving?"

"Anbar Province."

The chief nodded. "I've heard that's a hot zone. Heavy casualties."

"I got out alive. I can't complain." Will's face was clear and open, as if the fact that a third of his body was missing didn't matter.

The chief smiled a little. "A marine platoon saved my life once in Vietnam. I make it a habit to thank jarheads when I meet them. Thank you."

Will's mouth crooked up. "What branch were you in, sir?"

"Army."

Will smiled broadly. "Are you sure they only saved your life once?"

The chief laughed.

"Well. Goodness. We'd better get over to the gazebo." Dr. Anne's voice was bright and cheery. "We don't want Mayor Cameron giving the check away to somebody else." The Ellis men chorused good-bye, walking— and rolling—away.

"God." Hadley felt as if she had been holding her breath. "That's tough. He's so young."

"They always are. They're always too goddamn young." The squawk on the chief's radio was a welcome distraction. He keyed his shoulder mike. "Van Alstyne here."

"Where'n the hell is here?" Static made Deputy Chief MacAuley's voice crackle. "I been looking all over for you."

"I'm at the south end of the park, looking at the Rexall."

"I'm at the gazebo. Walk that way and I'll meet you. MacAuley out."

Within moments, Hadley saw the deputy chief's grizzled buzz cut bobbing toward them. "There you are," he said, as he came into sight. "They want you up on the stand."

"So I can stand next to John Opperman and smile? Not a chance."

"Opperman?" Hadley looked at the wooden pavilion, its spindled railing and octagonal roof draped in red-white-and-blue bunting. "As in BWI Opperman, the biggest employer in the county?" She could see Mayor Cameron, standing with a well-dressed middle-aged man and a woman whose twin set and glasses-on-a-chain said *teacher* or *librarian*. There were also three soldiers in camo: a young woman in a black beret, an even younger-looking man whose head was shaved bald, and an older guy twisting a bucket hat.

The young woman soldier turned, and Hadley saw it was Tally McNabb. The chief frowned. "What's she doing up there with Dr. Stillman and the Stoners' boy?"

"They're all veterans, aren't they? Jim Cameron's probably planned some patriotic foolishness and these were the folks he could persuade to get up on the bandstand." MacAuley gave Hadley a knowing look. "He's running for reelection this year. Nothing says 'vote for me' like supporting the troops."

"John Opperman's no damn soldier."

"Look." MacAuley sighed. "Opperman's announcing some new scholarship his company's putting up for our high schoolers. Cameron's got to know there's bad blood between you two—"

"I've never discussed Opperman with him."

"For chrissakes, Russ, you act like you smell dogshit whenever the man's name comes up. Everybody who knows you knows how you feel. Cameron probably figures this is a good time to pour a little oil on those waters."

"He's throwing around money, so I'm supposed to forget what he's done and play nice?"

"Russ—"

"No."

"It's a scholarship. For kids." MacAuley frowned, his bushy gray eyebrows drawing together like miniature thunderclouds. "I'm not going to argue with you. You want to turn the mayor down, you have to go tell him yourself."

◆ ◆ ◆

The chief stalked away, muttering. Hadley frowned. "What was that all about?"

"A whole lot of old business." MacAuley watched the chief for a few more seconds before turning toward her. "BWI Opperman came to build the new resort a couple years before you moved here. That was when they were just in the hotel trade, before they got into construction and what-all. Anyway, there were three partners in the business at that time, and before the place was completed, two of 'em were dead. The chief's always been convinced John Opperman was behind it, but he couldn't prove anything."

"Huh. Okay." She couldn't help sounding doubtful. It didn't seem very professional. Keeping an eye on someone you suspected, sure, but not acting like he burned down your house and shot your dog.

MacAuley gave her one of his deceptively lazy looks. "You're thinking that's not enough for him to be carrying on like this, right?"

She shrugged.

"Yeah. There's more to it. Right before she died, Linda—his late wife—spent a week at Mr. Opperman's private retreat in the Caribbean."

Hadley's mouth opened.

"She didn't have a romance going with Opperman or anything. She worked for him, making all the fancy curtains and frilly bits for the hotel. It was just a getaway." MacAuley's denial was so firm Hadley figured Opperman and the late Mrs. Van Alstyne must have been going at it like crazed rabbits from dusk to dawn. "But it stuck hard in the chief's craw. You know the intersection where her car wrecked?"

"Yeah. Eric pointed it out to me back when I was a rookie."

MacAuley gave her a look that said, *You're still a rookie, girlie.* "She was driving there because John Opperman dropped her off at the resort after the trip. He was one of the last people to see Linda Van Alstyne alive." He pointed at the pavilion. "Huh. Looks like the mayor got him up there after all." The chief was standing behind the soldiers, talking to the teen, turned away from the rest of the people on the stage. "Lotta folks around here owe their jobs to Opperman." MacAuley tapped his nose. "Jim Cameron can smell which way the wind's coming in."

Small-town politics was definitely on her list of things to avoid. "Do you want me to walk the loop, Dep?" Every merchant along the street circling the park had a sidewalk display set up, an open invitation to snatch and run. "Patrol the shops?"

"Naw, I'll take that. You stay here. Watch out for anybody who thinks it might be funny to set off a rocket during the speeches." He turned away, then turned back. "And keep an eye on *him*. Just in case he forgets to smile and play nice."

Mayor Cameron stepped up to the microphone stand. "Hi, everyone. I'm happy to say we're welcoming back our veterans to a strong and growing economy, thanks in no small part to BWI Opperman, whose commitment to hire locally has made a big difference in our community's life." Tally McNabb dropped her head as if she would have rather been anywhere than in front of the crowd. Four days ago, she had been hiding from her husband and her boyfriend. Hadley wondered what had changed since then. "Now the CEO of BWI is here to make another commitment to our town, and to tell you about it, please welcome Millers Kill High School principal Suzanne Ovitt."

There was enthusiastic applause as the woman in the twin set took the microphone. "Thank you. Mr. John Opperman has generously established a scholarship for four years' tuition, room and board at any State University of New York campus."

Holy shit. If Hudson could land that, she wouldn't need that lousy ten bucks a week.

"The winning scholar must be a graduating senior with a strong academic record who serves his or her community and encourages others to do so. This year's inaugural recipient of the BWI Opperman scholarship is Olivia Bain."

More applause, along with some whooping from the winner's friends. The oldest of the three soldiers cheered. A slim girl mounted the pavilion steps and shook Ms. Ovitt's hand. Hadley got her first good look at John Opperman as he came forward, greeted the teen, and handed her an envelope. His clothing was expensively casual, and he boosted his middling height with three-hundred-dollar shoes. His darkish hair hadn't been cut in any Millers Kill barbershop, that was for sure. If they had been in L.A., she would have pegged him as a corporate lawyer, with an office in Century City and a mistress in Bel Air.

"Thank you, Principal Ovitt, and congratulations to Miss Bain." Opperman's voice wasn't warm, but she figured that was normal from someone more used to giving orders than speeches. "I'm pleased BWI Opperman can, in this small way, give back to the town which has so wholeheartedly taken us into its bosom."

Hadley glanced at the chief, standing behind the soldiers. He looked like he wanted to spit.

"However, being up here with these fine representatives of the armed forces has made me realize that one scholarship is not enough." The men and women around her who had been discussing the scholarship and the high school and the Bain girl fell silent. "Therefore, I have decided to establish a fund that will provide one thousand dollars to each and every graduate of Millers Kill High School who has had a parent serve in a combat arena."

The crowd went wild. The teenaged soldier grinned and said something to Van Alstyne.

"Now. I understand Mayor Cameron has a certificate of appreciation to give to these brave soldiers behind me." The mayor stepped toward the microphone, but Opperman pulled several note cards out of his back pocket and continued. "First, Lance Corporal Ethan Stoner. Ethan will be heading back to Afghanistan shortly for his second tour of duty with the 2nd Battalion, 3rd Marine Division."

The kid the chief had been talking with stepped forward, shook the mayor's hand, and accepted an envelope. He looked at Opperman, clearly uncertain if there was more to do.

The CEO brought the mic up again. "Corporal Stoner, I'd like to add my thanks by offering you and all our honorees a complimentary weekend at the Algonquin Waters Spa and Resort." Stoner grinned and pumped Opperman's hand until it looked as if the CEO's gold watch might fly off.

Van Alstyne put his arms behind his back and assumed a parade rest posture. He didn't even glance toward Opperman this time. His grudge match against the Algonquin's owner was starting to look like a vendetta against Santa Claus.

"Dr. George Stillman is a lieutenant colonel in the National Guard and has just gotten back from his second tour of duty in Iraq." Opperman put down the mic and clapped. Stillman seemed much more assured than the Stoner boy when he stepped up to get his certificate. Hadley thought it was weird, that a guy as old as her father could be sent off to war.

At the other end of the pavilion, Olivia, the outstanding senior, was bent over the railing, making come-on-up gestures. Hadley cut through the crowd until she spotted Will Ellis, talking back to the girl, shaking his head. Will could only be a year or two older than Olivia. Maybe they'd been in drama together, or band. Maybe prom dates. Now she was going off to college and he was stuck in a wheelchair for the rest of his life. She couldn't make out what they were saying, but evidently Opperman could. He left the doctor and the mayor, who, having retaken the mic, was going on about "the ethos of service."

Olivia straightened as Mr. Opperman approached. He asked her something. She shook her head. *No.* Opperman made a gesture, smoothing, dismissive. He turned away and spoke directly to Will. The wounded boy's family closed ranks around his chair, blocking Hadley's view.

The mayor glanced at Opperman before introducing Tally McNabb, but Hadley didn't pay him any attention. The chief had given up his attempt to ignore Opperman and was glaring at the CEO. The other guy, Dr. Stillman, had come over and was talking with Opperman and Olivia. The crowd applauded at something the mayor said, Tally McNabb scooted behind the marine, and John Opperman took two steps toward the center of the pavilion and held up his hands.

"Ladies and gentlemen." He used what her daughter would have called "his big voice." "It's come to my attention that we have another veteran here today, a young hero who was gravely wounded in combat. Naturally, he doesn't want anyone making a fuss over him, but I think bravery in the service of our freedom ought to be rewarded. What do you say?"

All around Hadley people began cheering, whistling, yelling out, "Bring him up!" and "USA! USA!" Most of the spectators couldn't see Will, she realized. They were thinking he had been wounded and gotten better.

Her radio crackled. "Knox?"

She looked up. The chief was talking to her from the gazebo. She pulled the mic off her shoulder and raised her hand so he could see her. "Here, Chief."

"Get over there and help the Ellises. Don't let anybody lay hands on that wheelchair."

He snapped his mic into place without signing off and strode toward Opperman. Hadley caught glimpses of the action as she wedged her way through the crowd toward the Ellis family. Van Alstyne's hand coming down on Opperman's shoulder. Turning the CEO away from the spectators. The chief's face, like a stone wall, saying something to Opperman. Hadley reached Dr. Anne's side as the chief plucked the microphone out of Mayor Cameron's hand and said, "Enough." The chanting died away. "That's enough. You want to thank these folks, give 'em a big round of applause and let 'em go enjoy the rest of the holiday with their families."

The crowd cheerfully complied, clapping and hooting. "Chief Van Alstyne wanted me to assist you," Hadley yelled in Dr. Anne's ear.

The doctor bent toward her son. "Will, let's go."

"No. Dammit, Mom, I want to see Colin get his award." The kid was pale, with bright splotches over his cheeks, but his voice was steady.

"How 'bout I stand behind you and make sure your family isn't bothered?" Hadley offered.

"Thanks. That would be great." Dr. Anne gave her another of those tight smiles.

Hadley stepped behind Will and his dad. Just before she turned away from the gazebo, ready to present her best do-not-mess-with-me face to the rest of the crowd, she caught a glimpse of Opperman. His genial, satisfied look was gone. Instead, he was staring at the chief. The loathing and contempt in his expression raised goose bumps on Hadley's arms. Then his face smoothed to a bland calm. Hadley shivered.

TUESDAY, JULY 5   Russ was amazed to see Clare's car parked in the chaplain's spot at the Washington County Hospital that night. He had only had a few minutes with her after the dog-and-pony show at the pavilion. Her face had been tired and pinched with pain, and she had assured him she would let Dr. Anne look at her injuries and then go straight home and rest. If the

Fourth of July wasn't always so crazy busy he would have carried her to the rectory himself.

Russ got out of his cruiser and released the back door. His passenger slumped sideways. Russ wrapped a hand around the young man's arm and dragged him across the seat. "Wha?" The kid blinked at the neon EMERGENCY sign. "Wherezzat?"

Russ got the guy on his feet, held him with one hand locked over his skinny shoulder, and retrieved his backpack. "Come on, buddy. Just a little way further."

The kid stumbled, nearly falling, as Russ steered him through the clunky double doors and up the short hall to the intake desk.

"Heya, Chief." Alta Brewer, the head ER nurse, came out of her cubicle. "What have you got for us?"

"A drunk and disorderly call. The kid was weaving his way down Main Street thumping against storefronts."

Alta leaned up close and sniffed. "He doesn't smell like booze."

"That's why I brought him to you." He shook the backpack with his free hand. "There's nothing in here, so I couldn't tell what he's on. I figured you folks ought to have a look at him."

Alta flicked a penlight on and peered into the kid's enormous pupils. "Good call." She leaned over the intake counter. "Get me a gurney," she called to an unseen co-worker.

"Hey, I saw Reverend Fergusson's car outside in the chaplain's spot. Can you tell me what she's here for?"

Alta looked up from the blood pressure cuff she was strapping to the kid's wiry arm. "Reverend Fergusson's back?"

"Yeah. She got in last week." He kept his voice neutral.

Alta grinned at him as an orderly trundled a bed through the inner ER doors. "Well. I bet you're right happy about that."

So much for his cool outward demeanor. He helped Alta hump the semiboneless kid onto the gurney. "I'll be right there," Alta told the orderly as he rolled the guy—who was now making outboard motor noises—away. She wedged herself back behind the intake counter and tilted the computer monitor down. "She can't be on call again as chaplain yet. I would have heard about it." She punched a few keys. "Oh. Here it is.

By request of the family." She looked up at Russ. "Patient in for heart failure. Must be one of her parishioners."

"Where can I find her?"

"Third floor, in CIC. I'm sure you remember it from your own stay."

"Vaguely. Most of what I saw was the ceiling tiles."

She laughed as he headed for the elevator. Upstairs, the doors opened on the central care station. He had spent a lot of time on this floor after he'd made the mistake of stepping in front of a desperate drug dealer two years ago. The shots to his chest and thigh had laid him out for a long time. The big counter looked different from an upright and unmedicated position.

One of the two nurses manning the monitor screens looked up. "Mr. Van Alstyne?" He recognized her—she had been his night shift nurse, a sturdy woman with a voice like a glass of warm milk. She had hummed sometimes, when she got busy. He had liked it. Now she left the central station, smiling, looking him up and down just a bit, as if she were still assessing his condition. He wouldn't have been surprised if she'd whipped out a stethoscope. "It's nice to see you fit and on your feet."

"Believe me, it's even nicer to be here under my own power." The corridor on either side of the station was empty. Cardiac intensive care didn't have ambulatory patients, and visitors were strictly limited. "I'm looking for Reverend Fergusson."

The night nurse's smile stretched into a grin. Yeah, she would have remembered Clare. He suspected ministers didn't usually stay at a parishioner's bedside for twenty-four hours straight.

"You're in luck," the nurse said. "One of the care team has just gone in to flush his shunt and tap his lines. The family should be coming out any—" Her prediction was proved true before she could finish it. Five doors down the hall, a group emerged from a room: two men in their sixties in rumpled business wear that looked like it had been slept in, a grandmotherly sort in hospital-sensible sweats, and a tired-faced priest in black clericals with a long white satin stole about her neck. She glanced his way and stopped, blinking her surprise. She said something, low, to the family. He caught the word "cafeteria." They drifted toward the elevators, passing behind him and the night nurse with scarcely a glance at his uniform and gun, too emotionally wrung out to be curious.

Clare limped toward him. She had traded the donated crutches for an ugly but functional hospital-issue cane, and the first thing that came out of his mouth was "Did Dr. Anne take a look at your ankle?"

She stuck her foot out. The ACE bandage had been replaced with a plastic-and-Velcro cast. "She gave me this. It makes walking a lot easier, I can tell you."

"What about your shoulder?"

"I'm on antibiotics for that. Took my first dose this afternoon." Her eyes shifted away.

"Really?" He didn't try to hide his skepticism.

She looked straight at him. "I really am taking antibiotics, yes. What are you doing here?"

"Picked up some guy so stoned he couldn't tell me his name. Thought he'd better get seen." He shook his head. "Druggies."

Clare glanced at the night nurse, back behind her curved counter. "Nancy? Will you let me know when Gail is done and I can go back in, please?"

"Of course I will, Reverend."

Clare gestured with her head toward the CIC lounge across from the elevators. He resisted the urge to wrap his arms around her and tote her into the room, settling for walking just behind her to catch her if she fell. The waiting room was done in early modern Valium, all mellow colors and soft lights. The well-sprung modular seating said, *Stretch out here and have a nap, everything will be fine.* Clare looked at the couch facing the door with distaste. "Not there. In the corner." She limped toward a pair of chairs half-hidden behind a banana palm and dropped into one of them like a marionette who had had its strings cut.

"Mr. Fitzgerald's in congestive heart failure. The family called me."

"You've got a sprained ankle and a banged-up shoulder. You need to rest. Couldn't the priest who filled in for you be doing this? He's still around, isn't he?"

"Father Lawrence is at his daughter's house in Glens Falls, not here. It wouldn't matter anyway. Mr. Fitzgerald is my parishioner."

He leaned forward. Her face was drawn, but despite being smudged purple with fatigue, her eyes were as bright and alert as ever. She must have downed a thermosful of coffee. "Okay. How long will it take you to hear his confession, or whatever? I'm finishing up my shift. I'll drive you home."

"Russ."

"It's the least I can do. I would have done it for—" He cut himself off before ramming his boot all the way down his throat.

"For your wife?" She spread her arms as if to emphasize the black clericals and the symbols she wore. Collar. Cross. Stole. "I'm not Linda. I don't want you to feel like you have to *do* for me." She let her arms drop. "Mr. Fitzgerald is dying." She smoothed a hand over her stole, dimpling the heavy satin. "He's dying, and his children are afraid, and I'm going to stay until the end."

He took off his glasses. Polished them against the knee of his trousers. He thought of her reaction to the couch. Realized she must have sat there after he'd been shot, not knowing if he would live or die. He'd been back on the job within five months. Linda would have insisted he retire. Clare had never said a word, other than "Be careful." She understood his job was what he did.

So this was what she did.

He put his glasses back on. "Can I do anything to help?"

She smiled. "Not unless you've taken up prayer while I was gone."

He made a noise.

"I have a question for you."

He cocked an eyebrow at her change-of-subject tone. "What?"

"How is Eric McCrea doing since he came back? In your judgment?"

"Why? Is there something I should know about?" She flipped her hand open. *Answer the question.* "Okay," he said. "I haven't seen or heard anything that worries me. He's taken several sick days since he came back from Iraq. Which is a lot, for him. I told him he could have more time before he returned to duty. I figured this is his way of pacing himself."

She nodded. "He seemed . . . charged up when he responded to the call from the soup kitchen Friday. Aggressive. As if he were perceiving a threat where none existed. Could he be using something? Steroids?"

"It's possible, I suppose. That sort of behavior's not unusual, coming off a war zone. I remember trying to clear some underbrush from behind Mom's house the summer I got back from Nam. I couldn't do it. Couldn't walk into the trees and the tangle without my M-15 in my hand."

She smiled faintly. "I wonder if that's one of the reasons you became a cop. So you'd never have to go without your gun."

"No." Involuntarily, his hand fell to his service piece. "I haven't fired my gun off the range since the Christie hostage incident. Before that, it had been seven years."

"I didn't say use it. I said go without it."

He opened his mouth to argue. Closed it. "Hmm." He nodded. "I'll keep an eye on Eric. If he seems stressed, I can partner him up with one of the other officers or give him some time off. We've got access to a psychiatrist the town contracts with. Although having done my mandatory fatal fire session with the guy, I'm not wild about sending anyone else to him."

Clare's smile was broader this time. "Lowest bidder, huh?"

"That's my guess." He thought about where they were, thought about who might see them, thought *the hell with it*. He stood. Bent over her, bracing his hands on the arms of her chair. Kissed her. "Call my cell phone after—when you're ready to come home. I'll drive over and fetch you."

"From your mother's? That's ridiculous."

"Just call me."

"Russ, I told you. I don't need you riding to my rescue because I'm out late or because I got a little banged up. I can take care of myself."

"Clare." He touched his forehead to hers. "Listen." He pulled back so he could see her eyes. So she could see his. "Every day you were in Iraq, I woke up wondering if this was it, if this was the day I'd get word that you'd been killed. Every night I watched footage and commentary and reporting and statistics until I wanted to put a boot through the damn TV. I had to see it, and hear it, and think about it, and there wasn't a damn thing I could do about it." He straightened. "For God's sake, now you're home, let me do something. I'm not trying to turn you into—I don't know—the little woman. I just need to—to—" He ran out of words.

"Take care of me." Her voice was balanced between understanding and dislike. "Russ—"

"You'd be helping me out." That stopped her. "Please?" He didn't need to see her expression to know that phrase had won her over. The day Clare could resist helping someone was the day cows would fly over Millers Kill and start grazing on the roof of St. Alban's.

"Okay." She sighed. "I'll call you. But—"

"Reverend Fergusson?" A different nurse was standing in the wide doorway. "I'm all set."

"Thanks." Clare leaned forward and braced her aluminum cane. "I have to go. I don't want him to be alone."

Russ stood. Took her hand and pulled her upright.

"Thank you," she said.

"You told me once that saying you couldn't do something alone wasn't the same as saying you couldn't do it at all."

She paused. "I remember."

"Think about that, hmn? Next time you're dead-set on going it alone?"

She looked at him. "I'll try."

He watched her limp off to Mr. Fitzgerald's room, to watch the night through with a dying man. That was what she did. He turned, and left to go back to what he did.

FRIDAY, JULY 29   Hadley was heading back to the station to clock out when she got the squawk. "Fifteen-seventy, this is Dispatch, what's your forty?"

She unhooked the mic. "Dispatch, this is fifteen-seventy, I'm inbound at the east end of Burgoyne."

"We've got multiple reports of a three-car crash on the Sacandaga Road near the entrance to the new resort."

Shit. Home late again. "Roger that, Dispatch, I am responding." She switched on her light bar and sirens, checked her mirrors, and made a U-turn back toward the shortcut to Route 57.

The entire month of July had been crazy with tourists, and things didn't look like they were going to let up in August. She called home but only got the answering machine. "Granddad, I'm going to be late. I have frozen barbecue chicken breasts and those green beans the kids like in the freezer. All you have to do is nuke them. *Don't* take the kids to Mc-Donald's again." It wasn't so bad for Hudson and Genny—they would have a couple small cheeseburgers, some onion rings, and milk—but

Granddad's idea of a fast-food meal was two Big Macs and a super-sized order of fries, washed down with a large milkshake. Not what the doctor ordered for a man who had heart disease, hypertension, and diabetes.

She swung onto the Sacandaga Road and saw red-and-whites ahead. She triggered her mic. "All channels, this is MKPD fifteen-seventy responding to an accident on Sacandaga Road, over."

"Fifteen-seventy, this is fifteen-sixty-three." Kevin Flynn's unit. "Responding same. I am westbound on Sacandaga Road. Over."

Right on his heels came Eric McCrea's voice. "Fifteen-seventy, this is fifteen-twenty-five. I am southbound from Old Route 100."

Hadley's stomach churned. As overworked as they were during the summer months, it had to be one hell of a mess for Harlene to send three officers.

She slowed as she approached the final rise before the entrance to the Algonquin Waters. At the top of the hill, her gaze swept the horizon, the scene laid out before her like toys thrown about by a sulky child. Two cars parked on the shoulder. A Ford Taurus skewed across both lanes, an old Saab rammed halfway into its rear quarter. The third car way off in the field. Upside-down, its grill and side crumpled and scored, its make or model unidentifiable. People—good Samaritans or uninjured drivers, she couldn't tell—on the road and in the field.

Holy shit. She and Kevin and Eric were it, for the next however many minutes it took for the ambulance and the fire trucks to get here. Hadley followed Flynn's squad car down and parked in the travel lane, leaving her lights whirling. Flynn swung wide, between the accident and the parked cars, stopping on the other side of the tangle, blocking the northern approach as she blocked the west. In the next second, Eric McCrea's unit came over the hill. He slowed and pulled in behind her.

She and Eric got out of their cars. Eric popped his trunk and removed a crowbar. "Kevin!" His shout carried over the wreckage. "Meet me at the off-road vehicle!"

"I can—" Hadley began.

"If there's a fire risk, we're going to have to get the occupants out." He strode toward the field, gesturing toward the other two cars. "See if anybody there needs help."

I can do that, she wanted to say, but he and Flynn were already heading downslope—steeply downslope, she could see, as they rapidly disappeared from view. Hadley turned her attention to the cars blocking the road.

A young woman barely out of her teens sat sideways in the front of the Saab, her hands cradling her very pregnant belly, her face red and raw and terrified. A deflated air bag covered the steering wheel. A big, bearded guy crouched in front of her saying something in soothing tones.

"Hey there." Hadley squatted beside him. "What do we have here?"

The man looked as relieved as a con with an eleventh-hour pardon. "Thank God. She says she's, uh, leaking. Down there."

"Are you"—he looked easily old enough to be the girl's father instead of the baby's, but you never knew—"related?"

"No, ma'am. I was just driving home to Millers Kill and came across 'em. There's an older couple in the Ford, but they were just shaken up some, so I thought I'd better stay with her."

"Please help me." The girl's voice was wild. "I don't want to lose my baby."

"It's going to be okay. There are ambulances on the way. They'll be here any minute. What's your name?"

"Christy. Christy Stoner." Her chest rose and fell in quick, shallow bursts. Shock, or panic? Either way, it couldn't be good.

"Christy, how far along are you?"

"Seven months."

"Are you having any contractions?"

She shook her head. Gulped a breath. Let out a bleating, gasping cry.

"Okay, Christy, listen to me. Are you listening? You need to calm down. Your baby needs all the air it can get right now."

Christy nodded, panting.

"Is this your first pregnancy?"

The girl jerked her head up and down. Hadley spotted the rings on her third finger, a skinny little diamond and a big fat band. "Why don't we call your husband? You can talk to him while we're checking you out." That might help the girl relax.

"He's in Afghanistan. He's a marine."

Oh, great. Hadley gestured the bearded man to come closer. "Okay, Christy. I want you to hold—what's your name?"

"Dennis Walker."

"I want you to hold Dennis's hands and squeeze them tight." She did so, her knuckles whitening. Walker let out a grunt. "Now I want you to close your eyes and take slow . . . even . . . breaths."

Christy shut her eyes and opened her mouth.

"Dennis, I want you to pull her upright. We're going to move her to the backseat so she can lie down."

Christy groaned, then gasped, as they helped her out, but between the two of them, they got her relocated. Hadley had her lie on her left side, a vague memory from her own pregnancies that the left was better for circulation or something.

"You said she was leaking." Hadley addressed Walker over the roof of the car. "Any idea what?"

"Are you kidding?"

She ducked back down into the Saab. The girl was wearing a maternity sundress, rucked up around her knees in the move. "Christy, did it feel like your amniotic fluid bursting? Or maybe letting go some pee?"

Walker made a strangled sound.

"I couldn't tell! I don't know what it feels like when your water breaks."

"Okay. I'd like your permission to check your panties to see if I can tell what's happened."

"Oh, jeez!" Walker twisted this way and that, finally turning his back to the car.

"Okay." Christy brought her knee up. Hadley bunched the girl's skirt in her hands and took a look. *Oh, shit.* She was worried she was going to have to get more personal, but that wouldn't be necessary. Christy's white maternity undies were soaked right through with clear amniotic fluid—and streaked with blood.

"What's going on?"

Hadley snapped the girl's dress back into place and whirled around. She had thought Flynn's face seemed more mature since his TDY. His bones a little more defined, maybe, or his expression a little more tempered. Standing in front of her now, he looked years older.

"The other car?"

He shook his head. "Dead." His mouth compressed. "No seat belt." He looked over her shoulder. "Her?"

"Seven months pregnant." Hadley dropped her voice. "I think it might be a partial placental abruption."

"What's that?"

"The placenta peels away some from the uterus. It's all kinds of bad." She glared at the road. "Where the hell is that ambulance?"

"Hey! Officer!"

They both turned. Walker had squeezed himself between the front and rear seats so Christy could hold his hand again. "She says she's getting her pains!"

◆ ◆ ◆

Hadley opened her mouth to either pray or swear, but she was cut short by the *whoop whoop whoop* of the ambulance cresting the hill, followed by the fire department's chemical response truck, two volunteer fire police pickups, and, praise God, a second ambulance.

Duane Adams, one of their own part-time officers, led the EMTs. He prided himself on being fast. With good cause. Within two minutes, he had Christy Stoner on a stretcher, an IV in her arm and a fetal monitor strapped across her belly. They were pulling out, hospital bound, before Walker managed to extricate himself from the floor of the Saab. The last Hadley saw of the pregnant girl was a flip of her sundress over her tan legs as they slid her into the ambulance. *God, look out for her and the baby.*

Flynn went over to see what he could get from the elderly couple while they were being examined by the remaining EMTs. Hadley pulled out her own notebook. "Dennis, can I get your statement?"

The big man tore his gaze away from the now vanished ambulance. "Sure."

Hadley checked her watch to note the time. She blinked. It had been exactly ten minutes since she had gotten the call from Harlene. She shook her head to clear it. "Can you tell me what you saw?"

"I was headed up to town on the Sacandaga Road"—he pointed to a spot south of the accident site—"and the Ford and the young lady's car were coming down the hill toward me. All of a sudden, that Mini Cooper comes bombing outta the resort road. Musta been going seventy, at least. Those folks"—he thumbed toward the Ford—"kinda spun. I figured he slammed on the brakes and tried to skid himself. Probably woulda gotten by without more'n a scare if, uh, Christy hadn't been behind him." Walker gestured to the front of the Saab, accordioned into the rear corner of the Ford. "Wasn't her fault, I don't think. She mighta left more room between 'em, but, you know, unless she was a NASCAR racer in her spare time, there's no way she coulda swerved." He rubbed his big hands together. "Damn, I hope her and her baby come out okay."

"Me, too. Then what happened?"

"Then? I called nine-one-one and got out to see if I could help. There was a lady come down the resort road after the Mini Cooper. She said she was a friend of the woman in the car. She took off down the field to check on her, I guess." He glanced toward the pasture spreading out beneath the road. The car that had caused the accident, its driver, and her friend were invisible from where Walker and Hadley stood. As they watched, one of the paramedics toiled up the grassy slope into view. "What happened to her?" Walker asked. "The other driver, I mean."

"She was killed."

"Damn." He shook his head, his beard swaying along in somber disapproval. "I hate to say it, but I figured something like this was gonna happen sooner or later. There's a blind spot at the end of that resort road with all them trees and bushes there. Folks build up a good head of steam coming off the mountain and don't have the sense to stop and look both ways." He sighed. "It ain't like it used to be."

Hadley was quite sure of that. There were a number of increasingly dangerous intersections in the area, roads meant for farm vehicles and pokey local traffic overwhelmed by tourists and trucks and commuters rushing to get to Saratoga or Albany. Chief Van Alstyne's wife had died in a collision less than ten miles from this spot.

She took Walker's contact information and thanked him again for stopping to help.

"Anybody woulda done the same." He rubbed his hands again. "I just hope that girl and her baby do all right."

The fields around them were gold and green and bright with the summer sun, still high at six o'clock, but the accident site slid into the cool blue shadow of the mountain as she and Eric and Flynn processed the scene. The elderly couple elected to go to the hospital for a more thorough checkup, and the wrecker arrived. The fire police set up detours, and Hadley called for another tow truck.

The chemical response truck inched down the steep grade to the pasture and sprayed the remains of the Mini Cooper with fire retardant. The Ford, a total loss, was chain-winched to the side of the road, and the Saab, also a goner, got loaded on the flatbed and started for town.

The mortuary transport rumbled up, never in any hurry, and the body was removed. The driver, a middle-aged woman named Ellen Bain, had been coming from her job at the Algonquin Waters Resort after having "just one drink at the bar," according to her sobbing co-worker. Ellen was also "a very safe driver!"—although the friend admitted she never used her seat belt.

"She used to tell us about a driver who got burned right up because he couldn't get out of the car." The woman could hardly speak. "She always said she wanted to be thrown clear in case of an accident."

Hadley, who had hiked down to the crumpled Mini Cooper to take pictures, had to turn her head away.

Eric and Kevin took photos and measurements of the skid marks, and the second wrecker came to impound Bain's car until the final report had been written, and the chemical response guys sprayed the torn and flattened grass once more for good measure.

They gave the all clear to the fire police volunteers, and the road was reopened. Hadley watched as the volunteers' pickups jounced past. Nothing now but three cop cars and some broken glass on the roadbed to tell what had happened here. Everything else had faded into twilight.

"I never understood why people made those roadside shrines until I became a cop." Flynn stood beside her, his hands tucked up under his arms.

"It doesn't seem right all cleaned up," she agreed. "It shouldn't be so easy to ignore. Or forget." A harsh growl, a sound of anger and pain, jerked her around. "What the hell?"

Thud. Thud. Thud. A dull hammering, punctuated by McCrea's voice, low and vicious. Coming from the slope below the road. "Eric?" Kevin's hand went to his gun. "Are you okay?"

No reply. She and Flynn headed toward the noise, both their guns out now. McCrea was halfway down the slope, straddling a deep gash where the Mini Cooper's bumper had dug into the earth and wrenched off. He was flailing at the dirt with the crowbar, beating—Hadley peered into the gloom, looking for the snake. There was nothing there.

"Goddamn fucking stupid *bitch!*" Eric smashed the bar down. "Goddamn fucking *drinks*—" *Thud.* "And *speeds*—" *Thud.* "And doesn't wear a goddamn fucking *seat belt!*" *Thud.*

"Eric!" Flynn sounded appalled. "What are you doing, man?"

McCrea looked up at them, his eyes gleaming in the darkness. "We live in the safest fucking place in the world." Eric's voice was grating. "We have air bags and seat belts and traffic signals. We have highway inspectors and road crews and goddamn designated drivers. And that stupid bitch just *throws*—" *Thud.* "It *all*—" *Thud.* "*Away!*" *Thud.*

"I know. It sucks." Flynn stepped toward Eric. "It really does. Why don't you give me the crowbar, and we'll go get a beer. Blow off some steam."

"I don't want to *blow off some steam!*"

Hadley shook herself. Eric McCrea was acting like a three-year-old lashing out at feelings he couldn't name or express, and one thing she knew how to deal with was a cranky three-year-old. "Okay, Eric." She kept her voice calm. "We're not in any hurry. We'll wait for you." Flynn shifted his weight—going for McCrea or going for his car, she couldn't tell—and she wrapped her hand around his forearm. "We'll keep an eye on you to make sure you don't accidentally get hurt. Go on. Go right ahead."

Eric's arm twitched. He kicked at the gouged and torn soil beneath his boots. "Just—leave."

"No, man, that wouldn't be right." Kevin's tone told her he had caught on to what she was doing and was running with it. "We came on the call together, we'll leave together."

"Jesus." McCrea stepped toward them. Stepped back. Shook his head. "I can't do it with you watching me."

"Take your time," Hadley said. "Just ignore us."

McCrea barked a laugh. Harsh, but genuine. He tossed the crowbar at Kevin's feet. "You two are assholes, you know that?"

Flynn picked up the crowbar. "Takes one to know one, big guy. C'mon."

She drove back to the station with her heater on, despite the lingering warmth from the day. It took that long to get the chill inside her under control. In the squad room, they checked in and went straight to their reports. No joking or chatter tonight. Eric was the first to finish.

"The offer's still open if you want a beer," Kevin said.

Eric paused at the door. "Thanks, Kev. I think I'd better just go home. G'night, Hadley."

"Goodnight," she called. He left, his footsteps echoing down the hall. She glanced over at Flynn. It was just them now. Harlene had gone off duty after the last emergency vehicles had been dispatched; calls to the station would be routed through the Glens Falls board until morning. Ed and Paul were patrolling; if the need arose, one of them might stop by the station. A lot of times over the past year, she would have found the chief working late, but since Reverend Clare had gotten home, Van Alstyne bolted out the door as soon as possible and didn't show up again until the morning briefing, blissed-out and yawning.

Nope. It was just her and Kevin Flynn. The situation she had been dreading since he came back from his TDY. It wasn't that they had slept together. Yeah, he was a lot younger than she was, and yeah, it was against departmental regs, but, hey, things happen. In fact, if he hadn't gotten all emotional about it, she would have been tempted to keep on as friends-with-benefits, because it had been pretty good. Okay, really good, if she was being honest. Flynn had acted as if she were the final exam in sex ed and he was determined to make honor roll. How could she have known it was all book-learning with no hands-on experience?

She had been very hands-on—and because of that, he thought he was in love. With her. Right.

Flynn shut his computer down and scraped his chair back. "You done?"

"Yeah."

"I'll walk out with you."

They went down the granite steps into the sweet warm night. Hadley fished her keys out of her pocket. "See you tomorrow."

"Hadley?"

Here it comes. "Yeah?"

"You were great with that pregnant girl. I'm glad you were there for her. I'm pretty sure she was glad, too."

"Uh . . . thanks."

"Good night." Flynn clicked open his Aztek. He hopped in and was pulling out of the department's parking lot before Hadley managed to fit her key into her car door.

She sat in the driver's seat and looked at herself in the rearview mirror. Well. Evidently, she was no longer irresistible to Kevin Flynn. The small sting of that made her laugh, and laughing, she backed out and headed home to her kids.

YOU ARE NO LONGER
STRANGERS AND SOJOURNERS,
BUT FELLOW CITIZENS WITH
THE SAINTS AND MEMBERS OF
THE HOUSEHOLD OF GOD.

—*Morning Prayer II, The Book of Common Prayer*

"Personal relationships." Sarah let the phrase hang in the air while she looked from one member of the group to the other. In his wheelchair, Will Ellis stared at his knees. He was without prosthetics this session. Clare Fergusson sank lower in her seat and examined the ring she wore on her right hand. She buffed it against her short-sleeved black blouse. Tally McNabb lifted her hair away from the back of her neck and sighed.

They were having a spell of Indian summer on their third session, and the eighty-degree temperature would have been welcome, if the community center had better ventilation. Sarah could see, from the row of damp swimming suits and towels, how the preschool had escaped the heat. Unfortunately, she couldn't move her therapy group to the kiddie pools in the playground.

"It's a well-known phenomenon that a child who has been well behaved and cheerful at day care or on a play date will fall apart into tears and tantrums at home. Why? The child bottles up any negative emotions during the day and lets them all out with his or her parents." Eric McCrea and Trip Stillman were nodding. "Even familiar caretakers and friends might not be safe—but parents can be relied upon to still love the child no matter how badly he or she behaves."

Will Ellis absently kneaded his thigh muscles. His disengagement worried her. It might be time to refer him to more one-on-one care.

"As adults," she continued, "we carry on these same patterns. We unload our baggage on our partners or family members because we learned as kids that it's safe to do so. The problem is, of course, that we're not kids anymore. We're not dealing with all-powerful, all-forgiving parents, either."

Clare Fergusson shot a glance at Will Ellis. He looked at her and shifted in his seat. Sarah realized Will was, in fact, still dealing with his parents. Better cut the metaphor short.

"Let's talk about how we're dealing with our loved ones."

WEDNESDAY, AUGUST 10   Eric was trying to keep his temper over being checked up on like a little kid. "I just wanted to make sure you didn't forget," his wife was saying over the phone.

"For chrissakes, Jen, I can remember to pick up my own son from practice." He was running a little late, but jeez. He pushed back from his chair in the squad room and headed for dispatch. "I'm leaving the station now."

"I didn't put a dinner in the freezer, but there's a bowl of meat sauce in the fridge, so all you have to do is boil some pasta—"

"I can handle feeding us. Relax, will you?" He logged himself off the board hanging next to Harlene's communication center.

She sighed fretfully. "I'm sorry. I'm just not used to—I haven't spent a night away from him since you were deployed."

Which was a big part of the problem, Eric thought. Jennifer was so used to doing everything she practically tried to wipe the boy's mouth for him while he ate. All the mothering had turned Jacob into a sulky, self-entitled brat.

"Maybe I should just come home."

"No." He shifted his grip on his phone as he walked down the hall and out the door. The long, slanting rays of the western sun struck him full in the face as he jogged down the granite steps. He held up a hand to shield his eyes. "Your mom needs you there. We'll have a good time. Don't worry." As he turned the corner into the department parking lot, he held the phone away from his face. "Honey? You're fading out." He could hear her talking, shrill and distant, like a bird afraid of a stranger under her nest. "Honey?" he said to the phone, now at arm's length. "Talk to you later." He flipped it shut.

He stowed his service piece and duty belt in his cruiser's lockbox and slid into the seat. He had parked in the shade, so the car hadn't heated up too bad. He eased the cruiser across the bump where it interrupted the sidewalk and pulled into Main.

The pedestrians bothered him. He'd noticed it before, in the weeks since he'd been home. He was okay with people walking when he was walking, and he was as relaxed as he ever was with other drivers when he was behind the wheel, but driving past pedestrians—getting flickering views of faces, backpacks, hands, shopping bags—made his shoulders bunch up around his ears and his scalp tighten.

He went through his litany of reminders. *Relax your shoulders. Breathe. Don't drive too slow. Don't pull toward the center of the road.* That was another thing he had a tendency to do—steer himself away from the sidewalks and parked cars. His brain knew nobody in Millers Kill was going to lob a grenade into his cruiser or blow up an abandoned vehicle at the side of the road. Unfortunately, his balls hadn't gotten the update.

He grew easier as soon as he left the town center. Away from the small shopping district, the sidewalks emptied except for an occasional kid on a bike or a dog walker. The high school was at the east edge of town, as far as you could go before hitting the rolling farmlands of Cossayuharie. He took the looping drive past the admin building, around the sprawling one- and two-story complex, and parked in the lot nearest the athletic fields.

There were still a handful of minivans and SUVs waiting while the remaining members of the middle school cross-country teams dispersed: long-legged graceful girls talking and laughing; gawky boys, some a head shorter, shouting and bashing into each other.

Eric was surprised to see a familiar grape-Popsicle-colored Escort. Hadley Knox was leaning against her car, watching her little girl cartwheel clumsily through the shaggy grass at the edge of the bleachers. Unlike him, she'd taken the time to change into her civvies.

"Hey, Hadley." He slammed his door shut and strolled over toward her. "What are you doing here?"

She twisted to look at him. "Eric. Hi." She gestured toward the bleachers, where a clump of boys stood looking at somebody's Game Boy. "Hudson's starting on the track team."

"The cross-country team?"

She rolled her eyes. "Whatever. It's all running around in circles to me."

"He's in middle school?"

"He's eleven. Starting sixth grade this year."

"God. I can't believe it."

"Yeah, well, I guess time flies when they ship you over to a desert and shoot things at you."

He laughed. "It didn't fly fast enough."

"Your son's on the team?"

"Yeah. This'll be his third year. He qualified for all-state last season." Anger twisted his voice. "And I missed it." He tamped the heat down. Shrugged it off. "Oh well. He's been putting in a lot of time training over the summer. I expect him to make state again this year."

She looked past the bleachers to the center of the track, where Jacob and two other boys were vying to outdo each other in push-ups. "Training during the summer? That sounds pretty hard core for a kid who's in, what—eighth grade?"

"It is. We're looking ahead. Millers Kill High School has two traditional strengths, basketball and cross-country track and field."

"That makes sense. Neither of those takes a lot of money."

"You got it. Anyway, MKHS has fielded several kids who got running scholarships to college. That's what we're shooting for."

"You're kidding me." Hadley's eyes sharpened. "You can get scholarships for running?"

"Sure."

"Huh." She chewed her lower lip.

One of the other parents honked, and the Game Boy–playing group broke up. Hadley's son pelted over and gave his mom a hug, despite the presence of other kids. He was short, dark-haired and dark-eyed like his mother, and Eric's heart squeezed as the boy started babbling on about his practice, his arms unself-consciously wrapped around Hadley's waist. When Eric had left for Iraq, Jake had been like that, still a little guy, still wanting to be his dad's best bud.

". . . so Coach says he needs an assistant and we should all ask our parents for a volunteer," Hudson was saying.

"Not me." Hadley shook the boy's shoulders slightly. "Hudson, do you remember meeting Sergeant McCrea?"

"Oh. Yeah. Sorry. Hi, Sergeant McCrea." The kid peered at him more closely. "Hey, aren't you the one who was in the war?"

"That's me."

Hudson's eyes brightened. "Cool! Didja shoot anybody?"

"Hudson!"

Eric laughed. "Sorry, no."

"Our priest went to Iraq, but she just flew helicopters. I don't think she even had a gun."

"And you're not going to ask her, either." His mom shook him again and swatted at his rear. "Get your sister and get in the car." She grimaced. "Sorry about that."

Eric shook his head while Hudson thundered toward the bleachers. "Don't worry about it. It's a boy thing. They all think guns are cool."

"I just don't get it." Hadley shuddered. "I hate guns."

"You're kind of in the wrong profession, then."

"Don't I know it." She swiveled toward her kids, now roughhousing in the grass. "Into the car, you two!" She corralled them, and with a final "See you tomorrow!" she was off down the access road, along with most of the other vehicles.

"C'mon, Jacob!" Eric shouted. "Let's go." In contrast to Hudson Knox, Jake was taking his own sweet time, disappearing into the bleachers while Eric shifted from foot to foot. His stomach rumbled. Finally, Jake reappeared, water bottle in hand. He slouched toward his father.

"What the hell took you so long? The McIlverys are probably sitting down to eat by now."

Instead of answering, Jake eyed the squad car with disapproval. "God, Dad. Did you have to drive that thing here? It's so embarrassing."

"You used to love riding in the cruiser."

"I used to love Barney the Dinosaur, too." Jake ran a hand through his hair, exposing pimples on his forehead. "I was talking to Iola Stillman."

"Who's Iola Stillman?"

"She's on the high school team. They had practice before us."

Eric, who was opening his door, paused. "She's still here?"

"Yeah. Her dad's supposed to pick her up. She forgot her phone, so she can't call."

Eric scanned the empty parking lot and the vacant school beyond it. The sun sinking into the western mountains. The only thing likely to show up here on a hot night in August was trouble. "I'm going to see if she needs a ride."

"Dad! She's Iola Stillman. She's a sophomore. And you're driving a cop car. She's going to think I'm the biggest dweeb in the world. Dad! No!"

Eric strode off toward the bleachers. He rounded the corner and saw the girl, huddled in a tangle of bony knees and elbows. She started up when she saw him, then sank onto the bench again.

"Iola?" He stopped straight in front of her. The poor thing looked miserable. "I'm Eric McCrea, Jake's dad. Jake says your father was supposed to pick you up? Do you know when?"

She looked down at her running shoes. "He was supposed to be here an hour and a half ago. I woulda left with one of my friends, but I was sure he was going to show."

Eric tried to relax his fists. What the hell kind of father left his daughter all alone out here, with no phone and no other way home? Hadn't the bastard ever heard of sexual assault? "You come with me and Jake," he said. "We'll take you home."

"But what if my dad—"

"You can use my phone and let him know." If it were up to him, Eric would let the son of a bitch make a run out here. Maybe finding his daughter gone would put the fear of God into him.

She grabbed her tote bag and followed him to the parking lot. "Wow," she said, when she saw the cruiser. Jake had already gotten in the passenger side and was trying, when Eric opened the back door to let Iola in, to make himself invisible through immobility.

Eric handed the girl his phone and climbed into the driver's seat. He unlatched the reinforced Plexi barrier and slid it to one side, so Iola could talk to them. She leaned forward and looked around, big-eyed. "I've never been in a police car before."

"I'm glad to hear it. Buckle up."

Jacob shot him a glance without moving his head. "Ooo," Iola said. "There aren't any door handles back here." Eric started up the cruiser and pulled out of the lot. "This is really cool. Thank you so much for giving me a lift, Mr. McCrea."

Eric shot Jacob a look. Jake stared stonily ahead. "Where do you live, Iola?"

"Mountain View Park. Off Sunset Drive." About as far west of the town as the high school was east. Eric drove with half his attention on the traffic, half on Iola's call to what must have been her dad's office. "He didn't?" she said. "Okay. No, I'm fine. Thanks." She hung up. "My dad's a doctor. I thought maybe . . . there might have been an emergency."

"No?"

"Nope. He's not on call. He left a couple hours ago." Her voice had the wavering quality of someone trying not to show hurt. Eric's hands tightened on the wheel. *Bastard.*

Mountain View Park was a new development, built when the skyrocketing real estate prices in Albany and Saratoga began to drive families farther and farther up the Northway. In exchange for a two-hour daily commute, they got sprawling, shining-windowed houses tucked in among trees well away from the quiet dead-end road.

"This is it," Iola said, and he turned up a broad, square-paved drive leading to a brick-and-timber Tudor manor that Henry the Eighth would have been right at home in. He shook his head. *If you want to know what God thinks of money,* his dad would say, *just look at who He gives it to.*

"Is anybody home?"

"I have a key," Iola said.

Eric got out and released the back door, leaving the cruiser running. "I'll walk you up." Inside, unseen, Jake let out a low moan.

They were almost to the front door when it swung open. An older man in rumpled khakis and a half-buttoned shirt came out to the top step. "Iola?" He looked at Eric, alarmed. "What happened?"

"Dad!" Iola stomped up the steps. "You were supposed to pick me up two hours ago!" Her voice broke. "Where were you?"

"I . . . I . . ." Iola's father's eyes shifted back and forth. He looked like an animal pinned in a trap. *Cheating,* Eric thought. *He forgot his kid while he was banging the girlfriend.* "I'm sorry, baby girl." Stillman wrapped his arms around Iola, who stood stiff and unyielding. "I must have gotten my schedule mixed up. I'm so, so sorry."

You sure are. "Iola," Eric said. "Can I have a word with your father?"

Iola wiped at her face. "Okay. I'm going to go inside and call Mum."

She drew herself up with all the dignity a fifteen-year-old could muster. "Thank you again for bringing me home, Mr. McCrea." She glared at her father, then swept past him into the house.

Stillman rubbed his close-cropped hair. "Thank you, Officer. I don't know how I dropped the ball on that one."

Eric stepped closer. Stillman didn't smell drunk. Pills, maybe? Doctors could write their own prescriptions. "I don't know if you're new to the area, Dr. Stillman, but despite our quaint, small-town look, we're not crime-free."

"I know that. My family's lived in Millers Kill for generations, for God's sake."

"Then you ought to know that there have been several sexual assaults of young women over the years. You ought to know that a girl was gang-raped on high school property once. I worked that investigation. I saw what they did to her."

The color drained from Stillman's face.

"You ought to know enough not to leave your teenaged daughter alone out there with night coming on and no way to contact you."

"I didn't mean to!"

"I don't know what you were doing instead of being a father, and frankly, I don't care. Get your act together."

Stillman's mouth opened. Closed. He spun on his heel and vanished into the house, slamming the door behind him.

Goddamn rich guy. He probably sat on his ass watching a wide-screen TV while his daughter waited for him. Yet guys like Eric had to push their kids to run in order to have a hope of sending them to college. Life was no damn fair, and it made him mad. So mad, he could—he stalked back to the cruiser, the last hot rays of the sunset matching the red pounding in his head.

SATURDAY, AUGUST 20   Tomato juice. Worcester sauce. Onion salt. Celery. Clare sat the ingredients on the counter and retrieved her big glass pitcher from the cupboard. She banged through the swinging kitchen doors and headed for the foot of the stairs, trying not to favor her right ankle. She was working to rebuild its strength, and limping around babying it wasn't going to help.

"You want a virgin Bloody Mary?" she yelled up the stairs.

"God, no. Just coffee. I hate tomato juice."

"More for me." She snagged the vodka off the drinks tray and carried it into the kitchen. She removed a package of paper-wrapped sausages from the freezer and started them defrosting in the microwave while she mixed up a Bloody. She glanced at the clock hanging over her bare pine table. Glanced at the pitcher. It was noon in Nova Scotia. Close enough. She poured herself a tall, stiff one, swizzled it with a celery stick, and drank half the contents in one pull.

She smiled as she heard the shower go on. Russ had arrived unexpectedly last night, late from patrolling. Woke her up, despite the sleeping pill she had taken. Woke her up again at dawn, his hands moving over her, slow, intense, the two of them gathering like storm clouds over the mountains until they exploded: heat lightning and rolling thunder. She had dropped back into a deep, dreamless sleep, not surfacing until close to eleven. She stretched, snapping her spine. Lord, she loved Saturdays. She'd never really appreciated them before.

She threw the sausages into an enameled pan and started the coffee brewing in her press. Switched on the radio and refreshed her Bloody Mary. Pulled a carton of eggs from the icebox and turned around. She saw the face through the kitchen door at the same time she heard the knocking. She shrieked, clutched at her robe, dropped the eggs.

The door swung open. Anne Vining-Ellis burst into the kitchen. "Oh, Clare, I'm so sorry. I didn't mean to startle you. Are you all right?"

Clare felt something wet and viscous against her bare foot. She looked down. Three broken eggs were oozing across her cheap pressed-vinyl floor.

"Oh, God, I did startle you." Anne snatched a dishcloth off the rack and turned on the cold water. "I should have—"

"Clare, are you okay? I heard—" Russ came though the swinging doors before Clare could say anything. At least, she thought stupidly, he was wearing a towel slung around his waist. She had discovered that wasn't always a given.

"—called first." Anne's voice was faint.

Outside, birds caroled and chirped in the rustling trees. On the radio, the audience of *Wait, Wait, Don't Tell Me* was laughing. A puff of hot August air rolled into the kitchen. From somewhere deep within her, Clare's southern upbringing rose to the occasion. "Russ," she said, "I believe you know Anne Vining-Ellis."

Russ's lips twitched. "Clare, why don't you shut the door."

She did so, leaving a trail of egg-white droplets across the floor. Anne abruptly twisted the running water off. She squeezed the dishcloth into the sink. "Um." She waved the cloth toward the egg carton. "Better get that up before it dries."

Russ looked at Clare. "Is it all right if I go get dressed?" She nodded. "Okay. I'll be back in a few minutes." He sniffed. "Whatever you're making, it smells great."

Clare and Anne both watched in silence as Russ disappeared through the swinging doors. Clare listened to the thump and creak of his footsteps going up the stairs. She turned toward Anne. Chair of the stewardship committee. Important donor to the church. Parishioner. *Friend.* She hoped. She took a deep breath. "Well . . ."

Anne shook her head. "Oh. My. God."

Clare's heart sank.

"He is totally hot. Even with the bullet scars."

"What?"

"What is he, fifty? He's got to be close to my age, right?" She fanned herself. "Let me tell you, my husband sure doesn't look like that in a towel."

"What?"

Anne dropped the wet cloth on the counter and crossed to Clare. She hugged her. "Oh, Clare. It's not exactly a surprise. I mean, yeah, seeing him here half naked was definitely a surprise, but the fact that you're doing more than meeting for lunch at the diner isn't." She released Clare, grinning. "Besides, everyone knows priests and ministers don't have sex. So I'll just assume his shower is broken and he was borrowing yours."

Clare buried her face in her hands. "I think I need another drink."

"I'll join you."

Clare took down a second tall glass and filled it to the brim while Anne mopped up the broken eggs. "So." She stood and traded the eggy cloth for a Bloody Mary. "Is this a new thing? I mean, since you've been away for a year and a half."

"When I found out I was being deployed, we . . ." Clare made a vague gesture. "We only had two weeks, though, and everything was crazy, with me trying to take care of all the details at St. Alban's and get ready to go and all." She looked into her drink. "This feels very new. I mean, we've known each other for how many years now? But we've never actually been out on a date."

"What are you using for birth control?"

"Good Lord." Clare could feel her cheeks turning red.

Anne pulled out one of the ladder-back chairs and sat at the pine table. "I'm a doctor. I'm concerned."

Clare swallowed a large gulp of her Bloody Mary. "I'm on the pill."

"That's foresighted of you."

"I've been on for years. Erratic periods and army flight schedules don't mix." She dropped into another chair and covered her eyes. "I cannot believe I'm discussing this with you."

"Then make an appointment and go talk about it with your regular doctor. I know you have this *thing* about medical treatment, but—"

"Anne, what did you come here for?"

Anne paused. "Sorry." She took the celery stick out of her drink. Tapped it on the rim of the glass. "Sometimes it's easier to talk about other people's issues than your own."

"I know. Believe me, I know."

Anne looked up at her, smiling a little. "I just bet you do." She laid the celery stick on the table. "It's about Will."

"What about Will?"

"You . . . know what happened to him."

"Yes. I'd heard. I haven't seen him since I've been back, though."

"Of course you haven't. No one has. He doesn't go anywhere. He doesn't do anything. He lets us drag him to physical therapy and to the orthopedist, but he refuses to go anywhere else. Remember how he loved to play his guitar? We've encouraged him to get back together with his old band. We've offered to pay for shop classes over at ACC—you know how he was always fooling around with cars."

Clare nodded.

"Nothing. He won't do anything."

"Is he acting depressed?"

"No! I mean, not to my face. If he has to interact with anyone, he behaves as if everything's fine. He cracks jokes, he carries on a conversation, but it's all an act. When no one's around . . . I can hear him, in his room. Just sitting there. No music. No movement. Like a machine that's been turned off." Clare laid her hand open on the table. Anne took it. "I've tried to talk to him about seeing a psychiatrist, but he wouldn't listen."

"Can you place him in treatment? Without his consent?"

"Only if he's a danger to himself or to others. And I'm afraid—" Her voice broke. "I'm so afraid that by the time he shows he's a danger to himself it will be too late."

"How can I help?"

"Will you come talk to him? Not officially or formally. Just come for dinner and then, you know, casually talk to him."

"Of course, but Anne, I'm not a trained mental health professional. If you think he's suicidal—"

Anne shook her head. "I don't think it's his mind. I think his soul has been wounded, and souls are your profession."

Clare held out her other hand, and Anne squeezed both of them, hard. There was a polite throat clearing at the doorway. Russ stood there, barefoot, in jeans and an untucked shirt. "Am I intruding?"

"No." Anne released Clare's hands and stood up. "I am." She smiled at Russ. "I'll leave you to enjoy your brunch, Chief Van Alstyne."

"I think you ought to call me Russ, all things considering."

"You got it. Clare? Tonight? Six o'clock?"

"I'll be there."

Anne opened the door, letting in another puff of warm air. "Thanks. Sorry for the eggs and all. As for you"—she pointed to Russ—"if you're going to eat this woman's food and run up her water bill, the least you can do is take her out on a date."

The door clicked shut behind her. In the kitchen, the coffee press whistled faintly and the sausages popped in the skillet. Russ looked at her. "No more sleeping over."

"Noooo!" She stood up, nearly knocking over the remains of her Bloody Mary.

"Yes. We've gotten away with it for eight weeks. That was too damn close for comfort."

Clare flung an arm toward the door. "Anne's fine with it! She's happy for me."

"Dr. Anne's fine with it because she's your friend. What if it had been one of the conservative guys on the vestry, like whatsis-name, with the scarf?"

"Sterling Sumner."

"How do you think he would have reacted? What if it had been Elizabeth de Groot?"

Clare winced. Her deacon, who was tasked with keeping Clare on the straight and narrow, had a serious thing for clerical reverence and priestly authority. "She'd be on the phone to the bishop right now."

"Damn right she would—and I don't think his reaction would be 'Fine, I'm so happy for you.'" He reached out and pulled her into his arms. "Would it?"

She shook her head against his chest. "It's not fair."

"It's your organization, darlin'. I may not be a member, but I know we gotta play by the rules."

"But I sleep better with you here!" It was true. She had used prayer and sleeping pills and warm milk and brandy, but the only thing that centered and settled her was Russ. Curled against the warm solidity of his back, she could let down her guard. She was safe.

When did it stop being safe to fall asleep? She shuddered.

He tightened his hold on her. "Just for a while."

"It's not going to stop being an issue."

"It will if we're married."

Married. He had asked her once, the night they had found out she was leaving for Iraq. It was a spur-of-the-moment proposal, an age-old instinct to seize the moment when war was howling outside the door. She had turned him down, gambling that they would have a second chance. Confident that when he truly put his wife's death behind him, they would both be ready.

"Clare?" His lips were curved slightly, but his eyes were wary. He was, she realized, unsure of himself. It wasn't an expression she was used to seeing on Russ Van Alstyne's face.

"It's just . . . we haven't talked about that. Marriage."

He jammed his hands into his jeans pockets. "We have to be realistic. Living together isn't going to be an option."

"That's not what I meant." She was barefoot, wearing her old summer pajamas. Sausages sizzled and popped in the skillet. NPR had moved on to *Car Talk*. Even at her most down-to-earth, this wasn't what she envisioned when she thought of a proposal. "I mean we haven't discussed the issues. The details. Marriage is a big, huge deal."

His mouth quirked. "Believe me, I take marriage very seriously."

She flushed. She of all people had reason to know "divorce" wasn't in his vocabulary. Which, when you got down to it, was the reason for the sinking feeling in her stomach. The fact he was mentioning marriage for the first time after being caught with his pants down smelled unpleasantly like *shotgun wedding*. With her vestry, instead of her father, holding the 12-gauge. Russ loved her. She knew that. She just didn't know if in some deep well of emotion he was still choosing Linda over her. "Maybe this isn't the time or place for a big 'what do we want out of marriage' discussion."

He got that expression again. The uncertain one. "Is there that much to discuss? 'Cause I can tell you what I want in under five words. You as my wife." He shrugged. "The rest of it, I figure we'll make up as we go along. That's pretty much how it goes, in my experience."

"Why do you want to get married? I mean, other than the sex thing."

"There has to be more than sex?" He grinned. "It's not because I'm chomping at the bit to be the preacher's husband, I can guarantee you that." She laughed a little. He ran his hands up her arms and rested them on her shoulders. "I want to be married because I like those easy-to-understand, boring definitions. Husband. Wife. I want to be married because life is short, and I want to spend whatever I have left of it with you, every day, every night. I want to be married so that everything I have and everything I am is yours, and everything of you is mine. And I want to be married so I can lay you out on the dining room table if I feel like it and have you six ways from Sunday in the middle of the afternoon and if one of your parishioners walks in on us, it's tough titties for them."

She started laughing.

"I'm not a complicated guy, Clare. I keep trying to dress it up with flowers and stuff, but that's what it all comes down to with me."

She touched his cheek, smooth from his morning shave. She was afraid her heart would break open from feeling too much. "I told you. You don't ever have to dress anything up for me. Just be yourself."

◆ ◆ ◆

The phone hanging on the wall between the door and the window rang before he had the chance to ask her the same question. What did she want out of marriage? Specifically, marriage to a guy fourteen years older, who thought God was a myth and whose job could get him killed.

Clare sighed and crossed the floor. "Hello?"

Maybe he was pushing it. She didn't talk about Iraq, but he had held her while she thrashed around with bad dreams. He had seen the fatigue on her face as she tried to be everything for everybody in her church. Of course, that might argue for the two of them getting married as soon as possible. He knew he'd do a damn sight better job of drawing boundaries than she did.

Maybe he should just ask her right now. Get the damn thing settled. But Christ, the ring was back at his mother's house, and she deserved something special. Memorable. Not him blurting it out before breakfast. Maybe he could make an excuse to swing by his mom's place. He could take her on a picnic. Picnics were romantic, weren't they?

Clare looked at him oddly. "Um. Certainly." She handed the phone out. "It's Harlene, for you."

"What?" He took the receiver as if it might be booby-trapped. "Van Alstyne here."

Clare went to the stove to check the breakfast. "Sorry to bother you and the reverend," Harlene said.

"That's all right," Russ lied. "What's up?" Clare drew a long meat fork out of the utensil canister and started pricking sausages. He tried to remember if the IGA sold picnic lunches.

"Eric's called in sick, and Noble's gone up to Tupper Lake for the weekend. We're short and we need coverage."

"Have you tried Paul?" Russ watched Clare take down a glass bowl and open the carton of eggs. They'd need sunscreen—and bug dope. Bug dope definitely wasn't romantic.

"Well, I'm sure I could get ahold of him, but he'll be on overtime. You want me to try him anyways?"

The magic word, "overtime," brought his full attention back to Harlene. "No. No. I don't want to give the alderman anything else to complain about." He pointed at the egg Clare had picked up. He shook his head. *Don't bother.* "I'll be there in twenty minutes. And call Duane to see if he'll be available just in case. Last weekend before the holiday, we might need him for traffic and parking."

"Let's hope he remembers to turn his darned phone on so I can at least leave him a message. Unlike you."

He slapped the front pocket of his jeans and drew out his blank, inactive cell phone. "Sorry." He thought for a second. Did he want to know? "Harlene? Why did you call Clare's number to reach me?"

She laughed in his ear. "I may be old, but I haven't forgotten what it's like. I figured you two would be making up for lost time."

"Oh."

"And Erla Davis mentioned to me that she saw you walking down her street and getting into your truck real early last week when she was headed out to open up the diner."

Oh, shit. "Okay. Thanks. I'll see you soon." He hung up. Clare raised her eyebrows.

"Eric's called in sick, and Harlene can't raise Noble. I've got to go in."

"How did she know you were here? Did you leave word at the station?"

"Are you kidding? No. She called my cell, and when that didn't go through, she called here next. Seems the waitress from the Kreemy Kakes diner spotted me picking up my truck a few mornings ago." He pinched the bridge of his nose. "I guess I'm not as good at sneaking around as I thought."

Clare laughed. "Don't look so grim about it." She crossed the floor and wrapped her arms around his midsection. "I'm not complaining."

"God. I'm sorry." He pressed his lips against her hair. Over the aroma of the sausages, he could smell her, vodka and tomato juice and Clare. "I've got to go. If it's anything like last weekend, it'll be crazy today. I don't want you to feel like I'm running away from this conversation, but I don't know when I'll be able to get back."

"I'll be at the Ellises' tonight anyway."

"Tomorrow?"

"Sunday."

He groaned. "I'm in the seat all day Monday, but I'll be free by dinnertime."

She shook her head. "I've got a premarital session at six and a building and grounds committee meeting at seven." She slanted her eyes up at him. "You could sneak over later that night."

"No." His voice was stonier than he intended. Probably because the idea was so damn appealing.

Clare growled with frustration and pushed him away. "Go. Finish getting dressed. While you're at it, consider that I've been taking it easy on summer schedule. The Sunday after Labor Day is Homecoming Sunday, and everything starts up again: adult ed and weekly community suppers and all the committees. I'll be twice as busy as I am now."

He stumped upstairs, worrying about how much of herself she was going to pour into those meetings and suppers and lessons. Wondering how long after he asked her they could get married. Assuming she said yes. He was pretty sure doing it at lunchtime in Judge Ryswick's chambers was out of the question.

When he returned, feet in boots and his less than pristine uniform blouse tucked into his jeans, she handed him a paper sack. "I've put a sausage in a bun for you."

He grinned.

"Don't say it," she warned.

He took it with a quick kiss instead of a joke. "I'll call you."

"Oh, yeah. That's what they all say."

He thought about it all the way to the station. He hadn't set the scene very well. Hell, he hadn't set the scene at all. She hadn't gotten any courtship, just awkward years of being the semi-sorta Other Woman, followed by hush-hush sex. Maybe he ought to put on the brakes and do the dating thing for a while.

But dammit, he didn't want a girlfriend. It was ridiculous, for a man his age to have a *girlfriend*. He wanted a wife. He wanted a house with both their things in it, and joint bank accounts, and someone saying, "Hi, honey," when he got home at the end of the day.

He just had to come up with a decent time and place to ask her.

◆ ◆ ◆

The first thing he saw when he arrived at the station was Lyle MacAuley, coming through dispatch from the squad room. "What are you doing here?" Russ asked.

"Paperwork for a shoplifting bust." Lyle shook his head. "Used to be, you'd show up at the Super Kmart, and it'd be some kid with a CD jammed down his pants. Now it's professionals. You should have seen this pair. Slits sewn in their jackets and everything." He followed Russ into his office. "Don't need a fence anymore. Sell the stuff on eBay."

Russ picked up the BOLO sheets Harlene had left on his desk and leafed through them. "Hmn. Anything going on I should know about?"

"Not particularly. Anything going on that I should know about?"

Russ's head came up. "What's that mean?"

"Oh, I dunno." Lyle crossed his arms over his chest.

"You overheard Harlene, didn't you?"

Lyle dropped his arms and his pretense at casualness. "Reverend Fergusson's had to deal with a lot of gossip around this town over the past few years. Now, when she went away to Iraq, it all sort of died down. So I can't figure why you seem hell-bent on making her the subject of conversation again."

"What are you, her father?"

Lyle splayed his hands on Russ's desk and leaned forward. "Why'n't you just ask the lady to marry you? God knows why, but she seems pretty fond of you. Just make an honest woman out of her before talk spreads. If it was anybody else, it wouldn't make a damn bit of difference, but she's a minister, Russ. What are the people in her church going to think when it comes out you've been spending your nights over to her place?"

Russ threw the sheets on his desk. "I know that. You think I don't know that?"

Lyle opened his hands and raised his bushy gray eyebrows.

"I was ready to ask her the day she got back. There just didn't seem to be a good time to do it."

"It's been two months already. I think you'd be able to find five minutes somewheres."

Russ glared at his deputy chief. "Clare's had too much to deal with, readjusting to civilian life." He pushed away from his desk and walked to one of the high windows overlooking Main Street. "She's not sleeping well. She's drinking too much." He rapped against the glass pane, and a startled mourning dove flew off the granite windowsill. "She's trying to be there for her congregation, and it's sucking the life out of her. I didn't want to put one more thing on her plate."

"Give the reverend some credit. Near as I can tell, she's never shown any reluctance to tell you to go soak your head." Russ let out an involuntary laugh. "If you're crowdin' her," Lyle went on, "she'll let you know."

The intercom buzzed. "You two done in there?" Harlene's tinny voice asked.

"Yeah," Lyle said. "You can stop pretending not to listen now."

"I got the manager from the new resort on the line." Harlene sounded tart. "Says she'd like to speak with Chief Van Alstyne, if he happens to be available."

Russ looked at Lyle. "She asked for me?"

"Maybe she knows you're gonna be in the market for a reception hall."

"Not if an asteroid hit and it was the last building left in New York." The resort might be the fanciest spot in three counties, but as far as Russ was concerned, it was the open vortex to hell. He wouldn't have been surprised to find the place had been built atop an Indian burial ground, like in the horror movies. "Put her through, Harlene." He punched the speaker button. Lyle moved a stack of old circ sheets off the wooden chair on the other side of the desk and sat down. "Van Alstyne here."

"Chief? This is Barbara LeBlanc, at the Algonquin Waters. Look, I have a problem here that I think is one for the police, but I need it to be handled sensitively."

"Okay. What's up?"

"A man came in about an hour ago, looking for one of our bookkeepers. The front desk associates told him she didn't come in during the weekend, and he parked himself in the lobby and said he'd wait. They were a little nervous, because it seemed, well, very stalkerlike behavior, so they called me, and I went to talk to the man and told him the lobby was for the use of guests only and if he'd like to leave a message for Ms. McNabb he could—"

"Wait a minute. Did you say McNabb?"

"That's her name. The bookkeeper."

"Tally McNabb?"

"That's right."

Russ glanced at Lyle, who pursed his lips thoughtfully. "What does this man look like?"

Barbara LeBlanc paused. "He's, um, maybe five ten, very muscular, um, in his late twenties or early thirties . . ."

Russ sighed. He knew when someone was tiptoeing around. "Is he black?"

"Yes!" she whispered. "How did you know?"

"I've met him before. Go on, what happened?"

"When I told him the lobby was for guests only, he insisted on renting a room! He said he'd stay here until Ms. McNabb showed up, even though I gave him my word we didn't expect her until Monday." She dropped her voice again. "We're a public accommodation, Chief Van Alstyne. We have to have an iron-clad reason to refuse someone's trade. This whole waiting-around-for-a-woman-to-show thing makes me very nervous, but I was afraid turning him away would just open us up to a potential lawsuit."

"So you rented him a room."

"Yes."

Russ pinched the bridge of his nose beneath his glasses. "Where is he now?" Rousting Quentan Nichols out of a room at the hush-and-plush Algonquin Waters was going to be problematical.

"He's still sitting in the lobby."

Okay. One thing going right today. "You did the right thing by calling me, Ms. LeBlanc. I'm heading over now. I'll talk with him."

"He is a stalker?"

"He was here looking for Tally McNabb two months ago. There was some trouble. I don't have any reason to think she wants to see him now any more than she did then."

"You'll be discreet?"

"I'll keep things as low-key as possible."

She sighed. "Thank you so much, Chief. I'll see you in about half an hour." A dial tone replaced her voice.

Lyle looked at him. "This that guy who got up that fight at the Dew Drop?"

"One of 'em." Russ shook his head. "God knows what he's doing here now. I can't believe he got leave again so soon."

"That's right. He's military police, isn't he? Like you and Eric." Lyle pushed at the arms of his chair and stood. "Well. Let's get going."

"Who said you're going along?"

"It took Hadley and Kevin both to stop him last time, didn't it?"

"I'm just going to talk with the guy."

"Yeah? That's your intention. You don't know his." MacAuley let his half-smile drop. "Seriously. The only young MP I know is Eric McCrea, and I'll tell you, if I had to go pick him up for something, I sure wouldn't do it without backup."

Russ nodded. "Yeah. Okay. You're right."

"I usually am. It'd save us a lot of time if you'd just start from that premise."

They took separate cruisers to the resort. If everything went according to plan, they'd split up afterward, Lyle heading back to Fort Henry, Russ taking the Cossayuharie loop. Of course, not much had gone according to plan today.

They parked in the wide drive curving through the portico. As Russ stepped out into the shade and the mountain scent of balsam and juniper, his stomach turned. The world had been howling white with snow the last time he had been here. The polished oak-and-brass doors, open to the August air, had been draped in plastic sheeting. The oriental rugs and leather chairs of the gleaming pine lobby had been covered in paint-spattered tarps, and the people descending the stairs to the spa below had been electricians and carpenters, not tanned, toned matrons.

Linda had been alive.

Funny how he always thought of her by name these days, instead of as "my wife."

"You okay?" Lyle's voice was low in his ear.

Russ gestured toward the swags of lined and slashed fabric framing clerestory windows beneath the arching cathedral ceiling. "Linda made those."

Lyle slapped his upper arm. Gave his shoulder a squeeze.

"I'm all right." Russ coughed to get the thickness out of his throat. "I'm fine," he said in a more normal tone of voice. He brought his attention back to the lobby. There was a pair of white-haired gents in candy-colored pants swapping newspaper sections with each other, and a mother and daughter reading the daily activity board, their identical golden blond heads close together, but no Quentan Nichols. "He's not here."

Lyle nudged him. A slim brunette emerged from a door behind the granite reception counter. She had a flat walkie-talkie clipped to the waist of her short skirt, and a name badge pinned to her expensive-looking silk blouse. She crossed toward them, her heels clicking on the pine floorboards. "Chief Van Alstyne." She held out her hand. "Good to see you again."

"Ms. LeBlanc." He shook her hand. "This is Deputy Chief Lyle Mac-Auley."

Lyle straightened his spine and expanded his chest. He held LeBlanc's hand a second longer than necessary.

"The chief and deputy chief. I'm honored." Her wide mouth stretched into a smile that didn't quite make her eyes. "Or should I be worried?"

"Don't you worry about a thing." Lyle radiated confidence, with just a hint of amusement that anyone might think he couldn't handle a heavily muscled thirty-year-old MP. Russ had to admit, he was good. "Where is Mr. Nichols right now?" Lyle asked.

LeBlanc gestured toward the almost empty lobby. "He went up to his room about fifteen minutes ago." She held up a plastic card attached to a card- and key-heavy ring. "I put him on the top floor, as far away from anyone else as I could. Just in case."

"Good thinking." Russ glanced at Lyle. "See if we can get him back down here?"

Lyle nodded. "Be a lot less messy, if he doesn't want to come with us."

"Oh." LeBlanc lowered the card. "I'm sorry. I should have tried to keep him in the lobby."

"No," Russ said. "You did exactly the right thing."

"We're the ones with the law enforcement experience," Lyle reassured her. "Not you."

"Years of experience," Russ said. "Years and years."

Lyle shot him a look.

"Could you get him on the phone?" Russ said. "Tell him there's been some difficulty with his credit card and that you've got to swipe it again." He thumbed toward the far wall. "We'll wait between the elevators and the stairs. Whichever way he comes down, we'll have him surrounded before he has a chance to kick up a fuss."

LeBlanc nodded. She headed back to her office, giving them a chance to appreciate the view as she walked away. "Mm-mm," Lyle said. "That woman could rent me a room anytime."

"She's a little young for you, isn't she?"

"Oh, I dunno." Lyle slanted him a look. "I figure her to be about Clare's age."

Russ shut up. They crossed the lobby, Lyle gawking at the antler chandeliers and the stone fireplace, big enough to roast an entire cow in. He gestured toward the wide, carpeted stairs.

"It only goes as far as the second floor," Russ said. "Then it's your standard interior staircase up to the fifth."

Lyle craned his neck to see to where the lobby angled into a hallway past the bar. "What about that side?"

"The offices. There's a fire door, but it's alarmed. No exterior fire escape. The night of the fire, all the guests exited out the lobby or the alarmed door."

"Sounds easy. Just the way I like it."

Russ positioned himself at the edge of the elevator bank, where, if he leaned forward, he could see all four elevators. Lyle propped up the wall next to the stairs. Russ tried to look relaxed, but there wasn't any way to disguise two cops hanging around waiting for someone to show. The blond mother-daughter pair stared as they gathered up their tiny purses and headed for the door. Lyle waggled his fingers and winked. Jesus. That guy would hit on anything.

The elevator dinged. He tensed, but it was only an elderly couple, who looked at him warily and sidled past him before heading downstairs to the spa. He resumed his watch. He envisioned Nichols collecting his wallet and his key card. Maybe putting his shoes back on. Leaving the room. Walking down to the elevator. Pressing the button. Waiting. Waiting.

The elevator dinged again. The far set of doors opened, but no one stepped out. Russ strode toward the car, slapping his hand against the side of the door to keep it from closing, but there was no need. The thing was empty. He glanced over at Lyle, who ducked around the corner of the stairs. He reappeared a few seconds later. Shrugged.

Russ crossed the expanse of lobby again, making for the manager's office. LeBlanc met him at the door. "Did you reach him?" he asked.

"Yes, right after you and I talked. He said he'd be right down." She glanced at the thin gold watch on her wrist. "He should have made it by now. Do you want me to try him again?"

"No. Can you shut down the elevators for a few minutes?" She blanched, then nodded and disappeared into her office. When she came back, she dangled a rectangular metal key from her ring. "Follow me," he said. "He's not coming down," he told Lyle.

"Stairs or elevator?"

"I'll take the stairs. Ms. LeBlanc"—he turned to the manager—"I want you to shut down every elevator except the one Deputy Chief MacAuley is using. Got it?"

"I'm coming with you." Before Russ could object, she went on. "I'm the manager. What happens here is my responsibility."

He compressed his lips. "All right—but stay behind Lyle, and do what he says." She nodded. They headed for the elevator bank. Russ hit the stairs.

If it had been ten years ago, he would have taken the steps two at a time. If it had been two years ago—well, no, two years ago he'd been in a bed in the Washington County Hospital, recovering from two .357 bullets in his chest and one in his thigh, but the rehab and the PT and the exercise program his therapist had put him on had left him in the best shape he'd been in since leaving the army. His heart rate was up, and his knees twinged, but he could make five stories without breaking a sweat. As long as he wasn't trying to carry Clare at the same time.

The interior stairwell terminated at the fifth floor, which was just what he wanted to see. No way to go but down. He pushed through the heavy door into the hallway, in time to see Lyle and the manager walking toward him. Lyle's face was grim. "He's flown."

"How?" He frowned at LeBlanc. "Could he have cut the door alarms downstairs?"

She shook her head. "They're wired into the electrical system, not after-market add-ons. We'd have to have a complete power failure to turn them off."

"Then he's got to be hiding in the stairwell on the other side of the building."

"Or he's on one of the other floors." Lyle's face creased in frustration.

"The two of us aren't going to be able to smoke him out. We can't cover all the exits."

"The only way out is through the lobby or one of the alarmed fire doors. We can—"

"Oh, no." Barbara LeBlanc slapped her hand over her mouth. "There is another way." She shouldered through the stairwell door, kicked off her heels, and scooped them up one-handed.

"What?" Russ followed her.

"The second floor." She hiked her already short skirt up and bounded down the stairs two at a time. Russ and Lyle clattered after her, their boots thudding and echoing up and down the stairwell. "We have a collection room there," she shouted, already a flight and a half ahead of them. "So we don't have to haul loads of dirty linens through the lobby."

She was out the second-floor doorway before she could say any more. Russ burst though, Lyle right behind him. LeBlanc was pelting noiselessly down the hall, the thick carpeting absorbing even the vibrations of her passage. They caught up with her as she skidded to a halt in front of an unmarked door next to the elevator. She snapped the key ring off her waist and thrust a plastic card into the flat lock pad. The door clicked.

A teen in a maid's uniform looked up from a rolling cart, her hands full of tiny soaps. The collection room was the size of a guest bedroom, lined with towers of toilet paper and gallon jugs of disinfectant. Canvas-and-steel cleaning carts jammed end to end, filling the center of the room. In the back corner, Russ could see white-painted double metal doors. A freight elevator.

"Kerry," LeBlanc said, "did a man come through here?"

"Yeah. Just a few minutes ago. He said he was security." She stared at Russ and Lyle. "Did I . . . should I have . . . ?"

"Don't worry about it." LeBlanc weaved through the carts to the elevator.

"Where does this go?" Russ asked as she jabbed at the button.

"Broadway. The main behind-the-scenes corridor in the basement. It opens onto the kitchen, shipping and receiving, the employees' lounge—"

"Could he get out from there?" Lyle asked.

"Yes. The employees' exit and the door next to receiving are exterior-locking only. You can't lock them from the inside."

The elevator doors rattled open. Unlike the wood-and-mirror-paneled guest elevators, the service car was lined with hanging furniture pads. Russ and Lyle followed LeBlanc in.

"No alarms?" Russ said.

"No, of course not."

Russ pointed to the walkie-talkie hanging off her waist. "Check in with the departments he might have reached from Broadway."

The manager twisted the mike off its clip and triggered it. By the time the elevator shuddered to a stop, she had confirmed that no one had seen a stranger going through the kitchen, the receiving dock, or the spa.

"He must have split out the employees' exit," Lyle said. They stepped out into a concrete-floored corridor, inadequately lit by long fluorescent tubes high overhead, crowded on either side by crates and canisters stacked three and four atop one another. It looked like a pessimistic paranoid's bomb shelter.

"I don't understand how he found the collection room in the first place," LeBlanc said. "There's nothing to indicate it. It doesn't appear on any of the hotel maps."

"He was looking for it." Russ didn't like the level of thought and preparation that went into Nichols's flight. In his experience, innocent men didn't make escape plans.

"The employees' exit is this way." LeBlanc led them to where the corridor T-stopped at a set of steel doors. "This is the kitchen." She pointed. "Employees' exit to the right, stairs to the spa and the lobby to the left."

"This place is blown," Lyle said. "He's headed for his vehicle."

Russ nodded. "Get to your unit. Have Harlene send a car to Tally McNabb's house. I'll take the back way." Lyle jogged toward the stairs. "Thanks, Ms. LeBlanc. I don't think he'll come back here, but if you spot him, let us know." Russ turned toward the employees' exit.

"It's always exciting seeing you, Chief," she called after him.

The employees' way out was another nondescript door, marked only by a red exit sign and a litter of papers and posters taped on either side. Russ walked into blinding sunshine—no columned portico on this side—and found himself on a gravel path wide enough to accommodate a golf cart. It curved through manicured grass until it rose and disappeared into the trees that ringed the resort. The employee parking lot was somewhere back there, he guessed, tucked out of sight of the guests whose rooms overlooked the rear of the spa.

Would Nichols have stashed his vehicle there? He doubted it. Easier and less obtrusive to park in front. A quicker exit if things went south. He jogged up the walkway as far as the corner of the building, then struck out across the grass. He stayed tight to the hotel, avoiding the rock gardens and flower beds scattered across the lush lawn.

At the front of the hotel, a solid, waist-high yew hedgerow separated him from the looping drive. It was there he finally saw Nichols, in khakis and a polo shirt, a windbreaker in one hand, a leather-and-canvas attaché case in the other. The MP had crossed the drive and the crescent-shaped upper parking lot and was striding down the steps to the lower lot. Fast but not hurried. He looked like a businessman running late for a meeting at a Lake George marina.

"Nichols!" Russ spotted a break in the hedgerow a few yards away, where a crushed stone walk led into the gardens. "Police! Drop your bag and put your hands in the air!" He ran toward the opening. Nichols turned his head but kept walking. Russ skidded though the gap in the yew, stones flying, and spotted Lyle getting out of his squad car, headed for the upper lot. Russ ran in a straight line, ignoring the steps to his right and the concrete ramp to his left, picking the most direct line toward Nichols's rapidly receding back. He bounded over low rock outcroppings and pounded across the ground cover, leaving crushed flowers and scattered wood chips in his wake.

At the upper lot, he lost sight of Nichols. He ran across the asphalt and paused, teetering, at the top of the next set of stone stairs.

"There!" Lyle, above him, pointed. "He's behind the blue SUV."

Russ leaped down the stairs, knees screaming, and broke for the SUV. He was maybe ten yards away, closing fast, when a late-model Crown Vic, anonymous in government green, reversed out of the space behind a blue Explorer. It lurched forward, straight toward Russ. Then Nichols slammed on the brakes. Russ could see the man's face though the tinted windshield, see his lips moving, and had a heart-stopping second to think: *Pull my gun? Or jump?*

Nichols twisted in his seat. The Crown Vic exploded into reverse, screeching backward through the lot, bumping over one of the low rock curbs. It spun in a tire-squealing half circle and surged up the entry ramp the wrong way.

"Get in the car!" Russ yelled to Lyle. "Get in the car!" He turned, back up the stairs, across the upper lot and staggered up the second set of stairs in time to see Nichols's car disappearing down the drive. He hadn't gone through the portico, thank God, which by now had filled up with bell-hops and parking attendants and wide-eyed guests. Lyle's cruiser pulled forward into a tight U-turn. He rolled past Russ, pointing to where Nichols had gone. Russ nodded. Lyle punched his lights and siren and accelerated after Nichols. Russ yanked the door of his own unit open, hurled himself into the seat, and was rolling in the opposite direction before he had fin-ished buckling in.

As soon as he was safely away from the crowd, he stomped on the gas. He tugged the mic off its clip. "Fifteen-thirty, this is fifteen-fifty-seven."

"Got you."

"See him?"

"Just dust. We coming out at the same place?"

"Yeah. The loop joins up about a mile above Sacandaga Road."

"Will he head for town? Or south on Route 9?"

"Depends on what he's carrying in that case." It was damn small for an overnight bag, but there was plenty of room for a couple automatics and any number of magazines. "You get that car sent to Tally McNabb's?"

"Kevin's on his way."

"Good." At least she wouldn't be surprised, alone, by Nichols wanting to "talk." He heard a faint siren. "I'm coming up on the Y." He took his foot off the gas. The last thing he wanted to do was broadside Lyle. The road was clear. He accelerated forward. "I'm through."

"I see you."

Russ glanced up at the rearview mirror. There was Lyle's unit, lights whirling, sun sparking off the hood and grille. He shifted his focus ahead: narrow private road twisting through dense pine and hemlock forest. "No sign of him ahead."

"Jesum. That guy drives like he's at Watkins Glen."

And he was headed toward an intersection that had already seen one fatal accident this summer. Russ hoped to hell Nichols was a better driver than Ellen Bain had been. The two squad cars flew down the remaining stretch of mountain road, Lyle a prudent six or seven lengths behind Russ. Approaching the roads' T-stop, Russ took his foot off the gas again. He keyed the mic. "I'll take east toward town. You head south toward 9."

"Roger that."

Russ slowed, slowed some more, and made damn sure no other vehicles were coming along the Sacandaga Road. He swung left, past the enormous carved and painted Algonquin Waters sign. Behind him, he could see Lyle's cruiser pull into the road and head in the opposite direction. Before him, the road rose over a treeless peak. Russ sped up, crested, saw the fields and pastures spreading out below, green and gold and brown, like a ragged quilt stitched with stony brooks and sagging barbwire fences . . . and there, halfway to the horizon, a Crown Vic.

Russ tromped on the gas as he reached for the mic again. "Fifteen-thirty, this is fifteen-fifty-seven."

"Go."

"I got him."

"I'm coming around."

Russ signed off and immediately keyed the mic again. "Dispatch, this is fifteen-fifty-seven."

"Go, fifteen-fifty-seven."

"Be advised both units are in pursuit of late-model Ford Crown Vic, U.S. government plates 346-638, headed east on the Sacandaga Road."

"Roger that, fifteen-fifty-seven. Do you require assistance?"

"Alert the state police. He may be headed for the Northway via Schuyler-ville Road." Or he could take Route 57 into town. That was Russ's fear. Seventy miles an hour along country roads was dangerous enough—speeding through Main Street on a Saturday afternoon during tourist season was a guaranteed disaster. "Harlene, make sure they know our guy is an MP. Resisting, evading, speeding. Possibly armed. Fifteen-fifty-seven out." He punched the accelerator. The big-block Interceptor engine roared and the cruiser surged forward, pressing Russ into his seat, blurring the fences and fields outside, turning the steady thrum-thrum-thrum of his tires into a high-pitched yowl. He drove over another rise, the road curving farther to the east, and he saw Nichols smoking past the Stuyvesant Inn and out of sight again. His gaze flicked to the speedometer. Eighty-five. *Jesus.* His hands were steady, but his heart pounded, the adrenaline rush pricking under his arms and sparking up his spine.

He had time to think, *This was a lot more fun with Clare in the car,* and then he reacquired Nichols, popping over a hillock and disappearing again. Illinois driver's license. He remembered that from Nichols's billfold. He figured that meant crowded urban streets or country roads so straight and flat they made billiard tables look bumpy by comparison. Here in Washington County, you couldn't find a level stretch of road running more than a quarter mile.

He hit the same hill he had seen Nichols going over, up and then down, down, into another rolling valley, and there was Nichols, Christ on a crutch, overtaking a tractor and combine so fast it looked like the farmer behind the wheel was going backward.

Nichols shifted into the other lane and blew past the tractor. Ahead of him, an ancient Plymouth wagon crested the opposite hill and descended straight into his path.

"Shit," Russ said. "Shit, shit, shit."

Nichols jerked to the right, skidding half off the narrow blacktop, spraying dirt and grass before catching the road and straightening the Crown Vic out again.

Despite Russ's lights and siren, the Plymouth still hadn't pulled off the road. It continued to barrel toward the tractor, even as Nichols kicked his car into gear and began the climb up out of the valley. Russ was getting closer to the rear of the combine every second. "Get off of the road, you idiot," he said to the Plymouth. He took his foot off the gas and feathered the brakes, slowing, slowing, watching helplessly as Nichols hurtled over the far rise and was gone again.

The Plymouth finally got the message and wobbled to the edge of the road, leaving just enough space for Russ to squeeze between it and the tractor without transferring the JOHN DEERE lettering onto his cruiser. The driver, who looked about ninety years old, eyed him disapprovingly as he inched by. As soon as he cleared the tractor's grille, he hit the gas. His speedometer crept up. Forty. Fifty. Sixty. He remembered the stop sign at the T-intersection just as he crowned the hill.

He swore again. Hit the brakes, skidded down the road toward the stop. No sign of oncoming cars, thank God. Of course, no sign of Nichols, either. Russ had a half second to make his decision. West to the mountains? Or north toward town? He thought about Nichols at the resort. Scoping out his escape route as he was going up to his room. An old army maxim every grunt knew: *Know how you're getting out before you get in.*

Russ heeled his cruiser north. Too bad none of the brass ever thought like that. He was damn sure Nichols wouldn't get stuck in Iraq with no clear exit strategy.

His radio cracked on. "Fifteen-fifty-seven, this is fifteen-thirty."

He grabbed the mic. "Go, Lyle."

"Where are you?"

"Heading northeast on River Road." One car, then another, then another, pulled to the side of the road as he roared past. "Traffic's picking up." The Crown Vic would have to get past vehicles that moved out of the way for a cop car, slowing Nichols down. Unless Nichols didn't give a shit about who got hurt. If that were the case—Russ's shoulders twitched. He had no reading on Nichols. None. He didn't know if he had come back to town on a stupid romantic impulse and was panicking, or if he was hell-bent on murder-suicide.

Over the next hill, he spotted the fleeing MP again, a quarter of the way down the long slope that bottomed out at the intersection with Route 57. The light facing him was red. Along 57, a rusty pickup, an SUV, and a station wagon rolled southbound toward Glens Falls or the Northway. Russ trod on the accelerator. The pickup rattled through the crossroads.

"Get out of the way," Russ said between clenched teeth. The SUV crossed the intersection, its driver's head swiveling, trying to spot the siren source. "Get out of the way, get out of the way, get the hell out of the way!"

Then he saw it, a monster eighteen-wheeler, probably straight off the Northway, the trucker's mind already in Millers Kill, finding a place for lunch. Driving north at a comfortable, legal fifty-five miles an hour. Straight toward the intersection. Straight toward Nichols.

Russ's mouth went cotton-dry. He was close now, close enough to see the terrified face of the woman in the station wagon, close enough to make out Nichols's head, bent, intent, looking neither left nor right, close enough to hear the drum-popping squeal of the Mack's brakes as the trucker made a futile attempt to stop forty tons of steel before he reached the green light.

Russ stood on his brakes. The station wagon spun to the right, plunging nose-first into a culvert. The Crown Vic shot across the intersection an inch ahead of the eighteen-wheeler, which screeched and groaned and rumbled to a dust-plumed stop with its tail quivering.

Russ sat for a second, his mind wiped clean. *Get out of the car. See if anybody's hurt.* It took him three tries to unbuckle his seat belt, his hand was shaking so hard. He stepped out of the unit, and there was snow under his boots, he knew there was, and there was a different truck, its driver sobbing and apologizing, and there was a rental car crushed into a ball of flesh and metal and Linda was dead. She was dead.

"Holy shit!" the woman said from across the road. "Did you see that? Did you see that? Hey! Are you okay? Is he okay?"

Lyle found him bent over the ditch, puking his guts out. He waited until Russ had wrung himself dry and then handed him a fistful of tissues. "Sorry," Russ said, his voice clotted and harsh.

"So'm I." They both looked at the intersection, where the woman was now shouting into a cell phone and the truck driver squatted by his near tire, checking something underneath his rig. Lyle hadn't been there that day, but he had seen the reports. He scrubbed one hand over his face. "So'm I."

Russ coughed. Spat. "Nobody hurt?"

Lyle shook his head.

"You contact the staties?"

"They'll be looking for him. You want me to pull everybody out on patrol?"

"No. I want you at Tally McNabb's." Russ wadded up the tissues, started to shove them in his pocket, then thought better of it. "We don't have the manpower to dragnet him. Protecting McNabb is our priority. If he shows up, you and Kevin will have him. If he doesn't, let the staties have the sonofabitch."

He stayed behind to clear the intersection and write up the accident report. The routine task helped settle his spasming stomach and aching chest. He drove back to the station expecting to hear at any second that Nichols had been captured, but the radio remained stubbornly silent.

"Anything?" he asked Harlene as soon as he was within earshot of dispatch.

"Not from the state police. Kevin called in to say Lyle's over to Tally McNabb's and that her husband's being a pain in the ass. Says they don't need any protection." Russ grunted. "You got a call from some lawyer representing the new resort, complaining about you scaring off the customers with your"—Harlene picked up her message pad and read from it—"'unnecessarily violent and confrontational approach to removing a guest who had manifested no threatening behavior whatsoever.'" She put the pad down. "He wants to know who's going to pay for damage to a flower bed."

Russ tipped his head back. "Anything else?"

"Roxanne Lunt called. Said she's been trying to track you down." Harlene's face was as bland as vanilla pudding. "I guess she didn't try the St. Alban's rectory."

Russ narrowed his eyes.

"She says she's got someone interested in that piece of land on Lick Springs Road you were looking at, and if you want it, you got to make an offer now." She ripped off the messages and handed them to him, wrinkling her nose as he stepped next to her. "What in the Sam Hill did you get into? You smell awful."

The only thing that improved during the rest of the day was his odor; he washed up and brushed his teeth in the men's room before changing into his spare uniform. The state police turned up nothing; he had a long conversation with Sergeant Bob Mongue, who managed to imply that Russ had overreacted and overexaggerated and maybe the MKPD needed some training in suspect management? His attempt at getting intel about Nichols from Fort Leonard Wood was met with "I don't know, sir," and "I can't release that information, sir," from a series of brush-off artists who became wordier and less informative as he ascended the ranks. No one showed up at the McNabbs' house; when he arrived to persuade Tally to relocate to somewhere more anonymous, Wyler McNabb accused him of carrying out a vendetta against them.

"Has the husband done anything? Gone anywhere?" Russ and Lyle were standing in the driveway of the small house, conferring between the McNabbs' Escalade and Navigator. The two hulking SUVs effectively isolated them from anyone watching from the house or its neighbor.

"Nope. He spent the afternoon working on his ATV. Kevin said he was trying to boost the performance so's he could drive it faster. Dumb-ass."

"Nichols hasn't shown up yet—"

"He hasn't shown up anywhere," Lyle said. "He could be laying low until we clear out."

"Are we looking at this wrong? You think maybe she was going to meet Nichols and we stepped in it?"

Lyle shrugged. "Hard to imagine setting up a love nest in the hotel where you work as a bookkeeper, but stranger things have happened." He and Russ exchanged a look that said, *To you and me both, brother.*

Russ rubbed his lip. "They got guns?"

"Are you kidding?"

Russ kicked at the driveway paving. "Screw it. We'll put the house on the patrol list and tell them to call nine-one-one if anything happens. It's the best we can do."

Lyle frowned. "I don't like it."

Russ didn't like it, either. It gnawed at him while he drove back to the station, while he was filling out the remainder of his incident reports, while he watched Harlene close down her board and switch all incoming calls to the Glens Falls dispatcher. After he left, he drove back to Musket Way and cruised past the McNabbs' house. They lived in one of the last of the 1960s neighborhoods put up by optimistic developers back when there were still a few good jobs to be had at the Allen mill or down the Northway at General Electric. Small houses with deep yards, the kind of neighborhood folks said was a good place to raise kids. He parked just up the street and watched the lights coming on in the small houses, a pair of boys running in and out banging screen doors, one guy trying to get the last of his lawn mowed before it was too dark to see. Two doors down from Tally McNabb's house, a car pulled into a drive. A woman and a teenaged girl got out and went into the house. Five minutes later, a man came out, followed by the woman, who was twirling some long shawl-thing over her shoulders. They got in their car and drove off. Mom and Dad, out on one last date before school started up again.

God, he was lonely.

Lights were on at the McNabb house as he drove past again. The flicker from a wide-screen shone through a gap in the curtains. He shifted into gear and let himself roll away into the end-of-summer darkness of his hometown.

◆ ◆ ◆

For Clare, dinner that night at the Ellises' was surreal, like being in a play where one character had turned into a seagull and everyone else pretended not to notice. Dr. Anne told some amusing stories about the Glens Falls ER, and Chris described his latest furniture project, and Colin went on at great length about the odd tourists he encountered in his summer job at Great Escape, and the whole time Willem smiled and nodded and ate, a caricature of the cheerful, careless young man she had known.

Seeing him in the wheelchair made her heart ache. She knew prosthetics were highly advanced these days, she knew he would have every advantage his parents' money and the VA doctors could give him, but dammit, he had been a tall, strong, athletic young man, and now he was cut down—literally—before he had even had a chance to flower. She wondered if any of the Ellises had given Will, or themselves, the space to grieve that loss.

She broached the subject when the rest of the family conveniently disappeared on assorted after-dinner chores, leaving her and Will alone in the dining room. "I haven't seen you at church since I got back," she said.

"Did my mom ask you to talk with me?"

"Yes." She poured herself another glass of merlot.

"I don't need a talking-to. I'm doing fine."

Clare propped her chin on her hand. "Are you angry about losing your legs?"

He made a face. "At who? The Iraqi insurgents? My CO? The government?"

"For a start, yeah."

"What's the use?" He smoothed over his expression. "It's done. I need to move on."

"In the first place"—Clare ticked off a finger—"anger isn't useful, or therapeutic, or rational. It just is, and when life hands you a shitty deal, you have the right to be angry."

Will looked shocked. She almost smiled. Who would have thought she could scandalize a nineteen-year-old marine?

"Second"—she ticked off another finger—"we're all so in love with the idea of moving on and growing through loss and making lemonade when life hands us lemons that we don't take time to mourn. Before you can move on, you have to stand still and account for what's been lost. Sometimes, you have to throw the damn lemon against the wall and yell, *I wanted chocolate chip cookies, not this bitter fruit.*"

Will hiccupped a laugh. "Yeah. Well."

"You know, your mom is hoping I'm going to set you to rights over the dessert plates and biscuit crumbs."

"'Cause you have the awesome power of God behind you. Like a double-magic throw in D and D."

She smiled. That was the first thing he had said that sounded like the old Will. "She told me you don't want to go to a psychiatrist."

"No. No. Absolutely not. I'm not going to have somebody banging on about sibling rivalry and my parents' expectations when what my problem is, is that I got royally fucked up in Iraq and I'm never going to walk normally again."

He looked at her, challenging her to be offended by his vocabulary.

"You know what I think you could use? A veterans' group." She slid the black-and-white brochure out of her pocket and smoothed its crumpled edges on the tablecloth. "There's one starting up at the community center the week after next. It's not analysis. It'll just be a few other guys who know what you're talking about because they've been there, too."

He picked up the brochure and rolled his eyes at the overearnest pictures of waving flags and solemn soldiers. "What, another bunch of cripples? No thanks." He tossed the brochure back onto the table. "I did that at Walter Reed."

"Will. There are a lot of us who came back wounded. Some of us just don't show it on the outside."

"Yeah?" He leaned forward, his muscular forearms contrasting with the flowered tablecloth. "Where were you hurt, Reverend Clare?"

When did it stop being safe to fall asleep?

"I didn't mean me personally."

"You said us. You said there were a lot of us."

Her fingers clutched around the stem of her wineglass. "I'm fine. We're not talking about me, anyway."

"That's what you want me to do, though. Talk about what happened. Talk about how I'm feeling. With other vets. Like you. So. Are you like me?"

"No! I mean, yes, of course I'm like you, but no, I'm not . . . I don't have . . ." She thought about the noise in her head, the constant roaring tumult she tried to keep in check with booze and pills. For a moment, she could see it all, the dark tunnel vision, the brilliant explosions, the blood, the broken bodies—she picked up her wineglass and swallowed the entire contents in one gulp. She reached for the bottle and emptied it into her glass. "I'm fine." And she was. There were stresses coming back into civilian life. Everyone knew that. There had been stress in the seminary, for God's sake. Lord knows, she'd experienced stress as the rector of St. Alban's. So she ran hard—when her ankle wasn't wonky—and relaxed over a glass of wine and maybe used a sleeping pill to help get a good night's rest. That was dealing with stress in a healthy way.

"You're fine," Will said.

She nodded. Smiled at him. Her heart rate was coming back down. She hadn't realized it had been pounding.

"Then I'm fine." He leaned back. Unlocked his wheel brakes. Rolled away from the table.

"Will, wait."

"No." He looked at her, his eyes hard. He looked, she realized, like a man, instead of the boy she always saw. "Either you're telling the truth, and I'm some sort of freak who needs a blankie and a blow job to get over what happened to me, or you're full of it, in which case, you're dealing with it the same way I am. By keeping your head down and bulling through from one day to the next."

"Will, just because I don't think I need help—"

"I'll make you a deal, Reverend. If you go, I'll go." He wrapped his hands around the edges of his wheels and jerked himself into a turn. "Do you remember what you said to us in confirmation class? You said we should accept ourselves as God accepted us. And if we did that, no person, or job, or experience could define who we were. Because we were God's beloved. Remember?"

She nodded. "In all these things, we are more than conquerors through Him who loved us." The verse seemed to come from very far away.

"How's that working out for you?" He rolled out of the wide dining room arch before she could come up with a response. "Dad," he called from the other room. "I'm tired. Will you help me to bed?"

Anne poked her head in from the kitchen. Listened as Chris pushed Will up the hall, the wheelchair's hard rubber tires rumbling over their wooden floorboards. She dropped into the seat next to Clare. "How did it go?"

Clare rubbed her hands over her face. "Not so hot."

Anne pressed her lips together.

"I'm sorry, Anne." She took another drink of wine to quiet the other, older noise, the one that named her a failure as a priest. "I thought we were establishing some rapport, but then I got him mad at me. He's not really tired, he's angry."

Anne's mouth dropped open. "He's angry?"

"I'm sorry."

Anne grabbed her arm. "No! That's great! He hasn't shown any anger in—God, I don't know how long. Oh, Clare, I knew you could do it." She threw her arms around Clare in an awkward hug. "Will you come and talk with him again? Soon?"

The dark tunnel reappeared outside the limits of sight. "Of course I will." Clare swallowed more wine. "Of course."

◆　◆　◆

Chris Ellis gave her a ride home. She had planned on walking back, but it was a mile, and her ankle was wobbly—she thought it was her ankle, messing up her balance—and so she accepted the lift. He let her out in her drive. She waved as he drove away, feeling guilty for not finding the right words to reach his son. She limped up the kitchen steps and paused at her dark door, breathing in the scent of night jasmine and honeysuckle, listening to the mad chorus of crickets singing for love before the frosts came and mowed them all down.

She remembered something Russ had told her once. *I was drinking pretty heavily then. Of course, I never felt drunk. Just numb.* When would that happen to her? When would she get to stop feeling so bad?

She opened the door. Shut and locked it. Flicked on the kitchen light. "Don't be alarmed," Russ said from the living room. "I'm here."

"What?" She limped through the swinging doors. She could see him, the outline of him, sitting in one of the chairs in front of the empty fireplace. "I thought we weren't doing this anymore. Why on earth are you sitting here in the dark?"

He stood up. "You didn't leave any lights on. I didn't want to draw any attention."

"Well, I'm here now." She snapped on a lamp. She looked at his face, set in deep lines. "What is it? Is everyone okay?"

"I had . . ." He shook his head. "God. A day." He looked down at his feet. He was still wearing his boots. As if she might not let him stay. He looked up at her. "I . . ." He opened his hands, palms out.

"Need someone?" She smiled a little. Stepped toward him, arms open. He embraced her with a force that startled her.

"Not someone," he said into her hair. "You." He buried his face in the crook of her shoulder. "Only you." His lips were on her neck. "Always you." Then he was kissing her, and it was a different kind of need, catching in her like a spark in dry pine needles, desire like a hot wind pressing them together, whirling them around and around, sending them staggering up the stairs, shedding their clothing on the way.

He flung her onto the bed and dropped on top of her with none of his usual careful control. He twined his fingers in hers, forcing her hands deep into the mattress and surging into her with a rough urgency that tore a cry out of her throat.

"Oh, God," he gasped. "Did I hurt you?"

"Yes. No." She gulped for air. Cried out again. "Don't stop. Don't stop!"

"I can't. Oh, God." His voice was like a raw wound. He pounded into her, stretching her open and more open, going deep, deeper, hard and harsh and unspeakably good.

She clenched his hands, shaking, all wetness and straining muscles. Her mouth was open, her throat working, but his ferocious battering left her breathless, wordless, mindless. She spiraled up, tighter, sharper, closer, until he groaned, "Oh, God, Clare, I'm going to—" and that was it, that was enough. Her head snapped back and it was the dark tunnel reversed, all white hot light and an explosion of joy that turned her inside out and left her trembling. Russ's voice broke and he shuddered, once, twice, three times, then collapsed heavily on top of her, his face once more hidden in the crook of her shoulder.

She stroked his back while he worked for air, his rib cage rising and falling beneath her touch. He made a feeble attempt to push off of her. "No." She tightened her grip. He relaxed then, sagging against her. She ran her fingers through his hair, watching the strands of brown and blond and gray catch around her knuckles, feeling the shape of his skull beneath her hand.

"Don't leave me," he whispered.

"I won't."

"When I say don't leave—"

"I know." She pressed a kiss into the top of his head. "You mean don't die."

At some point, he fell asleep. She kept on stroking and smoothing his hair, watching her hand rise and fall, rise and fall, until she could admit to this exhausted, sleeping, damaged man what she couldn't admit to herself. "I don't think I'm fine," she whispered. "I don't think I'm fine at all."

THAT IT MAY PLEASE THEE
TO GRANT THAT, IN THE
FELLOWSHIP OF ALL THE
SAINTS, WE MAY ATTAIN TO
THY HEAVENLY KINGDOM.

—*The Great Litany, The Book of Common Prayer*

MONDAY, SEPTEMBER 26   Sarah was late to her own group session. She scurried down the hallway, her footsteps slapping the linoleum flooring and echoing off the walls in a syncopated beat to the shouts of young men and the thud of the basketball. She opened the door too hard, slamming it against the wall accidentally. They were all there; McCrea and Stillman bookending the group, Fergusson hunched over her cup of coffee, McNabb stuffing an iPod into her too-tight jeans, Will Ellis smiling at nothing. Sarah felt like pitching her notebook and pen and shrieking at them all to go home. She wasn't reaching these people. She wasn't helping them. She'd never been any closer to a war zone than downtown Newark. What in the name of little green apples did she think she could accomplish here?

Fergusson looked up at her, her face pale with fatigue. Studied her for a moment that must have been shorter than it felt. Then she rose from her rickety metal chair, smiling. "Sarah. Thank goodness. We were getting worried." She crossed the floor and touched Sarah on the arm, once, giving her a squeeze that seemed to say, *I know, and it's all right.* "Let me get you something. Coffee? Somebody's made hot cider in the Crock-Pot. Probably fresh from Greuling's Orchards." She looked at Sarah again, more closely, and for a second, Sarah wanted to lean against the priest, to feel someone taking care of her for a change, and then she snapped herself like a sheet and thought, *Oh, no, you don't. I've got your number now.* Fergusson was a caretaker. That explained the way she only really became engaged when she was bucking up Will or settling down McCrea.

"Thank you, Clare, that would be nice." She let Fergusson fetch her the hot cider while she sat down, surreptitiously rolling her shoulders to get the last of the tension out, smiling at the others. When Fergusson handed her the paper cup, she let her eyes open just a bit wider than usual, showing her vulnerability and her gratitude. A little manipulative,

127

maybe, but if she could use the moment to crack open Fergusson's closed book, it would be worth it.

"We've talked about homecoming," Sarah said. "We've talked about work, and about personal relationships." She took a sip of the cider. Heavenly. "But all that is background. Reconnoitering the terrain. Tonight, we're going to begin to dig deeper. The real issues, and the real work, are inside each of you. Tonight, we're going to talk about why you decided to attend this group, and what you hope to get out of counseling."

Tally McNabb glanced at McCrea, who bent over to rub a nonexistent speck from his hiking boots. Trip Stillman shifted in his seat. Clare Fergusson pinched her ring between two fingers and stared at it. Will Ellis looked up toward the sound-tiled ceiling.

Sarah let the silence lengthen. "Anyone?" More shifting, more looking at the floor or knees or coffee cups. "Somebody has to be first."

"I came here because I want to know how to leave what happened in-country behind."

They all stared at Tally McNabb. Her chin was tucked down, and she wasn't meeting anyone's eyes, but she went on. "I did some things I shouldn't have. Stuff I thought would stay there." She pressed her mouth into a hard line. Sarah waited, one beat, two, for her to go on.

Finally, Fergusson leaned way forward so she could look up into Tally's face. "But it didn't."

Tally shook her head, sending her straight, blunt hair jerking left, right, left. "I didn't mean to hurt anybody." She lifted her eyes and looked around the circle. "Everything seemed so clear-cut over there. Now I'm home, and I can't get a fix on anything anymore. My relationship with my husband's totally screwed up. My job is—" She dropped her head again. "My boss told me today he wants to send me back. As part of the construction team."

"What?" McCrea stared.

"You're kidding!" Stillman rocked back in his chair.

"Oh, no," Fergusson said.

"It's not like being on frontline duty. I'd be financial administrator for the ongoing projects. Probably get to spend ninety percent of my time behind a desk in the Green Zone."

There was an awful silence. Everyone, including Sarah, knew there was no such thing as "behind the lines" in Iraq.

"How do you feel about this?" Sarah asked.

Through the thick cotton of her hooded sweatshirt, Tally rubbed the spot where her arm was tattooed. "How do I feel?" She looked at Sarah. "Like I've been locked in a box."

"Do you feel like you'd like to discuss your options with the group?" Sarah kept her voice low and level.

"No. I don't have any options."

"You can always find something positive about any situation," Will Ellis said.

"Oh, for God's sake. Why don't you just grow up and drop the damn pep talks already?" Tally shoved her face toward Will. "At least I can admit my life's in the toilet."

"What?" Will glared at her. "What do you want me to say? That I lost my goddamn legs? That I'm never going to walk again, I've got no goddamn prospects, and I'm going to wind up spending the rest of my life with my parents taking care of me? That make you happy?"

Trip Stillman shook his head. "There's no reason you can't—"

"And what's your problem?" Will turned on the older man. "I haven't heard anything out of you other than it's been a pain cycling in and out of country for three-month rotations."

Stillman sat up straight and angled his body so that he somehow seemed to be wearing an invisible white coat. "I, um, believe I'm showing symptoms of post-traumatic stress disorder."

"From what?" Eric McCrea said. "You didn't get the DVDs you wanted in your air-conditioned lounge? You guys live like four-stars in those combat support hospitals. What the hell kind of stress could you have?"

"I wasn't in a CSH. I was at a Forward Response Station, and the only AC we had was in the operating rooms."

"Oh, cry me a fucking river. You wanna know what stress is? Try guarding a bunch of insurgents who'd just as soon kill you as look at you. Trying to get intel out of these fuckers, knowing they've got information that will kill Americans locked up in their heads, but for God's sake, you gotta respect their rights and their religion and their culture. Then a bunch of fucking pictures that never should have been taken get out into the damn media—from another fucking prison entirely!—and suddenly everybody looks at you like you've been putting electrodes on Achmed's balls."

"Were you?" Fergusson asked.

"What?"

"Were you torturing prisoners?"

"No! Jesus! Whaddaya think I am?"

"I think you're a good cop. I'm also thinking maybe a good cop who gets coerced or convinced to do bad things is going to wind up feeling pretty awful about it, later on."

Sarah cut in before Fergusson could take over as therapist. "Hold it." She made a time-out gesture. "Just hold it. Group therapy means we're working together to find out what we need to know. We offer observations in positive ways. We don't gang up and attack each other." She looked around the circle, taking her time, making eye contact with each one of them. "I repeat. We're going to talk about why you decided to get into the group." She zeroed in on Fergusson. "Clare, we're starting with you."

FRIDAY, AUGUST 26   Clare eyed the glass of Macallan's balanced on her porcelain sink. Why had she brought it in here, when she was brushing her teeth? Was she going to gargle with it? She spat, rinsed, wiped her mouth dry. She considered lipstick. She didn't usually wear makeup, but this was a special occasion. She thought it was a special occasion. She thought she might be getting engaged. She closed her hand around the heavy square glass and downed half the Scotch in one gulp.

The bell rang. She put down the glass and hustled down the stairs to her almost-never-used front door. "Why so formal?" she was asking as she opened the door, but the sight of Russ in a suit and tie made her lose whatever else she was going to say.

"What?" He peered down at his tie. "Do I have a spot?"

"I've never seen you dressed up before." She splayed her hand against her chest. "I'm speechless."

"That'll be the day." He stepped in, and she backed away to circle around him.

She whistled. "You clean up real nice, Chief Van Alstyne."

"You like it? You should see my dress uniform. Makes me look like an extra in *Naughty Marietta*."

"Does it have a Sam Browne belt?"

"No, thank God. That's a little too disciplinarian for my tastes." He caught her hand. "Nice dress. You wore it at that dance in the park."

"Mm-hmm." She twirled, letting yards of poppy red silk wind around her legs. "I remembered you liked it."

He smiled slowly at her. "Maybe we should just order a pizza and stay here."

"Tempting." She considered it for a moment. True to his word, Russ hadn't been to her bed since the night she had found him waiting for her after the Ellises' dinner. On the other hand, she had been promised a date. One date in four years. That didn't seem like asking too much. "Maybe later. I want my chance to go to the ball."

"Okay, Cinderella. Grab your wrap and let's go."

Outside, he opened his truck's door and handed her in. "Where are we going?"

"You like miniature golf?"

She stared at him. "You're joking." He got behind the wheel and backed out of her driveway. "You are joking, right?"

He grinned at her. The windows were open, of course—he didn't believe in air-conditioning unless the truck was going sixty—so she braced her elbow on the edge and showily propped her chin on her hand, staring outside as if the end-of-the-day shoppers and dog walkers were the most interesting things she'd seen that week. Russ looped around to Barkley Avenue, and she spotted the director of the Millers Kill Historical Society unlocking her car. Clare waved. "Hi, Roxanne!"

"What are you doing?"

"Just making sure we maintain our status as a hot topic of conversation."

"Great. Now I know what'll be first on the agenda at their next board meeting."

"What? The two of us in your truck on a Friday evening? That's positively wholesome. It's not like anybody's been able to see you sneaking into the rectory at all hours."

"Jesus, it's been less than a week. I had no idea you were such a sex fiend."

Clare crossed her arms. "There's such a thing as carrying discretion too far."

"Not when you're a minister in a small town, there isn't."

She sighed. "I know—but I don't have to like it."

He laughed. "How you made it through seminary and into the priesthood remains a mystery to me."

"To you and the bishop both." They had left the town behind, headed northeast. "Are we going to Lake George?" Russ didn't say anything. "We are. We're going to Lake George. Okay, what do you have to get dressed up for in Lake George?"

"Maybe I'm being all whimsical and we're going for Italian sausage on the Boardwalk."

She gave him a look. "Whimsical?"

"Hey, I can be as whimsical as the next guy."

"That's because to you, the next guy is a humorless law enforcement agent."

He laughed and took her hand, rubbing his thumb over her knuckles. She had a hunch about where they were going, but she kept her mouth shut over her smile. She didn't want to take away a second of his pleasure at surprising her. She leaned back and watched the road slice between the lake and the mountains.

Sure enough, he slowed and pulled into a long drive marked by an understated white and green sign.

"The Sagamore!" She clapped in approval. "I've never been here, but I've heard Mrs. Marshall and Sterling Sumner talk about it." Two of her vestry had summer homes on the lake. "Oh, it's lovely."

The drive crossed a wooden bridge and wound past clay tennis courts and crisp white bungalows before terminating at the entrance of the grand old resort. The parking valet opened her door before she had a chance to do it herself. "Checking in, sir?" the young man asked.

"Just dinner." Russ handed him the keys.

"Darn," Clare said, under her breath.

"Be good." Russ ushered her up the porticoed steps. "We may be out of town, but this place gets a lot of local business. I figure we still have a twenty-five percent chance of running into someone we know."

"So, no footsie during dinner?"

He gave her a sideways look. "Let's see how long the tablecloth is."

It was very long, and very white, in a dining room with the understated elegance that came with years of service to old money. Clare could see other diners, silver gleaming, glasses raised, but the heavy carpets and the plush chairs seemed to absorb the sound of clinking and conversation before it could reach them.

She blanched when she saw the prices on the menu, then thought of her grandmother's dictum, *A lady never notices the cost of her dinner,* and kept her eyes left. In deference to Russ's budget and his nondrinking status, she skipped the wine list and had the waiter bring her a whisky neat before the meal, and a single glass of merlot to accompany her beef Wellington. Oh, and all right, a nice little aperitif after, but she didn't order dessert, and only took two bites of Russ's key lime pie.

They talked nonstop through dinner, about the volunteer fair at the church and firearms training at the department; about gun surrender programs and going green at work. She admitted she was still trying to find a way to talk Will Ellis into therapy, and he told her he was worried about Eric McCrea's two unexplained absences the last two weeks.

The coffees came and went, and she started to think she must have been wrong, that he wasn't going to pop the question that night, when the waiter returned with the bill tucked inside a leather folder and Russ asked, "What's going on outside? I keep hearing music."

"Private party. The two weekends around Labor Day are our busiest of the year."

Russ looked up from where he was signing the charge slip. "Oh. Can we still get down to the landing?"

This is it, she thought. *Is this it?*

"You certainly can, sir. The terrace isn't closed to the public."

Russ looked at Clare. "Feel like a little walk? There's a great view of the lake from the boat landing."

"Absolutely." She pushed her chair back, and the waiter nipped in to pull it out of her way. Russ stood at the same time, snagging her wrap and draping it over her shoulders. She hid a smile, thinking how much her grandmother would have loved his manners. Her highest praise for a man had been "His mother raised him right."

The back of the resort—or front, she supposed, if one arrived by boat—consisted of wide wings with deep porches leading down to a terrace thronged with people drinking, dancing, and talking too loudly. A white tent had been set up on the side lawn, sheltering tables, and a four-piece band tucked between the porch steps and the flower beds played Motown classics. Russ took her hand, and they walked down to the flagstones, skirting the party.

"What's going on?" Clare craned her neck, looking for a bride and groom. Someone shrieked, there was a flurry of movement, and a heavy-set young man stumbled into their path. Russ caught him by his coat sleeves before he could fall on his face.

"Easy there, buddy." Russ righted the man, who swayed for a moment like a potted plant teetering back to level.

"Whoa. Thanks. Guess I'm a li'l juiced."

"Is this a wedding?" Clare asked, amused.

The young man shook his head, which set him to swaying again. "'Sa company party. BWI Opperman." He smiled proudly. "Great year, with alla construction."

She wasn't looking at Russ, but she could feel him stiffen. Talk about spoiling the mood. She wasn't any fan of the owner of the Algonquin Waters Resort, but Russ held a personal grudge against the man he felt had driven a wedge between himself and Linda. She hooked her arm in his. "Have a great time," she told the genial drunk, steering Russ toward the lawn.

She dragged him the first few steps, and then he gave himself a shake. "God. Opperman."

"Forget about him. He's here, he's a part of the landscape, there's nothing you or I can do about it." She looked up into his frowning face. "Weren't you going to show me the boat landing?"

He made a noise. Pointed away from the terrace. They walked across the lawn, sloping gently toward the black waters of Lake George. "Why the hell did he relocate up here? What was wrong with Baltimore? Isn't that where the business originated?"

"Easier to hide the bodies up here in the mountains."

He stopped. "Not funny."

She sighed. "I'm sorry." She turned to face him again. "I'm guessing he's relocated because there's a large pool of affordable workers up here. The resorts are only the tail end of the business, remember. It's primarily development and construction."

"I know that. What I don't know is why the hell he can't go to Alabama for his cheap labor, like everyone else."

She paused again. They were nearer to the water than to the terrace now. She could hear the lapping of the waves and the wind sighing through the leaves of the trees shading the paths leading down to the landing. Mellow lights picked out the texture of crushed rock and velvety lawn. The sweet and peppery scent of unseen carnations drifted up from stone planters. "Russ."

"Yeah?"

"I think this is very romantic, don't you?"

"Yeah, I suppose so." He led her onto the landing, their shoes thunking and clacking on the wood. He stopped. Looked at her. "You do?"

"Yes, I do." She smiled at him in an encouraging fashion. "I think this is just about the most romantic place I've seen in the entire North Country."

He grinned at her. "This is your way of telling me I should keep my mind on the business at hand, isn't it?"

"That's not precisely how I would have stated it, but . . ."

"This isn't a surprise to you, is it?"

She started to laugh. "I haven't the faintest idea what you're talking about."

"God." He wiped his hand over his face. "Okay, let's see if I can get this done without making a complete idiot of myself."

"Please feel free. I don't mind."

"That's good. Because half the time, just being with you reduces me to a state of idiocy."

She couldn't stop smiling. "What about the other half?"

He took her hands. "The other half of the time, it's like being at the summit of one of the high peaks with a stiff wind blowing. Terrifying and exhilarating and everything in the world in a completely new perspective."

Her smile fell away.

"You make me . . . not better than I am, but more of who I am. Which *is* better. Do you know what I mean?"

She nodded. She didn't think she could speak if her life depended on it. He glanced down at the wooden deck with a dubious expression. One side of his mouth quirked up. "I hope you didn't have your heart set on me getting down on one knee."

She shook her head. He reached inside his coat pocket. Took out a small box. Pried the lid open. Even in the dim light from the lanterns, the ring sparked like white fire. "Marry me. Please."

She tried to answer him, but all that came out was a whispery rattle as her lungs emptied. She took a deep breath. Tried again. "Yes."

"You don't need to tell me right away," he said. "I mean, maybe you ought to think about it."

"Yes," she said more firmly.

"I am fifty-two. And I'm planning to stay in Millers Kill. I mean, I suppose I could move after I retire, but I'm committed to heading up the force as long as—"

"Russ. I'm trying to say yes, here. I will marry you. I want to marry you. Let's do it."

"Really? I don't want you to jump into anything without thinking it through."

She laughed. "You're kidding, right? Can I put it on?"

He pulled the ring out of its holder. Her hands were shaking so, she almost dropped it. He helped her slide it onto her finger. It was smooth and heavy, with three diamonds set low in fat circles of gold. "It fits."

"I, uh, took your UVA ring off your dresser to size it."

"Very sneaky." She grinned up at him. "I like that in a man." She flung her arms around him and he squeezed her back. "I love it." She kissed him, a jubilant smack that turned into a long, sweet kiss that left her breathless. "I love you."

"Good. How soon can we get married?"

"Let's see. First, I have to get permission from the bishop."

He released her. "You're kidding."

"Nope."

"Holy—I don't have to go and ask him for your hand, do I?"

"No, it's more like—a professional courtesy. Once I have his blessing, let's see. We'll get married at St. Alban's. I could ask one of my friends from seminary to take the service . . . or maybe Julie McPartlin here in Lake George could officiate. She could do our counseling."

"What counseling?"

"We have to have three or four sessions of premarital counseling before being married in the church."

"For what?"

"For all sorts of things. When I meet with engaged couples, we discuss issues like sex—"

"I'm for it." He kissed her neck.

She smiled. "And money—"

"You can handle it," he said into her ear.

"And children."

He stopped. "We haven't talked about children." He pulled away from her, his hands still on her shoulders. "How do you feel about having kids?"

"How do you feel?"

"Honestly?" He blew out a breath. "I like kids. I hoped—when Linda and I were young, we tried for a long time."

She bit her lip. "How about now?"

He rubbed his thumbs along her collarbone. "I think I'm too old. Even if we had a kid right off the bat, I'd still be seventy-two or seventy-three when he graduated from college. If I make it that long. I just don't think it's fair, to give a child an old guy with bad knees as a father."

She nodded.

"How about you?" His face was intent, serious. It should be serious. They were deciding things that would affect the rest of their lives tonight. The immensity of marriage, everything it would be, suddenly stretched out before her like the waters of the lake, wide and deep and full of unfathomable mystery. *How about you?* She weighed her answer.

"I like children, too, and there's a part of me that would very much like to be a mother. But my ministry takes so much of my time and attention and emotional energy—all the things I'd have to give to a child. I don't know if I could be a good priest and a good parent."

"So . . . no?"

She paused. "No." Then she hugged him hard, burying her face in his shirt, because even though it felt right, it was still a kind of a loss.

"Maybe a dog."

"A big, hairy dog?"

"Sure. It can hang around the church office with you and terrorize the vestry when they get out of line."

She laughed. "It's a deal." She stepped back, tugging at his hands. All at once she couldn't wait another minute to let everyone know. "Let's go home. I want to call my parents, and your mother, and Dr. Anne, and everybody."

"Whoa." He laughed, but he let her drag him off the landing and onto the path anyway. "You still haven't told me when."

"Advent's out, and Christmas and Epiphany are crazy. Late January? That's when I usually take a week off. Of course, that might be a difficult time to travel. I don't know if I can persuade my family to leave southern Virginia when we've got three feet of snow and single-digit temperatures." She stopped. "Oh, good Lord. My mother is going to birth a live cow over this. She didn't ever think I was going to land a husband."

"January?" He shook his head. "Can't we just do it quick and simple? The last time, all I needed was a license and twenty-five bucks for the justice of the peace."

Clare bit her lip. "Oh, God, Russ, I don't know. Yes, we could get married within sixty days of notifying the rector."

"Consider yourself notified."

"You have to understand, though, my mother's been planning table arrangements and picking out silver patterns since Grace and I were toddlers. She never had the chance to put on her dream wedding for Grace."

"Is that what you want? A big blowout?"

"No, of course not."

"Then let's make it easy and quick. You don't need any more stress in your life than you already have. Get a pretty dress and some flowers, we'll let your church ladies bake us a cake, and boom, it's done." He did something she had never seen him do before. He lifted her hand and pressed a kiss into her palm. "We've lost too much time already."

And we don't know how much time we've got.

She nodded. "The end of October, then."

A woman screamed. Russ's head jerked up and Clare whirled. Above them, on the terrace, a knot of bodies thinned out to reveal two men stripping off their jackets, circling each other. The band wheezed to a stop. She could hear the woman again, shrill and tearful, and excited shouts, egging the fighters on.

"Oh, for chrissakes. Why do people drink if it just makes 'em mean?" Russ pushed past her, tugging his badge holder from his pocket and flipping it open. "Stay back."

She nodded, but of course, he couldn't see her. She watched him force his way into the crowd gathering around the spectacle, then lost sight of him. She stood on tiptoe. Cursed under her breath. The lawn in front of the tent would give her a better vantage point. Admittedly, it was closer to the fight—a lot closer—but she could argue that it still qualified as "staying back."

She clutched her wrap more firmly around her shoulders and strode toward the tent. Over the eager sounds of the crowd, she thought she could hear Russ's deep voice, trying to calm things down.

Call 911. The thought was immediately followed by the realization that she'd deliberately left her cell phone in Russ's truck. No calls from parishioners on her big date, nosirree. She could have whacked herself in the head. Then she spotted a woman with a phone. She was talking into it, rapidly, quietly, her shoulders set in an angry line. "Fine," she said. "Fine. If that's the way you want it." She snapped the phone shut.

"Excuse me." Clare hated to break up someone's special moment, but Russ needed backup. "Could you please call nine-one-one?" The woman turned to her. It was Tally McNabb.

"What? Why?" Tally frowned.

"The fight?" Clare gestured to the melee. Above the shrieking woman and the jeering guys, she could hear Russ's voice, hard and authoritative.

"A fight?" Tally shook her head. "Christ. Sorry. I didn't notice. I was . . ." She made a vague gesture in the direction of her phone. She teetered on the balls of her feet to peer over the heads of the crowd. "I think somebody's already busting it up."

"That's Chief Van Alstyne, yeah, but he's alone and—" Clare didn't want to say "unarmed." She compromised with "And the Lake George police ought to know."

Tally looked at Clare more closely. "Hey. I know you." Her mouth opened, and even in the dim light, Clare could see red rising in the younger woman's cheeks. "It's you."

Clare took a breath. Attempted a smile. "Please? Call nine-one-one?"

Behind them, a smooth voice said, "No need. The hotel has already been notified." Clare and Tally both turned.

The CEO of BWI Opperman stood behind them. His suit and shoes were hand-sewn perfection, an expensive difference that set him apart from every other man on the terrace. He held a half-empty wineglass and was looking at the knot of cheering spectators with a pained expression.

"Mr. Opperman. Hi." Tally sounded like a high schooler dismayed to see her principal at a picnic.

"Tally McNabb. Are you enjoying yourself?" Opperman turned to Clare. "You don't work for me." He tilted his head to one side, as if trying to slide her image into place. She twisted her wrap, tightening it across her exposed shoulders. She could see the moment when he recognized her. "Ah. The Reverend Clare Fergusson. What a surprise. I haven't seen you since that little hearing we had before my insurance company's adjustment board."

"Mr. Opperman."

"Insurance company?" Tally said.

Opperman answered her without turning his gaze from Clare. "Reverend Fergusson went joyriding over the Adirondacks in the BWI company helicopter a few summers back and crashed the thing. It was a total loss."

"I was trying to save the life of a man who was trapped in the mountains. He was badly injured. I didn't have time to ask for permission to use the ship."

"As you said, yes." The corners of his mouth tilted upward, but the smile didn't reach his eyes. "It was fortunate for you the insurers accepted your version of the event. Pilot error would have been an ugly thing to have on your record."

"As opposed to sabotage?"

"I believe you mean mechanical failure. That was, after all, the official verdict."

Clare found herself wringing the ends of her shawl. Opperman had never been linked to the mysterious collapse of the fuel pump that had nearly killed her and Russ, and he never would be. *Let it go.* She forced her hands to relax.

He went on. "I was under the impression you had gone back to being a captain in the army. I certainly hope you haven't wrecked any of their helicopters as well."

She jerked her chin up. "I'm a major. In the Guard. And no, I haven't broken any Black Hawks yet."

"She was in Iraq, too." Tally spoke brightly, like a woman who wanted to change the subject away from who did what to whom.

Opperman turned to her. "Did you know each other over there?"

"No. Oh, no. No reason our paths would have crossed." Tally looked at Clare. "We've really only ever met once before this. Accidentally. Right?"

Clare nodded. Tally clearly didn't want her employer to know she'd been living off the streets and using the soup kitchen. "Right."

He smiled. "Then may I ask what you're doing at my party? I don't recall seeing your name on the guest list."

Clare flushed. "Excuse me. I walked up from the landing to see if anyone had called the police. Now I know you have, I'll go back and wait for my date." Involuntarily, she looked over her shoulder to the place where Russ had disappeared.

Opperman stretched up to get a better view. "Is he fighting?" His face creased, as if a row of figures didn't add up. "No. Of course not. Van Alstyne." His voice changed, so that when his gaze snapped back to Clare she had to keep herself from flinching. "Yes. I had heard rumors about you two . . ." He looked her up and down, as thoroughly and impersonally as if he were doing the last-minute flight check of a helicopter. "I'm surprised. I didn't think Van Alstyne's interest in you would survive his wife's death. He adored her, you know. Still . . . a man in mourning needs some distraction, and you are reasonably attractive." He zeroed in on her hands. He stared for a long moment. Finally, he said, "What an exquisite ring. I take it best wishes are in order?"

She resisted the urge to hide it from view. Grandmother Fergusson pried open her mouth and made her say, "Yes. Thank you."

He leaned in toward Clare, close, where no one else could hear. She forced herself not to back away. "Do you really think you can compete with his wife?" His breath was hot on her face, his voice a slither in her ear. "Linda Van Alstyne was beautiful, creative, sharp-witted, loving— everything except faithful." He blinked in slow motion. "She was certainly the best fuck I ever had."

Clare's jaw unhinged. "That's a lie!"

Opperman shrugged. "Take it as a friendly warning, before you get in too deep. A man doesn't forget a woman like that. He compares every other woman to that perfection and finds her lacking. Is that really as high as you can aim for yourself? To be the consolation prize for someone who can't have what he really wants?"

Clare couldn't speak. Couldn't speak, couldn't breathe, couldn't move. She stood, trembling, like a battered boxer one punch away from going down. Opperman stepped toward her and she twisted away, but he walked past her as if she were already a ghost.

"Tally." His voice was cool and even. "Enjoy the rest of the party."

"Thanks, Mr. Opperman."

Clare wanted to grab hold of Tally and drag her away from Opperman. She wanted to find the nearest shower and scrub down until she felt clean again. She wanted to look Russ in the eye and ask him, *Are you really over her? Is it truly me you want?*

No. That was crazy. She knew Russ, knew him like she knew the Book of Common Prayer, carried him as a lamp beneath her breastbone. Opperman was playing her.

He stepped back into her line of sight and smiled. "Excuse me, please. I'd better go see how the rest of the party is getting along." His smile faded into a concerned expression. "Think about what I said, Major Fergusson." He walked away into the crowd.

Clare was shaking. Tally looked at her. "What was that all about? What did he say?"

Clare shook her head.

"Hey. I owe you big-time. I was a total asshole that day at the soup kitchen. Let me make it up to you. You want a drink or something?"

Clare wanted a drink very much. She nodded. "Hey, Drago." Tally hailed a hulking man bumping his way through the bystanders with two full glasses cupped in one giant hand. "Get this lady a drink, will ya? What are you having, Major?"

Clare took a breath. "Whisky."

"I got a Canadian Club I was taking to Zeller." The big guy held out a glass brimming with amber liquor. His fingers were covered in black hair. "I'll give her mine."

"Oh, I couldn't—"

"Go ahead." He deposited the glass in her hand. "You look like you need it more'n she does right now."

"Thanks, Drago." Tally punched him in the shoulder. Clare downed half the contents in one swallow. "Whoa. Easy there, Major."

She squeezed her fingers around the drink until she could feel the cut edges of the crystal digging into her skin. She swallowed the rest of the whisky.

"Hell, lady, take the other one." Drago tugged the empty glass out of her grip and placed the second drink in her hand.

"I don't want to . . ." Clare's voice trailed off. Her ring, her engagement ring, glittered and winked in the light of the torches.

Is that really as high as you can aim? To be the consolation prize for someone who can't have what he really wants?

She held the glass close to her nose and inhaled the golden oaken smell of the whisky, closing her eyes. She could hear Tally and the big man whispering, and then Tally said, "How long you been back, Major?"

"Nine weeks." Clare took a long drink. "Isn't that funny. I counted every day I was in-country. I didn't realize I was still counting here."

"Sandbox messes up your head." Tally ruffled her dark brown hair as if shaking bad thoughts out. "Running that soup kitchen probably doesn't help. There are some weird people there."

"I don't—" Clare began.

"She doesn't work for BWI?" Drago asked.

"Hell, Drago, does she look like a riveter or something to you? She's ex-army. Like me."

The big man's face creased. "I was just gonna tell her the company's got a doctor you can talk to for free. If she didn't know. I dunno about the army. Can you see a VA shrink for free?" He looked down at Clare, worried.

Even shaken and slightly sloshed, Drago's misplaced concern made her smile a little. He had clearly figured a soup kitchen employee didn't have deep pockets.

"The problem with VA isn't the cost. It's getting in in the first place." Tally unsnapped her purse and dug inside. "Look. Here's something you should think about. No pressure, and the lady, when I called? Said they didn't report anything to anybody if you didn't want them to." She handed Clare a photocopied brochure showing an American flag, an earnest and multiracial group talking, and a soldier silhouetted in the glow of a desert sunset. It was the same brochure she had tried to press on Will Ellis.

Clare let out a barking laugh. "The community center veterans group." She handed the brochure back.

"You heard about it? Yeah, they're starting up next week. I, um, I'm thinking of trying it out."

"Why?"

"Jesus, Dragojesich." Tally slugged him. "Try and show a little sensitivity here."

"Clare?"

Over Dragojesich's backhoe-sized shoulder, she saw Russ striding across the flagstones. Even in the flickering light, she could see his worried frown.

"Here," she called.

He crossed to her. Took her by her upper arms and shook her slightly. "I thought you were going to stay put."

"I'm sorry, I . . . I wanted a drink. Is everything all right?"

"Yeah, just a couple assholes who didn't learn how to use their words in preschool." He spotted Tally. "Pardon my French." He did a double take. "Ms. McNabb?"

Tally was looking from Clare to Russ and back to Clare. A knowing smile spread over her broad face. "That's why you told me to drop your name with him."

Russ wrapped his arm around Clare. "What?"

There was a swirl of bodies near the bar. Clare caught a glimpse of an expensive suit. "I'll tell you later," she said. "Are you done? Can we go now?"

"Sure. A couple uniforms from Lake George showed up. It's their problem now."

"Tally, thank you."

"No prob. We even about that soup kitchen thing?"

Clare waved her free hand. "It never happened."

"Good enough." Tally leaned forward and snapped Clare's clutch open. She stuffed the brochure inside. "Think about what I said, huh?"

"I will." Clare handed the empty glass to Dragojesich. "Thank you for the drink."

He shrugged, a movement akin to the uplift of mountains in quick time. "No thanks necessary. Those of us who been over there gotta stick together, right?"

The expensive suit seemed to be moving. Coming their way. "Right," Clare said. "Thanks. 'Bye." She headed off toward the porch stairs at such a clip it took Russ three or four seconds to catch up with her.

"Are you okay?"

"Yeah."

"You were awfully chummy with McNabb. Considering she's the reason you sprained your ankle. You were complaining about not running just a couple days ago."

"She apologized. I forgave her. Can we go now?"

"Are you—" He looked around them at the dancers as they passed. "Are you mad I left you alone to go stop that fight?"

She nearly tripped over her own feet. He steadied her. "Are you kidding? Of course not. That's your job. It doesn't end when you take the uniform off. That's one of the things we have in common." The booze was hitting her system, warming her from the inside out, calming her down. She smiled. "You ought to know that by now."

He looked down at the steps as they climbed to the wide, winged porch. "I guess . . . Linda would've been. Upset, I mean."

She caught his arm. He turned to her. The light spilling from the resort's open doors washed him golden, picking out his crow's-feet and smile lines and frown lines. He was the most attractive man she had ever met. He was fifty-two. He had been married twenty-five years. *Someone who can't have what he really wants.*

"I'm not Linda," she said.

"I know." He took her hand, interlacing his fingers with hers. "I'm not trying to compare you two. It's just that I have this whole set of reflexes that come from being Linda's husband. They're gonna come out now and again. I figure the best way to deal with that is to be up-front about it, and ask you what's going on instead of just assuming I know."

A laugh that was very close to a sob bubbled out of her chest.

"What?"

"That's my entire third marital counseling session condensed to one sentence."

He looked at her closely, a sliver of a smile on his face. He carefully rubbed one thumb along her cheek. "Are you sure you're okay, love?"

She could feel Opperman out there, gliding through the press of bodies like a malignant presence just under the surface of the water.

"Just . . . overtired. Overwhelmed."

"Yeah, I have that effect on women."

She laughed.

He tugged her toward the door. "C'mon, tired girl. Let's get you home to bed." He shook his head when she opened her mouth. "Alone."

SATURDAY, AUGUST 27   In her dream, Clare was flying. The radio crackled and spat with an endless flow of chatter, air-to-air, ground-to-air, reports from the AWACs flying miles above them.

Clare checked the airspeed, yawed the rooters another ten degrees so that they were looking at the ground through the windscreen. Drying fields. Irrigation pumps. And there, the narrow Nile green river that led to the town. She picked up speed. "Target coordinates in. Unlocking missiles."

"Confirmed. Range five hundred," her copilot said.

Clare tapped her mic. "Alpha Tango, this is Bravo Flight five two five, ranged three hundred meters from one-three Company Foxtrot. Do we have a confirm to go hot?"

Her helmet's headset blared. "Bravo Flight five two five, you are confirmed to go hot."

"Roger, Alpha Tango." She flicked the switches. "Missiles on."

The radio cracked again. "Bravo five two five, this is the one-three Foxtrot. Not to rush you or anything, but where the hell are you?"

"We'll be on top of you in two minutes, one-three. Are you still under fire?"

"Hell, yes, we're still under fire. We fell back to the house across the street. There ain't no more place to go. We've got wounded. We need an extract, and we need it five minutes ago."

"We have signal," her copilot said, and she glanced at him and saw it was her SERE instructor, Master Sergeant Ashley "Hardball" Wright, his lanky frame taking up all the cockpit space and then some.

"Master Sergeant? I didn't know you were flight-certified."

"Pay attention, Fergusson. You might live longer." The sun on the water flashed unbearably bright as they overflew the river. Then they were roaring over low buildings, dun and cement, and he said, "Target acquired," and she said, "Fire," and the Black Hawk's frame shuddered as the AGM-114s launched out of their cradles, and they streaked away faster than the eye could follow and half the target building exploded into dust and fire and oily black smoke. They flew into the black roiling column, the sound of the explosion carrying over the rotors, through her helmet, and she rode up, up, up on the high hard thermal, rising out of the smoke as the remains of the building burned beneath them.

"One-three Foxtrot, I need an LZ," she said into her mic. "Do you have enemy fire?"

"Negative, Bravo five two five. You smoked 'em. We're establishing a perimeter now."

She dropped the helo like an express elevator, leaving her stomach somewhere above the floating debris. The ambulatory of the one-three had cordoned off a dirty square flanked by burning rubble and mortar-pocked houses. She touched down and cut the engine. She looked around. There were bodies everywhere. Everywhere, circling her landing zone, heaped over the dirt and the cement, men, women, children, white shattered bones and black burned skin. "Oh my God," she said.

Then they were standing outside. The stench was beyond bearing, shit and burned insulation and rotting meat. Hardball said, "The lawyer, testing Jesus, asked, 'Who is my neighbor?'"

So many bodies. So many lives. So much death. The wounded of the one-three squad were lying on the broken concrete, body after bloody, blasted body, all in urban camo except for one. One was in khaki and brown. "We need extraction!" a sergeant yelled.

The helo was gone. Clare looked around, panicked.

"What does the Lord require of you," Hardball asked, "but to do justice, love mercy, and walk humbly with your God?"

"Where's the ship?" Clare cried. "Where's the goddamn ship?" A pair of EMTs hoisted a gurney. The man in khaki and brown was on it, packed with blue emergency bandages that had bled through in ragged purple blotches. "Where are you going?" Clare screamed. "We're extracting as soon as I find the ship! Bring him here!"

The EMTs passed her and she saw him in fragments: his sandy hair, the oxygen mask, one boot lolling off the stretcher. She saw his hand, tan, limp, still wearing his wedding ring. She lunged toward him and Hardball was in the way, soaking in blood, reeking of it, and he caught her and held her, saying, "This is my commandment to you; that you love one another as I have loved you."

Then the EMTs threw Russ Van Alstyne's dead body into the charnel house flames and she sat bolt upright, screaming and snot-faced in the darkness of her bedroom.

"Oh, God, help me!" Her heart was pounding so hard she thought she might stroke out. She half fell, half crawled out of her sweat-tangled sheets and staggered to the bathroom. She braced her hands on the cistern and vomited into the toilet, spasming over and over again until there was nothing left. She sank weeping onto the tile floor.

She sat there for a long time, tears smearing across her cheeks, her whole body shaking. She squeezed her eyes shut against the flashes of shattered and burned flesh, afterimages imprinted on her retinas. She tried to pray, but the vision of Russ, bloody, broken, dead, wiped all the words from her mind, and she was left with nothing but the most elemental plea. *Help me, God. God, help me.*

I don't think I'm fine at all.

She had left her clutch on the shelf over the towel rack, emptied of the lipstick and compact she had carried earlier this evening. Yesterday. She pushed against the edge of the tub and listed to her feet. Reached for the clutch. Pulled out the creased brochure. There would be somebody at the community center starting at eight o'clock when the gym opened. Nine at the latest.

She looked out the bathroom's small window. Venus blazed large and bright among the fading stars. She could see the silhouettes of rooftops and chimneys and trees against the sky, but she couldn't make out any colors yet. She smoothed the brochure against her aching stomach, over and over again, and then sat down on the cool tiles to wait out the coming of the light.

SATURDAY, SEPTEMBER 3 Hadley Knox stretched her legs out on the grass and watched the other parents waiting for the Millers Kill Middle School cross-country team to reappear from walking the meet course.

There was a trio of mothers near her, women she had seen at the school but never met. They were chatting and laughing in canvas camp chairs with their pedicured feet propped up on coolers. They wore crop-legged chinos and drapey cotton sweaters, bits of gold dripping off their wrists and circling their necks. Hadley was in jeans and her police acad-emy T-shirt, with nothing but a Goodwill windbreaker to keep the grass from staining her butt. She must have missed the memo that said they were supposed to dress like they were going to the damn country club.

She recognized a few faces here and there, from school concerts and open houses. There was one man she knew she had seen at St. Alban's, and another she had ticketed for doing fifty in a thirty-five zone, but there wasn't anybody she knew well enough to wave over and start shoot-ing the breeze with. Two years she had been living in Millers Kill—two and a half—and she didn't have a single friend.

Jesus, listen to your pity party. She drew her knees up and wrapped her arms around them. Her life was exactly the way she wanted it. She had

Hudson and Genny and Granddad. She had a job, and a house to run, and she even went to church every Sunday, although that was more for the kids' benefit than her own. The occasional bout of loneliness was the fee for controlling her own life. It was a fair trade.

A stir of excitement brought her attention to where the woods opened up to clear land. She recognized the Minutemen blue-and-white on the ragged clump of middle schoolers emerging from the trail, spotted Hudson and his best friend Conner and Eric McCrea's boy, and a grown-up in the midst of them, impossibly tall and redheaded and *what* the *hell* was Kevin Flynn doing with her kid's cross-country team?

Hudson was half a length ahead of Flynn, who seemed to be hanging back, talking to the stragglers. Hadley propped a smile on her face as she approached the snapping tape dividing the runners from the spectators. "Hey, babe. How's the course? Any cow patties you have to watch out for?"

Conner and Jacob McCrea cracked up. Hudson looked as if he didn't know whether to laugh or be embarrassed. "Oh, man, can you imagine," Conner said. "Stepping in one and it sticking to your shoe?"

"Stepping in two!" Jake started clomping around, his sneakers encased in imaginary cow patties. Hadley thought about Eric, already planning for this kid's future in college. Hard to believe these boys would ever be mature enough to leave home.

"Okay, guys." Kevin's voice carried over the boy's snorts and moos. "Go see Coach. He'll get you signed in. Remember what I said about the final downhill stretch." He paused in front of Hadley while the team moved on toward the crowded starting line, Jake demonstrating the double-manure maneuver to everyone. "Hey, Hadley."

"What are you doing here?"

He frowned. "Coach Bain needed an assistant. I'm helping him out."

"You're not a parent. Why on earth would you be hanging around a bunch of dopy middle school kids?"

"You don't need to be a parent to volunteer." His face stiffened. "Wait a minute. Wait just a goddamn minute. Are you trying to imply something?"

"Yes. I want to know if you volunteered because my kid is on the team."

"What?" He stared at her a moment, then snorted a half-laugh. He scrubbed his hand over his face. "Shit. Okay. I thought you were accusing me of being a pedophile."

"Euww! No!"

"Well, euww, no, I didn't sign up for this gig because Hudson is on the team. I didn't know the roster until I got to the first practice. I volunteered because I used to run for Coach Bain, and because none of the *parents* stepped up to the plate."

"I'm busy!"

"Then you ought to be grateful that somebody who has a little more time stepped in to take up the slack."

"Is that what this is about? Me being grateful?"

"Oh, for God's sake—" He blew out a breath. "Look, I gotta meet up with the team and see them off. Will you be here?"

"Of course. Are they going to—" He was already loping toward the throng of kids at the middle of the field, giving her a nice view of the arch of his thigh and the spring of his calf. *Stop that.* Most of the trouble in her life began with the fall of a guy's hair over his eye or the edge of his narrow hip bones peeking out from the low-slung waist of his jeans. She'd start out thinking *he's hot* and end up cosigning a loan for the loser.

The starting gun cracked, and an uneven line of boys surged toward the forest. She could see blue and white shorts and singlets, but she couldn't make out Hudson as the runners quickly closed into a pack and disappeared into the trees. Then there was Flynn, walking back toward her, oblivious to the appreciative glances from a couple of well-groomed moms who must have been twice his age, for God's sake. He held the tape up with his forearm and ducked under it. His hands were filled with two sweating water bottles. He gave her one.

"Thanks." There. She could be gracious.

"Did you bring a chair?"

"I brought a windbreaker." She gestured toward the crumpled nylon, weighted down with her purse. He collapsed onto the grass next to it in a tangle of long, pale limbs. As she sat—with a lot more care and a lot less athleticism—she caught a glimpse of the chino-and-gold-bangle crowd checking them out. *That's right, bitches,* she wanted to say. *You may have the goods, but I have the young stud.*

Oh, God, what was wrong with her? They probably thought Hadley was his aunt or something. Big sister. She popped open the bottle's flip-top and swallowed half the contents in one go.

"So, not to put too fine a point on it, do you want to tell me why you have a hair up your ass about me helping Coach Bain?"

She spluttered water and swiped the back of her hand over her mouth. "Look. I'm sorry. I was surprised to see you, and I leaped to a not very nice conclusion."

"That I did it because I knew Hudson was on the team?" He shook his head. "Hadley, I see you every day at the shop. It's not like I have to manufacture reasons to bump into you."

"I know that. It's just . . ." She could feel her cheeks heating up.

"Just what? Just you can't imagine me volunteering with no ulterior motive?"

"No! Of course not." She drew her legs up again and stared intently at the spot on her knee where the denim had worn threadbare and white. "Look. Before you left on TDY, you were all up in my face with 'I love you' and 'Let's be together.' Now you're back. I guess I'm waiting for it to start again."

"You told me to stop. Several times."

She looked at him, then. "Yeah. But you didn't."

His eyes shifted away from hers. He examined the tips of his running shoes. "I'm sorry. That was wrong of me." He took a breath. "When I was in Syracuse, I worked a stalking case. This couple, they had dated for a while, then she broke it off, but he wouldn't let go. He started hanging around the mall where she worked, and when security chased him off, he did drive-bys of her town house. Took pictures of her and e-mailed them to her. Left her flowers and stuffed animals everywhere—her gym, her hairdresser's, her parents' house. We pulled him in. She had a restraining order, and he violated. He kept saying—God, he was so delusional. He kept saying how much they were in love. To him, all this shit was roman-tic. In his mind, he was courting her. He didn't see, he couldn't see, that she was terrified. And the whole time we were talking to him"—he tipped his face up to the wide blue sky—"I kept thinking that was me."

"No." She touched his arm. "Flynn. Really. No. You never scared me. You just mistook one night for a relationship."

He shook his head. "It's not that. I didn't fool myself into thinking you felt what I felt. It's that I didn't listen to you. No means no and stop means stop and I didn't hear you, I didn't respect you when you said that and I'm sorry." The last of his sentence came out in a husky rush.

She thought for a moment. "Are you saying this so I'll drop my defenses and maybe sleep with you again?"

His whole body jerked. "God! No!" He looked at her, appalled. "Is that what you think of me? That I'd manipulate you like that?"

She took a deep breath. Reminded herself that there were a few good men out there. "No. I don't." She picked up her water bottle. "I think you're a nice guy who actually learns from his experiences and uses them to become a better person. Which makes you a rarity, in my book." She took a drink of water. "Apology accepted. Don't worry about it anymore."

He nodded. Picked up his water bottle and studied the label. "Thanks. It's been kind of eating at me since I came home, but bringing it up at the station seemed . . ." He looked at her. "Thanks."

She toasted him with her bottle. "Friends?"

He looked up from the label. His eyes were almost gray, she realized. Like mist and clouds over an autumn sky. "Yeah. Friends. That would be . . . that would be good." He sounded so relieved, she felt a flash of annoyance. So much for her fatal allure.

He looked past her shoulder toward the woods. "Here they come." He unfolded from the ground. "I have to be at the finish gate and get the times." He sprinted toward the far end of the course. Hadley got to her feet and made her way to the edge of the track. She could see them now, one kid, then another, then another, popping out of the forest trail and pelting down the grassy slope toward the cinder track. The sight of the end must have juiced them, because she swore she could see them pick up speed. A kid in Millers Kill colors pulled even with and then ahead of the front-runner, a lanky boy from Argyle Central. The crowd was screaming, she was screaming, and she saw it was Jake McCrea and she screamed even louder.

Then Jake glanced behind him, looking for the kid in maroon and white, and that was all it took. His leading foot slipped in the grass, skidded, and he flipped, tumbled, head, shoulders, tailbone, through the air, landing with a thud Hadley could swear she heard from where she stood.

The crowd's scream became a collective indrawn breath. The other runners kept on course, racing past Jake toward the finish, but Hadley lost sight of them as she waited, two seconds, four, six, for Jake to get up and run or walk to the edge of the field. He did neither.

"Shit." She ducked beneath the tape.

"Lady," someone yelled. "Hey, lady, you can't go out there!"

She pulled her badge out of her back pocket and flashed it toward the voice without stopping. She wasn't the only noncontestant on the field now—Flynn was running toward Jake, and a woman weighed down with clipboard, walkie-talkie, and stopwatches, followed by a graying man she recognized as the Millers Kill coach. She and Flynn reached the boy first.

"Jake. Hey, buddy, how are you doing?" Flynn knelt next to Jake and pressed his fingers to the side of the boy's neck.

"My chest hurts." Jake was pale and sweaty, but his pupils were normal, symmetrical, and he tracked Flynn's finger from left to right and back again without a problem. "Maybe I just—" The boy curled up into a sitting position and gasped. Hadley took his hand and let him squeeze it until her knuckles cracked.

"Where does it hurt?" Flynn gently touched Jake's rib cage, first one side, then the other. "Here?"

Jake shook his head then winced. "Higher."

Hadley looked at Flynn. "Collarbone."

Flynn laid four fingers over the boy's collarbone. Jake yelped. "That's it." Flynn looked at Hadley. "I can already feel it swelling up."

"I broke my collarbone at the first meet of the season? Oh, God, that's so lame."

"No way, dude." Flynn smiled brilliantly at the boy. "You're a wounded warrior. The chicks are going to be falling all over themselves to help you in the lunch line, carry your books. You wait and see."

"Should I call an ambulance?" Coach Bain asked.

"Quicker if we take him in my vehicle," Flynn said.

"The division regs state any injured child should be transported professionally unless released into the care of a parent or guardian," the time-keeper said.

"We are professional." With her free hand, Hadley flapped her badge at the woman. "Officer Flynn's car is equipped with a light bar, siren, and emergency service radio. I'll ride along."

"Oh. Oh. Well, in that case . . ."

"I'm sorry, Coach." Jake blinked fast and hard as Hadley and Flynn helped him to his feet. "I'm really sorry. I know I shouldn't have looked back. I knew it, and I did it anyway."

"You did great out there," Coach Bain assured him. "You ran a great race. You go with Kevin and Mrs. Knox—I'm sorry, with Officer Knox—and after this little ding heals up, we'll see about you breaking some records for the indoor track season. Kevin, I'm going to grab his medical authorization out of my truck. I'll meet you at your car with it." Coach Bain strode off, the track official double-stepping to keep up with him.

"Here." Flynn stripped off his T-shirt, pulled the neck over Jake's head, and ran the body of it under and over Jake's arm. He tied some sort of three-way knot with the hem and the sleeves and presto, Jake's arm was snug against his chest in an all-cotton sling. "Better?"

"Yeah."

"Oh, my God," Hadley said, "You really were an Eagle Scout."

"Yeah." Flynn looked surprised. "How'd you know?"

Then she saw the other tattoo. A second, smaller Celtic knot, this one circling his left nipple. "Jesus, Flynn." Even with the injured boy standing between them, she felt a jolt low in her belly at the sight. It was . . . erotic. Not what she wanted to be feeling around Kevin Flynn. "If the chief sees that, you'll be pulling the dog shift for the rest of your natural life."

He grinned. "Good thing I'm not planning on stripping down for the chief, then, isn't it?"

In Flynn's car, away from the other kids, Jake let himself lean against Hadley and shut his eyes. While Flynn turned on his lights and began the drive back to Millers Kill, she tried to reach Jennifer McCrea. She left a detailed voice mail at Jennifer's home and cell numbers, and when she had clicked off, she said, "I'm sure she'll get the message soon, and your dad will be on his way. The dispatcher will tell him what happened."

Jake bit his lip. "He'll be mad."

"No, honey, he won't. It wasn't your fault you broke your collarbone, and even if it was, he wouldn't be mad at you."

He blinked again. "It hurts."

"I know it does, honey." She glanced out the window. "We'll be there in five minutes. I promise you, I'll stay with you until your mom gets there, okay?"

"Okay."

Kevin parked in the MKPD spot outside emergency and they both helped ease Jake out of the car. The boy looked pinched and scared and about nine years old. Hadley tried his mother's numbers again while Kevin checked him in at the admission desk.

The ER nurse let Hadley wait outside the blue curtained area while he helped Jake change. Hadley stood at his bedside while the resident cheerfully agreed that yep, it sure looked like a broken collarbone to her. They ice-bagged the spot, now purple and swollen, and started an IV, which left Jake groggy.

"We need him for fifteen minutes in radiology," the resident said. "Then the orthopedist will be in to talk with you." She glanced at Jake's chart. "You're not the mom?"

"We're trying to get hold of her." Hadley squeezed Jake's noninjured arm. "I'll call your mom again while you're getting X-rayed." He nodded sleepily as they rolled him away.

Kevin Flynn was shivering in the waiting area, his arms wrapped around himself for warmth, looking for all the world like an extra from *Braveheart* who had mistakenly swapped his kilt for a pair of baggy shorts. "Here you go, Celtic warrior." She handed him his T-shirt. "The goose bumps don't go too well with the tats."

"They didn't have AC in ancient Ireland." He pulled the shirt over his head. "How's he doing?"

"They've doped him up and taken him in for X-rays." She glanced around the ER waiting room while she redialed Jennifer McCrea's home and cell numbers. Tired institutional paint, wide, armless sixties-style couches and chairs, a goateed teen, a grandmotherly type in a cardigan, a weather-beaten man asleep and listing. Jennifer's recorded voice invited her to leave a message. Hadley started to repeat her message when the ER doors whumped open and Eric McCrea strode through. He spotted them.

"How is he?" He must have come straight out of his unit; he was still wearing his rig, radio at his shoulder, his service piece holstered at his hip.

"He's fine," Hadley said. "They're pretty sure it's just a broken collarbone. He's in radiology now. They've given him Demerol for the pain."

"What happened?" Eric said.

"He pulled the lead maybe two hundred meters from the finish," Flynn said. "He was really flying. You would have been proud of him."

"What *happened?*"

"He couldn't resist checking out where the closest runner was. He looked behind him . . ." Flynn shrugged. "That's all it takes to put a foot wrong."

"Oh, Christ. Of all the boneheaded moves." Eric clenched his fists. "He knows better than that. He knows better!"

"It's a broken collarbone," Hadley reminded him. "Which is a lot better than a broken leg. Or a broken neck. He'll be running around again by November. December at the latest."

"By which time the season will be over."

Hadley looked at Flynn. The puzzled uneasiness she saw on his face matched her own concern. She had spent a fair amount of time riding with him back when she was a newbie. That Eric had been smart, patient with her mistakes, with a sense of humor that eased him over the rough spots of the job. This Eric looked like he was going to pop a vein because his kid busted a bone. Playing in middle school, for God's sake. "Where's Jenny?" he demanded.

"I've been trying to reach her." Hadley held up her phone. "I've been leaving her messages to keep her up to date. She'll know everything as soon as she checks her cell."

"Where in the hell is she? Why wasn't she at the meet in the first place?"

"Eric." Flynn moved in, close enough to drop his voice to a confidential hush. "I understand that you're worried and scared for Jake, but you're not going to help him or yourself by flying off the handle. Take a deep breath and let it go, man."

Eric hooked his thumbs in his rig and spread his arms and chest. "Don't try to talk me down, Kevin. I've been a cop twice as long as both of you put together. Don't give me some bullshit line about how you understand me, because you don't. You're not a father."

"Well, I'm a mother, and I can tell you that if you walk in there acting like Dirty Harry, you're going to scare your son to death and probably get hospital security to escort your ass outside."

"I'd like to see them try!"

"Luckily for them, there are two MKPD officers here to help them!"

Eric stepped toward her. "You think you can take me?"

"Cool it." Kevin's voice was sharp and unfamiliar. "Both of you. Eric, you're in uniform. If you can't pull it together and act like a professional, you'd better leave."

"Or what?"

"Or I report you for duty code violation, and we'll let the chief sort it out." Eric glared up at Flynn, who glared right back. "I'll do it. You know I will."

"God." Eric was the first to look away. "You're such a fucking Boy Scout sometimes." He glanced at Hadley. "Where is he?"

"Follow me." At the nursing station, she asked, "Is Jake McCrea done with his X-rays?"

The nurse glanced at a large wall-mounted whiteboard. Names and numbers and treatments had been written and erased so many times the surface was a permanent gray smear. "Yup. He's in bay four with the orthopedic surgeon."

Through a gap in the limp blue curtains Hadley could see a glimpse of a white coat. "Jake?" she called out. "Your dad's here, honey."

She opened the curtain. The orthopedic surgeon, reassuringly middle-aged and gray-haired, was scratching notes on the back of a folder. He looked up. "Hi. Are you Jake's mom?"

"No, she works with my dad—" Jake's explanation was cut off by Eric's loud voice.

"Oh, hell, no." He jabbed a finger at the doctor. "You're not touching my kid."

"What?" The doctor and Hadley spoke at the same time.

"I'm sorry," the doctor said. "Do I know you?"

"Don't play dumb, Stillman. I'm not letting a guy who abandons his own daughter to bang his girlfriend treat my son."

The doctor's face turned a mottled red.

"Dad!" Jake sounded horrified. He struggled to sit up.

"Eric! Jesus Christ!" Hadley was torn between dragging Eric away and going to Jake.

McCrea yanked the curtain open. "I want somebody competent in here to treat my kid," he roared toward the nursing station.

"Dr. Stillman?" The nurse spoke to the orthopedic surgeon, but he kept his eyes on McCrea.

The doctor turned toward the nurse. "Call security!"

"Lie down, honey." Hadley pressed the flat of her hand against the middle of Jake's chest. The boy was crying now, his face screwed into a twist of misery and mortification. "You'll hurt yourself. Lie down."

"You can't throw me out! I'm his father! I know my goddamn rights!"

Hadley opened her mouth to call for Kevin, but he was already there, long legs eating up the floor, holding his badge up for the gathering crowd of nurses and doctors and technicians to see. He wrapped one arm around McCrea's shoulder, turning him, saying something low and fast into his ear. Eric elbowed Flynn away. "Goddammit, I'm not the one being unreasonable here! I'm trying to protect my son and no one fucking appreciates that!"

Two white-shirted rent-a-cops bulldozed through the gawkers. The doctor jerked his thumb toward Eric. "Get this maniac out of the hospital and see that he stays out!" One of the guards unstrapped a restraint from his belt.

Eric's hand went to his SIG SAUER .45.

Hadley reacted without thinking. She screamed, "Gun!" and tackled Eric.

They went down in a sprawl, Eric and Hadley and Flynn. Eric twisted, bucked, then gave up. He began to curse, quietly, steadily, and his voice had more heartbreak than anger in it now.

She looked at Flynn. They were restraining a brother officer. A man who had mentored them both. "Now what?"

He drove McCrea back to the station in the cruiser. Hadley waited with a tearful Jake and the white-faced orthopedist, who wrote note after note after note, undoubtedly working up a full-blown complaint against Eric. When Jennifer McCrea arrived, she took the news of her husband's outburst with her lips pressed tightly together. "I'm sorry," she told Hadley. "I don't know what's going on inside his head anymore. It scares me."

Weary and just wanting to go home, Hadley still had to pick up Flynn. She drove to the station, parked, and let herself sink into a funk of could-have-should-have-would-have. The door opening startled her. So much for her ever-alert law enforcement instincts. Flynn hoisted himself into the passenger seat. "You mind driving back to the field? I'm wiped."

She shifted into gear and backed out of the parking lot. "What did you do?"

He closed his eyes. "I wrote up a report of the entire incident. I showed it to him. Then I saved it without logging it in."

"What? Christ, Flynn, he was ready to draw on that security guard!"

Flynn dragged a hand through his hair. It was getting overdue for a cut. "There was this brochure for a veterans support group—I saw it in the chief's office Thursday. I gave it to Eric and told him to call them, or the VA Hospital, or that department's therapist in Saratoga, and set up an appointment and get some help. Today."

She signaled and turned onto Route 117. "Did he do it?"

"He signed up for the veterans group at the community center."

"You're sure?"

"I sat right there while he called." He leaned forward and cranked the blower up. Cold air roared through the car. He collapsed backward again. "God. I don't know. He's a good cop."

"He was."

"He wasn't like this before he went to Iraq."

"I know, Flynn—but he went for his gun. In the emergency room. What if he loses it again with a suspect? Or at home, with Jennifer and Jake?"

Flynn crossed his arms over his chest. "You and I will keep an eye on him." He looked out the window. They were out of the town, entering the rolling hills and pastures of Cossayuharie. "He went off to war for us. That's what people say, isn't it? They're doing it for us? Don't we at least owe him a chance to make it right?"

HELP US, WE PRAY, IN THE
MIDST OF THINGS WE CANNOT
UNDERSTAND, TO BELIEVE AND
TRUST IN THE COMMUNION
OF SAINTS . . .

—*The Burial of the Dead: Rite One, The Book of Common Prayer*

MONDAY, OCTOBER 3   This week, it was Will who was running late. Sarah looked at the round white clock hanging above the preschoolers' construction-paper pumpkins and ghosts. It was already five past seven, and the rest of the group had been in their places for ten minutes, listening to the thuds of the basketball and the squeak of sneakers next door. Stillman scratched on his ancient PalmPilot with a stylus. Fergusson's head was tilted back, and her eyes were half closed; evidently even her coffee wasn't keeping her awake tonight. McCrea kept glancing at McNabb, frowning, then looking away, only to repeat the whole cycle again a minute later.

Sarah glanced around the circle. "Does anyone know if Will had any VA appointments? Maybe some difficulty with his ride?"

Fergusson roused herself. "His father brings him after dinner. It could be Chris was running late."

"Okay. Well, I don't want to waste any more time. Let's get started, and he can catch up when he gets here." Sarah looked at McNabb and Stillman. "Last week, Clare and Eric opened up about some of the ways they're expressing their emotions or not expressing their emotions, as the case may be, and we all talked about some strategies for dealing with those difficult moments when the pain or the anger or the fear breaks through. I want to explore those healthy responses further, but first we need to go back to hear from Trip and Tally about their reasons for attending therapy. Trip, we didn't have time to get to you last week. Will you start us off?"

"Well." The doctor fidgeted in his metal chair. "I've been under a lot of stress since I came home. Some of it's the usual—my practice, a surly teen in the house, my older daughter's financial troubles. Some of it's been new. A death in the family, problems with—" He clamped his mouth shut. After a moment, he said, "I've been having these migraines."

163

A pager went off. Fergusson started. She put her paper coffee cup on the floor and dug into the pocket of her ankle-length black skirt. She pulled out her cell phone and read the display. "Excuse me." She rose. "I have to take this." She vanished into the hallway.

Stillman sat there. "Migraines," Sarah prompted. The doctor touched his forehead. There was a small white scar threading across his skin into his bristle-brush gray hair. "I sustained a head injury when a clinic I was working at was blown up by insurgents." He lapsed into silence.

When nothing else seemed forthcoming, Sarah asked, "Was this the forward response station you were posted to?"

"No. No, this was a civilian clinic. Part of the mission was to treat as many Iraqis as we could. We were supposed to have an actual, honest-to-God reinforced building with a generator and a sterile room, but that never materialized, so we had to make do in whatever facility we could set up shop in. We were in a local medical clinic school when this happened." He rubbed his scar with his forefinger.

"Mortar fire?" Eric asked.

"Yeah. We had an escort, and marines patrolling the town, but they couldn't be everywhere at once."

"Where was this?" Tally asked.

"Haditha, in the Anbar. It was the closest population base to our FRS."

The hall door opened. Clare strode in, fastening the top two buttons of her black shirt. Beneath the room's fluorescent light, she looked sickly and washed-out. "That was Chris Ellis. They're in the hospital. Will tried to kill himself."

◆ ◆ ◆

Surprisingly, Sarah and the others arrived before Clare. Tally had stood up, said, "Let's go," and gotten her jacket off the hooks on the wall. The men followed her without comment, as if it were simply expected they would all reconvene at the hospital. "Maybe we should wait," Sarah said, but it was already too late. Nothing to do but get in her car and force herself to drive toward the ultimate verdict on her fitness as a therapist: a client's suicide.

Attempted suicide, she reminded herself in the ICU waiting room. The pills Will Ellis had swallowed by the handful had been pumped out of his stomach. Now they had to see if that would be enough. Through the archway leading to the hallway and nursing station, she heard a soft ding. The elevator opened. Sarah caught a glimpse of Clare Fergusson, a white collar around her neck, a long satin scarf-thing draped over her shoulders, a black leather box in her hand. The satin flapped around her knees as she strode up the hall and out of sight.

Tally, who had taken the chair kitty-corner to Sarah's, leaned forward. "Was that Clare?"

"Yes."

"Geez. I guess she really is a minister." Tally leaned back. "You'd think if you put that much faith in God, you wouldn't need to be in counseling."

"No. Well. God's not big into talk therapy."

Stillman rounded the archway, his eyes on his PalmPilot, scratching something with his stylus at what looked like a hundred words a minute. He sank into the chair opposite McNabb.

"Did you find out anything?" Sarah asked. He didn't look like the bearer of good tidings.

"His respiratory and circulatory systems are collapsing, and he's experiencing serious bradycardia."

"What's that mean?"

Sarah was feeling desperate enough to be glad Tally asked the question, allowing her to look at least marginally competent.

"He's got what we call combined drug intoxication. He apparently took all his painkillers, his antidepressants, a bottle of cough syrup, a whole lot of acetaminophen, and then washed it all down with booze. Simplified, his system is shutting down. His heart's pumping too slow, his blood isn't circulating, and his lungs aren't working." Stillman glanced at his PalmPilot. "He's damaged his liver, too. How much, they won't know until and unless he survives." His face was bleak.

"God." Tally sat for a minute. "Do you think he meant it to work? Or was he just, you know, crying for help?"

"He made a pretty credible attempt." Stillman rubbed his knuckles hard against the scar on his forehead. "I can't believe I didn't see any warning signs."

That same phrase was chasing itself around and around in Sarah's head. "Why would you?" *Why didn't I?*

"I'm seeing him for his amputation follow-up. He's doing PT at my practice."

"And I was his therapist." Sarah stood. Walked toward the archway. If she could, she would have stepped right out of her skin and kept on going. "If anybody should have recognized that he was potentially suicidal, it should have been me."

"You guys are forgetting something."

Sarah turned toward Tally, who spread her hands. "He's a marine. You don't think of it, because his legs are gone, but he's still a marine. You know, the jarheads, they do what they gotta do. Maybe he just woke up this morning and realized his body was the enemy." Tally rubbed her jeans over her thighs and knees, as if trying to feel what Will must have felt. "And you know, he knows what to do with an enemy."

◆ ◆ ◆

Eric left first; he had a wife and kid at home, after all, and had to be at work the next morning. Stillman was next, after several short conversations with Will's red-eyed, lank-haired mother. Tally hung around, whether through curiosity or empathy Sarah didn't know. Sarah couldn't leave, couldn't push herself forward to talk to the parents, couldn't ask anyone, once Trip Stillman took off, what Will's prognosis was. She was ready, if approached, to describe her impressions, show her notes, pass on anything that might be useful. She was ready, but she couldn't bring herself to volunteer. Her thoughts and self-recriminations chased themselves around and around in her head like disease-raddled rats on a rusty wheel.

She didn't realize she had sunk into a reverie until she heard Tally say, "Major. I mean, Reverend." Sarah opened her eyes.

Clare Fergusson collapsed onto the chair opposite McNabb. "What are you still doing here?"

Sarah's heart turned over in one slow despairing beat before she realized Fergusson was speaking to Tally.

"I dunno," Tally said. "No place better to go, I guess. My husband's away gambling for a few days." Her voice made it clear she thought games of chance were a monumental waste of time. Unless, Sarah thought, it was that the husband wasn't alone at whatever casino he had fled to. "How's Will doing?" Tally asked.

"He'll live." Fergusson slid down until the back of her head could rest against the top of the upholstered chair. "God. I'm so tired. I'd sell my grandmother's wedding ring for a drink right now."

"Let's find a bar," Sarah said. "I'll buy the first round."

Tally's mouth opened. "What happened to encouraging her to deal with her stress in a healthy way?"

Fergusson started laughing.

"At this point, I'm going to consider alcoholism a viable alternative. All things considering." Sarah bent over and rubbed her hands over her face.

Fergusson's smile faded away. "Are you implying I'm an alcoholic?"

Sarah looked at her. "Based on what little I've been able to pry out of you, I think you have a problem with alcohol." She folded her hands and rested her chin on her knuckles. It made a hard, uncomfortable perch, which was just what she needed right now. "Then again, what the hell do I know? I completely missed Will's suicidal intent."

"Oh, for chrissakes," Tally said. "Quit beating yourself up over it. Anybody who's seen a public service announcement on TV knows what the three or five or seven warning signs are. Will's not stupid. He didn't *want* to tip anybody off. Because then somebody woulda stopped him. It's the same reason Clare doesn't want to talk about drinking. Because she's afraid if she does, somebody will stop her from doing it."

Fergusson opened her mouth. Closed it again.

"It's like we're all sick, you know? Like we all got something wrong with us, but we won't tell the doctor and get it treated. Because we're afraid the cure is going to be worse than the disease."

Sarah was surprised at Tally's outburst, and by her insight. The young woman hadn't struck her as being that tuned in to others.

"You don't cure PTSD," Fergusson said. "You learn to live with it. I don't think taking a drink now and then or using a sleeping pill when you can't get back to sleep after a nightmare is necessarily a bad thing."

Tally scooted to the edge of her chair and stared at the priest. "Aren't you tired of being afraid all the time? I am."

"Then why in God's name are you thinking about going back to Iraq? What's that about? Facing your fears? Unit cohesion with the rest of the construction team?"

Tally crossed her arms over her chest. She rubbed the tattoo on her arm. "I'm not going back. I've decided."

"Oh." Fergusson deflated. "Okay."

"What's that going to mean for your job?" Sarah asked.

"I don't know." She rubbed her arm again. "Maybe lose it, I guess. It's not the worst thing that could happen to me." Her gaze shifted toward the corridor. Somewhere down that hall, Will Ellis lay, broken. "It's not near the worst thing that could happen to me."

WEDNESDAY, OCTOBER 5   It was Bev Collins and her home health aide who heard the noise. A boom, then a crack, loud enough to make the aide start and say, "What was that?"

"Gunshot." Mrs. Collins laid down a set of threes. She and Tracy played canasta every Wednesday, and Tracy allowed her one beer for the game. Her doctor said the sugar in it would kill her, but by God, if she had to do without beer, too, she'd just as soon go anyways.

"It's too close to be a gunshot. It sounded like it came from next door."

"Young lady, I have hunted and shot for nigh on seventy years. I'd still be doing it if I could see worth a damn." Mrs. Collins's upcountry accent changed "worth" to "wuth." "That was a small-caliber sidearm. Either somebody's gotten sick and tired of those damn raccoons taking down the garbage cans, or he don't know jack about cleaning his weapon and accidentally discharged it."

"Raccoons aren't out at three in the afternoon." Tracy got up from the kitchen table and went to the window. "I can't see anything through the safety fence. I better go out and take a look."

"Safety fence." Mrs. Collins shuffled to the icebox and took out another beer. What Tracy didn't know wouldn't hurt her. "Swimming pool. The river's too good for folks nowadays." She hadn't taken more than a few swigs when Tracy tore back into the kitchen.

"It's—she's—call the police! She's killed herself!"

◆ ◆ ◆

"I would say a single shot, through the mouth, to the back of the head." Emil Dvorak, the Millers Kill medical examiner, pushed against his silver-headed cane to straighten from his crouched position at the edge of the pool. "I can confirm that, at least, as soon as you remove her from the water."

There was a faint clicking noise as Sergeant Morin of the New York State Police Criminal Investigation Unit snapped off picture after picture on his digital camera. Tally McNabb was floating on her back, ribbons and streamers of blood trailing over and around and beneath her. Tiny pieces of bone and brain floated on the surface of the pool. "I'd like you to take prints from all the exterior doors," Russ said.

"Sure." Morin dropped his camera into his kit. "What about the inside?"

"Depends on what we find in there." Russ looked up to the open second-floor window. Sheer white curtains fluttered out of the frame to catch in the wind rising from the mountains. From McNabb's backyard, he could see the edge of the hills, russet and brown and yellow, and a dark wall of clouds moving toward them.

"You think there's somebody in there?"

Russ shook his head. "Not alive." He turned to Lyle MacAuley. "Have you raised the husband yet?"

Lyle shoved his phone into his jacket pocket and shook his head. "Nothin'. The foreman at BWI Opperman says he's on leave for the next two weeks. I got the names of a couple friends, and we can probably get a few more if we canvass the Dew Drop. He was a regular, right?"

"That's what the owner said." His eyes were drawn, again, to the open window.

"You thinking murder-suicide?"

"Maybe."

"If McNabb killed her out here and then offed himself, what in the hell is that .38 doing down there? Or are you going to suggest he switched weapons midstream?"

Both men looked into the pool. The gun, black and malignant, lay in twelve feet of water, according to the warning embossed on the plastic lip of the pool gutter.

Russ pinched the bridge of his nose. "She locks all the doors to her house, comes out to the pool in jeans and a sweater, and shoots herself at the very edge of the water."

"It does keep things nice and neat. If that matters to you."

"Maybe McNabb did her and tossed the gun in. Chlorine washes away a lot of evidence. He could already be at the Albany airport."

"We got a BOLO out on him. If he tries to run, somebody'll spot him." Lyle zipped his jacket against the chilly air. "Maybe the disappointed boyfriend did her. Or both of 'em."

"Quentan Nichols? He hasn't been back here since August."

"That you know of. Maybe he just figured out how to keep a lower profile." Lyle looked up as the locksmith on call crossed the yard, his tools out. "C'mon. Let's see what's in there."

The house was clean and orderly, with no evidence of a struggle and no indication that anyone had been there. The locksmith confirmed that the back door he opened would have latched automatically behind anyone who exited the garage. Lyle pointed out the spare key, hanging from a nail next to the door. "Looks like she didn't intend to come back inside."

Russ grunted. "Or someone didn't intend her to."

They found a gun locker in the unfinished basement. Russ asked Morin to print the battered metal chest, without much expectation of finding anything.

The message light was blinking on the kitchen phone. Russ tugged on his purple evidence gloves and hit the PLAY button. The first message was a shade above a whisper, as if the woman speaking didn't want to be overheard. "Tally, where are you? Kirkwood's having a hissy fit because you haven't called in sick." The second message was professionally warm. "Tally? This is Elaine Kirkwood in human resources. Are you ill? Please remember we need you to either phone in or request a personal day in advance." The final message was a voice that made his skin crawl. "Hi, Tally. This is John Opperman. Please call me at your earliest convenience."

"Whatever happened, she didn't plan it in advance," Lyle said.

"Get back to the HR woman. Let her know we're investigating Tally's death. I want to know her work history. Did she report directly to Opperman? Does she have any incidents on her record? Maybe lodged a complaint against him?"

"Russ." Lyle stepped closer. "There must be two hundred people employed by BWI Opperman, if you count the construction crews and the part-timers. I know how you feel about Opperman, but you can't automatically make him a person of interest because one of them decides to snuff it."

"He doesn't get my back up because he took Linda to the Caribbean, Lyle."

His deputy chief looked at him.

"Okay, he does, but that's not the *only* reason he goes on the list. The man built his company over the dead body of his former partner."

"Accordin' to you."

"If I'm wrong, it'll be easy enough to find out. It shouldn't take more than a phone call."

Lyle sighed. "All right."

Russ moved on to the den. He poked at a stack of documents and bills next to the computer. "I want her e-mails. Bank statements, travel reservations. Run down her friends. Did she talk to anyone about killing herself? Or about trouble with her husband?"

"I'm going to need Eric."

Russ blew out a breath. "Okay. Kevin and Knox must be done taking the neighbors' statements. I'll release them and set them on patrol."

"They'll be on overtime."

"I know, I know." He looked at his watch. "I'll have to take a break soon. Clare and I have another premarital counseling session this evening. I'll have my phone on, so you can reach me for anything, and I'll head back here as soon as we're done." He pinched the bridge of his nose again. "I'd reschedule, but we've only got three more weeks to the wedding."

"You don't need to reschedule. Eric and I can handle—"

"Russ?" Dr. Dvorak's precise European voice cut Lyle off.

"Yeah, Emil." Russ crossed into the kitchen. Its open door led into the garage, and from there to the yard. "You all set?" The wind had risen, the temperature low fifties and dropping fast. As he and Lyle emerged from the garage, Kevin and Knox rounded the side of the building.

"Yes, the body is in the mortuary transport." He gestured toward the pool, its bloodstained waters turning gray beneath the looming clouds. "I will want to be able to compare the weapon's particulars against the cranial damage the deceased sustained."

"Uh . . ." Russ looked at Lyle. "Get a diver?"

"You want to call in the staties to get a gun out of a pool? Hell, you can see the thing from here. Just have somebody strip down and jump in."

"You volunteering?"

"Hell, no. Rank hath its privileges. That's a job tailor-made for a rookie."

Russ, Kevin, and Emil Dvorak all looked at the newest member of the department. Russ was trying to manage his newly integrated force in a gender-blind fashion, but he didn't think letting Hadley peel down to her skivvies was going to fly. Hadley stared back at them wary-eyed.

"No, no, Jesum, not her. I didn't mean her." Lyle, for the first time in the nine years Russ had known him, looked embarrassed.

"I'll do it." Kevin unbuckled his rig and handed it to Knox. "Can I use one of their towels, Chief?"

"Sure. Don't leave your prints on anything."

The young officer disappeared into the garage. Russ looked at Emil. "You said you could confirm she'd been shot through the head when you got her out."

The medical examiner nodded. "I don't need to autopsy her to see the bullet went through the back of her throat and exited out the upper rear of her skull."

"She ate her gun," Russ said.

"It does have the hallmarks of the classic suicide technique used by someone who wants to leave no chance that his attempt might fail. However, I cannot confirm the wound was self-inflicted. The time of death will be difficult, due to the temperature of the pool, and the presence of water creates a capillary osmosis, drawing blood out of the body even after the heart ceases."

Lyle translated. "You're saying there's a chance she was killed elsewhere and dumped in the pool."

"I have no evidence yet with which to express my opinion. I do want to make you aware there is a slight possibility you are dealing with a homicide."

Kevin emerged from the garage wearing his T-shirt and purple evidence gloves, a large floral towel wrapped around his waist. Lyle coughed, a sound suspiciously like a laugh, and Knox said, "Don't you want to take your shirt off? So it'll be dry after?"

Kevin shot her a look. "I'm fine." He dropped the towel, revealing striped boxers, and plunged into the pool. Twenty seconds later, he emerged from the water, teeth chattering, the .38 in one hand. Lyle held an evidence bag out. Kevin kicked to the edge of the pool and dropped the gun in. "D-d-do you want me to look for the casing, Chief?"

The afternoon hour and the approaching storm meant they were losing light fast. Maybe Kevin could strike it lucky. "As long as you're wet, yeah, go ahead."

Kevin dove again. He went under two times, three, each time breaking the surface gulping for air and shaking his head. After his fourth dive to the bottom, his lips were tinged blue.

"Come on out, Kevin. No sense in you getting hypothermia." Russ wondered how difficult it would be to get the pool drained. If Emil Dvorak confirmed the .38 caused her death, they'd be fine. If not, he'd sure like to know if there was a shell casing down there or not.

Kevin hauled himself out of the water and wrapped up in the towel. Russ pointed him toward the garage. "Get yourself dried off and then take a break and go home for dry, uh, clothes. I want you and Knox both back on patrol while Eric and Lyle are working this scene."

"I've g-g-got a complete change at the sh-sh-shop," Kevin said.

"Go ahead, then." Russ looked at Knox, who was peering at her watch. "Knox, do you have your kids covered? Or do you need to make arrangements?"

"No, sir. I'll just call my granddad and let him know I'll be home late."

"Do it." He turned back to Lyle. "The husband." He held up one finger. "Quentan Nichols." A second. "Work problems." A third. "We clear those three, and if Dvorak's autopsy doesn't contradict it, we can close this case. Death from a self-inflicted gunshot wound."

"Hell of a thing," Lyle said. "Make it through two tours of duty in Iraq just to wind up capping it in your own backyard."

Russ glanced at the pool again. A trio of sere yellow leaves tore away from a dipping, flailing birch and whirled through the air to touch down on the surface of the water. "Yeah," he said. "Hell of a thing."

◆ ◆ ◆

Clare parked across the street from St. James and turned off the engine. She dropped her head back and simply sat for a moment, as gusting rain rocked her Jeep and rattled across the roof. She'd been going nonstop all day; morning Eucharist and visiting the hospital and dealing with her mother's drama over the phone and counseling and the teen mothers group. Somewhere in there she had written Sunday's sermon, which was probably three pages of *All work and no play makes Clare a dull girl.* The uppers she had popped that morning had long since worn off, and she was craving that kick right now like she craved a good night's sleep. She felt it in the pressure behind her closed eyes and the hot ache of her muscles.

Around her, the world exploded. Clare hurtled out of the vehicle, flat on the hard, packed ground, shellburst and fireworks and her own terrified shout echoing around her, and there was the road, and the burning truck, and the blood-soaked body with its throat gaping wide and she heard the relentless hail of automatic weapon fire and the dogs barking and her heart pounding out of her chest and they must be everywhere and they were surrounded—

—and then the world tilted again and she was lying on a wet street in Lake George, hard needles of rain pelting her as a late-season thunderstorm roared and crashed overhead.

She staggered up off the road and got back into the Jeep. Her stomach lurched with nausea. She covered her face with her hands and breathed. Eventually, her pulse slowed to something close to normal.

"Okay," she said. "Okay. Let's try this again." She left her umbrella in the car, figuring the damage had already been done, and crossed the street. Inside, she took the stairs two at a time to the office hallway.

Julie McPartlin's door was open, but she was on the phone. She flashed Clare five fingers and pointed toward the parish hall. Okay. Her little whatever-it-had-been hadn't made her late. Clare peeled off her coat and continued down to the large, wooden-floored room.

"Hey, darlin'." Russ gave her an obvious double take. "What happened to you? You're half soaked."

She hesitated. "It's really coming down out there."

He frowned as he took her coat. "Here. You're going to want this." He handed her a tall cardboard cup of coffee.

"Ohhh, God." She took a drink. The hot, sweet brew cut through her exhaustion and settled her tight, queasy stomach. "Thank you. You have no idea how much I needed this."

He wrapped his arms loosely around her. "You look like hell."

"Flatterer." He kept on looking at her in that way he had, the way that wouldn't let her evade or change the subject. "It's been a long day," she finally said. "I think this thing with Will Ellis has . . . shaken me up more than I'd like." She didn't want to leave it there. She wasn't ready to talk to Russ about everything that was going on in her head. "Also, my mother's driving me crazy about the wedding."

Russ nodded. "How is the Ellis boy?"

"Better. It looks like he may have missed out on liver damage after all. The hematologist said that aside from his amputations, Will's about the healthiest teen he's ever seen."

"Kids are hard to kill at that age."

"Thank God for that."

He smoothed a wet strand of hair away from her face. "What's going on with your mother?"

She took another long drink of coffee. "You have to understand, she wanted a ballet-dancing, debutante-party-going, white-wedding sort of girl. Instead I fixed airplane engines, played basketball, and joined the army. *Grace* was the one who fulfilled all Mother's fantasies."

"Except for the part where she died."

"Except for that, yeah. So now I've finally found someone willing to marry me—"

Russ snorted.

"—but I only gave her eight weeks to plan the party of her dreams."

"It's down to two and a half weeks now." He smiled. "Anyway, isn't it supposed to be the party of your dreams?"

"Clearly you do not understand southern women. So all day today I've been barraged with photos of mother-of-the-bride dresses, because she has to change her outfit to go with the dress *your* mother's chosen, which she does not like. 'Go with' in this case means 'blow out of the water.' She also called me three times to listen to selections from the DJ she's hired."

"Why do we need a DJ?"

"Because there wasn't enough time to hire a live band, which would have been much more tasteful."

He stared at her. "But . . . there's going to be dancing? Where? The

Stuyvesant Inn doesn't have enough space for that, not with all those Victorian knickknacks all over the place."

"The dancing will be in a tent, with a dance floor, which she has rented. I'm supposed to drop in Friday after the morning Eucharist to personally agree to everything she's already decided."

He shook his head. "And she's running the whole thing from Virginia. I'm beginning to suspect that if the southerners had put their women in charge, they would have won the Civil War."

She put her cup on a long table scattered with flyers and brochures and leaned into Russ, laughing because she wanted to scream. "I'm sorry. This isn't what either of us wanted."

He hugged her hard and kissed her wet hair. "I don't mind. As long as you're there, and you say the right thing at the right time, I'm good with it. You've got more than enough on your plate. Your mom can do what she wants as long as it doesn't add to your burden."

She let herself rest against him, her cheek pressed into his name tag. She rubbed her hand over the departmental patch on his shoulder. "You didn't have time to change?"

"I've got to go back after we're done. You remember Tally McNabb? The woman at the center of that bar fight the night you got home?"

Something uneasy slithered through her gut. "Yes . . ."

"Her neighbor found her dead this afternoon. It looks like she killed herself. Her husband's missing, so we have to find him and get his story before we can definitely close the case as a suicide, but—"

She opened her mouth, but she didn't seem to have any air with which to speak. Russ broke off. "Clare? What is it?"

Her skin felt clammy. She shivered. "Tally McNabb."

He chafed her upper arms. "Yeah."

She found her voice. "She was in my veterans therapy group. She was in the hospital with me just two nights ago. When Will was admitted. They all came. We all came."

"Wait. She was in your counseling group?"

Clare nodded.

"Jesus. And she was there the night the Ellis kid tried to off himself." He rubbed his lips. "That certainly gives more weight to it being suicide."

"She couldn't have killed herself. She couldn't have."

"C'mon, let's sit down. You look like you're about to keel over." He snagged her coffee and steered her across the high-ceilinged room to a more human-sized alcove furnished with several overstuffed armchairs. "Now." He handed her the cup. "Tell me why you say she couldn't have done it."

She plopped into one of the chairs. "She didn't have any warning signs. Not one. I think in many ways, she was the least troubled of us."

Russ sat down opposite her. "Who else is in the group?"

"Russ! I can't break their confidences. Why do you think I never mentioned Tally to you?"

"It's not like they were confessing to you as a priest. You're one of them."

"Anyone who's in therapy deserves privacy. It's not my place to break that trust."

He held up one hand. "Never mind. Telling me what McNabb said about herself won't bruise your conscience, will it?"

She glared at him. "No."

"Good. Did she ever talk about Quentan Nichols?"

"Sort of. She said she regretted what she had done in Iraq, and that she had never expected it to follow her home, but she never specifically mentioned Chief Nichols. I got the feeling she was ashamed of the whole episode."

"Did she mention him coming to see her again? Or being in contact with her?"

"No." Talking it over with Russ made her realize how little of herself Tally McNabb had revealed.

He nodded. "How about her husband?"

"I think things were bad with her husband. She was stressed. Plus, she was being sent back to Iraq with the BWI construction unit. She told me—she told us, on Monday, that she was going to quit instead."

"Would that have left her with money problems?"

"Not that she mentioned." She leaned back into the chair's corduroy-covered embrace. "She said her husband was away gambling, and didn't seem too happy about that. I thought it was because he had gone off without her, but maybe they couldn't afford his losses."

"Away gambling? Where?"

"She didn't say." She tilted her chin forward to look at him. "Is he really missing?"

"No one knows where he is. The scheduler at BWI Opperman said he hasn't been working for the past week or so."

She buried her nose in her coffee cup and breathed in the scent before taking a sip. "Maybe money problems, then—and she has to choose, Iraq or the unemployment office."

"Not if she quits. No benefits. Maybe no recommendation."

She thought about Tally in their last group session, frustrated and angry. At the hospital, cynical and resigned. "Her back was up against a wall. She's alone and upset, with her life and with her husband. Then he finally gets home from a weekend of blowing their money at the casino, and everything she's been feeling comes to a head. She lights into him, and in the heat of that moment, he kills her."

"There's zero evidence of that. The house was clean and orderly. We won't have any autopsy info until tomorrow, but I can tell you right now, there weren't any defensive wounds on her hands."

"He could have restrained her, killed her, and then cleaned up afterward."

"We're investigating that possibility right now. That's why I have to go back after our meeting with Reverend McPartlin."

A possibility struck her. "Are you sure it wasn't an accident?"

He shook his head. "She was shot in the head. Through her mouth."

"Oh, God."

He flipped his phone open and dialed. "Anything else? Drugs? Alcohol?"

"I never saw any sign she was using." Her rapidly dwindling secret stash swelled in her conscience, filling her mouth with the words that would confess; *uppers, downers, pain pills.* She swallowed her own guilt. "There was very open access to sleeping pills and stimulants in Iraq. She may have brought some back with her."

"Hmn." His glance shifted toward his phone. "Lyle? Russ. How's it going?"

Across the hall, the Reverend Julie McPartlin came through the door. She spread her hands. *What's up?*

Clare flashed her the same five-fingered signal Julie had given her earlier. *Five minutes.*

"No, no, that's fine. Look, evidently Wyler McNabb was away gambling as of Monday night."

Julie shrugged and tapped her watch.

"I have no idea. Could be Las Vegas or Atlantic City, could be Akwesasne or Turning Stone. Find a picture and have Kevin pick it up. He can start faxing it around to the state casinos."

Clare nodded. This might be a short session.

"Then call Ed in to cover for him. Yeah, I know he's on overtime. Just do it."

Julie disappeared back down the hallway.

"McNabb was in a veterans support group over at the community center." He covered his phone with one hand. "You don't mind if I tell them you were in the group with her, do you?"

She shook her head.

"Yeah, Clare's taking part in it, too. She said McNabb never mentioned seeing Nichols but that she was stressed about work and her marriage." He paused. "Yeah, it does. She might have been under treatment for depression or something." He cupped his hand over the phone again. "Can your therapist prescribe?"

She shook her head.

"Clare says she would have had to get scrip somewhere else if that was the case. Have you found anything?" He paused. "Okay. Yeah. The husband's the number one priority. I'll see you when I'm finished up here. I know." He let out a weary laugh. "I'm going to be the only guy not on overtime."

Russ snapped his phone shut and pinched the bridge of his nose. "You know what I want for Christmas? Another officer."

"She didn't commit suicide, Russ. I know she didn't."

He stood up. Held out his hand to help her. "We're not closing the door on the possibility someone else was involved, but I wouldn't get your hopes up. Perps may try to hide evidence, but outside of movies, they don't create elaborate scenarios making it look like the victim killed him or herself."

"Tally McNabb, death by gunshot, probable suicide." The chief flipped open a folder and draped it over his knee.

Hadley stifled a yawn and flipped her own notebook to a fresh page. She had gotten in last night at eleven, to discover Hudson half-asleep over an unfinished history project. She had sent him up to bed and stayed up until midnight gluing bark onto a cardboard longhouse.

"I got the medical examiner's report this morning." The chief picked his mug off the scarred wooden table he preferred to sit on and took a long drink of coffee. "*Earlier* this morning," he amended. "His finding is death consistent with suicide, but he won't go further than that. Her injuries were caused by a Taurus .38 ACP, the weapon at the bottom of the pool"—he pointed toward one of several color pictures pinned to the corkboard—"which has her prints all over it."

"Nitrate patterns on her firing hand?" Lyle MacAuley asked.

"If she had 'em, they were washed away by the chlorinated water."

The dep straightened from his slouch and jotted the facts on the whiteboard.

"There's no way she was killed anywhere else on the property," Eric McCrea said. "We sprayed with luminol. The place was clean."

The chief nodded. "Dr. Dvorak felt the"—he glanced down at the file—"the residual biological matter in the pool was consistent with her dying at that spot."

Hadley tried not to think about what "residual biological matter" meant.

"The neighbors heard one shot at approximately two P.M. and discovered her shortly thereafter," the chief went on. "Dr. Dvorak places TOD between noon and two o'clock. Nobody was seen coming or going from the place, although that's not definitive since it was during the workday and most folks weren't even home."

"It reads like suicide to me," MacAuley said.

"But we're still missing the husband," Eric pointed out.

"Wyler McNabb." The chief took another drink of coffee. "The victim described him as 'away gambling' on Monday night, but at this point, we haven't gotten any hits from the casinos Kevin sent his picture to. The Albany airport doesn't have a record of him transiting this past week. His Escalade and her Navigator are still parked in the driveway of their house."

"He could have driven home Tuesday or Wednesday, done her, and then fled the scene," Eric said.

The chief tilted his head in agreement. "Besides his boat and his ATV, he has no other vehicles registered in his name. Which doesn't mean he doesn't have access to something."

"Hadley and I checked out the backyard yesterday afternoon," Flynn said. "There's kind of a tangle behind the utility shed, and then a beat-down fence, and then you're onto the neighbor's property. Someone could've gone straight through to the next street over."

"Did you include them in the canvass yesterday?"

Flynn looked at Hadley. "I did," she said. "There was no one at home at the Saber Drive address behind McNabb's house, or at the ones on either side. There was a retired couple across the street, but they didn't see anything."

"Where's that street come out?"

Noble answered the chief. "Musket, Drum, and Saber all dead-end at the western side. Easterly, they all join up with Meersham Street. No other way out."

"Eric's right." The chief rubbed a finger over his lips. "If McNabb had a car waiting for him, he could have done her, walked to Saber Drive, and been five miles down the road before the FR arrived."

Hadley, who had been the first responder, nodded. "I got there eleven minutes after logging the call."

"Of course, now you're talking conspiracy to murder, with at least one accessory." Lyle tapped the tip of his marker against the board. "That's awfully complicated, for something that looks like suicide to begin with."

"I agree. Eric. What did you get from the electronic trail?"

Eric set his coffee on the floor and flipped his notepad back several pages. "No travel arrangements. No e-mails that seemed significant." He looked over the edge of his pad. "She shared the account with McNabb, though, so if she was still swapping love notes with the MP boyfriend, she might have had some Web-based mail service. She had a Facebook page that hadn't been updated in five months."

"That's it?"

"I'm not any sort of computer whiz, Chief. If you want the guts vacuumed out, you'll have to get the state cybercrime unit to do it."

The chief shook his head. "That'll be a last-resort item. Lyle?"

"She was a bookkeeper for BWI Opperman. Hired this past August, a few months after she got back. Wyler McNabb works there as well; he may have gotten her an in with the job. The company has a construction contract in Iraq. He's worked over there, and she's had"—he looked at his notebook—"two tours of duty, so it was a good fit. Our girl was scheduled to return to Iraq as part of the team's administrative support." He looked at McCrea. "Maybe she didn't like that idea."

McCrea picked up his tall cardboard cup. "Are you asking me my opinion? It's no tropical vacation paradise, but I wouldn't eat my gun to avoid going back."

Hadley glanced at Flynn, but he was busy writing notes. MacAuley continued. "The HR director described her as reliable, skilled, no problems with anyone she worked with." He shot the chief a meaningful glance. "At home, she kept their financial records real neat, like you'd expect. There might have been money stress—most of those fancy SUVs and stuff were less'n a year old, and they didn't have very much in checking or savings, according to her most recent statement, which is the only one I could find. There were some receipts for winnings and expenses from several casinos in an accordion file marked TAXES, so the gambling was not a one-off. There's a single mortgage on the house, payments current. The only thing that I flagged was his life insurance policy. It was underwritten by his employer to the tune of a cool half mil."

Hadley couldn't help it; she whistled.

"That's a helluva lot for a construction worker with no dependents," the chief said.

"Judging by the tax returns I saw, he was the big earner, not her. Which means if he was about to pull the plug on the relationship, she'd be pretty much left out in the cold, as far as money went." He made a gesture toward the chief. "You know, your first thought mighta been the right one."

"Murder-suicide?"

"Could be the reason McNabb hasn't turned up yet is that she did him somewhere else and hid the body."

"Then came back home to top herself? Maybe."

"I disagree. I think we're going to find the husband." Eric crossed his arms over his chest and tilted his chair back. "I think he did her."

The chief raised his eyebrows. "Based on . . . ?"

"I can't see her killing herself. She's got relationship problems, and job problems, but let's face it, there was obviously a lot of marital property to go around even if they did split up. And how hard can it be for a good bookkeeper to find employment?" Eric let his chair drop to the floor again. "I'm betting they had a roaring fight, he did her, and then dropped her in the pool."

The chief dropped the folder back onto the table. "We can all agree that finding Wyler McNabb is the top priority. Once we've got him, we'll be able to pin this thing down." He glanced around the squad room. "Any other questions? No? Okay, then. Lyle, Eric, with me."

Hadley glanced at Flynn, and then toward McCrea, who was following the chief and MacAuley out the door.

Flynn paused in the act of tucking his notebook away. "What?"

"She was a veteran."

"Yeah?"

She dropped her voice. "Eric was awfully insistent on her death being a homicide. Do you think it's a warning sign? Like he couldn't stand the idea that another veteran might have killed herself?"

"She might not have." Flynn collected his hat and handed Hadley hers. "Sure, it looks a lot like suicide, but she's got a missing husband who likes to throw money around like rice at a wedding. An Escalade. A plasma-screen TV. An *in-ground swimming pool,* for chrissakes."

She couldn't stop her grin. He sounded so outraged. "Flynn, *I* had an in-ground pool in California."

He stood to one side and let her precede him out the squad room door. "It makes sense out there. Here, where you can only use it a few months out of the year?" He shook his head. "It's just a big concrete sign that reads *Money means nothing to me*. They could have stapled twenties on the front of the house and sent the same message. At least that way, they wouldn't have had to keep the thing clean and chlorinated."

They walked down the hall side by side. *Money means nothing to me*. She bit her lip.

"What?" He opened the station house door.

Hadley zipped her jacket against the cool breeze. "What do you mean, what?"

"You thought of something. You always bite your lip like that when you're thinking." Flynn clattered down the steps toward the parking lot, a small smile on his face.

She forced herself not to bite her lip again as she followed him. "Of all the stuff they have at the McNabbs' house, what do you think cost the most?"

"The pool."

"Really? More than the cars?"

"Yeah. You have to dig them out crazy deep and wide, and surround them with layers and layers of crushed gravel and stuff to keep them from cracking when everything freezes. It's a huge job."

She paused by her cruiser. "I wonder . . . Eric and MacAuley didn't turn up a note."

He looked at her intently. "No."

"Maybe where she did it was her note. She kills herself in the most expensive, wasteful thing they own."

"What's her message? F-you?"

"No." Hadley opened the car door and tossed her lid and notebook in. "'Money means nothing to me.'"

◆ ◆ ◆

Hadley had been on patrol for three hours when she got the call to respond to army personnel trying to get into the McNabb house.

"Are you sure?" she asked Harlene.

The dispatcher's voice was tart. "That's what the neighbor said. If you go over there in your unit, you can find out for yourself."

Hadley was extra polite when she signed off. She was pretty sure Harlene liked her, but Hadley's position as low man on the totem pole meant she got the least amount of slack.

Quentan Nichols, she thought. Back for another shot at love. Boy, was he in for an unpleasant surprise. The surprise, however, was on Hadley, when she pulled in behind an anonymous government-issued car and found a tall white woman standing in the front yard, talking on a cell phone.

The woman hung up as Hadley opened the driver's side door. She was dressed in a green suit instead of those blurry camouflage outfits soldiers wore, with a lot of ribbons and stuff pinned to a jacket that must have been tailored but still didn't fit quite right. Hadley, whose uniforms came in any size as long as it was men's, recognized the look.

"Ma'am? Can I help you?"

A flicker at the corner of the garage. Hadley twitched toward the movement, then relaxed when she saw another army guy coming toward them. This one was in urban camo, like Nichols had been, but was younger and lighter-skinned. He was also carrying a sidearm.

"I'm Lieutenant Colonel Arlene Seelye." The woman stepped toward her. She was older than Hadley had thought at first, midforties at least. "I'm looking for Mary McNabb, also known as Tally McNabb."

"You're military police?"

Colonel Seelye nodded. "Specialist McNabb is absent without leave. We're here to return her to her battalion."

Hadley tried not to let that little piece of info rock her back. AWOL? They had all been working on the assumption that McNabb was quit of the army. The chief needed to be in on this. "Can you wait here a moment, ma'am? I've got to report back to my dispatcher and tell her what's going on."

Colonel Seelye cut her eyes toward the small houses flanking the McNabb place. "Observant neighbors."

"It's a small town, ma'am. We try to look out for each other." Hadley walked back to her unit with the cop strut she had picked up from watching Deputy Chief MacAuley—not too fast, not too slow. Owning the situation. Inside, she raised Harlene and let her know what was going on.

"Hold on a sec," Harlene said. "The chief's just calling in." Hadley's line went dead. She looked through the windshield at the two MPs. They had turned toward the house, so their backs were toward her. She wondered what they were saying to each other.

"Hadley?"

"Yeah. I mean, here."

"The chief is on his way. He wants to talk to 'em, so don't let 'em leave before he gets there."

Hadley almost asked how she was supposed to accomplish that, but she knew what Harlene would say. *Think of something!* "Will do," she said. "Knox out."

As she crunched across the leaf-strewn lawn, the colonel and her backup turned again to face her. *Detective and beat cop,* Hadley thought. *Plainclothes and uniform.* The look was familiar, even if the outfits were different.

"So . . ." Colonel Seelye squinted at Hadley's name badge, causing fine lines to radiate from the corners of her eyes. "Officer Knox. Can you tell us where we can find Mary McNabb?"

Harlene hadn't said anything about concealing the truth from them. "I'm sorry to tell you this, ma'am, but Tally McNabb is dead. She was found floating in her backyard pool yesterday."

The younger guy's head jerked toward Seelye, but the officer only blinked slowly. "That would explain the crime scene tape around the fence."

"Yes, ma'am."

"And your department is investigating this as . . . ?"

"Death by gunshot, probable suicide, ma'am."

The colonel held herself very still. Finally she said, "Who is the lead investigator on the case?"

"I guess that would be the chief. Although the dep—the deputy chief and Sergeant McCrea are working it, too."

"The chief of police." Seelye raised one eyebrow. "How many sworn officers does the Millers Kill Police Department have, Officer Knox?"

There was something in her voice that kind of went up Hadley's spine and made the answers to her questions pop out. "Eight, if you include the chief, ma'am. Plus two part-time auxiliaries."

"That's . . . small. Your department can't have had much experience with homicide or violent crime."

"You'd be surprised, ma'am."

Whatever the colonel was going to say was cut off by the grind of tires on asphalt. Hadley kept her eyes on the MPs. Behind her, a car door thunked. The young guy darted glances to Seelye, but Seelye simply watched, not asking anything, not registering any surprise. Hadley thought she'd never seen such a self-contained woman before.

"Officer Knox." When the chief greeted her, she turned to him. He gave her a nod and continued on toward the colonel. "I'm Russell Van Alstyne." He held out his hand. "Chief of police."

"Lieutenant Colonel Arlene Seelye, U.S. Army Military Police, attached to the 10th Soldier Support Battalion." They shook hands. "I came here to pick up one of our soldiers who was absent without leave, but your officer here tells me we're too late."

The chief nodded. "I'm afraid so."

"Can you tell me what your investigation has turned up so far, Chief?"

"Tally McNabb's autopsy indicated death consistent with suicide by handgun, although we haven't found any note. She seemed to be under some marital and job stress." The chief glanced at the younger, armed soldier. "Of course, if she was hiding out from you folks, that would have been a whole other problem that we weren't aware of."

"Are you considering her death as a possible homicide?"

The chief shot a look at Hadley. She straightened. "Her husband's been missing since before her body was discovered. We have a BOLO out on Wyler McNabb. I suspect that we'll be able to clear the case pretty quick once we find him." He looked assessingly at the house. "One way or the other. What's the army's story?"

The colonel shrugged. "McNabb went on leave in May, a couple months after her last deployment, and never came back. Her case kept getting shuffled to the bottom of the pile—you can imagine the sort of stuff we have to deal with when an entire battalion of young men and women get back to the States after a year. However, her company went back on alert this month, which shot her file to the top of our roster. So here we are."

The chief nodded. "So here you are. Was there anything else going on with her? Was she in trouble?"

"What do you mean?"

"Like you said, we ought to at least consider the possibility that she was killed. If McNabb was involved with something criminal, that would open up some new lines of inquiry for us."

Colonel Seelye smiled faintly. "I assure you, Chief Van Alstyne, as far as the army is concerned, not showing up for work *is* a crime. Let me ask you something. Other than the autopsy, what is your evidence for suicide?"

"Well"—the chief hitched his thumbs in his gun belt and spread his legs a little—"we checked for a note, like I said, and we went over her credit card statements and her mortgage book to see if she had money troubles."

"Did she?"

"Not that we could tell." He scratched the back of his head. In the two years she had been on the force, Hadley had never seen him do that. It made him look like a hayseed.

There was something wrong here. The chief was the original what-you-see-is-what-you-get guy. Why was he suddenly acting like an ignorant small-town sheriff?

"You know, it would be very helpful to us if we could take a look at her effects," the colonel said.

"For someone AWOL?" The chief huffed a laugh. "Why on earth for?"

Colonel Seelye tilted her head. "She may have had help in keeping out of sight and off the battalion's radar screen, so to speak. If she had any accomplices, we'd like to know."

"Hmn." The chief rubbed his chin. "Well, the problem with that is, this is Wyler McNabb's house, and you've got no cause to enter a civilian's home."

"He's wanted for questioning in a violent death."

"Yeah, but wanted ain't proved, as we say up here. If he checks out clean, my department could be in a heap of trouble if we let some army investigators paw through his things." He grinned at the MPs. "Unless you think her being AWOL had some bearing on her being dead."

Seelye shook her head. "No, of course not." She smiled back at the chief. "Still, you can understand our position, can't you? If we have soldiers evading their sworn duty, morale drops, training suffers, and eventually, you have men and women in harm's way who know that their brother and sister soldiers have sold them out." She clipped her jaw shut, as if she realized she had gone overboard.

"That's a problem, all right." The chief frowned. "Tell you what, let me run it by Judge Ryswick. If he says it's okay, we're covered. I wouldn't have an answer for you until at least tomorrow, though. Are you staying in the area?"

Colonel Seelye unbuttoned her jacket and slipped her hand into an inside pocket. "Let me give you my cell number." She retrieved a business card and a pen. She flipped the card over and scribbled on the back. "Just give me a call as soon as you know. Fort Drum isn't nearby, but it's not at the other end of the country."

She handed her card to the chief, who took it, smiling. "I'll do that."

"Then we're all set for now." She looked at the private. "Let's go."

The younger man nodded. He headed for their car, the colonel two steps behind him.

"And let me just say, on behalf of my whole department"—the chief had the solemn sincerity of a six-dollar Hallmark card—"thank you for your service."

Both the MPs paused. A twinge passed over Colonel Seelye's face so fast Hadley would have missed it if she hadn't been watching her closely. "Um. Thank *you,* Chief Van Alstyne."

The chief stood there, a sticky-sweet smile on his face, as they got into the government car and as they drove away. When the MPs were out of sight, the smile dropped away. His face set in grim lines.

"What was *that* all about?"

"I'm not sure, but it wasn't about Tally McNabb being AWOL." He dug his phone out of his pants pocket. "When a soldier's missing, the battalion's military police post sends a couple low-level warrant officers out. Like you and Kevin hauling in someone who's blown off a court date." His eyes narrowed. "That colonel is an investigator. She doesn't waste her time on fugitive specialists. She's not attached to the 10th Soldier Support Battalion in Fort Drum, New York, either. She's with the U.S. Army Finance Command. Which is based in Indianapolis."

"How could you tell?"

He tapped his shoulder. "Her patches." He flipped open the phone.

Thumbed a number. "Hi, Lyle? Russ. I have a question about the paper-work you went through at McNabb's house." He paused. "You said she was pretty well organized, right? Did you see any documents related to her service? Could have been enlistment papers, evaluations—yeah? Okay, did you see anything indicating she had been discharged or separated?" He nodded to the phone. "Okay. Thanks." Another pause. "I'll catch you up at the five o'clock. 'Bye." He flipped the phone shut. "Lyle says she had her whole service record in one folder. Including discharge papers from this past May."

◆ ◆ ◆

"Is it a bad time?" In the bright afternoon sunlight streaming through Will Ellis's hospital window, Clare could see the white-coated outline of the man sitting next to the bed, but she couldn't make out the details.

"No, it's me." Trip Stillman stood up. "I'm not officially here. I mean, I'm not here as Will's doctor."

Clare came into the room, half-closing the door behind her. "I'm not officially here, either."

"Does that mean you're not here as my priest or not here as my mom's friend?" Will's voice was weak but welcome. The fact that he had already been moved to a regular room was a testament to his physical strength.

"I guess I'm here as your brother in arms. Sister in arms?" She took Will's hand. "How are you doing?"

"Better." He gripped her hand. It felt like a small child squeezing a stuffed animal. "Really. Better. There's this hospital counselor I've been talking to, and Sarah's come to see me . . ." He took a breath, as if speaking two sentences in a row tired him out. "Mostly, I was finally honest with my parents about how freaking mad I've been." He looked at Clare. "It was like you said, remember? Everybody wanted so much for me to feel better. It was like I was letting the team down if I felt pissed off or screwed over."

"How do you feel now?" Clare asked.

"Like I want my damn legs back. Every minute of every day, I wish I was normal again. That's not going to change." He shook his head, a slow roll back and forth against the hospital pillow. "But, Jesus, I'm glad I'm not dead."

Stillman leaned forward and awkwardly touched Will's shoulder. "We're all glad you're not dead."

Clare took a deep breath. "Listen. I've got something to tell you, and it's not good news, but I think you should hear it first from me instead of stumbling over it in the paper or something."

Stillman rose. "I'll give you your privacy, then."

"No, Trip, wait. This is for you, too." The doctor sank back into his chair, frowning. Clare blanked for a moment. Then she remembered what Russ had said once about delivering bad news. *Get to the worst of it fast.* "Tally McNabb was found dead at her home yesterday afternoon."

"What?" Both men spoke at once.

"She died from a single gunshot to the head. The police are investigating. They say it looks like suicide, but they can't confirm it yet."

"Oh, God." Will shut his eyes. "Did I—do you think she got the idea from me?"

"No, I don't. I was here the night they brought you in. I talked with her. There wasn't anything in what she said or how she acted that made me think she wanted to do herself harm."

Stillman had slid his PalmPilot from his coat and was tapping through screen after screen. "I don't think she was suicidal," he said. "I don't see anything here suggesting that was an issue."

Clare raised both eyebrows. "You keep notes on our therapy sessions?" Her voice was pointed.

"Yes. Not to show them to anyone." He sat stiffly upright. "It's an old habit instilled in medical school. Over the years, it's been very useful. Lifesaving, at times."

"Don't you think it's a little—" She cut herself off. One of their group was dead. Another hospitalized. Compared to that, a crack in the wall of confidentiality was nothing. "Never mind. I agree with you. About her frame of mind. I don't think she killed herself."

"You mean she was murdered?" Will's shocked voice was a reminder of how young he really was.

"Do the police have a suspect?" Stillman asked.

"They're looking for her husband. He hasn't been seen since sometime before her body was found."

Stillman nodded. "I've heard it's usually the husband or boyfriend in situations like this."

"In Tally's case, you can take your pick. She had an affair with an MP when she was in-country. He came looking for her twice this past summer." Clare's shoulders twitched. "Maybe he finally caught up with her."

They all sat with that thought for a while. Finally, Will said, "I feel like we let her down."

Clare shook her head. "No. What could we have done? She didn't show any signs that she was in an abusive relationship." Even as she said it, she thought of Tally's disappearance back in the summer. Moving from friend to friend, eating at the soup kitchen.

"She said she was tired of always being afraid. Remember?" Will looked to Stillman for confirmation.

The doctor bit the inside of his cheek. "That phrase suggests to me she was tired of the fear you bring back with you." He spoke carefully, doling out his words one by one. "The stuff you know is foolish, but you just can't put it behind you. Like trying to find a mortar shelter when the town fire alarm whistle goes off."

"Or being afraid to fall asleep." Clare didn't realize she had spoken out loud until both men looked at her. She shrugged. "Nightmares."

"Me, too," Will said. "What if that wasn't it, though? What if she was afraid of something going on in her life right here and now?"

"The MKPD is looking into it. They'll get to the bottom of it." She took his hand again and squeezed it, ignoring the niggling voice in the back of her head reminding her of how sure Russ had been that Tally's death was a suicide.

A pretty young girl stuck her head in the door. "Bookmobile," she sang. "Ready to pick out a good read?"

"I'd better go," Clare said. "I don't want to tire you out. I'll be by tomorrow."

"As will I." Trip Stillman pocketed his PalmPilot as he rose. "Tell your mother I said hi."

"Thanks. For coming to see me." Will lifted his hand in a feeble salute.

The bookmobile girl rolled back to let them out of the room. Clare recognized her as one of the youngest and chattiest of the hospital's aides.

In her apron and ponytail, she looked like a nurse in a World War II flick, come to bring cheer to the wounded boys.

"I notice they're not sending him the grandmotherly candy stripers," she said.

"Might as well give him an eyeful of what he has to live for." Stillman pressed the elevator button. "My niece used to volunteer here. She would have loved to spend time with a good-looking boy Will's age."

"Tell him that."

"I will."

Clare looked at her scratched and blurred reflection in the elevator's doors. She was suddenly so tired she thought she might fall over. She leaned against the wall. "Do you think he'll make it? Not now, I mean. In the long haul. Are his doctors just patching him up so he can try again?"

"I don't think so. Will's already done the hardest work of recovery."

She made a little go-on gesture.

"His life's been divided into before and after, and he's in the after." The elevator pinged, and Stillman held the door open for her. "I think he's finally accepted that. That's the first step toward going forward." He stabbed the floor button.

The car jerked precipitously beneath them, and the lights dimmed.

Clare heard the sounds of the mortars in the distance as she looked frantically around the bunker. Dim emergency lights, and the smell of mouse shit and rotting wood, and *where* was the chem hazard locker and *where* was the bulkhead door and *where* was her mask and the blare of the klaxon and the thud of the shells getting nearer and the slosh of the river water rising higher and higher—

Clare found herself on the elevator floor, legs tucked, arms wrapped around her head. She opened her eyes. Trip Stillman was looking at her from exactly the same position.

The car jerked again, upward, quivered, and then began its descent. For a second, she couldn't move. *It's getting worse. It's supposed to be getting better, but it's getting worse.*

"Are you okay?" Stillman whispered.

She scrambled to her feet. Stillman got up more slowly. "Like I said. The foolish stuff." His voice was thin and dry.

"Trip, I need sleeping pills and amphetamines and Tylenol Three."

Like falling into the duck-and-cover, the words came out without conscious control. "I had them when I came back and I'm almost out and I
need more." She looked at him. "I don't have any good medical reason. I
just need them. Will you help me?"

He stared at her. The elevator dinged and the doors opened. They got
out. He glanced at the people walking past them; a pair of doctors, a tech-
nician in scrubs, a man toting a potted plant. He beckoned her around
the corner, into a niche formed by a vending machine and a stainless steel
crib frame. "What have you been taking?"

"I don't know. They're go pills and no-go pills. The only bags that had
labels were the antibiotic and the Tylenol." He frowned. "I'm cutting
back on the sleeping pills. Really. With everything going on, I've been
falling into bed at the end of the day. It's just—" She swallowed. "When I
wake up. If I have a nightmare. I need one then to get back to sleep."

"Are you mixing them with alcohol?"

"Sometimes. Yes. Usually."

He shook his head. "You don't need more, you need to get off them.
Amphetamines and sleeping pills just feed into each other."

"I can't!" To her horror, her voice cracked. "Trip, I've got nightmares
and flashbacks and parishioners to take care of and a wedding to get
through. I can't talk to my spiritual adviser about this, and I'm not going
to dump it on my fiancé. I just need to keep on an even keel for a few more
weeks."

Trip looked at the floor. Finally, he sighed. "I won't give you any painkillers. Forget about it." He pulled out his PalmPilot. "I'll give you a two-
week prescription for Ambien and Dexedrine. Here's the deal." He speared
her with a look. "You take the Dexedrine as prescribed—no more than ten
migs a day, to start. No booze when you take the Ambien and for twelve
hours after. I'm going to call you for a blood test some time during the next
two weeks. If I find you've been mixing, I'll cut you off. If I find you have a
higher concentration of dextroamphetamine than you ought to, I'll cut you
off. No second chances, no do-overs."

She nodded.

He tapped something into his PalmPilot. "I'm e-mailing myself the
instructions. I'll give you the scrip Monday, at group. Can you hold out
until then?"

She nodded.

"I shouldn't be doing this." He rubbed the scar along his forehead. "Thank you."

He sighed again. "I'll see you on Monday." He looked for a moment as if he were going to say something else. Instead, he turned and walked away. She stayed against the wall, half hidden, for a moment, turning the whole thing over in her head. Telling herself she was going to be okay. Wondering if this was her own before and after.

FRIDAY, OCTOBER 7   Clare hadn't taken a sleeping pill the night before, and she hadn't had a nightmare, but she was still sodden with fatigue when she rolled out of bed at 6:30 A.M. for the 7:00 Eucharist. She debated taking an upper for twenty seconds before popping one in her mouth. By the time she closed the rectory door behind her, she was feeling bright-eyed and bushy-tailed, congratulating herself for making a smart choice.

She wrapped up the Eucharist in thirty-five minutes and was standing by the great double doors, bidding farewell to the communicants—all seven of them—when Russ wedged his way past Mrs. Mairs into the narthex.

"I didn't expect to see you today. What are you doing here?" Clare asked.

Mrs. Mairs tittered. "Can't wait to see the bride-to-be. That's a good sign."

Russ smiled patiently at the octogenarian before turning to Clare. "You said we had to go to the Stuyvesant Inn, remember? To okay the napkins or mints or whatever?"

Clare waited until the last of the congregation left the narthex. She kicked away the stand and let the heavy double-braced door glide slowly closed on its hydraulic hinges. "I said *I* have to go. I didn't mean to drag you into this." She headed up the aisle. Russ fell into step beside her. "If I hadn't been sure my mother never would have spoken to me again, I would have just asked Julie McPartlin to do the deed in her office." She opened the door to the hallway. "It's still awfully tempting."

He laughed. "You may be the only southern woman in existence who prefers elopements to white weddings."

She went into the sacristy. "Me and every other clergywoman. Do you know how many weddings I've officiated at? And I haven't been ordained five years yet." She stripped her alb over her head and snapped it to get the wrinkles out. "Another five years and I'll run screaming when I hear the opening strains of Pachelbel's *Canon*." She slid the alb onto a wooden hanger and replaced it in the closet. "Which reminds me. If you have any musical preferences, speak now or forever hold your peace, because Betsy Young has announced she and the choir will be providing the wedding music as a gift to us." She removed the stole from around her neck, kissed it, and draped it over a padded dowel with the others.

"Hmn. I was thinking you could walk up the aisle to 'She Drives Me Crazy.'"

She gave him a look.

"Then we could come back down to "Goody Two Shoes.'" He swiveled his hips in a surprisingly agile figure eight. "Don't drink, don't smoke, what do you do?"

"I drink."

"Who says the song is about you?"

She shoved him. "I'll tell Betsy we'd like 'Jesu, Joy of Man's Desiring' and 'Come Down, O Love Divine.'"

He laughed. "Chicken."

She grabbed her keys and her coat from the hook inside the sacristy closet and ushered him out. "Seriously. You don't have to do this. I know you're flat out with Tally McNabb's murder investigation."

He let her lead him back to the narthex. "First, we're nowhere near to calling it a homicide. Second, if my department can't get along without me for an hour, I'm not doing my job right. Third"—he stepped into the early morning sunshine and stood to one side as she locked the great doors—"I put my work ahead of everything else when I was married to Linda. It didn't turn out so well." She turned to look at him, and he braced his hands against the wooden door, trapping her between his arms. "I want to do it differently with you. You deserve the best I can bring to the table."

She didn't know what to say to that. "Thank you."

"C'mon. I parked over in Tick Solway's lot across the street." It hadn't been Tick's lot since he died two years back and his son inherited, but that was the way things worked in Millers Kill. Clare was sure half the town still referred to the rectory as Father Hames's house, and that paragon of virtue had been gathered into Abraham's bosom six years ago.

It was five minutes before traffic thinned enough to allow Russ to pull his truck onto Church Street. "What's with all the cars?" Clare looked at her battered Seiko. "The morning rush to Glens Falls ought to be over by now."

"Leaf peepers. For the next two weeks or so we'll see almost as many tourists as we get during ski season." He braked as an Explorer with New Jersey plates cut in front of him to turn onto Main.

"I've never quite understood how driving an SUV three hundred miles expresses your love of nature."

"Don't say that in front of any local business owners."

A thought struck her. "Aren't you going to be short on manpower? With an investigation and a boatload of tourists in town?"

"Yep." He cut the wheel, and they made the sharp turn onto Route 57. "I can already hear Lyle. 'Ask not for whom the overtime tolls, it tolls for thee.' What we really need is another sworn officer."

"What about trainees from the police academy?"

"That was fine to plug the gap while Eric and Kevin were away, but in the long run, I need someone full-time. Someone who can cover me or Lyle or Eric when things get tight."

He swung onto the bridge. Up and down the river, the trees reflected in the calm water, red and gold, yellow and bronze, green and copper. It was made more beautiful by its brevity; the glory of a few days, a week, and then it was gone.

Russ sighed with pleasure. "Poor bastards."

"Who?"

"Those folks you were talking about who have to drive three hundred miles for this. Looks like someone set the river on fire, doesn't it?"

The river. The fire. The pale Nile green water and the buildings beyond, stone blocks and mud bricks baking in the endless sun. The car exploding, and the barn burning and the fire racing across the dry field. The column of oily smoke, and the chunks of masonry smashing into the hard-baked dirt. The blood. The screams.

"Clare?"

She shuddered back into the here-and-now.

"Are you all right?" Russ's voice was concerned.

"Yeah. I'm—" *not fine. Just tell him. I'm. Not. Fine.* "Okay. Just a little tired."

She was a coward. She was straight-up chickenshit. He thought she deserved the best he had to offer. She knew better. She had something ugly living in her, no different in its way than the colon cancer that had eaten up her sister from the inside out.

She just wanted it to be over and done with so she didn't have to think about it ever again. The moment the idea touched down in her head, her skin goosefleshed. Was that what Tally McNabb had come to?

"Do you want to go home? We can reschedule. Or, hell, just have your mother decide everything."

"My mother?" She breathed in. She was a big girl. She could handle a few bad memories. "You mean, my mother who wants you to wear a kilt?"

"What?"

The horror in Russ's voice made her laugh, thank God. "That was her suggestion after I told her it was unlikely you'd agree to your police dress uniform. She thought all the men could wear kilts."

"That's the nuttiest—"

"They did it at my brother Doug's wedding."

He was silent as he slowed the truck and made the turn onto the Sacandaga Road. Finally, he said, "It might be worthwhile just to see how Lyle reacts."

She laughed, and the moment was behind her, left beside the river as they rolled up and up through the stone-and-wire-rimmed pastures until they crested a rise and there was the Stuyvesant Inn, looking like a painted Florodora Girl in a wide green skirt sitting in the middle of dairy country.

It seemed Stephen and Ron were reaping the leaf-peeper bounty as well; their small three-car parking area was filled, and the sign pointing vehicles to the back was in its wooden frame. Russ ignored it in favor of pulling his truck half on, half off the grass beneath a blazing red maple near the road. "Fast getaway," he said, when she looked pointedly at the parking sign. "In case of a police emergency."

"Uh-huh." They walked up the curving drive and mounted the steps to the wide front porch. In honor of the season, the chintz pillows on the curlicued wicker furniture had been replaced with needlepoint. Lacy throws and plaid lap robes draped over scrollwork settees and fan-back armchairs.

Russ pressed the brass buzzer. "I always feel like I'm going to break some god-awful piece of bric-a-brac worth a fortune when I'm here."

"Maybe we can bypass the house and walk straight around to the tent for the reception," she said, and then the door opened and Stephen Obrowski was there. "Welcome! Welcome!" He pumped both their hands at once, so it appeared, for a moment, as if they were about to begin a folk dance. "Congratulations," he said to Russ. "You're a lucky man."

"Thanks. I agree."

Stephen tugged them inside. Gray-haired, red-cheeked, Obrowski always reminded her of some jolly British print of a century ago: *The Genial Innkeeper* or *The Happy Host*. Instead of a buxom wife in an apron, however, he had the tall and Teutonic-looking Ron Handler, emerging from the kitchen at the end of the hall wiping his hands on a dish towel.

"Great to see you, Clare." Ron kissed her cheeks. "And Chief Van Alstyne. You're looking as butch as ever."

"Ron," Stephen warned.

"I kid, I kid. Look, why don't you show them where everything will be set up, and then we can go over the menu and the notes Mrs. Fergusson faxed." Ron tilted his head toward Clare. "I don't like to leave the kitchen while we still have guests eating breakfast."

"Notes Mrs. Fergusson faxed?" Russ said, at the same moment Clare said, "If this is a bad time . . ."

"Of course not." Obrowski steered them toward the archway on the left while his partner vanished back down the hall. "Now, we thought we'd put the pianist here in the double parlor"—he pointed to a grand piano—"and leave the rest of the furniture pretty much as it is, to encourage folks to sit and talk."

"There's a pianist?" Russ looked at Clare. "I thought it was a DJ."

"The DJ will be outside, in the dancing tent," Stephen said.

Clare was starting to get a bad feeling. "When you say 'dancing tent,' does that imply there's going to be a *non*dancing tent?"

"That's right. The dining tent will have roll-down walls and heaters, to keep everyone comfortable through dinner and the toasts and all that." Obrowski looped them through the second parlor, emerging back in the wide entrance hall. "We're going to have the coat check back here, with a rolling rack tucked beneath the stairs, and then right here in the hallway, we'll have one of the bars." He looked at Clare hesitantly. "I know it's a little unorthodox, but I thought it would keep traffic flowing and prevent the guests from bunching up around the drinks."

"*One* of the bars?" Russ shook his head. "Christ on a bicycle. It's like the sacking of Richmond in reverse."

Clare caught the look on the innkeeper's face. "It's fine, Stephen. Russ's idea of a wedding is fifteen minutes in front of Judge Ryswick." And boy, wasn't that getting more appealing by the minute?

"Ah. Of course. I understand. Trust me, it sounds like a lot of fussy details right now, but the night of your wedding, when you're here with your beautiful bride on your arm, you'll be glad we took pains to get everything just so." Stephen hurried ahead and cracked open the doors on the other side of the hall. He peeked inside.

"Having you on my *arm* is not what I'm looking forward to on our wedding night," Russ said into her ear.

"Hold that thought."

Stephen beckoned to them. "We have a couple of guests eating breakfast, so we're just going to walk through the dining room and then on to the kitchen. We can collapse the dining room table by a few feet, but we can't remove it from the room, so the plan is to have the desserts and coffee served from here." He opened one door. "Excuse us, folks. We're just doing a wedding walk-through." He led them into the elaborately paneled room. "We'll take the chairs out, of course, and put the tea service on the sideboard—"

Beside her, she could feel Russ stiffen. He was staring at the other end of the mahogany dining table, where a forty-something woman in a starched shirt was buttering toast and a young black man with very little hair was working his way through eggs and sausage. The woman's eyes opened wide. She put her toast and her knife on her plate. "Chief Van Alstyne."

◆ ◆ ◆

"I see you decided not to head all the way back to Fort Drum. You hoping to become better acquainted with our little town?" Russ's tone triggered Clare's early alert system. This wasn't some tourist whose purse had been returned by the police department.

The woman's nose pinched in and her mouth thinned. "I did a little research and became better acquainted with *you* last night. Twenty-two years in the army, twenty of them as an MP, retired as a CW5. Purple Heart, Bronze Star, Presidential Commendation with Valor. Investigator in chief for the 6th Military Police Group, Fort Lewis, training command at Fort Leonard Wood . . ." She steepled her fingers. "So what was the Deputy Dawg act yesterday?"

His service records, Clare thought. The only place that information was accessible—and then only by authorized military personnel.

Russ crossed his arms. "Why don't you tell me why you really came here looking for Tally McNabb?"

The woman's eyes flicked toward Clare and Obrowski. Clare would go if Russ asked her, but she was damned if she was going to back down for anyone else. The innkeeper was another matter. "Stephen," she said, "can we meet you in the kitchen in a few minutes?"

"Absolutely," Stephen said, with the gratitude of a man whose job made him privy to more dirty laundry than he wanted to hear. He headed for the door. Paused. "I'll have Ron make a fresh pot of coffee." That thought seemed to make him happy again.

When the door swung shut behind him, the woman stared at Clare with a gaze like a dissecting knife. "Who's she?"

Instead of answering her, Russ pulled a chair away from the table. "Clare?" She sat. "I'd like you to meet Lieutenant Colonel Arlene Seelye of the U.S. Army Finance Command." He gestured toward Clare. "The Reverend Clare Fergusson."

She wasn't sure what was going on, but since it looked like Russ had already taken the role of bad cop, she figured she ought to be the good cop. She smiled, showing many, many teeth. "Hello!"

"This isn't a matter for a civilian, Chief. Even if she is a priest."

"Didn't I mention?" Russ took the chair next to her. "This is also Major Clare Fergusson of the 142nd Aviation Support Battalion."

The private, who had stopped eating when it was clear Russ wasn't going to keep moving along, straightened in his seat.

"I don't care if she's commander of the Big Red One. I'm not going to—" Seelye slapped her napkin down. She looked at Russ. Despite the heat in her voice, her gaze was cool. Assessing. Whatever she saw, she decided to change tactics. "Mary McNabb, a.k.a. Tally McNabb, was under investigation for peculation."

Russ cocked an eyebrow. "She had her hand in the battalion cookie jar?"

"We believe she made off with a considerable sum."

"I have a feeling the army and I probably have different ideas as to what constitutes a considerable sum."

Colonel Seelye paused. "In the neighborhood of a million dollars."

Russ whistled.

"Nice neighborhood," Clare said. Seelye looked at her as if she had just spat chewing tobacco on the table. Clare tried not to let her cheeks pink up.

"That's a hell of a lot of money to sneak off with under the army's nose," Russ said. "Didn't she have any oversight?"

"McNabb altered the records. Destroyed data. She was very skilled. And the chief financial officer of her unit was . . . lax."

Clare nudged Russ's thigh. He nodded to her. *Go ahead.* "Tally had been stateside since March," she said. "Her discharge came through in May, and she's been living openly in Millers Kill since then. How come you're only now showing up to investigate her?"

Seelye crossed her arms over her chest. The private stared at the eggs congealing on his plate. Clare looked at Russ. *What did I say?*

"I don't think it's because they've been taking their own sweet time. I think they didn't know about it before now." He twisted in his chair and propped an elbow on the table, for all the world as if he and Clare were having a postbreakfast chat over the paper. "Tally McNabb may have been a damn good bookkeeper, but she wasn't any sort of criminal mastermind. I think she had help covering the theft up. From the inside." He glanced toward Seelye, then back to Clare. She frowned. From the inside? The whole Army was one big "inside." "From another MP," he clarified.

Quentan Nichols. Clare's mouth formed an O. Russ swept his lashes low in acknowledgment.

Seelye didn't react. "I need to search that house, Chief."

"That house is the property of a civilian who isn't here to give his consent. You take what you have to a judge, you get a warrant, and I'll be glad to help you execute it. Hell, I'll have my whole department pitch in."

"This case is not in your jurisdiction."

"Maybe not, but Tally McNabb's death is."

"Your people searched their house."

"With probable cause, post death by gunshot."

"I want to see your files."

"You want a lot, don't you?" He stood. "C'mon, Clare. We have some faxes to decipher."

Clare rose to her feet. A hundred questions were screaming in her head, but she smiled and nodded at the soldiers. "Colonel. Private."

"Ma'am," the young man said.

Seelye shot him an icy look. She steepled her fingers again. "This isn't over, Chief. If you try to play hardball with the United States Army, I will have your ass hanging from my company flagpole. That's a promise."

Russ flattened his hands against the table and leaned forward. "I was playing hardball with the army back when you were still buffing up your butter bars and trying to memorize the ten-code." He straightened. "Get a warrant, and we'll talk. Until then . . ." He flipped his hand open.

He gestured Clare ahead of him. She felt as if she had a gun sighted between her shoulder blades as she walked to the kitchen door. As soon as the door had swung shut behind them, she opened her mouth.

Russ held a finger to his lips and dragged her around the industrial-sized center island toward Ron and Stephen, who immediately stopped talking. Ron twisted around and moved a stovetop percolator off the enormous gas range. "What was that all about?" Stephen asked.

"Police business," Russ said.

Ron rolled his eyes.

Russ ignored him. "How long have they been here?"

"They checked in late Wednesday night," Stephen said. "They were complaining about not being able to get a room at any of the motels."

"They were damn lucky *we* had a party cancel. The Adirondacks during peak foliage?" Ron blew a raspberry.

Stephen frowned at his partner.

"Don't give me that Mrs. Grundy look," Ron said. "I told you they weren't here for antiques and cider." He pointed to Russ. "Is there anything we need to worry about? Seeing as they're involved in *police business?*"

"No. They're cops. Military police." He turned to Clare. "I've got to get back to the station. Do you mind handling the rest of the wedding hoopla without me?"

"No-o-o. I would mind the walk back to town, though."

Russ made a frustrated sound. "Sorry. I forgot. Okay, let's go." He took off toward the hallway.

"Uh—" She looked helplessly at Stephen and Ron.

"Go, go." Stephen flapped his hands at her. "Call us when you're free. We can set up another time. Just don't leave it too long!"

"Unless you want to think twice about the whole thing." Ron indicated the door Russ had disappeared behind. "As I recall, Prince Charming is supposed to chase after Cinderella, not the other way around."

Russ had already backed the truck onto the drive when she caught up to him. She swung the door open and jumped in. He started down the road before she had finished buckling her seat belt.

He unhooked the mic from its mount. "Dispatch, this is Van Alstyne, IOV."

The radio cracked. "Chief, this is Dispatch, go ahead."

"Is Lyle or Eric in?"

"Eric's out interviewing friends and family. Lyle just headed to the courthouse with a warrant request. He's fixing to get into McNabb's bank account. The rest of 'em are in the seat."

"Anybody not on patrol yet?"

"Hadley. She got in late."

"Good. Have her contact McNabb's telephone carriers. Landline and cell. I want a record of all incoming calls for the week up to her death. She's looking for out-of-state numbers, especially ones originating from a Missouri or an Illinois area code."

"Roger that."

"And Harlene? Do we still have the hard copy of the intake file for Quentan Nichols? It would have been late June."

"Probably."

"Find it and put it on my desk. I'll be there in fifteen minutes. Van Alstyne out."

He hung up the mic.

"You think she and Nichols stole the money together."

"If she took it, she didn't do it alone. Do you know anything about how you draw pay during deployment?"

"Um . . . I showed up at the quartermaster's and signed for it. At the bigger camps, like Liberty or Anaconda, you could use a card at the CX or to get cash."

"Where's the cash come from?"

She blinked. "I never thought about it."

"It's just like a civilian bank. The army flies it in, shrink-wrapped on pallets. The cash is transferred under guard to a secure location, where it's locked into a vault and disbursed as necessary."

"Huh. So when Seelye said upwards of a million, she meant one million actual *dollars*?" Clare shook her head. "That's gotta be a big amount. Physically, I mean."

Russ flicked on his signal and turned onto River Road. "Yeah. McNabb was a finance company specialist. That means she only intersected with the cash at the end, when it was in a vault, under tight control. Or maybe not even then. It sounded as if she was in accounts management, not dispersal."

"A bookkeeper, not a teller." Clare scarcely noticed when they crossed the bridge. "She can cover up the loss, but not remove the actual loot from where it's supposed to be."

"That's right. She would have needed an accomplice who had access to the money earlier. One of the ground crew. Or a truck driver. *Or* one of the MPs assigned to guard the cash."

"Quentan Nichols. Do you think he gave Tally advance warning that the investigators were after her?"

"That's why I'm having Knox pull the phone records."

She stared out the side window. The sun made the autumn leaves look like they had been lit from inside. Almost too bright to look at against the white clapboard farmhouses and the October blue sky. She turned back toward Russ. "Maybe it wasn't love that kept him coming back trying to talk with her. Maybe it was one million dollars."

"Well, you know what they say. Nothing says 'I love you' like a cool million in the bank." His mouth quirked. "Either Nichols had already gotten his cut, and he called to warn her in order to save his own skin, or she still owed him money, and he called to warn her in order to keep the cash flowing."

"Or he showed up in person to collect." She watched as he swung onto Church Street. The gazebo in the center of the park was still hung with red-white-and-blue bunting. Maybe one more concert this weekend before the town boarded it up for the winter. "Where does her husband fit in?"

"I'm sure he was happy to accept whatever money she gave him, no questions asked." He braked to let a handful of shoppers cross the street. "I still want to question him, but unless there's some evidence of domestic abuse we haven't turned up yet, he's dropped down several notches on my list."

Clare could think of other reasons Wyler McNabb night have killed his wife. A million of them. Maybe she was going to break it off and take the money with her. Maybe *he* was going to break it off and he wanted it all for himself. Maybe only she knew where it was hidden, and his attempts to wring the location out of her went south. "Where do you suppose she stashed it?"

"That's not my problem, thank God." He drove past the church, past the boxwood hedge, and turned into her drive.

"What do you mean? A million in untraceable cash? If that's not motive for murder, what is?"

He engaged the parking brake but kept the engine running. He turned, slinging his arm across the seat back. "You're not seeing the whole picture. The McNabbs spent money like water in the past couple of years, buying cars, a boat, a swimming pool, and God knows how much in useless crap and rounds of drinks at the Dew Drop. Their relationship, by all accounts, was rocky. She was stressed by two tours of duty in Iraq, one of which included grand larceny. One of the guys in her group just tried to kill himself. Then she finds out the CID is about to show up. She's looking at fifteen years' hard time in Leavenworth and complete financial ruin from the restitution order." He laid his hand over Clare's. His voice gentled. "I know it's hard to accept—but her .38 must have looked like her only friend in the world at that point."

◆ ◆ ◆

Eric McCrea knew that most cases were cleared with systematic, step-by-step investigation, methodical and well analyzed. Still, there was an element of luck to police work, too, and he didn't know a single cop who'd disagree with him on that score.

Eric McCrea was about to get lucky.

He had been working his way down the list of McNabb's family and friends, trying to find someone who might give the weasel up or at least tell the truth about his relationship with his wife. Eric had spoken to two co-workers already that morning, respectable, solid family guys who lived on quiet streets and kept their lawns mowed. Neither of them had ever socialized with Wyler McNabb, except for the company parties BWI Opperman put on. Neither of them knew much about Tally McNabb other than that the couple had been together since high school. No one recalled Wyler talking about or spending time with another woman.

"He sucked when he was on construction," one man said. "Got fired off the resort here. He got rehired as a foreman, though, and he actually did better at that. He wasn't dumb. Just allergic to hard work."

An opportunist, Eric thought. *Lives off others.*

"He was kind of an asshole," the other man said. "Thought he was smarter than he was and wanted you to think so, too."

Arrogant, Eric thought. *Confident he can get away with murder.*

The next stop on the list was in an entirely different neighborhood— the Meadowbrook Estates Park, a tightly packed collection of rusting, rattling single-wides that had neither a meadow nor a brook to soften the hard-packed dirt between the concrete slabs and hook-ups. This was the home of Morris Slinger Jr. Fetch, as he was known, was one of those guys who managed to live off a combination of disability, small-time dealing, and the generosity of his friends. The most generous of whom was Wyler McNabb.

Eric was pleased to see Fetch's Camaro beneath a fabric-topped, PVC-pole car park. He had tried the place yesterday, but his target had been gone. He pulled in, blocking the Camaro, and got out.

He banged on the door. Behind and around him, he could hear the pop and scrape of aluminum latches on aluminum frames, as Fetch's neighbors stuck their heads out to watch the show.

"This is the Millers Kill police," Eric roared. "Open the door!"

The door opened. Fetch stood inside, tall, blond, and still gangly, even though his teens were well past him now. "Hey. Sergeant McCrea." He was trying for some enthusiasm. "What's up, man?" He plucked at his T-shirt. "I'm clean. You can walk right in and see for yourself. Clean as a whistle."

"I'm looking for a buddy of yours. Wyler McNabb."

"Wyler." Fletch's voice relaxed. He stopped tugging his shirt out of shape. "Yeah, man, I just dropped him off at his house, like, less than an hour ago. What's up?"

A flare of excitement shot up Eric's spine and detonated inside his skull. He kept his face blank and his voice hard. "Where were the two of you?"

"At the Mohegan Sun. They had this off-season special, Monday night to Friday morning. Our room was, like, dirt cheap and we got free breakfast, too."

The Mohegan Sun. The Connecticut casino was on Kevin's list of out-of-state locations. Easy to follow up on.

"You were both there. The whole week."

"Yeah." Fetch mimed pulling a slot machine lever with one long, skinny arm. "It was just for the gambling, man. The casinos, they're way strict. They even *think* you're carrying, next thing you know security's tossed your ass out the door and you ain't gettin' in again."

"Why'd you take your car instead of his?"

Fetch shrugged. "He asked me if I wanted to drive. He paid for the gas and tolls and shit." His face creased with concern. "You know, for real, Wyler likes a good time, but he don't party. He don't use shit, and he don't move it. If that's what you're looking for, you're going to come up with nothing."

Eric thought, for a moment, about calling in the CSI and impounding Fetch's Camaro. Just because they had spent four glorious nights in some resort didn't mean they hadn't snuck back home for a little wet work. In which case, there might be fiber or skin or hair inside that car. He decided against it. If they hadn't already cleaned and vacuumed after

McNabb's death, he was pretty sure Fetch wasn't up to the task of sanitizing the environment himself.

"I want you to stay here." He jabbed his finger at Fetch, not quite touching him. "You stay here, and the car stays here."

Fetch's Adam's apple bobbed. "Okay. Uh, for how long?"

"Until I tell you. Got it?"

Fetch nodded.

Eric gave him one more look, the one that said, *I will mess you up if you cross me*, and strode back to his unit. He waited until he had pulled out of the mobile home park to pick up his mic. "Dispatch, this is fifteen-twenty-five."

"Fifteen-twenty-five, this is Dispatch, go ahead."

"I've got a forty on Wyler McNabb. He was dropped off at his house within the last hour. He was supposedly at the Mohegan Sun in Connecticut since Monday afternoon. Can somebody verify that stay for me?"

"Roger that, fifteen-twenty-five."

"I'm proceeding to 16 Musket Way to bring the suspect in for questioning."

"Roger that, fifteen-twenty-five. Do you require backup?"

Did he require backup? Hell no. Not against a limp-dicked woman-killer like McNabb. "Negative on that, Dispatch." If McNabb did come after him, so much the better. He told Harlene what she would want to hear. "I'll proceed with caution, Dispatch. If anything looks off, I'll call for support."

He hadn't thought much of Tally McNabb's cheating. Sure, it had been common among troops in Iraq, but so were sand fleas—and he sure wouldn't have taken one of those into his bunk. Even if she had slept with every guy in her unit and then shown pictures of it to her husband, by God she had been one of their own. A brother in arms. He wasn't going to let her down at the last.

◆ ◆ ◆

Approaching the house, Eric saw the first sign McNabb was home. The garage doors were open, and McNabb's ATV had been rolled onto the blacktop. Eric entered through the overcluttered garage and pounded on the kitchen door. "This is the Millers Kill police. Open up!"

There was a long pause. Finally, a voice said, "Prove it."

Oh, for chrissake. "Look out your front window, asshole. You can see my cruiser sitting at the foot of your drive."

Another period of silence. Then, "Whaddaya want?"

"I want you to open up this goddamn door before I kick it in!"

The door cracked open. Eric slid his boot into the opening, leaned against the edge of the door with his shoulder, and greased right through. "Hey!" McNabb backed away, bunching his hands into fists. "You can't do that."

"We're like vampires, asshole. You open the door, we get to come in and stay."

"What the hell do you want?" McNabb was dressed for the outdoors: ripstop woodlands camo pants and a matching shirt. A blaze-orange vest and bill cap were hooked over a kitchen chair.

"Going someplace?"

"I'm meeting some buddies. We're going riding. No law against that."

"Riding where?"

"We got a course set up behind the resort. Anybody who works for the company can use it. You can check. Nobody's trespassing."

"I don't give a rat's ass whose woods you're tearing up on that oversized roller skate. I want you to come with me to the station. We need to have a talk with you."

"Am I under arrest?"

"Not yet."

"Then screw you. I know my rights. I don't have to talk with you or with anyone."

Eric lunged forward. Twisted his fingers in McNabb's collar and contracted his bicep, jerking the younger man up until he was dangling, boot toes pattering against the kitchen floor. McNabb gurgled. Clawed at Eric's hand. "You can come with me conscious, or you can come with me unconscious. That's as far as your rights go."

"Uck oo!" McNabb swung wildly, unaimed blows Eric deflected with his forearms.

"That's it, asshole, you just assaulted an officer. You're under—" McNabb's boot connected solidly to his knee. Eric howled, dropped the perp, staggered back, swearing, sweating, eyes watering. *Jesus!* It felt like his fucking kneecap was broken.

He raised his head. McNabb was at the other end of the kitchen. Gasping. Spitting. Receiver in one hand. Dialing with the other. Calling a lawyer. Calling the press. Calling his wife. Tattletale. Fucking little tattletale. He charged McNabb, knocking him into the wall. The receiver clattered to the floor. Eric stomped it, once, twice, until it broke into black shards and green chips.

"C'mon, asshole," Eric rasped. "C'mon. Just you and me now. Let's do it. Let's do it."

◆ ◆ ◆

"Fifteen-seventy, this is Dispatch, do you copy?"

Hadley unhooked her mic. "Dispatch, this is fifteen-seventy, go ahead."

"I've just had a nine hundred from the McNabb house. That's 16 Musket Way."

A nine hundred. A 911 call that was broken off before any communication could take place. Most times, it was a four-year-old after a preschool trip to the fire station. Occasionally, a teen who didn't realize his prank call could be traced. Sometimes, it was bad. Real bad.

"Eric McCrea reported Wyler McNabb had returned home this morning. Eric was headed there to bring him in. My last contact with him was at oh-nine-forty. He's not answering my hails."

Hadley's stomach rose and lodged in her esophagus, even as her hand flicked on her light bar and siren and her foot tromped on the gas. "Roger that, Dispatch. I am responding."

"I'm sending in whoever else I can raise, so you'll have backup." Harlene's matter-of-fact recitation faltered. "Be careful, Hadley. Remember what the chief says."

"Don't be a hero. Don't worry. I'm not planning on it."

◆ ◆ ◆

Hadley Knox hated suspense movies. Couldn't watch horror. Any scene involving the hero walking warily into an unknown situation had her holding a pillow over her face and fast-forwarding to the next part.

So she recognized the irony of her position. She had taken on a job that kept requiring her to do the exact same thing she wouldn't watch in a DVD. The training helped, and the past two years' experience helped, and practicing three times weekly at the range helped a lot, as she now felt sure she could hit a target smaller than the side of a barn if necessary.

Even so, she still felt as if a swarm of half-frozen ants were crawling up her skin as she pulled her unit in behind Eric's and got out.

One glance told her McCrea hadn't returned to his vehicle, either to call for help or to secure a prisoner. She unsnapped her holster. Drew her Glock 9. Positioned her arm, straight down and slightly outward, the carrying stance that would, her instructors at the Police Basic course had promised, keep her from shooting her own foot off.

She heard the first noise as she entered the garage. A thud, like a bag of flour being dropped from a height. Then a mangled, indistinct sound, something that had come out of a human throat, something that made those ants march double-time up the back of her neck.

The door that led into the kitchen from the garage was ajar. Not far enough to see inside. Another cry, or shout. Then another. No time to weigh the situation. No time. She took a stance at the door, shoulder-on, presenting the smallest target. Took a deep breath. Raised her near foot and kicked the door in, almost bouncing it back in her face because she overestimated its hollow-core weight. Came down hard on the same foot, still shoulder-on, swept the room with her Glock, yelling, "Police! Drop your weapon and get on the ground!"

She saw McCrea at the same instant, straddling a perp who was already on the floor, and she had a second to think *Oh, thank God, he's okay* and then she registered the blood, and saw that McCrea had his service piece in his hand, a big SIG SAUER .45, three pounds of steel, and he raised it up and *whack*, bludgeoned McNabb in the face with it. *Whack!* Blood sprayed across the no-wax flooring. *Whack!* McNabb wasn't moving, wasn't resisting, wasn't making a sound, so Hadley did it for him, let out a screech that would have embarrassed her if she had been able to think about it and launched her whole body forward. She tackled Eric, knocked him to his side, scrabbled for his weapon, all the while screaming, "Stop it! Stop it! Stop it!"

He rolled over her, banging her head so hard against the floor she saw stars. He gripped her wrist and banged it again, harder, then again, until her bruised knuckles released and her gun clunked to the floor. He hit it with his other hand and sent it spinning into an overturned chair. She kicked and bucked beneath him, thinking *he's snapped* thinking *rape* thinking *I lost my piece, oh, God* and the shame and fear and anger coalesced inside her and she head-butted him, then punched him one-two in the diaphragm as he reared back in pain, and as he turned red and choked for air she twisted, rolling to her stomach beneath him, and pushed onto her hands and knees, throwing him off her.

She scrambled for her gun. Seized it. Assumed the stance. Pointed it, not at the feebly croaking Wyler McNabb, but at her fellow officer.

An outline at the door made her jerk her gun up. The chief. His own weapon out, down, to the side. He raised his hands, showing his finger was off the trigger. "Knox?" He glanced at her, at McNabb, at McCrea, half-sprawled on the floor with blood dripping from his nose. "What the hell just happened here?"

"Sorry, Chief." She was amazed to hear her voice sounding so normal. She holstered her gun and saw that she looked normal as well, blouse still tucked in, service belt still centered. Her awful polyester pants weren't even creased.

"I asked what's going on." The chief's voice was hard.

She looked at Eric. His arms were shaking. The chief couldn't see his face, but she could. Terrified. Desperate. Just like she had felt, when he was on top of her.

She opened her mouth to tell the chief everything, and at the same moment she saw what would happen. She was the newest. The only woman. Not really from this town. Flynn would stand by her, but the rest of her brother officers would turn their backs on her. Freeze her out. Their conversations dying away. Her questions and comments ignored.

She would be alone.

"The suspect resisted arrest and assaulted Officer McCrea. Officer McCrea managed to subdue the suspect, sustaining injury in the process. I was about to cuff the suspect and Mirandize him when you came in."

The chief let his gaze travel around the kitchen. The blood spattered on the floor, the broken phone, the toppled chair. When he spoke, his voice snapped like a broken branch. "Subduing an arrestee means physically restraining him, not hitting him until he can't fight back."

Hadley swallowed. "I was knocked down and away in the struggle. I wasn't able to assist for several . . . seconds." She had no idea if that was plausible or not. "I wasn't able to control the situation with my sidearm until Officer McCrea was . . . until the perp was . . ." She made a motion like pulling dough apart.

"Eric?" McCrea got to his feet. He stumbled and listed to one side, favoring his right knee. The chief looked at him a long moment. "Get out to your unit and wait for me there."

McCrea nodded. He limped out the kitchen door, not looking at Hadley. When he was gone, the chief crossed the floor. Got down on one knee next to McNabb. Took the man's chin and gently turned his face side to side. McNabb moaned. "Jesus," the chief said.

He stood. Fished his phone out of his pocket. Punched a single button. "Harlene? Russ. I want you to send an ambulance to 16 Musket Way." He paused. "No. They're fine. It's for Wyler McNabb." Another pause. "Just tell 'em it's not a gunshot or a heart attack. And Harlene? Keep it off the radio. Use the phone."

He hung up. Looked down at Hadley, looked *into* her, like he could see everything she had hidden away. Her stomach fluttered. She had to force herself not to drop her gaze. God. No wonder he got such good results in interrogations. "Knox. Hadley. What really happened?"

"What I told you, Chief. That's what happened."

"What you told me."

She tucked her chin.

"That's your story."

She licked her lips. "That's what happened." To her horror, her eyes welled with tears. "I know I should have done better, Chief. I'm sorry."

The chief sighed. "So am I, Hadley. So am I."

◆ ◆ ◆

The fifteen minutes before the ambulance arrived were some of the longest in Hadley's life, and that included labor and delivery. When the EMTs finally bustled in, they were efficient and cheerful, taking McNabb's vital signs, reporting to the ER by radio, not by word or glance suggesting something had gone badly wrong in this kitchen. When they hoisted McNabb on a stretcher and wheeled him outside, the chief jerked his head, indicating Hadley should follow.

He stopped her with a gesture beside McCrea's car. Eric sat in the driver's seat, staring out the windshield with unfixed eyes. His usual sharp edges seemed blurred, as if someone had taken his picture and half-erased it.

"I want you to accompany the ambulance," the chief told Hadley. She nodded. "Eric?" McCrea looked up. "Knox maintains that McNabb was injured because he resisted and attacked you."

Eric glanced up at her, then dropped his eyes.

"*Even* if that is true, you used excessive force. I'm suspending you. Two weeks without pay. Starting now. You'll return your vehicle to the department and leave it there." The chief held out his hand. "I want your service weapon and your badge now."

McCrea gaped. "But . . ."

The chief braced a hand on the top of the car and leaned in. "If McNabb retains a lawyer, and if the board of aldermen demands an investigation, it'll be a lot longer. Now give me your gun."

"I have the right to a review." McCrea's voice was panicked. "I have that right."

"Call your union rep and set up an appointment. In the meantime, I'm exercising my right to suspend you."

McCrea looked at his lap, out the door, at the passenger seat of his cruiser. Anywhere except at the chief. Finally he retrieved his badge and passed it through the window to the chief. Then he leaned to one side and removed his gun from its holster. Handed it, butt side up, to the chief. The chief held the SIG SAUER up where they could all see it. He stared at the tracery of blood on the grip. "The authority we hold is based on the trust of the citizens of this town." His voice was hard and tight. "When you abuse that trust, you shame yourself. You shame *me*. You shame everyone who wears our uniform." He turned his head and stared at Hadley. She wanted to die. He pointed toward the ambulance, pulling into the road, its blue lights flashing. "Go."

She fled to her car. Dove in, slamming the door behind her as if she could keep the shrieking harpies of her own conscience out with steel and glass. She started the ignition with a shaking hand. Wondered, as she lurched into gear and rolled after the ambulance, if any amount of shunning from her fellow officers could possibly feel as bad as this.

◆ ◆ ◆

Russ stood outside the main entrance to the Washington County Hospital and shivered. The temperature had dropped twenty degrees when the sun went down, and there was for sure going to be frost on the pumpkin tonight. He should have worn his MKPD-issue parka.

The tap-tap of heels made him turn around. Lieutenant Colonel Arlene Seelye strode up the walk, her khaki skirt and trench coat standing in for a uniform. No matter how casually dressed, active duty military personnel never quite managed to look like civilians. Seelye didn't.

"I appreciate you for inviting me along on this, Chief." Her tone wasn't warm, but she held out her hand.

He shook it. "Don't thank me yet, Colonel. You can see if McNabb will agree to let you search the house. That's as far as it goes."

"I plan on asking him about his wife's finances."

He tilted his head. "After I find out what he knows about her death."

"As you say."

They entered the building side by side. It was eight fifteen, after visiting hours, and the corridors were mostly empty. Russ led her to the right elevator bank, and they rode to the third floor in silence. One of the hospital security guards was sitting outside McNabb's room, scratching away with a pencil in a fat, floppy book. Russ plucked the man's name from the back of his memory. "Hank. Hi. How's he been?"

"Heya, Chief. Quiet as a mouse. He had a couple guys from work come to visit, and his mama and then his papa. She left mad, promisin' she was gonna call a lawyer, and *he* left mad, saying the same thing. I guess they'll have to hash it out between 'em."

"Thanks. Why don't you take a break while I talk with him?"

"Don't mind if I do. My bladder can't sit still more'n two hours these days anyway." The guard ambled off, Sudoku puzzles flashing them at every step.

"He's already in custody?" Seelye said.

"For resisting and assaulting an officer." As much as it turned his stomach to do it, Russ was going to stand by the arrest. It was obvious, from Eric's limp and his bloody nose, that McNabb *had* gotten a few good hits in.

They entered the single-bed room. Seelye inhaled sharply. Unfortunately, it was obvious that Eric had gotten in a hell of a lot more hits. The colonel looked at Russ like he was something nasty she found underneath the leaf pile. He wanted to explain, wanted to tell her *We're better than this,* but what could he say? McNabb's pulpy, bandaged, purpling face spoke damningly for itself.

McNabb stared at them while Russ pulled out a chair for Seelye and then sat down himself. "Wyler? I don't know if you remember me. I'm Russ Van Alstyne, chief of police. I'd like to ask you a few questions."

"He hit *me.*" McNabb's words were slurred by the damage to his cheek and jaw, but his tone was clear. "That bastard hit *me.* I didn't do *nothin'.* I'm gonna sue him, and you, and the rest of the cops, and the goddamn town. You all gonna be taking tickets at the movies for a living when my lawyer gets through with you."

"I'm not here to discuss what happened today."

"Oh, I jus' bet you're not. How'm I supposed to work like this? I'm due to head off for another construction job at the end of this week. Who's gonna make up for that if the doctor don't clear me to go?"

"You're not going anywhere in the immediate future, Wyler. You're under arrest, remember?"

"Under arrest my ass. I was defending myself. No judge's gonna hold me when they see what your cop did to me."

Russ smothered a sigh. "I want to ask you about your wife."

McNabb went quiet. He turned his face toward the ceiling. "If you're gonna break the bad news to me, save your breath. M'mother told me. She killed herself."

"When was the last time you saw Tally?"

"Monday morning. 'Fore she went to work."

"How was she when you saw her? Happy? Sad? Did you two argue?"

"Argue? Hell. We fought. I was headed off with Fetch for the week. Going to a big casino in Connecticut. She din't like Fetch, and she din't like gambling, and she sure as hell din't like me being out from under her thumb."

"So you fought. Were you mad at her?"

"Not mad enough for her to want to kill herself." He rolled his head back toward them. "Look, she was screwed up in her head about the war. Lots of soldiers come back that way. I saw it on the news. She was going to this counselor. You go ask her if you want to know why Tally did it."

For the first time, his voice shook. His eyes sheened over. "Goddammit. She always was a pain in my ass. Always had to have things her way. Didn't even wait to tell me good-bye, the—" His voice cracked.

McNabb blinked ferociously and hacked. Russ handed him a tissue, and McNabb spat into it, balling it up in his fist. "When did you get back from the casino?" Russ asked.

"This morning. About an hour before your guy comes along like Vin freaking Diesel."

"Were you alone at the casino?"

"I told you, Fetch was with me." McNabb's mouth dropped open. "Ohh, I get it. You think I was cheatin' on Tally, and that's what set her off. Well, I wun't. One woman is more'n enough trouble for me. I don't need that kind of complication. Closest I got to girls was the tits and ass show."

"Did you leave the resort for any length of time?"

"Nope."

"Did you get any calls from Tally? Or call her?"

"Nope."

Kevin, who had been detailed the task of faxing McNabb's picture to area casinos, had already gotten in touch with Mohegan Sun's security. They were reviewing their camera footage and would send the MKPD the relevant pictures and a summary of McNabb's movements. It would have taken a seven-hour window to get from Uncasville to Millers Kill and back again. If McNabb had been gone that long, they would know it.

"One more question," Russ said. "Do you know of anyone who might want to kill Tally? Or any reason why?"

McNabb's mouth sagged. His eyes bugged. "What? No!"

Russ waited to see if more was forthcoming. It wasn't. "Okay. Thank you, Wyler."

"I'm still gonna sue your ass," the younger man mumbled.

Seelye leaned forward. "I'd like to ask you a few questions now, Wyler. About Mary—Tally's service in Iraq."

McNabb made a face that would have been a frown if his eyebrows could have moved. "Who're you?"

"I'm Lieutenant Colonel Arlene Seelye."

For the first time, Russ saw apprehension on McNabb's face. "What do you do? What, you know, branch are you in?"

Seelye hesitated. Glanced at Russ. "I'm with the military police."

McNabb turned toward the ceiling again. Clicked his mouth shut. "I'm not saying nothing without my lawyer."

◆ ◆ ◆

It was colder outside now. A raw, damp cold that promised more rain in the next day or two. Seelye shivered and buttoned her trench coat. "You folks ever have anything approaching warm weather?"

"July and August. First half of September."

"And you came here voluntarily?"

He shrugged. "It's home."

She made a noise. Fished in her coat for a tissue and blew her nose. "So what do you think?"

"He didn't do it." He jammed his hands in his jacket pockets. "Unless he's the greatest actor since Laurence Olivier. I'll take a look at the casino report, but I'm betting it'll show us he was there the whole time. Just like he said he was."

"You going to clear it as a suicide?"

He nodded. "I'll give the ME the results of the investigation. He'll make the ruling. Release the body."

"And that concludes your interest in McNabb."

"Unless you've got information suggesting someone else might have had the means, motive, and opportunity. Like maybe a co-conspirator."

She looked at him. "Did you find any anomalous prints at the scene?"

"No."

"Then, no. I have no reason to suspect anyone else is complicit in her death."

"Would you tell me if you did?"

She thought for a moment. "Yes. Unless it would torpedo my own investigation." Her wide mouth twisted. "The army's interest is in getting its money back, after all."

"Wyler McNabb knows something."

"Oh, yes. I'm quite sure Mr. McNabb knows a great deal about that money."

"Let me give you some free advice. John Ryswick is the judge you're going to be dealing with for the warrants. Give him more information than you think he could possibly need, and make sure you cross your t's and dot your i's. Have you gotten the federal district attorney in the loop?"

"Not yet."

"Hold off as long as you can. Ryswick doesn't like the Feds."

"Thanks for the heads-up."

He held out his hand. "Let me know if we can assist."

She shook it. "I will. I plan on wrapping this up and getting out of here as quickly as possible." She hunched her shoulders against the chill. "This weather is actually making me miss Iraq."

MONDAY, OCTOBER 10   The rain that had drifted in patchy showers through the weekend was on again Monday morning, a cold drizzle from a blank gray sky. Perfect weather for a funeral. Clare could have walked—the cemetery was barely a mile away—but she had pressed her Class A uniform and polished her regulation one-and-three-quarter-inch heels, and she wanted to look parade-ground ready for the interment. So she climbed into the rattleclank Jeep and drove.

The new cemetery, as it was called, had been new in 1870, when the dead from the Civil War had claimed the last of the original settlers' burying ground. Clare rolled through the iron-framed gate and crunched along the twisting gravel drive, past Victorian marble obelisks and yellow weeping willows, past Depression-era granite and dark red alders, until she reached a treeless plain of flat stamped-metal markers and high-gloss composite memorial stones. She parked behind a line of cars. She left her coat in the car but took her hat.

She picked her way through the grass, her heels sinking into the ground with every step. A small striped awning had been erected next to a large mound of excavated soil discreetly covered with bright green outdoor carpeting. She hated that carpeting. She always wanted to roll it away at her interments. Show the reality. Earth to earth.

There were more people than she expected; far more than the number of folding chairs set up beneath the awning. Good. She spotted Trip Still-man and Sarah Dowling standing near the back of the crowd, Sarah in

Quaker gray and Trip, like Clare, in an immaculate green uniform whose shoulders were blotched with rain. She joined them.

"Do you know the minister?" Sarah asked quietly.

"That's the funeral director." Clare spoke in the same undertone. "They're not having a religious service. Just a few people speaking. Mr. Kilmer will make sure things move along smoothly."

The first person to the podium was a cousin. Good choice. Close enough to have some warm anecdotes, not so attached to the deceased that she was in danger of losing it. Clare let her mind and her eyes wander. The woman in the front row who looked a thousand years old must be Tally's mother. With his face varying shades of purple, green, and yellow, Wyler McNabb was very visible a few seats down from her. Russ had told her Tally's husband had been discharged, been arraigned, and posted bail all on the same day.

Farther back, Clare spotted the kind-hearted Dragojesich, already wiping his eyes with fists the size of softball mitts. She caught a glimpse of army green at the other edge of the crowd and was surprised to see Colonel Seelye, also in her dress uniform. Perhaps not so surprising, though. Russ had told her the MP wanted access to Tally's house, bank accounts, and records. Maybe she was trying to get in good with the family. Or maybe she was watching to see who showed up. She spotted Clare looking at her and nodded coolly.

Next up was one of Tally's friends, a young woman with two-toned hair and way too much eye makeup for a funeral. She was only a few sentences into her remembrances of Tally and Wyler in high school when she started to gulp and cry and her mascara began to run black down her cheeks. Clare felt a nudge. Looked at Trip. The doctor nodded toward the line of parked cars. Eric McCrea, spit-and-polished in his own Class A's, was striding toward them. She was amazed. Given what Russ had told her about Eric's treatment of Wyler McNabb, she had expected the sergeant to be holed up with his union representative right now. Or with his lawyer.

McCrea fell in between Clare and Sarah, so that the four of them made a wall of hawkish green punctuated by dove gray. Like Trip, he stood at ease, facing the speaker. His eyes cut toward Clare. "The chief isn't here with you?"

Clare shook her head minutely. "He offered." She kept her own spine straight, her hands clasped behind her back, her eyes forward. "The husband is here. Is your presence going to be a problem?"

From the corner of her eye, she could see the ribbons on his chest rise and fall. "You know about that?"

This time she looked at him directly.

Eric's mouth compressed. "No one's going to notice me. They'll just see the uniform." He faced front again. "I had to come. She was one of us." Sarah leaned forward and glared at them, her finger to her lips. McCrea dropped his voice to a whisper. "She was one of us."

◆ ◆ ◆

There was no honor guard. Clare didn't know if that was because the area commandant was so overwhelmed with requests he couldn't supply one, or if the army didn't send a team for soldiers who had died after walking away with a million dollars of army money. There was a group from the local VFW, though, one big-bellied guy, a pair who looked too thin and frail to hold up their rifles, and a bearded man of about forty. Three of them fired the volley while everyone in uniform saluted and the older folks placed their hands over their hearts and the younger ones stared.

Clare and Eric and Trip and Colonel Seelye kept their salutes as the bearded man and the big-bellied guy—*Desert Storm and Vietnam,* Clare thought—folded the casket flag into a sharp-edged triangle and presented it to Tally's mother. She clutched it, as mothers always did, and for a moment Clare could see in her every woman standing at a graveside, left with nothing but a flag to hold. Those hands, digging into the star-spangled twill, seemed to reach into Clare's chest and squeeze her heart. She stopped analyzing the ceremony. Stopped comparing and critiquing it against the dozens of funerals she had officiated at. Her eyes filled with tears and the bitter, salt-rimed taste of grief stung the back of her throat.

She turned her face away from the childless mother, struggling to master herself. She stared hard at the trees fringing the older section of the cemetery, their autumn colors burning like banked coals against the heavy gray sky. She paid attention to the details, slick stone and dripping branch, because focusing on the sodden scenery meant she wasn't falling apart.

That was how she saw Quentan Nichols.

◆ ◆ ◆

"It was him. I'm sure of it."

Russ relocated a pile of reports and newsletters from the extra chair to his desk. "Sit down."

"I don't want to sit down." Clare paced from the desk to the filing cabinets to one of the tall windows. It was streaked and spotted, the watery afternoon light held at bay by the bright fluorescents inside the office. "I want you to do something."

There was a knock on the door. Harlene stuck her head in. "Would you like a cup of coffee, Clare?"

"I'd love one, Harlene. Thank you."

"Hey!" Russ crossed his arms and leaned against his desk. "What about me?"

"You got two legs, don't you?" The dispatcher nodded at Clare. "You look a right treat in that uniform." She shut the door.

"So what do you think?"

"Sorry, Major, the uniform doesn't do it for me. Too many bad memories of idiot officers."

"Russ!"

He raised his hands in surrender. "Sorry." He straightened and went around his desk. He picked up a file. "Here."

She took the slim folder. Inside was a fax from Fort Leonard Wood acknowledging the MKPD's request, blah, blah . . . she found the information halfway down the sheet. Nichols, Quentan L., posted to Fort Gillem, Georgia, September 26. Copies of the travel order and the transportation receipts. She flipped the page. A different fax headlined Office of the Commandant, Fort Gillem, told her Sergeant Nichols had arrived on October 4 and was currently listed as active duty assigned to the military police post.

She looked at Russ. "He's in Georgia?"

"Since a week before Tally McNabb's death." He took the folder from her. "Did you think I wouldn't take a look at Nichols? Rule him out as a suspect?"

"But I saw him. Today. At the cemetery."

"Did you go after him?"

"Of course not! I had to stay till the end of the ceremony, and then I had to introduce myself to Tally's mother and offer my condolences." She ground the sole of her ugly regulation pump against the floor. "I should be at her house right now."

"I bet you made a casserole."

She glared at him.

"Okay. So today you saw a youngish black man of average height, standing maybe a hundred yards away, through the mist and rain."

The door bumped open and Harlene entered, carrying two mugs and a sugar bowl on a wooden tray that looked as if it had been someone's shop project in high school. She set it atop the most stable stack of papers on Russ's desk. "I got one for you, too," she told Russ. "Don't get used to it."

After she closed the door behind her, Russ spooned a generous helping of sugar into one cup and handed it to Clare. The oversized mugs were decorated with fat, parasol-carrying geese. Too cutesy-poo for his wife, he had once told her, so they had donated the set to the department.

Clare took a sip of the sweet and bitter brew from Linda Van Alstyne's rejected kitchenware. "Yes, okay, I was a long way away and conditions were cloudy—but I have very good eyesight, and it's not as if Millers Kill is crowded with black men in uniforms."

"What about the private who's here with Seelye? Was he with her during the ceremony?"

"No, but—"

"She probably set him at a distance to observe. Maybe follow Wyler McNabb." He blew on his coffee. "If I were investigating the theft, I'd have him dogged. See if he led me to the money."

"I know what I saw! It was Quentan Nichols!"

"Clare, it doesn't matter. Let's say you did see Nichols. Let's say he took a leave of absence and drove a thousand miles north to lurk outside his girlfriend's funeral. He didn't kill her. Her husband didn't kill her. She committed suicide. The case is closed."

"I cannot believe you'd dismiss her death that—that—casually!"

He stepped away from the desk. "I'm not dismissing her death. I'm making a judgment based on physical evidence and solid investigating. You, on the other hand, are pulling crap from thin air because you don't want to believe the plain facts."

"The plain facts? You mean, like the fact that she may have a fortune stashed away somewhere? The fact that she must have had accomplices who helped her steal the money? The fact that she was troubled and under investigation—"

"Which led to her suicide!"

Clare stabbed a finger against his khaki-covered chest. "So she knew, one way or the other, that the party was over. Anyone who wanted to keep that money or keep their involvement in the crime a secret had a million reasons to shut her up before she could talk to anyone. I don't see how you can just blindly ignore that!"

He leaned forward in a way she had seen before, when he was trying to use his size to intimidate people. "The theft of U.S. Army property is outside my jurisdiction."

"Tally McNabb's death is in your jurisdiction—and you're failing her."

His mouth thinned until it was a hard line. "I'm sorry you can't accept the death of someone in your therapy group. I'm sorry you didn't see where she was going ahead of time and stop her. But I'm not going to waste my department's resources on an imaginary murder because you feel guilty for not helping her."

His words hit like a sucker punch. When she could find the air, she said, "I see. Clearly, I should keep out of your business. Like Linda did."

"Goddammit!" He slammed his mug on his desk, sloshing coffee over folders and papers and blotter. "That is *not* what I said."

"You think I'm overreacting because—what? She was in Iraq, like me? Because she was in therapy, like me? Because she was screwed up, like me?"

He looked at her. "Yes." His voice was flat.

"I'm out of here." She grabbed her purse and hat from the top of one of the filing cabinets.

"Clare—"

"And I want you to think, very carefully, about whether you really want to marry someone like me." She swung open the door and dropped her voice. "Because God knows, I might snap and decide to kill myself for no good reason."

BUT I HAVE SQUANDERED THE
INHERITANCE OF YOUR SAINTS,
AND HAVE WANDERED FAR
IN A LAND THAT IS WASTE.

—Reconciliation of a Penitent, The Book of Common Prayer

They were sitting around Will Ellis's hospital bed, all five of them together. At the end of the sad, short ceremony at the graveside, Sarah had said, "It's Monday. I expect to see you all tonight." Trip Stillman had pointed out Will hadn't been discharged yet. "That's why the group is meeting in his room," she had told them.

The three soldiers had changed back into civilian clothes, but Sarah could still conjure the way they had looked, pressed and contained and ramrod straight, as if they were double-exposed in photographs. Sarah wondered, not for the first time, which was the original image and which one had been superimposed.

Fergusson told Will about the people who spoke, and Stillman described the rifle salute. Sarah mentioned how beautiful the flowers were. Everyone tried to keep it upbeat, but there wasn't really any way to put a good face on the violent death of a twenty-five-year-old woman. Will grew pale and paler as they spoke, as if the light inside him were being turned down by degrees and would soon be extinguished. "I can't believe it," he finally said. "I can't believe she really did it."

It struck Sarah that the only difference between Will and Tally was lack of access to a gun and seven days of stomach purges and antidepressants. Coming close but no closer seemed to have stripped death of its glamour in Will's eyes.

Fergusson shook her head. "I don't believe she did." Sarah was sure she had been drinking. She was in control—no slurring or listing—but her color was high and her expression unguarded.

"Forget it." McCrea lifted his head and spoke for the first time. Something was clearly bothering him beyond Tally's suicide. "I thought she was killed, too, but we're wrong. Her husband turned out to have an airtight alibi before, during, and after the time of death."

"Yeah, yeah, yeah. And her boyfriend from Iraq couldn't have done it because he was on duty at Fort Gillem. I'm not saying she was killed in some sort of lovers' quarrel. I think she was killed for money. A whole lot of money."

"Excuse me?" Sarah said.

"You saw the other officer at the funeral?"

"Yes. I thought she was from Tally's company."

"She was. Sort of. She's with CID, assigned to FINCOM. She's investigating the theft of a million dollars from the army's coffers."

Stillman leaned forward. "She thinks Tally was involved?"

"She thinks Tally's responsible."

"What?" Will said.

"That's ridiculous," Stillman said.

McCrea rubbed a finger over his mouth and made a humming noise.

Sarah's first impulse was to view Clare's statements as a symptom of denial or anger. A projection, thrown up because the bald truth of McNabb's suicide was too painful. On the other hand, she *was* engaged to the chief of police. Maybe she knew something the rest of them didn't. "What evidence does this investigator have?"

"I don't know. She's here trying to get a warrant to search Tally's house and all her financial records. Russ—Chief Van Alstyne believes she'll probably arrest the husband as an accomplice."

"Where's the money?" Will asked. Sarah was glad he had said it first.

"I have no idea. The *where* isn't the point. It's that someone—maybe several someones—had a pretty damn good motive to kill her."

McCrea shook his head. "If the chief is calling it a suicide, the evidence has got to be locked up solid. He doesn't cut corners."

"I know that!" Fergusson sounded exasperated. "I'm not saying it doesn't look an awful lot like she did it. But think, Eric. You were at the scene. Would it have been impossible for another person to have staged it?"

He paused. "Not impossible, no. Although it would've required a hell of a lot of fine-tuned planning to carry it off that convincingly."

"The sort of planning a lot of money could help with?"

He frowned. "Maybe. Provided the perp had enough brains. Most criminals are dumb as dirt."

Sarah raised her hands. "I'm feeling as if we're wandering off track here. We were talking about dealing with Tally's death—"

"You know what we say in the Corps?" Will's voice was stronger than it had been. "Nobody gets left behind. Alive, dead, it doesn't matter. Nobody gets left behind."

"It's over," McCrea said. "There's nothing else we can do for her."

Will gave the police officer a look that reminded Sarah of how young he really was. "You can. You could at least dig into it some more."

"No. I can't." Eric bent over in his chair and locked his fingers over the back of his head. Hiding his face from the world. "I've been suspended. I can't do jack shit."

Will and Stillman stared. Fergusson glanced away. *She knew.* Sarah leaned toward McCrea. "What happened, Eric?"

"I don't want to talk about it." Before she could prod him into revealing more, he said, "I lost it with a suspect. I was mad, and I couldn't . . . I lost it."

Will flopped back onto his pillows. "Oh, God. Look at us. A cripple, a drunk, a washed-up cop, and—" He looked at Stillman. "I don't even know what you are. An obsessive note-taker with three-generations-old technology." The doctor drew his PalmPilot closer to his chest.

"I am *not* a drunk," Fergusson said.

"Reverend Clare, you've been to my house. I've seen you putting away wine like it was Kool-Aid. I've heard my parents talking about you."

Clare breathed in. "They were talking? About me?"

"And we're what Tally left behind. Her squad mates." Will closed his eyes. "Losers and failures. You wanna know who's going to give her justice? Nobody. Not a damn soul."

The silence that followed was painful. It wasn't thoughtful or contemplative. It was the silence of despair. Of ending. Of surrender. Sarah should remind them of the grief process. She should help them connect their feelings with their experiences. She should offer them something positive. She couldn't. The echo of Will and Clare's words were drowning out all her other ideas. *Who will give justice to the dead?*

She opened her mouth. "We can try."

"What?" McCrea looked at her.

"I said we can try. There's no law against asking questions, is there? Talking with her friends or co-workers?" As she said it, Sarah realized she wanted someone to blame as much as the rest of them. She wanted to know she could not have prevented Tally's death. *This is not a therapeutic response,* she told herself. "I suppose we could . . . we could . . ." She spread her hands. "Actually, I have no idea what we could do."

"There might be some people I could call," Stillman said hesitantly. "To find out about her service in the 10th Soldier Support. I can probably get some information on the man she met in Iraq as well." He smiled vaguely. "The old doctors' network."

Sarah made an encouraging noise.

"I've met the officer who's investigating the theft," Fergusson said. "I can see if she'll tell me anything about what they've discovered so far."

"Why don't you just *pump* the chief for information?" McCrea asked.

"Euw." Will made a face. "She's my priest, remember? TMI."

"What? It's okay if she drinks, but it's not okay if she—"

"That's enough." Fergusson sounded every inch the officer. "I know you're angry with Russ. I'm pretty pissed off at him myself. But don't take it out on me, Eric."

McCrea couldn't meet her gaze. He dropped his head and mumbled something.

"I don't have any special contacts or anything," Will said. "I don't think any of the marines I knew can help us out."

"She was closer to your age than to any of us," Fergusson said. "Maybe you can spread the word among your friends. You never know what somebody may have heard on the grapevine."

Will looked skeptical. "Most of my friends left for college."

"So e-mail them. Pick up the phone. They'll be so happy to hear from you, they'll tell you anything."

"Well . . ." He kneaded his thighs. "I guess. It's been a while since I've talked to anybody. Maybe I can call a few guys. Okay."

If Sarah hadn't been watching Fergusson instead of Will, she would have missed the flare of triumph on the priest's face. *Doing well by doing good, Reverend?* One way or another, something positive might come from this folly. Which made her think. "What about you, Eric?"

McCrea glared at her. "I told you. I'm suspended. I can't help you."

"Maybe you should try helping yourself. A structured, goal-oriented activity with no pressure from your work or your family? It could be a good place to work on containing your anger."

"C'mon, Eric." Fergusson leaned forward. "We need you."

"In the first place, I don't have either my badge or my service piece. In the second, pursuing an active investigation while suspended is grounds for termination."

Fergusson snorted. "You don't need a badge to be good at asking questions and figuring things out."

"Besides, if Tally's death has been ruled a suicide, you can hardly call it an active investigation." Stillman didn't lift his eyes from his PalmPilot while speaking.

"That's right," Fergusson agreed.

"Barracks law," McCrea said.

"Join us, Eric." Fergusson looked far too sly for someone professing to be religious. "You know you want to."

"Oh, my God." McCrea snorted. "This is how you got the chief to do all that crazy stuff with you, isn't it? You just badgered him until he gave in."

"Yup."

"Okay. Okay." He sighed. "I can question her co-workers. Lyle took statements over the phone from a couple people, but we were looking for evidence of suicidal intent at that point. I'll see if I can get an idea as to how she might have laundered the money." He huffed a laugh. "I think you're all freaking crazy, though." Then his breath broke, and he bent over again. "I think I'm freaking crazy," he said in a cracked voice.

TUESDAY, OCTOBER 11   Eric had hoped that somehow he could get by without telling Jennifer. Dawdle in the morning, maybe, so she didn't see him not getting into his uniform. It wasn't until he tried that he realized how set the three of them were in their morning routine. Jen in the shower first while he got Jake up and started the coffee. Then he showered while she dressed and yelled at Jake to hurry up. Downstairs, he and Jake ate breakfast while she blow-dried her hair. He put away the milk and cereal while

Jake fed the cats and Jen checked to make sure the boy hadn't forgotten anything that ought to be in his backpack. Then out of the house, look for the bus, wave good-bye, slamming doors, and they were all on their way, to the middle school and the elementary school and the cop shop.

"What are you doing?" Jennifer bent over, towel-drying her hair. "You're going to be late."

He mumbled something. Went into the bathroom. Turned on the shower. Sat on the toilet lid and considered exactly how far he was going to go to keep Jen from knowing about his suspension.

What the hell, he had to take a shower anyway.

He sat at the table and methodically spooned Cheerios into his mouth while Jake read *The Last Olympian* and occasionally managed to get a bite in without taking his eyes off the book. Jennifer's blow-dryer cut off, and he could hear her putting it in the drawer. She came into the kitchen. Paused with her hand on the refrigerator handle. "You're not dressed."

Eric looked down at his khakis and shirt. "Sure I am."

"Why aren't you in uniform? Is there something special going on today?" She frowned. "Are you working plainclothes?" Which he did, once in a blue moon.

It was so tempting to say yes. He wiped his mouth. Stood up. "No," he said. "I'm off for the next ten days."

Jennifer glanced at Jake, still lost in Percy Jackson's adventures. She beckoned Eric into the family room. "What do you mean, off? You don't have any vacation coming until Christmas."

He took a breath. "I'm on suspension."

Jennifer's eyes widened. "Suspension? Oh, my God. What did you do?"

He felt a flare of irritation at her instant conclusion that he was the problem. It could have been an administrative action. If he had been involved in a shooting, for instance. Which he would have told her about as soon as he got home yesterday. His anger deflated. "I got into it with a suspect who resisted arrest. The chief thought I was too . . . physical."

"Physical? As in what? You hit the guy?"

"Look, Jen, he was—"

"You hit some guy, right?"

He looked toward the bookcase, littered with pictures of Jake and half-completed craft projects. "Yeah. I hit him. Put him in the hospital."

She covered her mouth. "Oh, Jesus," she said into her palm.

"Listen—"

"No. You listen. First it was yelling at Jake and blowing up at me. Then it was threatening that doctor. Now it's beating up suspects."

"For God's sake, Jen, he threw the first punch—"

She shook her head. "You have a problem, Eric. A serious, serious problem. You need help, and your little group isn't cutting it. I don't know if you need psychotherapy or drugs or what, but you find someone who can help you and you get yourself sorted out." She gulped. "Or I'll leave and take Jake with me."

"What?"

"I'm not going to wait around for you to start beating on us, too."

Her words took his breath away. His stomach ached and his chest was tight. "I would never, ever harm you or Jake. I love you. You two are my whole life."

Her face fractured. "There was a time when you would have said the same thing about a suspect. That you'd never hurt anyone if you could help it." She pressed her fingers against her mouth for a second. "You were always the most conscientious, sweet-natured man I knew. Sometimes you had to do hard things, but you never let them make you hard. I loved that about you."

Loved that. Past tense. His gut knotted itself even tighter. "I just need some more time. To get my bearings again."

"You've been home four months now. It's getting worse, not better." She stepped back. Looked around the room. Lifted Jake's backpack off the desk. "Get help. Or I swear to God, I'm out of here."

◆ ◆ ◆

Clare had tried dropping by the Stuyvesant Inn, to see if she could meet with Arlene Seelye, but the two MPs had been out. She lingered as long as she could over her mother's menu options, but there was only so much time she could kill debating brown sugar versus mustard glaze on the Virginia ham, and eventually she had to leave unsatisfied.

When she got home, she had a message on her machine. "Hey, it's me. Are you there? . . . No? Huh. Look, I'm sorry. I know this whole thing with Tally McNabb has been hard on you. I shouldn't have hammered on you like that. I'm flat out today—I gotta meet with the board of aldermen about Eric's suspension—but maybe we can have lunch tomorrow? At the diner?"

She tried to reach him but had to settle for playing phone tag. Frustrated, she called her junior warden, Geoffrey Burns, Esq. Not about Russ—there was no love lost between the two men—but about Arlene Seelye. "She's investigating a theft from the army," Clare explained. "The suspect is dead, but her husband lives here, and Colonel Seelye thinks he knows something about the missing money. What does she do?"

"She'll go to Judge Ryswick for a warrant." Geoff didn't hesitate. "She'll want to search the house and, based on what she finds there, any accounts that might be in either spouse's name or further locations, like a second home, cars, boats."

"Can she arrest the husband?"

"As an accessory? Possibly. She might get the Feds involved. Undoubtedly, your fiancé as well, since the guy's in his jurisdiction. Are you sure you want to marry him?"

"Yes." Despite their disagreement over Tally McNabb. "And I expect you to at least pretend to have a good time at the reception."

Next, she phoned Assistant District Attorney Amy Nguyen. She had met the woman just enough times to justify calling her on a fishing expedition. Unfortunately, Amy hadn't seen anyone fitting Seelye's description at the courthouse, and she hadn't heard anything about a possible arrest involving the FBI in their area.

That evening, she sat for a long time with one of the sleeping pills Trip had prescribed in one hand, and a highball glass full of Macallan's in the other. *I shouldn't. I shouldn't.*

He's not going to spring a blood test on me the day after I got the prescription filled.

She chased the pill down with a long swallow of Scotch.

WEDNESDAY, OCTOBER 12   Wednesday morning, she told herself the same thing when she popped two Dexedrine. *It's too soon for a blood test.* The familiar jittery rush of heat went through her when the pills hit her system, and she thought, *Okay. I can get through today.* She wouldn't be tempted to drink before early evening, and she'd burn that bridge when she got to it.

It was a relentlessly busy morning: a 7:00 A.M. Eucharist, a stack of phone calls to get through, then a sermon to draft. She struggled with it; Sunday's gospel was Matthew, the Great Commandment, but her attention kept circling back to the beginning of the passage. *One of them, a lawyer, asked him a question to test him.* It brought back the nightmare she had had, with her old SERE instructor quoting scripture at her while Russ's body burned.

She was grateful when Lois, the church secretary, interrupted her. "Your mother phoned. She asked me to tell you the florist is coming over this afternoon to look at the space and take measurements." Clare had taken to letting Lois handle as many maternal calls as possible. The secretary actually seemed to enjoy debating the virtues of tulle versus netting for the sugared-almond favor bags. "Magnolia swags and gold-sprayed live oak," Lois went on. "Very romantic."

"For Tidewater Virginia in June. Too bad I'm getting married in November in the North Country." Clare looked down at her crossed-out paragraphs and scribbled notes. "I guess I'm not going to be able to leave until after I've spoken to the florist. If I get a call from a Colonel Arlene Seelye, will you keep her on the line and track me down?"

"I will." Lois retreated down the hall, humming "Here Comes the Bride."

"No *Lohengrin*!" Clare shouted.

Her practice of writing her sermon on Wednesday served two functions: It gave her enough time between then and Sunday to come up with something else if her first try was crap, and it made her positively happy to have her solitude broken by the lunchtime vestry meeting.

This week's meeting was brisk. Twenty minutes to cover Gail Jones's education budget and the feasibility of an energy audit; forty minutes of Clare listening to Terry McKellan and Norm Madsen and Mrs. Marshall waxing on about their own nuptials. It was sweet and charming, and it made her uncomfortably aware that Russ had been part of this club, too, long married and happy to be so.

Clearly, I should keep out of your business. Like Linda did. God, she was an idiot. As if Russ needed a reminder of the difference between Clare and his late wife. His beloved wife.

She was cleaning up after the meeting when Glenn Hadley stuck his head in the door. "Summun in the sanctuary to see you, Father."

She was always "Father" to the sexton. She handed him a tray loaded with uneaten sandwiches. "Thanks, Mr. Hadley. Would you put this in the icebox downstairs?"

"Ayuh."

She sniffed. "Were you smoking?" The sexton's granddaughter, Hadley Knox, had enlisted Clare's help in keeping the seventy-six-year-old diabetic away from cigarettes.

"Me, Father? You know the doctors told me not to."

She rolled her eyes as she walked down the hall toward the church. Short of following him around all day, she didn't know how anyone could keep the old fellow from indulging. She switched on the nave lights and hauled the oak door open. If a heart attack and a quadruple bypass couldn't convince him to—

Quentan Nichols was standing in the center aisle.

Clare froze. Behind her, the heavy door whispered closed. Despite the soaring space, the thick stone walls of St. Alban's seemed to close in around her. Lois was running errands on her lunch hour. Mr. Hadley was in the undercroft. No one would hear her if she screamed.

Nichols took a step toward her. Frowned. She tensed, ready to bolt for the hall.

"Major Fergusson?" His voice was uncertain. He took another step toward her. "I mean, Reverend Fergusson?"

Clare nodded. Cleared her throat. "Chief Nichols. I'm . . ." *Surprised* didn't begin to cover it. "What are you doing here?"

"It is you." He relaxed, which wasn't the relief it might have been, since he seemed to be all muscle. He was in mufti—khakis and a turtleneck sweater. "You look different." He touched his throat. "I mean, beyond the collar and all."

"I'm growing my hair out." *Idiot.* The man was a possible killer, a probable thief, and likely absent without leave as well. And she was talking about her hair. "There are several people here. In the offices. And I'm expecting a visitor any moment."

He held up his hands. "Whoa. I'm not gonna hurt you." He took one step, two, and as Clare rocked onto the balls of her feet, ready to run, he sat in the first pew. At the far side of the aisle. He spread his arms across the back of the pew and rested his hands over the smooth, dark wood. "I need your help."

Well. That, at least, was familiar. "Go on."

"You knew Tally."

"Yes, I did." She relaxed enough to take a more comfortable stance. "I don't know how you knew that, though."

"She told me about her therapy group. The doctor, the cop, the Marine and Episcopal priest." He shrugged. "I Googled 'Episcopal church in Millers Kill.' When I saw your name, I figured there's no way there are two woman priests who were also vets. Leastways not in a dinky town like this."

"Tally told you about her group."

"We talked, yeah. A couple times. I was—" He shook his head. "It's complicated. I don't know where to start."

"How about where you helped her steal a million dollars?"

"I didn't! I mean, yeah, I guess in a way I did." He looked ahead, at the stained glass triptych behind the high altar. Christus Victor. Christ, victorious over death and sin. "I didn't mean to."

This, too, was familiar. A person sitting opposite her, talking around and over and between the problem, taking his time because getting to the point meant getting to the pain. She sighed. Sat down in the pew on the near side of the aisle. Faced Nichols, her hands relaxed and open. Listening. "Tell me about when you met Tally."

He smiled a little. "It was my second tour. Hers, too. I was stationed at Balad. After the insurgency took hold, it was the most secure airfield in the country. Crazy busy. Planes flying in from everywhere, day and night. Everybody in the world passing through—reporters and security contractors and politicians. I saw that guy from *The Daily Show* once. Anyway, Tally's company was staging out of there. They had a construction project going, shoring up some old buildings. Tally told me it was going to be the in-country version of a Federal Reserve Bank. She was going back and forth between Balad and Camp Anaconda, which was stressing her big-time."

Clare nodded. Ground travel was tense. Taking long trips over the same highways, you figured every time you didn't get blown up just brought you closer to the time you would.

"We met at the club. She asked me if I knew where she could get some booze, and she just about died when I told her I was a cop." He glanced at Clare's collar. "We, um, started spending time together. You know."

"Uh-huh." She wondered where Wyler McNabb fit into the picture. "Did she ever mention her husband?"

"She said he was a civilian." He shrugged. "At the start, I didn't care. I mean, people were jumping in and out of the sack all the time. Nobody checking for rings. By the end"—he tilted his head back—"I pretty much convinced myself he was history." He looked at her. Smiled humorlessly. "To look at me, you wouldn't think I could get played so bad, would you?"

"She asked you to do something for her."

"Oh, yeah." He heaved a breath. "She did. Asked me to keep my patrol away from a storage building. Tell my team anything they saw around one of the hangars was authorized. For one day. That should have been the tip-off it was something big. People smuggle in booze or dope or other contraband, they've got drops. Regular customers. A supply chain. One-off, that's got to be something big."

"You didn't know what was going on?"

"I didn't *want* to know." He bent over, resting his elbows on his knees. "Jesus help me. She could have been smuggling those WMDs out of the country. I didn't want to know."

"So then what happened?"

"Nothing. The finance building got finished, and she went back to Anaconda for good. We e-mailed and IM'd back and forth as much as we could." He gave her a challenging look. "It wasn't just sex. She was really easy to talk to. I felt like—like she got me, you know? Even though she was from this pissant little town in upstate New York and I'm from Chicago. Like those differences didn't matter at all."

"I know." Did she ever. "When did you start to think there was something more than just a romance going on?"

"When she shipped home. All of a sudden, she's not answering my e-mails, she's not taking my calls. I knew she was separating, and I thought maybe the readjustment to civilian life was hitting her hard. I had leave after I cycled back stateside, so I decided to come out here and talk to her in person."

"Which is where you and I met."

"Yeah." He paused for a long moment. "After that's when I started looking into what actually happened. It took a while, because I wasn't officially investigating and I wanted to keep things on the down low."

"To avoid incriminating yourself?"

"Hell, yeah. She already made an idiot out of me. I didn't want to lose my career, too."

"So you found out she had gotten away with a million dollars."

"The building I was supposed to keep my patrols away from was a transshipping facility, right next to the airfield. Usually, any cash coming in would have been secured, but this stuff was transiting, off one Herky Bird and onto another within a few hours."

"Do you know how she moved it?"

He shook his head. "There were quite a few finance people at the base. She might have gotten help there. Or who knows, maybe she had a string of guys she was playing along. One with a forklift, another with a truck."

Clare rubbed her arms. "That doesn't sound like Tally."

"Yeah. Well. She had friends. It was her second tour. She knew people."

"I take it you don't know where the money is right now?"

He gave her a look. "Would I be here asking for help if I did?"

Clare spread her hands. "What sort of help are you looking for, Chief? What do you want? The money? Revenge? You want to find out who killed her?"

He frowned. "I thought she killed herself."

Clare made a noise. "Officially, yes."

"You think—oh, God. Yeah. If somebody was trying to get her out of the way." He closed his eyes. Opened them. "Will I sound like a sick bastard if I say that would be a relief? I called her just a couple days before she died to tell her the investigation had been taken away from me. I thought maybe the news—"

"Wait. She knew about the investigation?"

"That's why I'm here. I was putting together the pieces, slow, like I told you. I had a pretty good idea of what she'd done. I figured she doctored the manifests, so the paperwork that came from stateside matched the paperwork from inside the theater and the numbers all lined up. Nobody checks against the originals if they think they have authentic copies in hand, right?"

"I guess."

"I needed to see the original invoices. The ones that were generated stateside. U.S. Army Finance Command has a small group of MPs and CIDs attached—specialists in fraud and financial crimes and all that. I made the request through them. A week goes by, and then two weeks. Then I get a surprise visit in person from Colonel Arlene Seelye."

Clare blinked. "She's the one who's here, investigating the missing funds."

"She asks me to turn over everything I have on the case, which was weird, because I hadn't put any other info on my request form. Then she says she's taking over the investigation. I'm thinking I'm screwed, that somehow she's been able to figure out I was the guy who looked the other way and let it happen. So I handed over my stuff and sat down to wait for the arrest. The next day—two weeks ago—I was reassigned to Fort Gillem. Courtesy of Colonel Arlene Seelye."

Clare frowned. "That doesn't make any sense."

"That's what I thought. I went back and forth, trying to figure out the right thing to do. About telling Tally or not." He propped his elbows on his knees and stared at the floor. "Up to that point, I guess I was still hoping there was going to be some way I could have my cake and eat it, too. Get the money back without Tally taking the fall. At the end, I called her. Told her I'd been working on an investigation. Told her what I found." He glanced up at Clare. "I warned her that there was a CID finance investigator on her trail. The next thing I heard . . ."

"She was dead."

"Yeah."

They both sat with that in silence for a while. Finally, Clare said, "I still don't understand Colonel Seelye's actions. If she knew you were involved, why not place you in custody? And if she didn't know, why didn't she ask you to back her up, since you knew about the investigation? The only other guy she's got here is a buck-green private."

"Huh." He sat up again. "I figured at first she wanted the cred for the discovery all to herself. Policing in the army isn't all that different than policing on the outside when it comes to being judged on the number of collars you make or the cases you clear. Then I got to thinking. Nobody else in my chain of command knew what I was doing, and if she's the one who fielded my request for information, nobody else in her unit knows about the missing money, either."

"That sounds consistent with not wanting to give anyone else credit for the arrest."

"Yeah—but I think she's after more than a nice write-up from her superiors. I think she's after the money."

"You mean . . . for herself. To keep." Clare sat back in her pew. She stared at the reredos behind the high altar, at the dozens of saints and angels carved into the fine-grained mahogany. "Tally died last Wednesday."

"Yeah?"

"Stephen Obrowski, the innkeeper at the Stuyvesant Inn, said Colonel Seelye checked in Wednesday evening. He said she was upset there hadn't been any other accommodations available." If she had thought about it before, she would have passed it off as the normal annoyance of someone who was going to have to explain blowing her travel budget to the quartermaster. She would have missed the other implication. "Her trip was so spur-of-the-moment, she didn't take time to make any reservations." She turned to Nichols. "What if she came here to confront Tally? To see if she could force the location of the money out of her? Maybe she went too far. Or maybe she scared Tally into telling her and then decided to get rid of her." She stood up. "You stay here."

Nichols got up from his pew, frowning. "Where are you going?"

"To tell the chief of police that he can't rule Tally's death a suicide just yet."

◆ ◆ ◆

Entering the Kreemy Kakes diner, Russ spotted Clare in what he thought of as her usual spot, the red vinyl banquette against the wall, the wide window behind her showing the granite-and-marble facade of Allbanc and an unusual number of pedestrians on Main Street. Tourists, enjoying the last week of prime fall foliage.

She was in her clericals, of course, rosy-cheeked in the heat from the crowd. She was finally putting on some weight again, and it looked good on her. Real good. *Down, boy.* Russ dropped his jacket over the back of a chair and sat.

"Hey," he said.

"Hey."

He reached across the red-tiled table. "I'm sorry."

"I am, too." She took his hand. "Friends?"

He grinned. "Among other things."

Erla Davis appeared at his side, menus in one hand and a pot of coffee in the other. "Well, howdy, strangers!" She beamed at Clare, then at Russ. "It does my heart good to see you two back in the old spot. Reverend, you still partial to a cup?"

Clare turned her mug over. "Erla, I'll be partial to your coffee three days after I'm dead."

The waitress eyed Russ as she filled Clare's cup. "I heard you two are getting married the end of this month. Never saw *that* one coming."

Russ laughed.

Erla served up his coffee and then tapped the large plastic sheets against the table. "You need to look at the menu?"

"I'll have the chili, please," Clare said.

"Reuben with fries."

"That's what I like," Erla said. "Folks that know what they want without shilly-shallying." She winked like a burlesque performer and whisked away, menus in hand.

Clare leaned forward, but instead of making a joke, she said, "Quentan Nichols is here. In town."

The clatter and conversation in the Kreemy Kakes diner created a kind of homey white noise, loud enough to keep a private discussion private, soft enough to hear the person across the table. "Huh," he said. "Okay. It looks like I really do owe you an apology." He rubbed his lips. "I'd better tell Seelye." Then the meaning of her statement caught up with his brain. "Wait. How do you know he's in Millers Kill?"

"He's at St. Alban's, right now."

"Oh, for chrissakes, Clare—" Erla appeared again with their order. "'Scuse my French," he said as she unloaded the thick china dishes. He waved away the waitress's offer to bring them anything else. "Nichols may not have killed Tally, but he sure as hell has his hands dirty." He shoved against the table and stood up. "I'm going to take him into custody for questioning."

"Sit down."

The steel in Clare's command voice dropped his ass back into his chair before he could think about it. "Ma'am, yes ma'am."

"Oh, cut it out. I just want you to hear me out before you run off half-cocked."

"Right. Wouldn't want to do anything without assessing all the information and thinking it through carefully."

She gave him a look. "Listen. Nichols admits he enabled the theft by steering his patrols away from the transit warehouse where the money was stored." She dug her spoon into her chili. "He says he didn't know what she was doing and he didn't want to know. He thought it was all love's sweet bliss until she got back stateside and dropped him like a hot rock."

"More like a hot million," he said around a bite of his sandwich.

"After he came here to try to see her—that was the night I got home, you remember?"

He smiled slowly. She pinked up. "Yes, well. Anyway, after that, he decided to figure out what it was, exactly, that he had done for her back at Balad Air Base. He spent a month or two digging around and figured out she must have altered the invoices coming from the States to hide the theft. So he sent a request in to USAFINCOM's attached investigators, asking them for copies of the original invoices. Guess who shows up in person?"

"Colonel Arlene Seelye?"

She frowned. "Yes, Arlene Seelye. She confiscates all the stuff he's amassed in the course of his investigation, tells him she's taking over, and then—get this!—has him transferred to Fort Gillem."

He had a good idea where this was going, but he let her spin it out.

"*She's* after the money. For herself." Clare emphasized her point with her spoon, dropping a blob of chili on her paper place mat.

He finished chewing a bite of Reuben. Wiped his mouth. "Did he happen to say why he showed up at your church?"

"I was the only one of the therapy group he could track down. He needs help if he's going to find the money before she does."

Russ held up his hands. "I want you to repeat that last sentence to yourself. Tell me what it sounds like."

"He's not going to *keep* it!"

He looked at her steadily. She bit the corner of her lip. "He's going to keep it?" Sighed. "He's going to keep it." Then she frowned. "Wait, what about Colonel Seelye transferring him? That's way too easy to be checked. He couldn't have made that up, could he?"

"If I were running this investigation, and I suspected an MP of involvement in the crime, but didn't have enough evidence to charge him, the first thing I'd do would be to contain him. So he can't muck up any evidence or help out his co-conspirators." He shoved the last bite of his sandwich into his mouth. Clare stared into her coffee, still frowning. Probably trying to figure out a way to redeem Nichols. He felt himself smiling like an idiot around the bread and pastrami.

Clare raised her eyebrows at him. "What?"

He swallowed. "Just you." He stood up and pulled out his wallet. "C'mon. I want to talk to this guy."

"Russ. He came to me for help. I told him to wait in the parish hall. I can't lead the local police in to clap him in irons."

"I think we've been over the fact that the church as sanctuary doesn't fly in the twenty-first century." They had had this same lunch so many times he didn't have to see the bill to know the total and tip. He tossed the money onto the table and stood aside to let Clare out. "Besides. If Nichols is still there, I will wear a kilt to the wedding."

Nichols wasn't in the sanctuary. Nor in the sacristy, the parish hall, or the undercroft. He had picked up a great deal about church architecture for a nonreligious man, Russ realized.

"Sorry, Clare." They surprised her secretary eating freeze-dried tuna out of a pouch. "He must have left before I got back from lunch." She waved her plastic fork. "Obviously not lunch-lunch. I was running errands. I found a great dress for your wedding, and I'm getting it altered. It was a size six. A little bit too big." She beamed. "Hi, Russ."

"Hi, Lois."

"A little bit too big, Lois? Really?"

The secretary smiled smugly.

In her office, Clare tossed her coat onto her battered love seat and flung herself into her desk chair. "Dang it!" She tilted back with a creak and a snap. "What are you going to do now?"

He leaned against the tall bookcases lining one wall. "I'm going to call his command and find out if he's unauthorized absence. If he is, they'll have people after him. Then I'll tell Seelye. Based on what he told you, he's definitely an accessory. If she wants, we'll put a BOLO on him."

"What about her?"

"What do you mean?"

"Nichols may be after the money for himself. I'm willing to accept that."

"Gee, thanks."

She frowned at him. "There's still the matter of Colonel Seelye. She found out about the theft, got Nichols out of the way, and hightailed it here, conveniently just after Tally was found dead."

"What are you saying? Are you trying to implicate Seelye in McNabb's death?"

"The timing works. She doesn't have any airtight alibi. She could have—"

"Okay, first"—Russ held up one finger—"Tally McNabb committed suicide. All the physical evidence points to that conclusion. There is *no* evidence supporting any other conclusion. Second"—he held up another finger—"Colonel Seelye's a CID investigator chasing down the theft of one million dollars. Of course she hightailed it over here. What do you think she'd do? Sit on her ass until Tally McNabb finished laundering the money?"

"Exactly!" Clare sprang her chair forward, jumping to her feet. "One million dollars! Which is up for grabs now that Tally McNabb is out of the way."

"Oh, for chrissakes. Will you give it a rest already?"

She strode toward him, her cheeks flushed, her hazel eyes glinting brown. He wanted to shake her shoulders until she dropped this fact-free victim fantasy she'd dreamed up for Tally McNabb. He wanted to strip her naked and fling her on the lumpy love seat and not let her up until he had wrung them both dry. How could one woman make him so batshit crazy?

She stopped maybe two inches away, close enough for him to feel the heat she was throwing off. "You're wrong," she said. "You're wrong, and I'm going to prove it."

"Do *not* go chasing after Nichols on your own, Clare. You don't know what he's after or what he's capable of."

"I can take care of myself. As I've told you."

"Is that the deal? Either I knuckle under and drive an investigation in the direction you want, or you put yourself in danger? Is that how you're going to get your way when we're married? Forget about talking things out and making compromises, just go straight for the nuclear option?"

Her face went pale. She turned. Opened her office door. Pointed toward the hall.

"Clare. For God's sake. I don't want to fight like this." He put his hands on her shoulders. "Please, love. I don't understand why this is so important to you."

Her face wavered. He pulled her toward him. She resisted for a second, then collapsed against him. He wrapped his arms tight around her. "Why can't you trust me on this? Why can't you let it go?"

"It's all wrong." Her voice was muffled against his chest, but he realized she was crying. "It's all gone wrong, and I have to make it right."

He had a sick feeling that she wasn't talking about Tally McNabb. Not talking about Tally McNabb at all.

THURSDAY, OCTOBER 13   Hadley's notes for the morning briefing were about as abbreviated as she could get. *1. Tourists in town. 2. Check kiting IGA. 3. B and E 52 MacEachron Hill Rd. Cossayuharie, interrupted, no loss.* She wrote more detailed grocery lists. Well, this was all penny-ante stuff. There was only one really big case going on in Millers Kill right now, and it wasn't even theirs.

"I've been trying to get hold of Colonel Seelye, the Army CID who's heading up their investigation. I've left her a couple of messages on her cell." The chief squared his boots on the chairs again. "Here's the deal. The theft from the army isn't technically in our jurisdiction, as you all know."

Hadley glanced at Flynn, who looked disappointed. The man was way too invested in policing. He needed a hobby.

"However. Both Wyler McNabb and Quentan Nichols, whom some of you will remember"—he nodded at Hadley and Flynn—"are in town right now. Nichols has admitted to direct involvement with the theft, and it's a sure bet McNabb has some knowledge of it."

"Wait a minute." Lyle MacAuley rousted himself from his usual slumped posture against the whiteboard. "How do we know Nichols is back in town?"

The chief rubbed the back of his neck. "He came to St. Alban's looking for Clare. Asked her to help him find the money."

"I'll be damned. Where is he now?"

The chief shrugged. "Your guess is as good as mine. I faxed his name and description around to area hotels and motels last night before I left. Nothing yet."

"That guy is better at disappearing than a bowl of shrimp at the all-you-can-eat buffet. You sure he's not really a Green Beret or something?"

"I'm more worried about him reappearing. In Wyler McNabb's driveway." The chief pointed at Hadley. "Knox, I want you and Kevin to go by there and pick him up for questioning. I was willing to wait for Seelye, but she's dragging her tail. I want to find out what he knows *before* something bad happens."

Hadley felt her face heating up. He knew she had lied. He didn't trust her to pick up the guy by herself.

"Both of us?" Flynn asked. "I didn't think he was in any shape to put up a fight."

"I'm not worried about him resisting arrest. I'm worried about him being alone with an officer and no witness to say what happened or didn't happen. I don't want to give McNabb an opportunity to lodge a false complaint on top of the real one he's got going." The chief pinched the bridge of his nose beneath his glasses.

"What do we do if Colonel Seelye is already there?" Hadley asked. "She's going for a warrant to search the place, right?"

"If she's there, tell her unless she's immediately placing McNabb under arrest, we're taking him in for protective custody. She can come over to the station and question him here." He slid off the table and thudded to the floor. "That's all. Lyle?"

Kevin drove. She took shotgun. It was the first time they'd been alone together in at least a week. So of course, he led off with "What happened with you and Eric at this guy's house?"

"You know what happened. The guy swung at Eric, they got into it, eventually the perp was subdued."

"Right into the hospital. You know, I might have bought that story—*might* have—if I hadn't seen Eric go medieval on that emergency room doctor."

She looked out the window. "It doesn't matter to me what you believe. I made my statement. It's on the record. I'm not changing it."

"Hadley. Jesus. You're not a coward."

She turned on him. "Eric McCrea is a red-white-and-blue, yellow-ribbon war hero, Flynn. He's been on the force for nine years, and everybody knows if MacAuley retires, he's getting the deputy chief's slot. I'm the girl. The *new* girl. Who's going to get burned if I turn him in?"

"I'd back you up!"

She smiled a little. "I know. I knew. Now tell me who else will."

"The chief. He suspended Eric on the spot, and he'd stand by you against anyone in the department."

"Yeah, and what happens when he's not around? You know MacAuley and Noble and the other guys are Code Blue, all the way. I heard about what happened to the guy who was here before me. He got frozen out because he called the state police in on a murder case. He had to leave town to get another job!"

"Mark Durkee." Flynn shifted in his seat. "That was different."

"No, it wasn't. Let it go, Flynn. I made my choice, and I'll live with it."

His hand tightened on the steering wheel. "I just hate to see you forced to compromise yourself."

She almost whooped. "Compromise myself?" She leaned back into the seat. "Flynn, you're a world too late to stop that from happening."

He opened his mouth as they drove into view of the McNabbs' house. The driveway was empty, both her Navigator and his Escalade gone. Flynn changed whatever he had been about to say into "In the garage?"

"There wasn't room last time. Let's check."

They parked. She peered into the garage. He banged on the door. They both turned up empty.

"Now what?" Hadley said over the hood of the squad car.

"Could he be at work?"

"I don't think he'd be physically able to after—" She couldn't say it. "What happened. I'll check. Do you still have your notes from the interviews we did right after the suspicious death?"

Flynn brandished his pocket-sized notebook.

She pulled her cell phone out of her pocket. "Okay. I'll call BWI while you drive to the closest friend's house. He's gotta be around somewhere." She didn't have to point out that McNabb wasn't well enough to take off for another casino vacation.

The BWI Opperman receptionist transferred her to the construction department, where she hung out on hold for two minutes, three, four, while boring classical music tried to lull her into a stupor. "God." She turned to Flynn. "They must be hauling some poor guy off his bulldozer to talk to me."

The line went live. "Hi! What can I do you for?" The man was shouting over the sound of machinery grinding in the background. Her guess about the work site must have been correct.

"I'm looking for Wyler McNabb." She tried not to raise her own voice. "Is he working today?"

"Naw, he's off for a few weeks. Try him at home." The line went dead.

She stared at her cell, frowning. "Talkative guy."

"Don't worry about it. At least we know he's not on the job." Flynn handed her the notebook. "Do me a favor. Figure out who on the list is closest to us if we strike out on the first contact."

The first person listed was a co-worker. When they got to the address, a small house on Meersham Street, the only person home was a harried wife with a baby on her hip and a toddler shrieking behind her. Her look of alarm melted into an expression of relief when they asked about McNabb. "Don't know, and don't care," she said. "We didn't move in the same circles."

The next person on Flynn's list was labeled "drinking buddy." He lived in a much rattier house on South Street, and his expression wasn't so much alarm as it was sullen suspicion. He, too, looked relieved when they asked about McNabb, although in his case, Hadley figured it was relief that they weren't after him.

"I dunno where he is. I heard he was feeling pretty lousy." The drinking buddy rubbed his chin. "I wonder if he mighta gone to Tally's mom's house? She's a LPN. What with Tally being gone, she mighta taken him home for a little whaddaya call it."

"TLC?" Flynn said.

"Yeah. They always got on well. Mrs. Walters is pretty laid-back. Not like Wyler's mom." He shuddered.

Hadley glanced at Flynn. It sounded like a solid lead. "What's her address?" she asked.

"Fifty-two MacEachron Hill Road. Up in Cossayuharie."

Hadley kept her face neutral while Flynn thanked the guy. They got back into the cruiser. Buckled up. Pulled away from the curb. As soon as Hadley was sure she couldn't be seen, she turned to Flynn. "Did you hear that? The same place with the B and E last night!"

He grinned at her. "Oh, man. Maybe we'll have a major theft fall right in our laps."

"You know what the chief says."

"I don't believe in coincidence," they chorused.

Flynn's notes had more details than hers, including the complainant's name, Evonne Walters. Paul Urquhart had taken the call last night around eleven. A search of the area turned up nothing—knowing Paul, the search probably consisted of him waving his flashlight around the yard—and the complainant believed nothing had been taken. There hadn't been any mention of a connection to Tally McNabb, which didn't surprise her. She had heard Paul say that asking questions only led to more work.

They drove through fields and woodlots as they wound their way up MacEachron Hill Road. Most of the residences they passed were slightly sagging farmhouses, where solid nineteenth-century construction managed to keep the worst ravages of time and poverty at bay. Tally McNabb's mother's house, on the other hand, looked like something out of *Traditional Homes* magazine. The roof was so new it gleamed like fresh blacktop in July; the deep, wide gutters emptied into neat gravel beds; the windows were period reproduction, with built-in storms and freshly painted shutters.

"Geez," Flynn said.

Hadley nodded. "Unless LPNs get paid a lot more than I thought, I think we know where some of the stolen loot went."

They got out of the cruiser. At the door—also recently painted, with bright hardware and a fancy, chime-playing bell—Flynn stepped back, letting Hadley take point.

The woman who answered looked as if she belonged in one of those other houses—shabby, weathered, but with strong bones. She blinked at them. "May I help you?"

"Ms. Walters? I'm Officer Knox of the Millers Kill Police, and this is Officer Flynn. May we come in?"

"I already talked with one of your officers last night." Even as she spoke, the woman opened the door wider and made space for them. "There wasn't anything missing. I was more scared'n anything else." Flynn tucked his hat beneath his arm as she ushered them into the kitchen. "I guess you always think nothing bad can happen out here in the country. Tally told me I ought to get a security alarm, living out here on my own." Her voice cracked.

"I'm so sorry for your loss," Hadley said. "I can't imagine anything worse than the death of a child."

The woman nodded. Glanced at Hadley's ringless finger. "You have children?"

"Two. A boy and a girl."

There was a clatter on the stairs, and a young man in his late teens or early twenties loped into the kitchen. "Ma? What's going on?"

"My youngest, Danny. These officers came about the break-in."

"Did you find out who did it already?"

Hadley shook her head. "It's under investigation. Are you the only other person living here, Danny?"

"I don't live here. I'm a sophomore at Kenyon. In Ohio."

His mother put her arm around him. "First in the family to go to college."

He hugged his mom back without embarrassment. Hadley liked that. "I was planning on heading back this weekend, but I hate to leave Ma alone with this hanging over her head."

"Danny's worried it might'a been one of those crazy people who thinks God kills soldiers 'cause we got gay people in the USA."

Hadley decided to fudge a bit. "We think it's more likely someone who read that your daughter died and was hoping to steal some valuables in the confusion. It happens sometimes." The first time she had dealt with one—the burglary of a house left empty for a funeral—she had thought a human being couldn't go much lower.

Evidently Ms. Walters agreed with her. The woman's face screwed up in disgust. "Well, if that don't beat all."

"Did your daughter ever use your house for storage? Leave anything here for safekeeping?"

"When she was deployed, yes. I was the one kept her checkbook and paid what bills came due while she was in Iraq."

"Not her husband?" Kevin asked.

Mrs. Walters hesitated. "He's not so good with that sort of thing." She smiled a little. "Those two were together since tenth grade. Ten years later, Mary was still head-over-heels for Wyler. Never mind in some ways he's still in high school."

Danny made a face that suggested *he* minded his brother-in-law's immaturity.

"Anything else?" Hadley asked. "Other than the checkbook?"

"The cars," Danny said.

"Well, if the burglar was after the cars, he wun't too smart, now, was he? Looking in the house instead of the garage."

Flynn glanced at Hadley before looking at the Walterses. "What vehicles are you talking about?"

"Wyler and Tally's cars. They keep them—" Danny caught himself. "They kept them here when they were both overseas. Wyler and I brought them up here yesterday."

"I want you to have her SUV. It'll be a load off my mind to not have you driving halfway 'cross the country in that old beater of yours."

"Ma—"

"You brought both their cars here?" Hadley frowned. "Why?"

Danny looked at them. "Wyler's gone back over. To join the construction team in Iraq. He left yesterday."

◆ ◆ ◆

Clare hadn't intended to swing by the Stuyvesant Inn on the way back from the Infirmary. Her plan to fit in a short visit with two of her elderly parishioners expanded as she saw one senior that she knew, and then another, so that twenty minutes became an hour and a half of looking at photos and holding hands and listening to stories. Then the nursing director, Paul Foubert, had dragged her into his office to complain that she and Russ weren't registered anywhere and to unsubtly interrogate her about the perfect wedding gift.

"Nothing, Paul. We don't need anything. Make a donation to a good cause in our names if you have to do something."

"Hmph," he rumbled. "You only get married once, knock on wood. You ought to milk it for what it's worth."

When she finally emerged into sunshine and a brisk easterly wind, she realized she was never going to make the diocesan development committee lunch scheduled for noon in Schenectady. She had to admit giving up boxed sandwiches and a tedious meeting wasn't a hardship. Plus, she now had a legitimate couple of hours free before her afternoon counseling sessions.

She considered going back to the rectory for a nap. Trip's prescribed ten milligrams of Dexedrine was clearly a much lower dosage than she'd been taking out of her go-bag. She felt like she was wearing an overcoat of fatigue. Trip surely wouldn't call her in for a blood test this soon. He wouldn't know if she upped her dose for a day or two. She climbed behind the wheel of her Jeep and headed toward Millers Kill.

She thought about the therapy group. If she could get hold of Colonel Seelye, she could ask the others what they thought about the situation. Get their take on Quentan Nichols's surprise visit, too. He was obviously in it up to his neck, as Russ would say. In town and looking for his money. Which was . . . where? Who knew? Had Tally had someone helping her stateside? There must have been other people involved in Iraq, if only to move the cash from point A to point B. What if Nichols knew the other accomplice? Knew, and had struck a deal with him. Or them. After all, taking even one person out of the pool left considerably more money for everyone else to divide.

Clare drove over a hill and blinked at the sight of the Stuyvesant Inn. She had driven the entire way on autopilot. So much for her vaunted observational skills—and so much for her nap. She turned into the drive and pulled into one of two empty parking places. The leaf peepers must have decamped to the city.

The inn's enormous maple was half-stripped of leaves, the remainder looking like the tattered red pennants of a defeated army. The wind across the valley, which cooled the sprawling Victorian all summer long, was a cold slice against her back as she got out of her car.

The door opened while she was climbing the porch steps. "You must be psychic," Ron Handler said. "We just got another fax from your mother." He stepped to one side and let her into the wide front hall.

"Lord help us." Clare shucked her jacket off. "What is it now?"

"Oh, a bunch of stuff. She wants to make sure we're coordinating with the baker and the patisserie. A rundown on the linens. She has a sketch of how she wants the presents displayed—what's a 'sip and see'?"

"A party for silver fetishists." She glanced at the hallway's étagère, where an authentic nineteenth-century feather bouquet bloomed eternally beneath a glass bell. "Don't worry about it, though. There aren't going to be any presents."

"I hate to burst your bubble, Your Reverence, but they're already arriving. Your mother's been forwarding the ones sent to your parents' house."

"Oh, for . . ." She scrubbed her hands over her face. Wished she had some cold water to splash there. "Look. I didn't actually come over here to discuss the reception. I was hoping to talk to Colonel Seelye. She never returned my phone messages."

"Rude, but not unexpected. I'm sorry, but she's gone."

"Any idea when she'll be back?"

Ron shook his head. "I mean she's gone. Checked out. Took her luggage, her car, and her life-sized GI Joe doll with her."

◆ ◆ ◆

Russ was negotiating the turn off of Route 57 when his cell phone rang. He picked it up without looking. "Van Alstyne here."

"Hey. It's me," Clare said.

"Hey, you. Are you feeling better?"

"I guess so." She paused. "I think I know why we've been so snippy with each other lately."

"Snippy" wasn't the word he would have used, but what the hell. "Why?"

"Because we're not having sex."

He grinned. "I sure am thinking about it a lot, if that's any consolation."

"Oh, yeah? What sort of things are you thinking about?"

"Stop that. Are you calling about Nichols?"

"What? No. Why?"

"Didn't you get my message?"

"No. Sorry. I didn't check before I called you. What's going on?"

"Wyler McNabb has flown the coop. He left his car with his in-laws and told 'em he was off to join the BWI Opperman construction team in Iraq."

"Wasn't he out on bail?"

"Uh-huh."

"With a broken cheekbone?"

"Plus a hairline fracture in his skull."

"And they let him go to a construction site in a war zone?" Clare's voice carried all the disbelief his had when Knox and Flynn had reported in.

"That's what I'm about to find out. I called the construction depot in Plattsburgh, but the guy there didn't know anything except that the monthly flight to Iraq left yesterday evening. All the operations-level stuff is handled at headquarters. I'm headed for the Algonquin Waters to get the truth out of somebody."

"I'm at the Stuyvesant Inn. I'll meet you there."

"No. Do *not* go to the resort. I don't want you anywhere near there if you can help it."

"Why were you calling about Nichols?"

He hissed frustration as he swung his squad car onto the Sacandaga Road. "Clare, I mean it. I don't want you—"

"Oh, honestly, Russ, you're not going up against a terrorist cell holding the hotel with guns and explosives. You're going to ask the human resources manager if they authorized McNabb to get on their plane. I think I can survive the danger. I'll see you over there." She hung up.

He swore under his breath. The wedding, which she had just been complaining about, was in nine days. She was carrying her usual overfull schedule at St. Alban's. On top of it all, he knew, despite her being less than forthcoming about therapy, that she was still struggling with her experiences in Iraq. So what does she do? Go chasing after Tally McNabb's nonexistent killer.

He switched his light bar on and stepped on the gas when he hit the resort's road, causing a car speeding down the mountain to brake hard enough to spew dirt and leaf mold into the air. He was going to have to lobby the aldermen to install a traffic light on the Sacandaga Road, or sooner or later there was going to be another fatality like this summer's. Of course, the aldermen, who liked spending money as much as Clare liked sitting quietly at home, would make him choose: traffic control or a new officer's position.

He saw Clare's ratty old Jeep as soon as he drove into the parking lot. That was another thing on his list. The first weekend after they were married he was marching her over to Fort Henry Ford and buying her a reliable four-wheel drive with all-weather tires and side-door air bags.

She hopped out of her clunker when he got out of the cruiser. She tugged a wool cardigan over her clerical blouse. "So why were you calling me about Nichols?"

He zipped his jacket up. "I wanted to ask you if you had any idea where he might be. If he said anything to you. Why are you so keen on Wyler McNabb's whereabouts?"

She looked up at him. "I told you. I think Tally McNabb was killed for a million dollars. I want to find out everything I can about the money, because if I know that, I'll know who murdered her."

It came to him as he spoke the words. "You know, distracting yourself by playing private eye won't make the bad stuff in your head go away."

She opened her mouth. Shut it. "Is that why you became an MP? Because focusing on other people's problems helped you ignore your own?"

His breath hitched in his chest. Jesus. Sometimes she pulled truth out of him like a magician conjuring scarves. Then he saw her eyes, wide and white-edged, and realized she was feeling the same way he was right now. Because he had done the same thing to her. Truth for truth. He took her hand, holding her palm open as if he could see the future there. "You know what's scary about being with you?"

She shook her head.

"There's not anyplace to hide. For either of us."

She smiled a little. "You chickening out?"

"Not a chance." He started for the hotel's entrance. She fell into step beside him.

"So," she said. "Nichols."

"I figure there are three possibilities behind McNabb's disappearance. One, he really was shipped off to Iraq as a BWI contractor."

"That sounds flat-out strange to me."

"Yeah. Two, he told people he was going to Iraq on a job and skipped town for places unknown."

"Let me guess the third. Nichols took him out in a bid to be the last man standing."

"Like you said, a million bucks is a powerful incentive to murder."

They thumped through one of the revolving doors and crossed to the gleaming reception desk. A cute young woman with dark hair perked up at them. "Welcome to the Algonquin Waters Spa and Resort, Reverend. Chief."

Clare's title was self-evident, but how had she known he was—he spotted her first name pinned to her chest. "Christy McAlistair," he said.

"Yup. It's Christy Stoner now, though."

He knew Wayne and Mindy Stoner's boy had gotten married between deployments, but he hadn't put that fact together with the name on the Bain accident report. "How are you doing?" He glanced at her trim waistline. "Everything, uh, okay?"

"You mean after the accident? I'm fine. Zachary—our baby boy?— came early, but he was already almost six pounds, so my OB said it was probably just as well he was born at seven months." She laughed. "Then— because the driver who caused the accident had been working up here?— Mr. Opperman offered me a job. Wasn't that amazingly nice of him?"

Amazingly smart of him to avoid a lawsuit. Ellen Bain had been drinking at the lobby bar before taking her fatal drive.

"Zach and I are living with my parents while Ethan's in Afghanistan, so everything I earn can go toward a down payment on a house when he gets out of the marines."

"You're Ethan Stoner's wife." Clare put the pieces together.

Christy's eyes lit up. "Do you know Ethan?"

"We haven't met, formally. I know of him."

The girl laughed again. "Yeah, he was kind of wild when he was young. He's settled down now."

Clare glanced at him, and he knew just what she was thinking. *When he was young?* For all that she was a wife and mother, Christy Stoner looked to him like she ought to be cheering on the Minutemen football team. God, he was old.

"Well." The voice behind him was as smooth as a well-oiled gun. "What have we here? The Church and the State. Together." Russ and Clare turned around. Opperman's mouth curved up as he looked at them. "How unconstitutional."

"Oh! I'm sorry," Christy said. "I didn't know you were waiting for them, Mr. Opperman."

"That's all right, Christy." Opperman gestured toward the elevators. "My office is this way."

Russ threw out his arm, blocking Clare's way. He didn't want her anywhere near the resort's CEO. Irrational, but there it was. If he had kept Linda away from Opperman, she never would have gone to the Caribbean with the man, never would have been driving home from the resort in a blizzard, never would have died—and he never would have been marrying Clare, which brought him back to irrational. "We don't need to take up your time," he said. "I came here to speak to your HR director."

Opperman gazed at him coolly. "It's no bother. I should be able to answer anything you might ask her."

"Look, I just need to know—"

"Let's not keep our paying guests from the desk." Opperman strolled across the expansive lobby toward a riverstone fireplace big enough to roast an ox in. The small fire burning in its center made it look like the entrance to a prehistoric cave. Opperman sat in one of a group of chairs clustered to the side of the hearth. He held out his hand toward the remaining chairs.

Russ grudgingly sat down. Clare settled beside him.

"You just need to know . . ." Opperman began.

"If Wyler McNabb was transferred to your operation in Iraq."

"Yes. Employees working on the Provisional Authority contract are on a six-month cycle, six months in-country, six months at home. Wyler returned in mid-April, and so . . ." He spread his hands. His nails were clean and shining.

"Were you aware Wyler McNabb was out on bail?"

Opperman's eyebrows went up. "I was not. What are the charges?"

"Resisting arrest and assaulting an officer."

Opperman nodded. "Does he have a trial date?"

"Sometime in January."

"We have a monthly flight to and from Balad Airport. If you let us know the exact date, I'll have the crew supervisor make sure he's on it in time to make his appearance."

"Just like that."

"Even highly skilled construction workers tend to be, shall we say, rough around the edges. This isn't the first time one of my employees has been extra-jurisdiction, and it won't be the last." He placed his hands on the chair's arms and prepared to rise. "If that's all—"

"Were you aware McNabb was released from the hospital five days ago with several broken bones in his face?"

The hands relaxed. "I was not."

Russ waited, but Opperman didn't seem to have anything else to say. "Don't you have some sort of basic health requirement for your construction workers?"

"I'm moved by your concern, Chief Van Alstyne. Since you seem so much better informed than I, perhaps you can tell me how Wyler was injured."

Russ tried to keep the tension out of his voice. "As I said, he assaulted an officer and resisted arrest."

"And as a result, someone in your police department smashed his skull in?" Opperman shook his head. "Funny. You see it in the news, but you don't expect something like that in a small town like Millers Kill." He laced his fingers together and looked straight at Russ. "I hope this is an isolated incident of police brutality. The tourism-dependent businesses in this area can't afford to have their customers frightened of the very men and women they rely on for protection."

A scalding cloud of shame and rage surrounded Russ, burning his chest and face, tightening his throat. Clare laid her hand on his arm. "Mr. Opperman, have you met Lieutenant Colonel Seelye? She's an Army CID investigator."

Opperman blinked at her. Then looked at Russ. "Are you delegating your work to the clergy these days?"

"It's a simple yes or no question," Clare said. "Have you met the colonel?"

"Yes." Opperman's voice was short. "I met with Arlene Seelye a day or two ago. She was investigating something to do with the unfortunate Tally McNabb, and she wanted to know what kind of employee Tally was."

"All right. Thank you." Clare got up. Russ frowned. He wasn't certain what she had been after, but he stood with her.

Opperman rose as well. He smiled broadly. "I understand you two are planning to get married." He captured Clare's hand in both of his and raised it almost to his lips. "I imagine you'll be a ravishing bride, Reverend."

Russ balled his hand into a fist to keep from reaching over and tearing out Opperman's throat. Clare snatched her hand away.

"I hope you'll consider the Algonquin for your reception," Opperman continued smoothly.

"We've already booked the Stuyvesant Inn." Russ's voice was harsh.

"Now that's a shame." Opperman looked at him regretfully. "You're settling for second best."

Clare went pale. Russ put his hand in the small of her back and steered her toward the hotel's entrance. "Come back anytime," Opperman called.

Walking out into the cold mountain air was like bathing in a clear, clean fountain after wading through muck. "Are you okay?" he said.

"Yeah." She twitched her shoulders, a movement that became a full-body shiver.

"I'm sorry. God." He wrapped his arm around her shoulder.

"He was playing you. When he almost kissed my hand? He was trying to stir you up."

"It worked." He kept his arm tight around her as they descended the steps to the parking lot.

"He knew about Wyler McNabb's injuries. Before you told him. It's unlocked," she said to his outstretched hand.

He opened the Jeep's door. "What makes you think that?"

She climbed into the driver's seat and swiveled to face him. "He didn't ask anything about Wyler's condition, or about how you knew. The only thing he asked was the one thing guaranteed to embarrass you and throw you off balance."

"Hmn." He braced his arm on top of her door and leaned forward. "Why'd you ask him about Arlene Seelye?"

"She's gone. I went to the Stuyvesant Inn to talk with her, and she had upped stakes. I wanted to know if she'd investigated Opperman first."

"Gone? Huh. Although if she got a lead on Tally stashing the missing loot elsewhere, there wouldn't be any reason for her to hang around. Especially at what the Stuyvesant charges for a room."

"Do you think Opperman is involved? I mean, Wyler McNabb was working for him, then he hired Tally."

"What, with the theft? I'd like to think so, because I can't stand the smug sonofabitch. I believe right down to the bottom he got control of that company by killing off his partners." He shook his head. "That was for high stakes. Huge money. To you and me and Tally, a million bucks would be life-changing, but to a guy like Opperman? It's a couple months' salary. Not worth the risk."

"Shame." She smiled a little. "He makes such a satisfying bad guy."

"He is a bad guy. Just not the one we want."

"Who is, then? Wyler McNabb? Are you going to try to get him back?"

"Extradite him from Iraq? Hell, no. I can't even *imagine* what kind of hoops I'd have to jump through for that."

"Oh, come on. He's got to be in on the theft."

"Agreed. Unfortunately, it's not my case. It's the army's. If Seelye wants him, she can try to reel him in. He's left town, and she's left town, and if there's a merciful God—"

"There is."

He smiled at her. "Then Quentan Nichols will also have left town. Let 'em all chase their money somewhere else. We've got more important things to do." He kissed her, slow and easy, an apology for mixing her up in this business. Pulled away and looked at her, her lips parted, her eyes half closed. He kissed her again, harder, wrapping one hand around the back of her head, the other tracing the barrier of her collar until he found the tiny button in the back. He twisted, tugged, and her neck was bare.

"Smooth," she gasped, as he put his teeth and tongue to her throat. The sound she made jacked him up even higher. Beneath his coat, she clutched at his shoulders, his chest, his sides. Even through his uniform blouse and undershirt, the bite of her fingers into his muscles sent electric jolts skittering over his skin. She took hold of his rig, pulling him closer, rattling the baton, clinking the magazine pouch.

"Damn." Her voice was husky. "This thing is worse than a chastity belt."

He broke off, panting, hard, and realized they were still in the Algonquin's parking lot. Any guests looking out their windows were going to see a lot more than foliage. "Shit." His own voice was pretty far gone, too. "I'm sorry." He laughed harshly. "So much for discretion."

She shook her head. "It's Opperman."

He reached down to adjust himself. "Darlin', I can guarantee you it's not Opperman did this to me."

"No, I meant—" She grinned at him. "Never mind. Come back to the rectory with me. I've got a couple of hours before my afternoon appointments."

"No."

"Your mother's place."

"*God,* no."

"Your truck."

He paused at that one. Sighed. "Regretfully, no. Nice idea, though." He searched her face for a safe spot and settled for kissing the tip of her nose. "I've got to get back to the station. Hold that thought."

◆ ◆ ◆

At his desk at the end of the afternoon, his vision blurring from the small print the state used on its crime stats reporting forms, his mind kept going back to Clare. Not the good stuff: He packed the image of Clare, nude and in his pickup, into a box labeled LATER. Instead, he thought about her exchange with Opperman. Something about it was sticking in his brain.

Lyle came in without knocking, which made him grateful he hadn't been sitting there trying to figure out how to fit a mattress in the bed of his truck.

"I finished the rest of the midmonth stuff we gotta send on to CADEA for you." Lyle tossed a folder on his already overcrowded desk before collapsing in the one chair still empty of booklets, bulletins, and circ sheets. "Kevin says in Syracuse they got two full-time civilian employees to deal with the paperwork. Think about that, will you?"

"First another officer. Then a second-shift dispatcher. Third, Tasers. A paper pusher comes fourth after that."

"Tasers." Lyle snorted. "When I started out, all you needed was a club. My first sergeant taught me how to break open hippies' heads with a nightstick. Good times." He sighed. "You find out anything about Wyler McNabb?"

"According to John Opperman, he was, in fact, sent back to Iraq to join the construction team. They get six months on, six off, and his time card was punched."

"With a busted jaw. Right."

"Opperman claimed he didn't know the guy was out on bail."

"You believe him?"

"I did at the time. Now I'm not so sure. I don't doubt Opperman could have sent McNabb off and lied about it just to make my life more difficult."

Lyle shrugged. "No skin off his nose. He's not the one posted bail."

"Yeah. Here's the thing. He said Arlene Seelye had interviewed him. Asked him about Tally McNabb." Russ crossed his arms on top of the drifts of paperwork. "Wouldn't she have also asked him about Wyler McNabb? He was her biggest lead. She knew he worked for BWI Opperman."

Lyle nodded. "Makes sense. I would've."

"But she also knew McNabb was under arrest."

"So she told Opperman. You already said he might have known, and sent the guy off to Iraq anyway. He doesn't care if he takes a dump on Seelye's investigation."

"Maybe, but think about it. He's got a lucrative contract with the army. Why would he chance jerking them around?"

"What chance? When was the last time somebody complained and got rid of Halliburton? Or Blackwater?"

"Those are the big boys. The T. rexes of the contracting world. Opperman's one of the little guys, comparatively speaking. He's got to make nice and deliver the goods and keep his accounts clean, because there are five other guys just like him waiting to take his place if he goes down."

"Then what? It can't be the money. Opperman's the CEO and majority stockholder of BWI Opperman. The damn company's estimated worth is five hundred million."

Russ raised his eyebrows. "And here I was, thinking you were just a pretty face."

"I read more'n *Guns and Ammo,* you know."

"I'm agreeing with you. A million's small potatoes for him." He folded his hands. "It's a hell of a lot for a lieutenant colonel, though."

"Seelye?"

"The way things played out doesn't make a lot of sense if she went in there asking questions like we would, right?"

Lyle made a noise of cautious assent.

"What if she never mentioned Wyler McNabb because she had already suborned him? Or because they were already accomplices? She was in Iraq. She told me so herself."

Lyle sat for a moment, his woolly eyebrows drawn down in thought. "That's a mighty thin thread to hang her on."

"What if I told you she left town yesterday? The same day Wyler McNabb did?"

"I'd say it's likely her investigation petered out here and she went after the next lead. We're talking cash, stolen overseas by a bookkeeper. It's probably sitting in an account in the Cayman Islands right now."

"Which is one of the reasons Seelye wanted to search McNabb's house so bad. We were just looking for evidence pointing to suicide. She's a financial crimes specialist. If there's anything to lead her to an offshore bank or some other money-laundering operation, she's going to find it at Tally's house. Or at her place of employment. Or at her family's or friends' houses." He reached for the phone. "Hang on. I want to check something out." He dialed the courthouse.

"H'lo Washington County Courthouse Lila Greuling speaking may I help you please."

"Lila, it's Russ Van Alstyne." When he had worked for her dad back in high school, he'd always let talkative little Lila follow him around, "helping." His patience with an eight-year-old paid off when she became a clerk of the court.

"Well, hel-lo, handsome. What can I do you for?"

"I'm looking to find out if Judge Ryswick issued a residence-and-accounts warrant on Wyler McNabb, 16 Musket Way, Millers Kill."

"Not through me, he didn't. When would this have been?"

"Sometime in the past week. The investigating officer was an army MP, but it might have come through the DA or the Feds."

"Lemme check with the other girls." The line went to music. She was back in less than a minute. "Last thing fitting that description came out of your own department on the thirteenth. Deputy Chief MacAuley got a warrant against Mary McNabb's Allbanc accounts."

"Okay. Thanks much, Lila." He hung up. "Seelye never searched the house."

"Legally," Lyle said.

"Or the accounts. A suspect has money hidden away. What's the first thing you do?"

"Search all the accounts I can find." Lyle rubbed his lips. "Damn, I wish I'da spread the net wider when we asked Ryswick for that first warrant."

Russ shook his head. "Not your fault. We didn't know McNabb had stolen the money at that point."

"We'll never get another warrant out of him. The case is in Seelye's jurisdiction, not ours." Lyle straightened in his chair. "Wait a minute. If she's looking for the money for herself, how come she didn't go ahead and search those accounts?"

"Maybe she already found out where it's hidden. She might have talked to McNabb. Or like you said, she could've searched his place illegally."

"Or she might have been behind the B and E at Tally McNabb's mom's place."

"Maybe. If she's dirty, everything's up for grabs."

"Your fingers are twitching."

Russ looked down to where his hands were resting atop paperwork. "Yeah?"

"You do that when you're trying to figure something out."

Russ sighed. "Yeah."

"Army property. Stolen in Iraq. No way it's our case." Lyle buffed his nails against his pants. "Officially."

"It's definitely not our case."

"So there's no call for us to do any investigating." Lyle looked up at him again. "Officially."

"Nope."

"It sure is interesting, though." Lyle grinned at him.

Russ found himself grinning back at his deputy chief. "It sure is that."

◆ ◆ ◆

Russ picked up and put down the telephone three times after Lyle left. He had been an MP for a long time, but he was a civilian cop now, and he knew the kind of runaround he would get if he tried to trace Colonel Seelye through the usual channels. If he was going to ignore his good sense and pursue this, he had to figure a different way in, but it was getting late, and his brain kept stalling out. The mental snapshot of Clare in his truck had become a motion picture, complete with interesting sound effects. He'd have thought after all those years of holding himself in check, he'd be able to do without for a few lousy weeks, but Jesus, he was going cross-eyed from wanting her.

The hell with it. He shelved the problem of the out-of-his-jurisdiction theft in favor of loading the pickup with quilts and driving over to Clare's place.

Unfortunately, when he got home he discovered a dead furnace, a rapidly cooling house, and a mother who had been waiting for him to play handyman.

"I'm sorry, Russell, but you know the repairman charges sixty dollars just to come out, let alone the cost of fixing up the old beast." His mom fussed around him as he disassembled the pilot light, looking for the problem. "You didn't have any plans, did you?"

"No, Mom, it's fine." He managed a quick call to Clare between flushing out the draw line and his trip to Tim's Hardware for new spark plugs. She commiserated with his oil-stained, thwarted lust, told him he was a good son, and then hammered the nail in his coffin when she said she was headed out the door to the Foyers' dinner, and no, she didn't expect to be home before ten or eleven.

As a result, he went to bed as frustrated physically as he had been mentally, and he woke up like a man who had been bitten by bedbugs, his involuntary abstinence transformed into an itch to find out the truth about Arlene Seelye.

It was an itch he didn't have a chance to scratch until after he had given the morning briefing and taken an A.M. patrol. He got back to the station at lunchtime, shut the door to his office, and tossed his lunch bag onto his desk.

He needed a favor. Who did he know who could help him? He had been out of the army for a decade now, an eternity in an organization where twenty years meant a career and the unwritten law was up or out—rise in the ranks or leave. He flipped through his ancient Rolodex, passing on one name and discarding another until he came to the card for Major Anthony Usher.

Tony Usher had been a raw WO1 when Russ took him under his wing during the brief, intense days of Desert Storm. Impressed by Usher's combination of careful attention to detail and sheer smarts, he boosted him into the ranks of the CID. After several years of solid investigative work, Usher decided his true calling was on the other side of the aisle. He applied for and was accepted to OCS and from there went on to law school. He'd been with the Judge Advocate General's Corps for three years now, and if he didn't know everyone involved in army law enforcement, he knew someone who knew someone.

Russ had copied Usher's latest contact information from the annual Christmas letter he got. He figured it was a fifty-fifty chance the man was at the same posting, so he felt he'd already accomplished something when the private who answered put him through.

"Major Usher."

"Tony? It's Russ Van Alstyne."

"Chief Van Alstyne! Well, I'll be damned. How are you? Hey, Latice and I were so sorry to hear your news about Linda."

"Thanks. I appreciated the card. I'm doing well. I'm actually getting married again. End of this month."

"Well, hush my mouth. Good for you. Let me guess, high school sweetheart?"

"Nope. She's an Episcopal priest from southern Virginia who's fourteen years younger than me."

Usher roared. "Damn, Chief, you always could land in a pile of horse shit and come up smelling like roses." His laughter died down to a wheeze. "So. Sweet as your life is, I don't think you're calling me just to brag."

"Got a favor to ask." He outlined the situation with Seelye, what he knew about her so-called investigation, what he had heard about Quentan Nichols, and what he suspected, based on the events of the past week and a half.

"Hm-mm. It does sound like sloppy police work, to say the very least. Can I ask your part in this? I'm not seeing where you have a duty to investigate."

"I don't. Which is why I'm calling in a favor instead of going through official channels. There's been no crime in my jurisdiction—yet—but several persons of interest live in my town, or worked in my town, or keep popping up in my town. I want to be prepared, and for that, I need more info."

"Okay. I'll see what I can do. Might take me a while. I'll try and get back to you before the end of the day."

As it turned out, Russ had logged out and swapped his uniform for jeans and a flannel shirt and was headed to the parking lot before Usher called again. He checked the number on his cell phone to make sure it wasn't his mom—if her furnace acted up again, she could start a fire and wait till he got home. He was looking forward to an entirely different sort of hot date tonight.

"Van Alstyne here."

"Hey, Chief, it's Tony Usher."

Russ climbed into the cab of his truck to escape the cold wind blowing off the mountains. "You know, Tony, you can call me Russ. You outrank me now."

Usher laughed. "Right. How many people you know in that little burg of yours call you Russ?"

"Well . . . the Episcopal priest does, but I call her ma'am."

"Mm-hm. That's what I call Latice. You know the three little words every woman wants to hear? 'Right away, honey.'"

Russ laughed.

"Okay, I got the skinny on this lieutenant colonel of yours. She's U.S. Army Financial Command, attached to the 10th Soldier Support Battalion, but you probably knew that already. Her specialty is financial fraud and loss prevention, which makes her a logical go-to person when you've got a theft of this size. She has a good record, nose clean. Married, with two kids in college."

Russ started up the truck's engine. "That must call for some money."

"Tell me about it. The schools Kanisha's looking at run to fifty thousand a year. *I* may have to rob a bank next fall to pay for it."

Russ twisted the temperature control to hot and turned the blower on. "What about the investigation?"

"Well, that's the real interesting part. I asked a JAG who's prosecuted several fraud cases to talk to her contact in FINCOM. As far as she could tell, no one in that office has seen a major theft investigation come across the transom. Now, Seelye is high enough up there to take a case without having to run it by her colleagues, but regs state everything must be logged and a file started, both hard copy and electronic."

"Let me guess. There's no record of the missing million or Tally McNabb."

"You got it. No log, no file, no nothing."

Quentan Nichols had told Clare that he was the one who had started the investigation, and when he went looking for more help from FIN-COM, Colonel Seelye had shown up and taken the case away from him.

"Tony, did you get a sense of what Seelye was doing in Iraq? Could she have been part of the plot to steal the cash from the start?"

"She was doing loss prevention in Camp Anaconda, according to my contact. Reviewing contracts, running spot accounting checks, the sort of thing a bank's financial control officer does—and don't forget, we're running the biggest bank in the country. I have to say, though, you're not talking about a high level of sophistication here. This is basically a couple guys shifting a box out of a warehouse. It doesn't take any special knowledge."

"Except knowing that the box had a million inside."

"Right. My guess—and you can take it for what it's worth—is that she spotted something that tipped her off to the missing money. It was her job to pass on all accounts coming in and out of Anaconda. For whatever reason, she decided she could use that money more than the army could. I bet if you dug into her personal life, you'd find a major weak spot. Husband's business failed, or they lost all the kids' college money."

Russ smiled. "Good to know you can still think like a cop, counselor."

"Hey. I learned from the best."

"Thanks—and thanks for getting me the info. I owe you a big one."

"You can pay it off by sending us a picture of your wedding. I want proof you're not getting hitched to some gap-toothed second cousin. I know how you northern rednecks roll."

Russ was still laughing when he said good-bye. His smile faded as he thought about Seelye, and the money, and about Nichols and McNabb. McNabb and Seelye were out of his reach. Nichols, on the other hand . . .

He glanced at the instrument panel clock. Five thirty. He made another call, to the same Fort Gillem MP station that had sent him a copy of Nichols's transfer orders. "This is Chief of Police Russ Van Alstyne from Millers Kill, New York," he said when he had gotten hold of the officer of the day. "Chief Nichols was consulting with me about a veteran's suicide we had here." That wasn't stretching the truth *too* much. "I need to follow up with him."

"Sorry, sir, but Chief Nichols is off base at this time."

"Can I reach him later?"

"No, sir, he's been temporarily detached to Fort Drum to assist in an investigation. I can look the number up for you if you want to contact their MP station."

"Thanks, no. I'll try them later." Russ hung up. Fort Drum. Four hours away by car. *That* was quite a coincidence. He wondered who Nichols knew in their MP post. Obviously, Seelye wasn't the only officer who could pull a string and get someone reassigned.

Russ tried on the idea that Nichols had been telling Clare the God's honest truth. He wasn't prepared to credit the man with no interest in getting the monies for himself, but it was sure looking more and more likely that he had been right when he said Seelye was on the take.

He needed to talk to Clare. He shifted the truck into gear and pulled out of the station parking lot. Traffic at this hour was as heavy as it ever got out of tourist season. Brake lights bloomed and faded in the twilight as cars and SUVs stopped and started their way up Main toward Church Street. Which is why Russ was able to spot Clare, in jeans and a jacket, coming out of the Rexall.

He jerked his truck out of traffic and pulled into a no-parking tow zone. He unrolled the passenger-side window and leaned over. "Hey!"

She looked up, surprised.

"Didja walk?"

"Of course."

"Get in."

She hopped into the cab, stuffing the small paper pharmacy bag into her coat pocket. "When you said you wanted to take care of me, I didn't think it would involve driving around town looking for a chance to pick me up."

"I was on my way to talk to you. Were you getting a prescription filled?"

"Mmm. I know things are cheaper at the Super Kmart in Fort Henry, but shop local and all that. What did you need me for?"

He saw a break in the traffic and took it. "What? Oh. Quentan Nichols."

"You've found him?"

"Nope. Although I found out how he's been able to do his little appearing acts here. He's still posted to Fort Gillem, but he's TDY to Fort Drum."

"Ah."

He swung into the wide curve of Church Street. The single spot on the flagpole was the only light in the park now; the bandstand was a pale outline in the shadow of the maples. "Tell me what he said about Seelye."

"I already told you everything I heard. He applied to her office for the original shipping manifests, and she showed up in person a couple weeks later and took him off the case."

He turned onto Elm. They passed the stone bulk of St. Alban's. "How did he seem when he was talking about her? Emotionally?"

"A little frustrated, maybe."

"Did he seem angry? Make any threats against Seelye?"

She turned to him as he rolled his truck up her drive and put it into park. "Oh, my God. You don't think she disappeared because he killed her, do you?" She frowned. "No, that couldn't be it. Ron Handler at the inn saw her check out."

"I'm just trying to sort out the possibilities. Could she be after the million for herself? Or is she just an ambitious officer who doesn't want to share the limelight when she gets it back? Is Nichols trying to stop Seelye, or is he trying to screw her out of the money?"

"One doesn't preclude the other."

"No." He unbuckled and slung his arm over the back of the seat. It was familiar, talking to her like this, sitting in the cab of his truck in her driveway. There was a time—a long time—when it was the only safe and private place for them. "I want to find that cash."

"Get to the back of the line."

"We should be able to figure it out. There has to be some evidence of what happened stateside in her house, or her mother's house or her bank. If we had Nichols to tell us what went down at Balad Air Base, we could do it. It's an equation. Millers Kill plus Iraq equals one million dollars. Which means he ought to be somewhere around here, looking for that evidence." His chain of thought unlinked at the sight of her smile. "What?"

"Just you. I like watching your mind work. It's sexy."

"It is, is it?"

"Mmm-hmm." She smiled again.

He mentally tossed the missing million aside. "You know, I just happen to have a box full of quilts in the back. Feel like taking a ride?"

She laughed. "When I suggested the truck bed, it was a sunny afternoon. Not nighttime, thirty-eight degrees and falling."

"Chicken. What happened to army tough?"

"You're the one who always knows when the snowbirds have flown. Don't you have some friend or acquaintance with an empty house and a working furnace?"

The answer hit him hard enough to snap him upright in his seat.

"What?" Clare sounded alarmed.

"I know where Nichols is."

"You do?"

He buckled up and threw the truck into reverse. "He has a friend with an empty house and a working furnace."

Clare looked up from fastening her own seat belt. "Tally McNabb's place." Russ nodded. He threaded through the Friday evening traffic, surprising her when he turned off onto the Cossayuharie Road and began the twisting drive through the hilly farmland. He pulled into the driveway of a large, well-lit home and disappeared inside, returning five minutes later with a key and an expression of grim satisfaction. He dropped the key into her hand. "We have Evonne Walters's permission to enter her daughter's residence."

"Oh. Does this mean you can legally search the place?"

"Hell, no." He peeled out of the drive. "Anything I found would be tossed out before it reached trial. I don't want to search the house tonight. I want Nichols."

"Are you going to arrest him?"

"No. I want his cooperation." The truck jounced down the road. "Which is why you're coming along. He trusted you enough to talk to you. I want you to get him to trust me."

"He might not believe me. I'm a little biased."

"You? Darlin', if you thought he was right and I was wrong, you'd not only refuse to give him up, you'd hand over half your paycheck and drive him up to Canada personally."

She laughed.

"Which is why, if you say he can trust me, he'll believe it."

They left the truck on Saber Drive. Russ retrieved his Glock from the truck's gun locker and slipped it into a flat holster he hung from the back of his belt. She frowned at it. "Just in case I've misjudged him," Russ said.

They walked through the neighbor's yard silently. Past the tangle of brush between the properties it became much harder to stay quiet; no one had raked in a long time, and the ground was littered with dead leaves. "Don't walk. Shuffle," Russ whispered. He demonstrated. It looked like he was ice-skating beneath the leaves, and all she could hear was a rustle, as if the wind were passing by. Her attempts were less successful. She swish-crunch, swish-crunched past the pool fence to the far side of the garage, where Russ was waiting.

"Sorry," she whispered.

"It's okay," he said in her ear. "He probably thought you were a three-legged dog."

She stifled a snort of laughter.

"You got the key?"

She handed it to him.

"I'm going to turn the lights on as soon as we go in. Be ready. You do the talking, but stay behind me."

She nodded again. Followed him along the garage wall to the door. He unlocked it and swung it open without a sound. Clare tensed as his footsteps creaked on the wooden steps leading to the kitchen door. He slipped the key into the lock. Opened the door.

The lights coming on blinded her. She kept her eyes fixed on Russ's back as he strode through the kitchen, into the living room, turning on the overheads. "Quentan," she called. "Quentan Nichols! It's me, Clare Fergusson. We spoke in my church." She heard a faint thump overhead. Her heart thumped hard in response. He was here. A part of her hadn't believed it. Russ snapped on the stair light and mounted the steps. She kept close to his heels. He had his sidearm out. *In case I've misjudged him.* "Quentan, Chief Van Alstyne is with me. He knows you were right about Colonel Seelye. He knows she's after the stolen money. He needs your help to stop her."

The bathroom was at the top of the stairs. Russ flicked that light switch, too, and silently pointed at the razor and toothbrush by the sink, the damp towel on the floor.

Two bedrooms. Left and right. "Quentan. Please." She cast about for the right words. Was he thinking like a lover? A guilty man? A cop? "You can't break this case yourself. The Millers Kill police can't break this case by themselves. We have to work together." God, that sounded trite.

Russ pushed her against the wall on the far side of one door. "Stay here until I clear the room." He positioned himself on the other side and shoved the door open. Nothing happened. He reached around the jamb blindly until he hit the light switch. He turned the lights on in the same instant he stepped into the doorway, crouched low, his gun tracking left-right-left. He stood up. "Okay."

Clare peeked around him. *Guest bedroom,* she thought, furnished with mismatched chairs and a few framed posters. The queen-sized bed was brass, high off the floor, offering a clear view of a few see-through sweater boxes underneath. Unless he was hiding beneath the mound of coats and dresses tossed on the bed, he wasn't here.

Russ pointed toward the other room. He turned, and Clare turned with him, and then she caught his arm and looked at the bed again. The pillows were missing, and the clothes all had hangers in them, as if they'd been lifted bodily off the rack. Maybe Mrs. Walters had started sorting Tally's things already.

Clare looked at the closet door. Maybe someone else needed the space.

Russ nodded. Gestured for her to get against the wall next to the closet. He opened the door, stepping out of the line of fire as he did so.

Quentan Nichols was sitting cross-legged on the floor. He slowly lowered the book he was holding and butted it against the .45 lying in front of him. He gave the book a shove, and the gun slid across the floor. Russ bent down and picked it up.

◆ ◆ ◆

"Inside the damn closet was the only place I could turn a light on and be sure it wouldn't be seen." Nichols was scrambling up a huge skillet of eggs. He had announced that if his hideout was busted, he might as well enjoy a hot meal before they carted him off. "I can live without the Internet, and I don't mind missing a few games on TV, but damn, if a man can't read . . ." Clare glanced at the book, now resting on the mauve-and-gray-speckled counter. *At the City's Edge.* It had a silhouette of Chicago's skyline along the spine. She suppressed a smile. She supposed a big-city boy might get a little homesick, stuck in the closet in Millers Kill.

Nichols shoveled the scrambled eggs onto three plates and laid them out on the table. He opened the refrigerator and pulled out a bag of grated cheese and a bottle of hot sauce.

"I notice McNabb left in such a hurry he still had a full carton of eggs," Russ said.

"And a gallon of milk." Nichols smiled ruefully as he sat down. "Dig in." He paused for a second, his hand over his fork. "Unless you want to say a blessing, Reverend."

"Do you want me to?"

"Not particularly. My grandparents raised me up strict Baptist, but I've

slid some since then." He shoveled a bite in. Clare did, too, suddenly rav-
enously hungry. Nothing like a hunt through a darkened house for an
armed man to stimulate the appetite.

"Along with the groceries, McNabb left behind his calendar." Nichols
reached for the hot sauce. "Seems he had a man-date to some truck show
and a dental appointment next week."

"The head of the company told me the overseas construction unit did
a six-months-on, six-months-off shift, and it was McNabb's time to go."

Nichols shook his head. "Bullshit. Excuse me, Reverend." She glanced
toward Russ and found him looking at her, amused. "I mean, yeah, maybe
that's the drill, but no way he'd been planning to go this past Wednesday.
My guess is, he offered to swap with whoever really was scheduled to join
the crew in Iraq."

Russ nodded. "I think Seelye scared him and he ran."

"You don't think they're in it together?"

"No. She came with me to the hospital when I interviewed him. I'd lay
money he'd never seen her before. He didn't recognize her name, either.
When she asked him about the missing money, he lawyered up and
wouldn't say another word to either of us."

"Coulda been an act."

"Yeah, it could have—but then why bug out for Iraq?"

"Maybe he was personally afraid of the colonel," Clare said. "Maybe
she threatened him. Maybe she told him she killed Tally and she'd do
him, too, if he didn't cough up the money."

Russ propped his arms on the table. Its uneven legs clunked toward his
side. "Tally McNabb's death was a suicide. There's no doubt about that."

"Yes, there is!" Clare put her fork down and glared at Russ.

"Only in your imagination."

Nichols paused, his loaded fork halfway to his mouth. He looked at
her, then Russ, then back to her. "What . . . are you guys . . . ? You're a
minister, right?"

"Episcopalians use the term 'priest.'" Clare nodded. "But, yes, I am."

"Police chaplain?"

Russ snorted. "Only unofficially." He crumpled his paper napkin. "For
our purposes, it doesn't matter why McNabb ran. He's obviously in it up
to his neck. The thing to figure out is—"

Clare pointed her fork at him. "Why did John Opperman tell us he'd been assigned to leave?"

"Who's John Opperman?" Nichols asked.

"Opperman saw a chance to dick me over at no cost to himself and he took it," Russ said.

Clare turned to Nichols. "The CEO of BWI Opperman, where Tally worked. They run the resort, which you've seen, and the construction company where McNabb works."

Russ made a noise. "As I was saying—"

A sharp rap on the door interrupted him. "Millers Kill police," a voice called. "Please open the door and identify yourself."

Russ raised his eyebrows. He held his hands up, indicating Clare and Nichols should stay put. He rose and crossed the kitchen.

"I'm opening the door. I'm unarmed." Which wasn't strictly true. There were two 9 mm automatics on the counter next to the sink. Russ swung the door open to reveal Kevin Flynn.

"Chief?" His gaze swept the kitchen. "Reverend? Wait a minute, isn't that—"

"Quentan Nichols, yeah. Come on in, Kevin."

"Um ..." Kevin stepped past Russ, his eyes still on Nichols. "We got a report from the old lady next door that the place was lit up like Christmas. I figured maybe Mrs. Walters was here going through her daughter's things ..." His voice faded as he took in the three plates and the remains of a scrambled egg dinner. "What's going on, Chief?"

"Quentan Nichols, this is Officer Kevin Flynn." Kevin nodded warily toward Nichols, who still sat, seemingly relaxed. Clare suspected she was the only one who could see the pale crescents beneath his fingernails from pressing hard into the table.

"So ... I guess he's no longer on our BOLO list?" Kevin's voice had a pinch-me quality.

Russ crossed his arms and looked at Nichols. "I think Mr. Nichols is willing to cooperate with us."

Nichols nodded slowly. "I get the credit if we find the money. From the army, I mean."

"Still hoping to avoid a court-martial?"

Nichols dropped his gaze, but his voice was steady. "I got twelve years invested. Eight more to go. I'm not gonna flush it all down the toilet because of one stupid mistake. Not if I can fix it."

◆ ◆ ◆

It was the weirdest case briefing Kevin had ever been to. Him and the chief, in his civvies, sitting around the table in a dead woman's home with Reverend Clare and the guy they'd all been looking for as a POI.

"Report in your break," the chief said. "Keep your radio on in case you get a squawk."

Nichols got up and made coffee while Kevin signed out with dispatch. The chief let the guy have his run of the kitchen, so Kevin guessed that was all right. When they had all taken a seat, he ventured a question.

"Uh, Chief? What exactly are we doing here?"

The chief took a deep whiff of his coffee, a gesture so familiar Kevin could see an image of him, uniformed, sitting on the squad room table, superimposed over this flannel-shirted man in a pine-paneled kitchen.

"We're going to find the money Tally McNabb stole. Then we're going to use it to prove Colonel Arlene Seelye is dirty."

Nichols paused from getting the milk out of the fridge. "How the hell will finding the money get you to Seelye?"

"We'll let her think *she's* the one finding it."

"Set it up as bait?" Nichols thunked the carton onto the table. "That might work."

"You really think their army investigator is after it?" Kevin couldn't keep the doubt from his voice.

"Let's just say I'd like to see how she reacts to the opportunity to make off with the money undetected. What's that saying you told me, Clare?"

"Honi soit qui mal y pense."

"Evil be to him who evil thinks," Kevin translated. The chief raised his eyebrows.

Reverend Clare smiled. "Someone knows his English history." Kevin felt the color rise to his cheeks.

The chief spooned sugar into his cup. "I have a contact in the JAG Corps who looked into her alleged investigation. There's no file on the case. No log of Mr. Nichols contacting her office, nothing. My contact thinks she may have stumbled over the theft while she was overseeing the financial office in Camp Anaconda. I think Mr. Nichols's investigation tipped her off. Either way, she's in prime position to collect that million for herself."

"But she left town," Kevin said. "If a financial crimes expert thought she'd have better luck finding the loot elsewhere, why do you think it's here?"

The chief blew across his coffee. His gaze slid sideways toward Nichols. "Because Mr. Nichols is still here. The colonel may know all about money laundering and bank fraud, but Mr. Nichols knows Tally McNabb." He rested his arm on the table and turned toward the MP. "You told Clare you had talked to Tally a couple times since this summer. That's how you knew they were in counseling together." He glanced at Reverend Clare, then back to Nichols. "What do you know that we don't?"

Nichols was silent for a long moment. Finally, he pulled out his chair and sat down. "She never told me where it was. She just said that they had brought it back home."

"They?"

Nichols nodded. "She didn't say much about it. She never admitted right out that she'd stolen the money." He made a noise that resembled a laugh. "I guess she still didn't trust me. She talked around it. Talked about her feelings, you know."

"What were her feelings, Quentan?" The reverend's voice was quiet.

"She said money didn't make you happy. She said she didn't think it was worth it."

"*It* presumably being the theft?" The chief's voice was dry. "Yet somehow, she forced herself to hang on to the loot."

Kevin couldn't help it. "No, Chief, it tracks." Everyone looked at him. "The dep said most of the stuff here was new—within the last year or so. You know, the pool and the ATV and the pimped-up SUVs. She was spending money on *him*. Her mom said they'd been together since high school, and Tally was still head-over-heels for him."

He happened to be looking at Nichols, which is why he saw the expression flash over the man's face and disappear. *Poor bastard,* he thought, and on its heels came another, *just like me.* Only in his case, the woman he loved wasn't crazy about anyone else. She just didn't want him. Kevin tightened his grip on his mug of coffee and forced himself to continue. "Her mom's house in Cossayuharie looks like it's been renovated from the ground up. Inside and out. Now compare that to this house. They've got a giant flat-screen hanging in the living room, but everything else is kind of old and basic. So it's not that Tally had to have the best of everything herself. She just wanted the people she loved to have whatever they wanted."

"I think Kevin's right." Reverend Clare glanced around the room. "I can't imagine anyone with unlimited funds not updating this kitchen."

"That's 'cause it's the first thing *you'd* do." The chief smiled a little. "But I agree. Kevin has a point."

"There's your motivation for murder." The reverend thunked her mug on the table hard enough to slosh her coffee. "She held the purse strings and was feeling remorseful. Maybe she was going to give back everything she hadn't spent. So Wyler killed her."

The chief shook his head. "There's no evidence to support a homicide, Clare."

"Besides, McNabb made good money himself, working construction for BWI Opperman." Kevin leaned forward, addressing the reverend. "The guys who go overseas really rake it in."

The chief rubbed his lips. "Wyler McNabb's first shift in Iraq overlapped Tally McNabb's second tour of duty."

"He was *there*? In-country?" Nichols sat back. "She never told me that."

"They," the chief said. "*They* had brought it back home." He tapped the worn surface of the table. "Tally and Wyler did it together."

"Didn't Eric say he was the matériel guy?" Kevin tried to remember the rest of the case file. "Would that mean he'd have been the one in charge of getting stuff to and from the States?"

"Yeah. On their monthly flight out of Plattsburgh." The chief had that look on his face, the one he got when pieces started falling into place.

"How far away is Plattsburgh?" Nichols asked.

"An hour and a half, if it's not snowing," Reverend Clare said.

The chief shook his head. "I don't think it would still be there."

"Why not?" Nichols looked at him. "Just one more pallet, sitting around? Who's going to know?"

"They'd need to have it someplace Tally could access. McNabb could have manufactured an excuse for being at the depot in Plattsburgh once in a while, but if they were laundering cash, they needed to keep a small, steady stream going. I'm betting that would have been her job."

Nichols propped his elbows on the table, interlacing his fingers. "Okay, what about this: Either McNabb brings it back from Iraq himself, or he ships it back to their materials depot. Then he gets some of his co-workers to help him move the thing."

"More accomplices?" Kevin asked.

"Not necessarily. He could have it marked up as unused PVC or grout or whatever. Something nobody would care much about. All he needed was some muscle to help him get it into a truck."

"Then the television falls off the back of the truck." The chief's voice was knowing. Kevin found himself nodding along with Nichols.

"What?" Reverend Clare said.

"It means he reports it stolen. Or lost in transit."

"Okay." Her voice was cautious. "How does that tell us where it is now?"

That one stalled out the conversation. Kevin tried to imagine the places where you could hide two square meters of cash and not have it seen. Old barns. Abandoned houses. A root cellar or summer kitchen or even up on blocks in the woods, protected by a tarp. A lot of ground to cover. Too much ground. "We need to question other members of the construction team," he said. "Somebody must have seen something. Or heard about it."

The chief shook his head again. "We've got no jurisdiction. The crime was committed on army property by army personnel. We have no legal justification for investigating unless we're asked to by the army."

Everyone looked at Nichols. He raised his hands. "Not me. I'm supposed to be tracking down steroid pushers who've been supplying Fort Drum. If I raise my head on this case, Seelye will have my ass posted to Fort Wainwright before you can say boo. Excuse me, Reverend."

"Fort Wainwright?" Kevin asked.

"Alaska," the chief said.

"*Fairbanks,* Alaska." Nichols shivered.

The reverend wrapped her hands around her mug. "I know someone I can ask."

The chief frowned. "What? Who?"

"Dragojesich. The big guy Tally and I were talking with the night we got engaged." A look passed between them, tender and soft, like the last warm day in October. Kevin dropped his gaze to the table. "He was with the construction team in Iraq the same time as Tally. So he was probably there with McNabb."

"Do you know his first name?"

"No—but how many Dragojesiches could there be in the phone book?"

◆ ◆ ◆

She could find one. G. Dragojesich. In Fort Henry, not Millers Kill. Russ had sent Kevin on his way, with an admonition to say nothing about their less than legal visit to the McNabb house. Then they dropped Nichols off at his rental car—he had parked it on Morningside Drive and hiked the mile to his hideaway—with directions to the Sleepy Hollow Motor Lodge and a promise to call him first thing in the morning.

"Don't you worry he's going to bolt again?" Clare asked.

Russ glanced away from the road for a second. His mouth tipped up at one corner. "That sounds like something I'd say." He faced forward again. "No, I don't. First, even if he originally planned to get ahold of the money, he knows that's not going to happen now. If he disappears, I'll blow the whistle on him. His best bet is to do just as he said, help us out in the hope that returning the loot will squeak him past any damaging questions."

"And second?"

"Second, the man's a cop. I think he's probably a good one. Were you watching him when we were laying out the investigation? He wanted in. He wants to break this case as bad as we do. More."

"Do you think he's hoping it'll give him a lead on Tally's murder?"

"Clare . . ."

"I don't want to fight with you. Honestly, I don't. I just want you to admit—"

"That I should have ignored the evidence and the ME's report and kept the case open?"

"I'd settle for you keeping your mind open!" She looked out the window at the orange sodium lights of the Super Kmart. "I have a personal stake in this."

"She knocked you down, sprained your ankle—and gave you an infected gash in your back, remember that? Then you met her once a week for an hour with a bunch of other people. How on God's green earth does that translate into a personal stake?"

"She was one of us." Clare's voice was low. "I can't just turn my back on her."

"Look. I understand that. I meet a guy who served in Nam, I feel a spark of connection with him. It doesn't matter if we have nothing in common. It doesn't matter that we're old and gray now. He was there, and I was there, and we remember."

She turned toward him. Looked at his hands, big and steady on the wheel, his forearms exposed where he'd rolled his flannel shirt up.

"But here's the thing. That connection doesn't overshadow the ones I've made with people I've lived with and worked with and served with." He glanced at her. "We're supposed to be getting married in a week. You need to decide which connection is more important. The one with your brothers in arms? Or the one with your husband?"

"So I should support you, no matter how I feel? Pretend I think you're right?"

"No. You should respect my professional judgment and realize that I only rejected your point of view after careful consideration." He flicked on his signal and turned onto the street whose name they had copied out of the phone book.

We're supposed to get married. Was he having second thoughts? Linda never critiqued his investigations. Linda never called him names. Linda never, ever slammed out of his office, swearing she was going to prove him wrong. God. Clare hadn't even been married yet, and she was already a failure at being Mrs. Van Alstyne.

"We're here." Russ pulled into one of Fort Henry's small condo complexes, the sort of place where couples commuting to Albany or singles with good jobs in Glens Falls touched down until they'd saved up the down payment for a house. "Will you take the lead? Since you've already met him?"

"Of course." She half-expected Dragojesich to be out on a Friday night, so when the door opened moments after she rang the bell, the sight of him filling the entryway knocked her opening line out of her head.

"Can I help you?" he said.

"Mr. Dragojesich? I don't know if you remember me, but I met you at the BWI Opperman party at the end of August. I was with Tally McNabb?"

His forehead creased, then cleared. "The major! Who likes Canadian Club!" He looked past her to Russ. "And the boyfriend, right?"

"Fiancé," Russ said.

"We'd like to ask you a few questions about Tally, if we could."

"Oh, cripes, that was you at her funeral, wasn't it? Yeah, sure, come on in." He stepped back to let them pass. "She was such a sweet girl. Give you the shirt off her back." He ushered them into his living room and snapped off the television. "Can I get you something? Sit down, sit down."

"Nothing, thanks," Russ said as Clare perched on a chair wide enough to pass as a love seat.

"Mr. Dragojesich—"

"Call me Drago." He took the opposite seat. Dressed in a Syracuse Orange sweatshirt, he resembled a black-haired, black-browed snowplow. There was enough room on the chair for Russ to sit down next to her. "Are you sure I can't get you anything? A small whisky?"

Clare thought of the pills in her coat pocket and swallowed her desire for a drink. "No, thank you. You were in Iraq the same time Tally was, is that right?"

"Yeah, sure, during her second tour. She hadda spend a lot of time at Balad, setting up some finance thing. That was where we staged out of. She would hang out with the crew, 'cause her husband worked with us. We became buds."

"How about Wyler McNabb? Were you friends with him as well?"

Drago's face crunched in thought. "Not really. I mean, I got nothing against him, but Wyler was more of a party kind of guy. He liked to live large. Me, I like it nice and peaceful. Do my work, come home to my babies."

She could feel, rather than see, Russ's eyebrows rise.

"You haven't seen 'em yet." Drago whistled. "Hey, my puppies!" Clare heard yipping and the scrabble of nails, and then three toy poodles bounded into the living room. They leaped onto Drago's lap—he could have fit several more—and the big man crooned to them, lifting the whole pack in his hands. "Who's Daddy's good girl? Is it you? Is it you?"

Check your assumptions at the door, Clare reminded herself.

"We're trying to track a shipment McNabb would have made from Balad back to the States." Russ's voice was as coplike as ever.

"Anything more specific?" Drago let the dogs down on the floor. They immediately scuttled over and began exploring Russ's boots. "Wyler was in charge of ordering matériel. He was usually pretty accurate, but he did overestimate at times."

Russ reached down and scratched a tiny head. "This would have been a pallet, maybe a couple meters square, shrink-wrapped. It would have been marked for transit beyond your Plattsburgh depot."

"The bedding!" Drago nodded. "It's gotta be the bedding. Everything else stayed in Plattsburgh."

Clare and Russ looked at each other.

"It was a big, dumb mistake. We got sent a load of the sheets they order for the resort. They're all fancy and stuff, Egyptian cotton and a zillion thread count." His eyes, which had been lit with pleasure at being able to answer their questions, clouded over. "What's this got to do with Tally? We kept it on the q.t. so's not to get the clerk on the other side of the operation in trouble. But Tally couldn'tuv been responsible. She didn't work for BWI until this summer."

"Drago"—Clare tried to keep her voice neutral—"do you have any idea of the final destination of the, um, sheets?"

He looked at her as if she were cracked. "Where do you think they went? The resort."

SATURDAY, OCTOBER 15 I don't like this," Lyle said.

Russ didn't pause in his march up the stone steps from the parking lot to the Algonquin Waters Spa and Resort. There wasn't a leaf to be seen on the stairs or the flower beds beside them. The staff probably vacuumed them up when no one was looking. "There's nothing illegal in stopping by the resort to give our regards to the manager. We're off duty."

"Who are you kidding? If we're not made as plainclothes thirty seconds after we hit the lobby, I'll eat my shorts. I bet you're even carrying under that coat."

Russ glanced down at his navy jacket. "Can you tell?"

Lyle made a noise.

"How 'bout you?"

"Hell, yeah."

"You?" Russ looked across Lyle to where Quentan Nichols climbed in lockstep with the two Millers Kill police.

"I always carry. I figure it's like an American Express card. Don't leave home without it."

Lyle was right. With phone instructions to look "well dressed, but casual," they had all turned out in coats and ties. Too dressed up to be end-of-the-season golfers, not spiffy enough to be businessmen.

"And *him*. I don't see why he's gotta be here. You don't think they'll remember his face?"

"I'm not trying to sneak us in, Lyle. We just need to not be here in our official capacity. Now can it." They crossed the portico, Russ and Nichols smiling at the bellhops and the valets, Lyle scowling.

Inside, Russ steered them to the far edge of the reception desk, the one closest to the door leading into the offices. A quick glance reassured him that Ethan Stoner's child bride wasn't working this morning. No loud greetings of "Hi there, Chief Van Alstyne." He leaned on the gleaming rosewood counter. "Good morning. I'd like to speak to Barbara LeBlanc, please."

The young woman across from him looked at the three of them, stricken. "Is there anything wrong, sir?"

"No. We just want to speak to her. If she's in." He had assumed she would be. Saturday at 9:00 A.M. had to be one of the busiest times of the week.

The girl looked doubtful. "May I say who's asking?"

Lyle sidled up to the counter and gave her a smile to charm the birds out of the trees. "Just tell her Lyle MacAuley's back. With a . . . special request."

"Oh!" The girl blinked rapidly. "I'll go get her right away." She vanished through the door.

Russ glanced at his second in command. "It never gets old for you, does it?"

"Nope."

Barbara LeBlanc emerged from the office, her expression half welcoming, half wary. "Deputy Chief MacAuley? And—" Her gaze slid past Russ to Nichols. "Good heavens."

Russ stepped forward. "Can we talk in private, Ms. LeBlanc?"

The manager nodded, her eyes still on Nichols. She led the way back into her office. She was in a silk blouse and form-fitting skirt, just like the last time they had been here, and just like the last time, Lyle kept his eyes on her posterior, jerking his gaze up to a respectable height a scant second before she turned and gestured for them to seat themselves.

"First," Russ said, "let me explain that when Chief Warrant Officer Nichols was here at the end of August, he was working as an undercover investigator." That was sort of true.

"But—"

"I know. We hadn't been notified by the army." Definitely true. "We've sorted out the mix-up. We're here because we're assisting with the inquiry in an informal capacity."

"What does that mean?"

What did it mean? He was a terrible liar. He was getting spun in his own gobbledygook.

"Chief Nichols hasn't yet been authorized to involve civilian law enforcement." Lyle propped an arm against the edge of LeBlanc's desk and leaned closer. "I always thought we had it bad. You can imagine what army bureaucracy is like." He smiled. "He thinks there may be contraband, stolen from the U.S. Army, hidden right here in your hotel."

Barbara LeBlanc shook her head. "Impossible."

"I know, I know. He wanted to come in here with a warrant and a bunch of MPs." Before the expression of horror could settle on the manager's face, Lyle went on. "Now, the chief and I know BWI Opperman is the largest employer in town. We want to handle things discreetly."

LeBlanc nodded. She gave Russ a look of melting gratitude.

"So what we'd like to do is this. You allow us behind the scenes in the basement. We'll take a quiet, low-key look around the shipping dock and the storage areas and that big corridor."

"Broadway."

"Broadway, right. If we find anything, we'll consult with you about the best way to deal with it without kicking up a fuss and scaring off the trade. If we don't find anything"—he shrugged—"no one's the wiser."

Three minutes later, Barbara LeBlanc was opening the heavy door labeled EMPLOYEES ONLY that divided the hotel into above and below stairs.

"He's good," Nichols said to Russ.

"Uh-huh."

"I have to get back to reception," LeBlanc said, "but if you need me for anything, you have my cell number." More specifically, *Lyle* had her number. He ran a finger along one bushy eyebrow as she shut the door behind her, leaving them in the spottily lit concrete corridor.

"Let's start with the shipping dock and work inward," Russ said.

So they began the job of pushing and pulling and lifting and opening every box, carton, canister, and cart they could find. Russ discarded his jacket in the first five minutes and his tie in the next five. They cleared the shipping dock quickly. Its echoing, oil-stained interior had a few piles of boxes and several heaping laundry carts, but the efficient staff had obviously been moving goods in and out of the area as soon as they arrived.

The storage rooms were fast work as well—they were smaller spaces with industrial shelving up to the ceiling. Two were for the kitchen, stacked with ten-gallon jugs of mayonnaise and garbage cans loaded with cornmeal and flour. Three more looked like the staging room Russ had seen last summer—towers of toilet paper and tubloads of shampoo.

"Anything?" Russ emerged from the last supply closet with the smell of Lysol clogging his nose.

"Nothing." Lyle sounded personally offended.

They all gazed down the length of Broadway. It ran from one end of the hotel to another. Empty, it would have been as wide as a two-lane road, but the stacks and shelves and dollies crowding either side narrowed it to a concrete gulch just wide enough for a golf cart or a loader.

Nichols put his hands on his hips and whistled. "Looks like the Federal Depository in *Raiders of the Lost Ark.*"

"Why'n the hell didn't we bring more help?" Lyle asked.

Russ didn't point out that his deputy hadn't even wanted Nichols along. He thought for a moment. "Would they have wanted it nearer to the employee entrance, or farther away?"

"I think they'd have to load it wherever there was room." Nichols gestured toward a teetering jumble of gilt-painted chairs, some with cracked legs, some missing seats. "This is like a bad combination of your gramma's attic and Home Depot."

"Okay, then. Lyle, you and Quentan start up at this end. The left side. I'll take the far end and yell if I need help moving anything. We'll meet in the middle."

"About the time I'm due to retire," Lyle said.

Russ suspected his deputy was right, but he didn't say anything. He hiked down the corridor and got to work.

Boxes and cartons and bundles strapped to pallets. Vacuum cleaners and lamps and pillows in plastic. Russ looked into and behind and around everything, wondering if the money had been broken down into briefcase-sized packages, wondering if it had gone missing between Plattsburgh and the resort and they were barking up the wrong tree, wondering why he was spending his Saturday here, in a place he loathed, instead of looking at properties with Clare, wondering where she was, what she was doing, what she was wearing—

"Russ! Get up here." Lyle's shout snapped him out of his reverie. Jesus H. Mud-Wrestling Christ. Love was making him soft in the head.

He trotted back up the corridor. "Look at this." Nichols pointed to a narrow door set into the corridor. It must have swung inward, because boxes marked LATEX PAINT and H-455 AC FILTERS were stacked tight on either side.

"Locked?"

"Uh-huh. Deputy Chief MacAuley is on the phone with the manager right now."

"She's coming down with the keys." MacAuley stepped back within hearing range, snapping his phone shut.

Within minutes, they heard the brisk tap-tap-tap of LeBlanc's heels. She had pulled her chatelaine off her waistband and was flipping through the keys and cards. "Oh." She stopped when she saw where they were. "I'm afraid that's just the alcohol lockup. The wine cellar, if you will." She held up a key. "Do you want to look anyway?"

"Yeah." Russ tried to keep the doubt out of his voice.

She opened the door. It was, as promised, stacked with crates of booze and racks of bottles. No shrink-wrapped pallet. No stacks of cling-sealed money.

Russ walked away as the manager resealed the room. He listened with half an ear to Lyle, asking her about other rooms, asking her where a book-keeper or a construction worker might go with no questions asked.

"I'm sorry," LeBlanc said, "there's really no order to the storage in this area. It's just shove it in where you can. If it was important to be able to access something quickly, it would have been unpacked and put some-where else. The garage, or the tool shed, or the power plant—this is a big complex."

Important to be able to access something quickly. McNabb delivered a pallet here. He'd want to be able to find it again, no matter what outdated appliances or busted furniture got stacked on top or in front of it. So how would you mark it? Not on the floor. People would notice. Nothing right by the thing—it might get moved. He looked up, to the shadowy space above the hanging fluorescent lights. Cement blocks rose smooth and unmarked to where massive I-beams transected a dim, unfinished ceil-ing. Pipes and conduits and electrical wires, barely visible but there, open for fast repairs. Hard to reach, unless you were authorized to work in the area, but—he made a tossing motion, as if he had a ball in his hand. You could throw something.

He spotted it. A length of bright orange twine, the stuff you could pick up at any sporting goods store. Each end was tied to what looked to be, in the half-light, a stack of heavy-duty washers. A homemade bolo. Curled around a cold water pipe, hanging a few inches off either side. You'd never notice it unless you were looking straight up—and who would be staring past the lights instead of getting in and out as fast as possible?

"Here," he said.

"What?" Nichols trotted down the corridor toward him. "How do you know?"

Russ pointed at the dangling cord.

"I'll be damned," Nichols whispered.

"Help me move this stuff." He and Nichols started removing the plas-tic five-gallon buckets piled like a wall beneath the marker.

"Wait. Look." Nichols leaned against the stack of boxes to the left of the buckets and pushed. The cardboard tower slid away, revealing a dolly, empty except for a blue plastic tarp. Nichols pulled it toward himself. It rolled easily out into the open corridor.

Peering into the narrow, shadowy space they had revealed, Nichols breathed in. "I think this may be it."

"Let me see." Russ replaced Nichols in the gap. He could see white opaque plastic stretched over a cracked and splintered wooden pallet. The corner closest to the wall had been ripped open and resealed with duct tape. Russ tried to reach it, but he couldn't fit.

"Let me try." Lyle was five inches shorter and a good fifty pounds lighter than Russ. He squeezed into the angular space sideways. Past the rest of the buckets, he was able to turn toward the wall. He got down on one knee. Russ could hear the ripping sound of tape being torn away.

"Well?" Russ wanted to shove the buckets aside and get in there himself.

Lyle grunted. Stood up. Shifted to the side and edged back toward them. He had a wad of heavy plastic in his hand.

"Well?"

Barbara LeBlanc butted up against Russ. "What is it?"

Lyle stepped free. "This is one of the empties." He handed Russ the stiff, crumpled plastic, and then, like a magician producing a rabbit, held up more of the stuff, wrapped crudely around stacks and stacks of cash. Twenties, in bricks of five hundred, enough to fill a small suitcase.

"Oh. My. God." Barbara LeBlanc's voice was faint.

"Gotcha," Russ said.

FEAR THE LORD, YOU THAT ARE
HIS SAINTS, FOR THOSE WHO
FEAR HIM LACK NOTHING.

—Psalm 34, The Book of Common Prayer

Sarah was looking at the black cats and flying witches pinned to the walls of the community center's meeting room. Lots of black and purple and green crayon, with one defiantly pink-and-yellow standout, as if Glinda the Good Witch had taken to her broomstick. Some little girl was not lowering her princess standards, even for Halloween.

"Hey, y'all, look who I brought."

Sarah turned at the sound of the Virginia drawl. Clare Fergusson rolled Will Ellis through the doors. He smiled and waved, and if she hadn't known better, she would never have guessed the boy had narrowly escaped death by his own hand.

"Welcome back, marine." Eric McCrea got up from his folding seat and shook Will's hand. "You're looking a lot better than you did last week."

He was, too. His hair had been shaved away to a sandy brown fuzz, and he had some color in his face. He was still far too thin for such a big kid—after seeing his father and brother in the ICU, Sarah realized Will must have stood over six feet before the amputations—but he had lost that ghastly drawn expression he'd had in the hospital.

Will ducked his head. "Feeling better." He paused, taking in the smaller than usual circle of chairs. "Where's Dr. Stillman?" His voice had an edge of panic.

"He's fine." Sarah took the seat opposite Will. "He was on call this evening and had to go in to the Glens Falls Hospital. He told me he probably wouldn't make it tonight."

Fergusson put the brake on his chair and set off for the coffee table. "How are things now that you're home?" Sarah asked.

"Better. More honest." He rubbed his thighs. "We started family therapy while I was an in-patient, and we're going to keep it up for a while."

He smiled briefly. "Never saw myself as the kind of guy who'd be seeing two therapists a week."

"If you had diabetes and, say, an ulcer, you'd see a specialist for each condition. It's no different for mental health. Eric? How are you doing? You're still on suspension?"

"Yeah." He bent forward, bracing his elbows on his knees, his face toward the floor. "It's been . . . tough. My wife . . ." He looked up at her. His face changed. "She just doesn't get that I need a little time! I was gone for a fucking year, and she won't even give me a few months to readjust to being back."

"Have you thought about entering marriage counseling? Or family therapy, like the Ellises?"

"Oh, Christ, don't you start, too. That's what she said."

"So?" Fergusson dropped into her seat with her customary cup. "What's holding you back?"

"I'm a cop. Do you know what that means? I have the most fundamental job in the world. Because *nothing* else matters if people and property aren't safe and if the law isn't enforced." He smacked himself on the chest. "*We're* the line between civilization and the jungle. The *only* line. You trust me to do that job, you gotta trust me to have my head on straight."

Sarah waited a beat. "So . . . what does your suspension mean?"

Eric turned away. "I made a bad call. I'll take my punishment and that'll be the end of it."

Sarah waited, but he didn't seem inclined to continue. "Clare? How about you?"

"I think he ought to accede to his wife's request. Even if he doesn't think he needs it, it would strengthen their relationship."

Sarah pursed her lips. *The caretaker strikes again.* "I was asking how you are this week."

"Oh." Fergusson rubbed the end of her nose. "Good. Busy. Stressed." She paused, and Sarah opened her mouth to ask about drinking, but Fergusson went on. "There've been a lot of developments in the police investigation around Tally's death. They may break open part of the case soon."

That snapped McCrea out of his sulk. "What's going on? I called Lyle

MacAuley yesterday, and all he'd tell me is that they were bringing in somebody from the army for a possible arrest on the theft."

"There really was money stolen?" Will sounded bemused. "I wasn't sure if I'd imagined that conversation or not."

"The MKPD found it Saturday," Fergusson said. "Something like six hundred thousand dollars. It was hidden at the Algonquin Waters." Fergusson was quite effectively derailing any inquiries into her own emotional life. Sarah wasn't sure if the priest was aware of it or not.

"So what was MacAuley talking about?" McCrea said. "Why didn't they just tag it and ship it back to the army? Or hand it over to the Feds?"

"Russ—the chief—thinks Lieutenant Colonel Seelye may have been after the money for herself when she showed up here asking questions."

Sarah didn't want to get sucked into Fergusson's self-protective behavior, but she had to ask. "Was that the other officer we saw at Tally's funeral?"

"Uh-huh." Fergusson drank some coffee. "The MKPD and Russ's JAG contact—the Judge Advocate General's Corps—are trying to get her to incriminate herself."

"How?" Will asked.

"I don't know. I haven't seen Russ since last Friday. Most of this I got from a phone message he left me."

McCrea's glance sharpened. "Does the chief think this lieutenant colonel had something to do with Tally's death?"

Fergusson's face, which had been rosy and animated during her conversation, fell into disapproving lines. "He still insists she killed herself. He won't listen to any—" Her mouth worked, as if she were trying to find the right word.

"Other evidence?" Will offered.

"Sensible arguments." Fergusson frowned into her coffee.

"The ME's conclusion was pretty well grounded," McCrea said.

Fergusson gave him a look. "Don't you start, too."

Time to steer this into a therapeutic mode. Sarah looked around the tiny circle, gathering each of them in. "If Tally McNabb did, in fact, kill herself, we have some hard work to do. How do we accept an unacceptable death? How do we find meaning in an act that denies meaning?"

"I got the chance to talk with my other therapist about her while I was in the hospital," Will said. "It sounds weird, but looking at her situation helped give me a different view of my own stuff." He glanced at Sarah, as if for permission to continue. She nodded encouragement. "See, I can look at Tally and think, she could have returned the money, she could have gotten a different job, she could have kicked her husband to the curb. Things were hard for her, real hard, but she had options. She could've taken them." He rubbed his thighs. "It kind of made me see that even when I don't feel like it, I have options, too."

Fergusson put her coffee down and leaned toward Will. "Yes, you do. And you have your family and friends and a great cloud of witnesses all around you. Wherever you look, there's someone who loves you looking back."

"Oh, I know that. I knew it when I . . . when I did it. The problem was, they loved me too much. Too much to stand seeing me hurt and mad all the time. Too much to let me touch bottom." Will glanced across the room to where the Crayola witches flew between construction-paper cats. "And I had to touch bottom." He twisted in his chair, as if settling himself into the present. "Anyway, we're talking about it in family therapy. They're trying to see me the way I really am now. As much as they can."

"See? That's the hard part," McCrea said. "Getting the people in your life to admit that you've changed. Been changed."

Fergusson smiled crookedly. "Some days I fantasize about starting fresh in a new town. Nobody to have to put up a front for." She looked at Sarah. "Of course, in my business, you always have to put up a front. No one wants to see their priest spit and swear and fall apart."

"I dunno," Will said. "I'm getting kind of used to it." Fergusson laughed.

"So even you can find people to accept you as you are," Sarah said.

"Yeah," Will said. "Remember how you said I should get in touch with some of my old friends from school?" He smiled a little. "I did."

"Oh." Fergusson hid her pleased expression behind the rim of her coffee cup. "I don't suppose any of these friends happen to be girls?"

"Yeah." His cheeks pinked up, and the combat veteran disappeared, replaced by a teenaged boy. "I've been talking with Olivia Bain."

"Is she still here in town?"

"Naw. She left for SUNY Geneseo this fall. Got a full scholarship."

"That's a tough school to get into." McCrea nodded. "She must be a smart girl."

"A lot brainier than me. I can talk to her about anything, though. She knows what it's like to have something really bad happen to you. Her mom died in a car crash this summer."

"That's hard," Sarah said. Still, it made her a good choice for Will's confidant.

"This summer?" McCrea said. "Here? In Millers Kill?"

"Yeah."

"What was her name?"

"Um . . ." Will frowned in thought. "Eleanor? Ellen? Something like that."

"Ellen Bain." McCrea's mouth twisted.

"You know her?" Fergusson asked.

"I cleaned up after her. She went barreling down the resort road with no seat belt on after taking part in Happy Hour. I didn't have to follow up with the survivors, thank God. I didn't know she'd left a kid behind."

"Yeah, and it was just Olivia and her mom. Her dad took off when she was little." Will made a face, clearly unable to imagine a father like that. "Her mom did okay with her bookkeeping job, she said, but she would've had a hard time with college if she hadn't gotten—"

McCrea cut the boy off. "What did you say she did?"

"Who?"

"Ellen Bain. You said she was . . . ?"

Will looked at him, confused. "A bookkeeper. At the new resort."

Fergusson sat up straight.

McCrea extended his hand and tapped his palm. "Ellen Bain, who died in an auto accident at the end of July, was a bookkeeper at the Algonquin Waters. Tally McNabb, who committed suicide in October, was a bookkeeper at the Algonquin Waters."

"Yeah, but . . ." Will's forehead crinkled. "It's got to be a coincidence. Tons of people work for the resort."

"Chief Van Alstyne always says he doesn't believe in coincidence." Fergusson put her cup down. "Did Tally and Ms. Bain know each other? Did they have the same job responsibilities?"

Will shrugged. "I don't know."

"We've got to find out," Fergusson said.

"No, we've got to tell the chief," McCrea countered.

"Eventually." At his look, she spread her hands. "I'm just saying we should come up with something more solid if we want him to reopen Tally's case. I'm overdue for a visit with her mother. I can ask her how Tally got her job, and what she might know about Ellen Bain."

"Stop." Avoiding issues in group was one thing. Acting out that avoidance in real life was a whole other ball game. Sarah pointed to Fergusson. "You are not Velma from *Scooby-Doo*. We are not going to get into a purple van and ride around town looking for a spooky old house."

"All I'm proposing we do is ask a few questions."

McCrea studied the priest. "Are you sure you're not all hopped up on this idea because you'd like to show up the chief?"

"No!" Fergusson paused. "Well. Maybe a little."

"Okay. I'm in."

"Me, too," Will said. "What should I do?"

Fergusson gave McCrea a go-ahead gesture. "Get back in touch with Olivia," McCrea said. "Ask her if her mother was behaving oddly at any time before her death. Ask her if she ever mentioned Tally or Wyler McNabb."

Will nodded. "I'll IM her when I get home tonight."

"See if she can get us a look at her mom's bank balances and investment reports."

"Investment reports?" Sarah was losing control of the session. Again.

"It's clear Tally stole a million dollars, and it's a pretty sure bet her husband was in on it with her." McCrea had an expression Sarah had never seen before. It was, she realized, his cop face. "If the money's been found at the resort"—Fergusson nodded—"it's a good bet that they had an accomplice to help hide it. Accomplices usually get paid off."

"Unless," Fergusson said, "somebody decided to cut her out of the picture."

"Yeah." His mouth compressed. "I'll go talk to the HR people at the Algonquin Waters."

"But you're still suspended," Sarah said. "Isn't that—I don't know, illegal?"

"I'm not going to arrest anybody." He grinned suddenly. "Like Reverend Clare said, I'm just going to ask some questions."

Will looked at her slyly. "What are you going to do, Sarah?"

She shook her head. "I guess I'm going to put on an orange turtleneck and drive the van."

◆ ◆ ◆

It was one of the easiest stings Russ had ever set up, even given the tight time frame. Nichols contacted Seelye on Saturday morning and told her he'd found the money after a search of Tally's house tipped him off. Lyle had soothed Ms. LeBlanc's fears and assured her that no one would even know an arrest was occurring in her resort's basement—they would use the employee exit to get in and out. Even persuading Tony Usher to fly up to Albany and run the operation with him had been a cinch. Bringing down a lieutenant colonel could be tricky, politically, but the prospect of bringing home six hundred grand—they had counted the remaining bricks and scanned their FDIC routing labels before replacing them on the pallet—was enough to paper over his concerns. Within twenty-four hours, Tony had found an ambitious CID investigator to be another witness, and right now, at ten o'clock on Monday evening, the man was hidden behind a screen of empty boxes not five feet from the money. It was his small camera stashed in the piping above, recording everything that happened.

Russ and Tony were in another blind, this one with a partial view of the employees' exit. They could see Quentan Nichols shifting from foot to foot in front of the door. He was dressed in a cleaning-service uniform. They had gotten three of them; Kevin, mopping close to the hotel-side employees' entrance, had one, as did Lyle, who was playacting sleep in the darkened break room. At least Russ hoped he was acting.

"He's going to walk a trough in that cement if he doesn't stop pacing." Tony kept his voice down. They'd set up a blower farther down Broadway's corridor to mask any ambient sounds, but no one wanted to take any chances.

"He's got a right to be nervous." Russ shifted on his box. The combination of cold and inactivity was making his hip ache. "He's betting everything on this."

"Nichols isn't the first soldier to go stupid and start thinking with the wrong head." Tony sighed. "And Seelye, sad to say, isn't going to be the first officer to be tempted by all the money they've got floating around over there. The stories I could tell you—" He broke off as Nichols grabbed the handle and opened the employees' entrance.

Lieutenant Colonel Arlene Seelye stepped in. She was dressed as anonymously as Nichols—dark jeans, dark shirt, dark windbreaker. Nichols said, "Colonel," but she held up her hand. She glanced around her, then strode past him into the corridor. She walked up toward the hotel-side entrance and back down, past Russ and Tony, past the CID captain, past the loot itself, scanning left and right. She poked her head into the darkened break room but didn't turn on the lights. Evidently satisfied, she returned to Nichols's side. "Quentan Nichols." She looked him up and down. "I'm still not convinced you're not yanking my chain. What's really going on here?"

Nichols took two dancing steps into the corridor, like a nervous junkie about to make a deal. Now they were both under one of the dangling fluorescent lights. In perfect focus for the camera. "I told you. I waited until Tally McNabb's old man was gone and then I searched that house from basement to attic. I found a reference that made me think it might be here, and it is."

She shook her head. "I think you knew all along. I think she made you a partner when you agreed to help her steal that money from Balad Air Base. So why do you need my help now?"

"I didn't know where it was! I didn't even know what it was she was moving!"

Russ tensed. *Keep cool, Quentan. Don't jerk the line. Just reel her in.*

Nichols breathed in. "It's too much for me to shift. And it's too much for me to deal with. I'm offering you a fifty-fifty split. I show you where it's stored, you launder the money. If you don't want in, the door's that way." He pointed.

Seelye paused. "Okay. I'm in. Show me what you've got."

Beside him, Russ felt Tony Usher's muscles bunch as he clenched his fist in triumph.

Nichols and Seelye passed them. Russ could hear the soft scrape of the cardboard tower moving over concrete, and then the rumble of the dolly being rolled into the corridor. "Help me with this," Seelye said. "I want to see what we've got." There was a faint grunt and then the sound of plastic slapping onto the floor. There was a long pause. Russ looked at Tony. The JAG officer shook his head. Russ nodded. They wanted her to take the money into possession.

"FDIC tags and all," Seelye said. "I'd have to match it up to make sure, but it looks like the shipment that was stolen from Balad."

Tony frowned.

"Excellent work, Chief Nichols."

The employees' entrance slammed open. Russ leaped from his seat, his Glock already in his hand. He broke from the blind, empty cardboard boxes tumbling into the boots and black-clad legs of the men pounding up the corridor, and he shouted, "Stop! Police!" hearing his voice huge, reverberating off the walls, many voices, all screaming, "Stop! Police!"

A helmeted and armor-clad man skidded, faced him, M-9 semiautomatic braced and ready, bellowing, "Police! Put your weapon down! Put your hands in the air!"

From the other side of the hall, Russ heard Lyle roaring the exact same words. They were everywhere: shouted commands and weapons and body armor and bright yellow letters screaming MILITARY POLICE.

Russ reversed his Glock and raised his hands. The MP opposite him tore the sidearm from his grasp and shoved him around. "Lyle, give up your gun," Russ yelled.

The guy behind him pushed him hard enough to make him stumble. "Shut up!"

"MKPD, put up your weapons!" They could sort out this disaster, but if someone got shot—

"I said shut up and get on the floor!" His MP's voice was on the edge of wild. He shoved Russ with the bore of his M-9 this time. Russ shut up. He got down, one knee and then the other, but he was too slow for the kid behind him. The MP slammed him forward, jolting the breath out of his body. Russ lay panting on the cold concrete, craning his head to see while the MP cuffed him. He spotted Nichols cuffed and on the floor, saw the CID captain down on both knees, hands in the air and his mouth going a mile a minute, saw Seelye, dark shirt yanked aside, unstrapping the wire taped to her T-shirt. She was talking to an officer in BDUs whose body armor and MILITARY POLICE vest looked at odds with his fleshy body and fifty-something face.

She glanced down. Blinked. Blinked again. "Chief Van Alstyne? What the hell are you doing here?"

TUESDAY, OCTOBER 18 This time, the fight started because Eric *was* putting on a uniform.

"What are you doing?" Jennifer's voice caught him up short, laying out his BDUs after his shower. "It's Tuesday. You don't have anything Guard-related."

He had figured no one at the resort would answer his questions if he was in civvies, unless he wanted to misrepresent himself as a plainclothes detective. On the other hand, he was pretty sure no one would call his reserve unit to ask why one of their MPs was at the hotel, interviewing the human resources director. Not that that made it any less of a violation of the Uniform Code of Military Justice. He was edgy, already having second thoughts, and that was why he snapped at her instead of just blowing it off.

"What are you, my personal calendar?"

"You haven't done anything except mope around the house and go to those useless veterans group meetings since you got suspended. Now all of a sudden you're getting ready to report? What's going on?" She paled. "Oh, Jesus. You're not converting your enlistment to regular army, are you?"

"No." He tugged on his pants.

"Then what?"

He spun around. "I'm trying to help out a friend by asking a few questions. That's all. For chrissake, get off my back."

"Asking a few questions? You mean, like pretending you're working as an MP? You can't do that, Eric. If you get caught you could face charges. You could lose your job!" She moved in close, forcing herself into his line of sight. "For God's sake, what are we supposed to do if you get bounced off the force? You're in a precarious enough position as it—"

"Why can't you for one frigging time just support me?" He sat heavily on the edge of the bed and began yanking his socks on. "Why is it always criticizing and fault-finding and looking at me like I'm a goddamn monster because of what I have to do?"

"What are you talking about?" She stepped back.

"I am trying, Jen. I am trying *all the time,* and you never notice, and you never appreciate it. You have no idea what I've been through!"

"Then tell me! For the love of God, I'm here! I'm listening!"

He picked up one boot. "You don't want to hear it."

She made a strangled noise and spun around in a circle, something she did when she got too frustrated to stand still. "No, you just don't want to face your feelings. Because it's easier to get angry than it is to let yourself feel scared, or sad, or helpless." She jammed a finger toward him. "You're too cowardly to—"

"Mom?" Jake was standing in the doorway, staring, his eyes huge and afraid, his hands clenched in fists as if he were ready to wade into—

—to protect his mother—

—and the feeling roared over Eric, swamping him, and he rose, screaming, "Get out of here!" and hurled the boot, snapped it, hard, and it smashed Jake in the chest and sent the boy stumbling back into the hall.

Then the tide washed out again and he was standing there, dumbfounded, his hand empty, his son sobbing. His son, to whom he had never raised a hand in his life.

"Jake?" Eric's voice came out cracked and raw. "Oh, God, son, I'm sorry—" He moved toward the door, but Jennifer was there, blocking him.

"Jake." Her voice was calm. She never took her eyes off Eric. "Honey, I want you to get the big black duffel bag in your room, and your backpack, and get into my car. Can you do that, lovey?" Jake sniffled an assent and staggered off down the hallway.

"I need you to sit back down on the bed, Eric."

He backed up blindly and collapsed onto the bed. Jen crossed to her closet, still keeping her eyes on him. She bent down, reaching behind her, and pulled out her overnight bag.

"What are you doing?" he whispered.

"Right now, Jake and I are going to my sister's. I'm going to contact you in a few days and let you know what I've decided to do."

She didn't put anything in the bag. He realized she had already packed. She had prepared for this. She was leaving him.

He lunged off the bed and grabbed her by the arm. "Jen. For God's sake!"

She looked at his hand, wrapped around her forearm. Then she looked at him. "You can hurt me, Eric, but you can't hurt me enough to make me leave my son in danger."

He snatched his hand away, and a terrible sound broke out of his tight chest and aching throat. Jennifer backed away, one step, then another, and then she was gone; down the hall, down the stairs, out the door, out of his life.

He stood in the bedroom for a long time afterward. Then he wandered through the house, touching tabletops and pictures, stacking the books Jake had left behind. Finally, he went into the basement and unlocked the gun cabinet. He looked at his rifle and his .44 and the youth Remington he'd gotten Jake the Christmas before he deployed. He took out his Heckler & Koch 9 mm, his favorite for target practice, and he sat in the rocking chair by the television and rocked and rocked, holding the gun in his hands. He'd have to go back upstairs and unlock the ammo if he wanted to use it, of course. That was the right way to store guns. Not like the McNabbs, who had kept their firearms loaded. He thought about Tally McNabb, maybe feeling as bad as he was right now. All she had to do was take it out and pull the trigger. Permanent headache relief. He indulged in a little wouldn't-they-be-sorry fantasy, but it kept breaking into the reality of Jake or Jennifer having to see him with his brains blown off. "Jesus, Eric," he said to himself. "Teen drama, much?"

He was a grown-up. He was a grown-up who had screwed up unbelievably bad in almost every way there was, and he wasn't going to get out of it with some grand fuck-you-world gesture. He locked the 9 mm back in the cabinet and trudged upstairs. Put on the rest of his uniform. One thing at a time. He had questions about Ellen Bain to figure out. Then, if he played his cards right, he'd have his job. Then he'd fix things with Jake. Then he'd get his wife back.

Get one thing right. Doesn't matter if you have no idea how the rest of it will fall into place, or even if it *will* fall into place. It was just like his tour of duty. You take it one day at a time, one hour, sometimes one minute at a time, and that's how you get through it.

He set his beret on his head and went off to do one thing right.

◆ ◆ ◆

Eric parked as close to the hotel entrance as he could. He sat there for a while, hearing Jennifer saying, *If you get caught you could face charges. You could lose your job.* Hearing Will Ellis saying, *Nobody gets left behind.*

He got out of the car. Took the curving steps up to the wide cobblestone entryway, jammed with rich-looking retirees getting into Beemers or handing off the keys to the Mercedes to the valets. The parking guys were too busy to pay him any heed, but several guests stared at him. Curious, at first, because the resort was out of the pay grade of anybody lower than a full bird colonel. Then they got the look he had seen before. It was all sorts of warm and approving, like they had slapped a WE SUPPORT OUR TROOPS magnet on their faces. God, he hated that look.

It was less annoying on the face of the perky blond desk clerk. Hotel receptionists always looked like they were grateful for your service. "May I help you?" the girl said.

"Yes, you can." He tried to smile, but it felt off. "I'd like to speak to your human resources manager."

Her expression grew guarded. "I'm afraid we're not hiring at this time, but I can get you an application to fill out if you'd like."

Eric flipped his reserve ID badge at her, fast enough to register, not so fast she could make out the details. "I'm with the military police. I need to ask a few questions about Tally McNabb."

"Oh. Okay. Wait here, please." She disappeared through the door behind reception. Popped out again not two minutes later. "Ms. Kirkwood will be right with you."

Elaine Kirkwood, the Algonquin Waters HR director, had the softened skin of somebody's mother and the assessing eyes of a card shark. She led Eric around the edge of the resort's sprawling lobby, past the dark, leafy bar, into a side corridor punctuated by unmarked doors. She opened one and ushered him into a typical corporate space—copier, cubicles, and computers. Hermetically sealed windows displayed untouchable views of trees, mountains, sky. Several women's heads popped up like woodchucks out of holes. Eric thought, not for the first time, that he'd rather take a bullet than have to work in an office.

Kirkwood continued on to an inner door. "This way." She shut the door behind them, then sat at a desk that was almost as cluttered as the chief's. He took one of the two chairs facing her. There was a large box of tissues within reach. For employees getting the ax, he supposed. "I don't know if you've checked with them, Sergeant, but we've already given a statement to the local police."

"I'm not here about her suicide." He slid his pen and notebook out of his breast pocket.

"You're not? What, then?"

"How long had she been working for BWI Opperman?"

Kirkwood raised her eyebrows as if to acknowledge his sidestepping her question. "Almost three months. She started on August first."

"Can you tell me what, exactly, her job entailed?"

"I don't understand."

"Was she responsible for the accounting for the entire company?"

"Oh, no. We have an outside firm for that. Tally's job was to keep the books for the special construction projects."

"I'm afraid you've lost me." He gave her a look that said, *I'm slow.*

"Oh, well, let's see. Let me give you some history." She held up three fingers. "There are three divisions of BWI Opperman."

Not that slow, he wanted to say.

"The original division is the resort construction company. For its first twenty years, the company specialized in fulfillment. Building for others," she said in response to his questioning expression. "About fifteen years ago, the company went vertical. Designing, building, and operating its own resorts. In the past few years, BWI Opperman has spun its expertise off into special projects that require single-team, clearing-to-cap construction."

"Can you give me an example of that?"

"Well, the only contracts we've taken so far have been with the coalition forces in Iraq."

Eric blinked. "There aren't any resorts in Iraq. At least, not any that weren't blown up."

She smiled. "BWI Opperman was hired because of that vertical integration. We have earth movers and carpenters and electricians and roofers and anyone else you might require to turn a completely undeveloped piece of land into a school. Or a clinic. Or a mess hall. Anything that might be necessary. We're one-stop shopping for the Provisional Authority's building needs. All the American contractors are, as I understand it."

"So she did all the accounting for that. From here?"

"Yes. Well." Kirkwood paused and looked uncomfortable for a moment. "She had been reassigned. It was felt that having the specials' accountant in Iraq would be more useful. Lead to less cost overruns. Of course, she never actually went over." Her voice thinned.

"You had another bookkeeper here before Tally was hired. Ellen Bain."

"Yes, that's right."

"What was her job?"

Kirkwood lifted her brows. "Special construction projects. Tally was hired to replace her."

"Three days after she died in an accident?"

The HR director's face fell into smooth, untroubled lines. "It was too important a position to leave unfilled."

"How did Tally come to your attention?"

"I'm afraid our hiring process is confidential." Kirkwood placed her hands on her desk and rose. "If that's all, Sergeant, I have a busy day ahead of me."

Eric stood as well. "Who replaced her?"

"I beg your pardon?"

"Who replaced Tally? In the special construction position?"

Kirkwood blinked, hiding her shark's eyes for a moment. "We haven't found anyone suitable yet."

◆ ◆ ◆

"It doesn't make any goddamn sense." Russ paced from the squad room table to one of the windows to the whiteboard to the huge three-county map hanging near the door.

"Will you quit that? You're gonna give me motion sickness." Lyle handed Tony Usher a mug of coffee. "Don't worry. Harlene made it. It's safe to drink."

"You made a wrong call, Chief. It happens." Tony sounded pretty damn philosophical for a man who'd had to admit to a CID investigator and another JAG that he'd been running his own not entirely authorized investigation.

"Christ, Tony, I'm sorry. I'm sorry I dragged you into this."

"No harm, no foul. They think I was following the same case, just half a step behind them. I can stand looking a little slow. It's not going to hurt my career."

Tony was generous. Two light birds—the JAG had been a lieutenant colonel, too—now thought Usher was some sort of cowboy. Not the performance any major wanted on his record.

"I just don't get it." Russ picked his own mug off the table, wincing at the spasm of pain in his shoulder where the overeager MP had rifle-butted him. "She let her prime informant fly off to Iraq. She didn't search McNabb's house or her bank accounts. Hell, as far as we can tell, she never even questioned Tally's friends. That's not an investigation. That's dereliction of duty."

"Maybe she got your number when she was here," Lyle said. "She figured you'd never be able to stand not knowing what happened and you'd find the money for her."

"Do you think Opperman's in on it? He could have paid her off. Made McNabb disappear."

Lyle stared at him. "You think the CEO of a fifty-million-dollar-a-year company is going to hook up with one of his construction bosses and his wife in order to split a million in cash? Jesum, Russ, the man's vacation house in the Caribbean is worth more'n that."

"Maybe she stuck with Nichols," Tony said. "Let him lead her to the money."

"Poor Nichols. Christ." Russ wiped his hand across his face. His jaw stung where he had scraped it raw against the concrete floor. "The guy put it on the line to help us, and he winds up under arrest." His last sight of Nichols had been the man's despairing face as he disappeared into one of three personnel carriers Seelye's SWAT team had brought.

"Chief." Tony dropped his hand on Russ's shoulder for a second. "He knew the risk. It's not like he was Ivory Soap clean."

"I know, I know." Russ's frustration goaded him forward, window to whiteboard to map.

"The money's back where it belongs." Lyle raised his mug. "I count that as a win."

Russ turned on his second in command. "Does this feel right to you?"

Lyle pursed his lips together. "No," he finally said. "It doesn't. But I've seen enough incompetent kiss-asses rise to the top of the heap off of other men's hard work not to recognize it when it happens. She blew the investigation, then lucked out when Nichols called her. She gets the gold mine and he gets the shaft."

◆ ◆ ◆

Russ took Tony down to Albany to catch his morning flight. It was the least he could do. "You sure you don't want to stay for the wedding?" he asked, pulling into the departures lane.

Tony grinned. "The opportunity to see you doing the Chicken Dance is tempting, I must admit, but I better get home and start covering my ass."

Russ threw the truck into park. "I'm sorry about all this."

"Stop apologizing." Tony dug his travel voucher out of his coat pocket. "You're the one who taught me it's better to have backup and not need it than the other way around."

They both got out of the cab. Tony hoisted his bag from the truck bed. "If anything else like this comes up, anything involving the army, I want you to give me a call, okay? Even if it's just to bounce ideas off my thick skull."

Russ balanced on the edge of the curb, stretching his legs. "Forget it. My normal caseload consists of drunken fights and shoplifting from the Stewart's, not military justice violations. The nearest base to us is Fort Drum, and that's three and a half hours away."

Tony shook his head. "Your little burg's not a military town, that's true, but it's the kind of town where the military comes from. Small, rural, not much opportunity. Right? How many of your young people join up to get away?"

Russ thought of Wayne and Mindy's boy, Ethan. Of himself, all those years ago. "A few."

"Uh-huh. And how many of your officers and EMTs and firefighters got their training in the Guard?" He lifted his bag from the walk. "There are a lot of Millers Kills all over this country. It's where people like you and me come from, and sometimes it's where we go back to. As long as that's true, you're going to keep crossing paths with the Big Green." He held out his hand, and Russ shook it, hard. "You take care, Chief. Have fun being the preacher's husband. Send me and Latice the baby announcement when it's time."

Russ laughed. "Sorry, no kids. How 'bout you send me and Clare an invitation to Kanisha's graduation?"

"Invitation, hell. We're selling tickets at fifty bucks a pop. You've got to think creatively when it comes to funding college."

◆ ◆ ◆

Evonne Walters's greeting that morning was so enthusiastic Clare felt guilty for not visiting sooner. She brought out a loaf of pumpkin bread warm from the oven, and they settled on a sofa in a room Grandmother Fergusson would have called "the good parlor." Photo albums and boxes of tissues suggested that this had become the place to meet and mourn and reminisce.

Clare placed her mug on the coffee table and picked up an album.

"That's Mary in high school," Evonne said.

Clare flipped the cover open. A long-haired, makeup-wearing Tally McNabb smiled up at her. There were pages of friends and teammates, slumber parties and snow forts and the beach at Lake George. Tally in her prom dress, escorted by a boy in an ill-fitting tuxedo. "Is that Wyler?"

"Oh, yes. They dated all through high school and got married right after." Evonne flipped to a picture of Tally and Wyler leaning against the hood of a muscle car. "I don't mind admitting I was against it at the time. Wyler didn't even have a diploma, and I didn't want Mary to have as hard a life as I had. But she was crazy in love with him." She turned another page. Tally, in a white dress and veil. "They had their ups and downs. When she enlisted he was right ticked. Wouldn't leave Millers Kill, though it wun't like he had a regular job to keep him." Evonne sighed. "He took his own sweet time growing up. Then he got hired by BWI Opperman, and they got the house and all, and I figured he just needed some extra baking time."

"Were you worried when she signed up?"

"I always figured, what harm could come to a girl pushing a pencil?"

Evonne made a quavery attempt at a smile. "Who knew the trouble would come after she got home?"

"Sometimes . . ." Clare searched for the right words. "Sometimes the hard part is coming home. When you're in, you know exactly what's expected of you. After . . . you're on your own."

"But she had me, and Wyler, and her friends. She had that group of yours. She had the job with BWI Opperman, and money to burn. She could've done anything." Evonne blinked hard. "Somehow she just got smaller and smaller inside herself. Like she was hiding."

"From what?"

"If I knew that, I mighta been able to help her." The older woman sliced the pumpkin bread and held it out toward Clare. *Take, eat,* she thought. *This is my body, given for you.* They ate the bread together. It was warm and sweet on Clare's tongue.

"You were a chaplain," Evonne said.

"No. I flew helicopters. I was regular army for ten years before I became a priest."

"Then you must have seen action. Is that the right word? Fighting, I mean."

The pillar of smoke, before her, beneath her, around her. Blood on concrete. The screaming. The smell. "Yes," she said.

"Well, you came through fine." Clare almost laughed, but Evonne went on. "That's the part I don't understand. She was an accountant. The worst thing that should've happened to her was a paper cut. How did she get hurt so bad inside the only thing could cure it was a bullet?" Her voice broke. Clare held out her hands, and the older woman took them, squeezing tightly.

"I don't know. All I can tell you is that being over there changes you. War makes you different, and you can't go back to who you were before."

"I feel so . . ." Evonne shook her head, as if trying to rattle the words free. "Angry. At her. At Wyler. At the counselor. At the army."

"Not at BWI Opperman? They were going to send her back to Iraq with the crew."

"You know, she never did tell me that. I didn't find out until Wyler spoke to me." Evonne released Clare's hands and reached for a tissue. "I can't believe that was what made her . . . she could've just quit. She already had a couple good offers when BWI Opperman came after her."

"Came after her? She hadn't already applied?"

"Nope. The owner himself asked her, is what she said. Wyler greased it, I figure." She flipped back to the page where Tally and her new husband stood in their finery, eternally young, eternally happy. "He had his faults, but he was good to her. He always said he wouldn't have his job with BWI Opperman if not for her."

◆ ◆ ◆

Clare's phone rang as she was rattling down Route 137 on her way back to town. A number she didn't recognize. Maybe Eric had uncovered something good already? "Clare here," she answered.

"Clare Fergusson? This is Dr. Stillman's office. We've scheduled your tests at the Washington County Hospital Outpatient Clinic. Are you available at one this afternoon?"

Oh, God. Her brain whited out. How many pills had she had this morning? Did she drink last night? No, she'd come home from group and fallen asleep.

"Ma'am?"

Clare snapped to. "What?"

"Are you available?"

"Yes. Of course." Her voice sounded scratchy in her ears. "Where is that, exactly?"

The receptionist gave her directions to the outpatient clinic. She thanked the woman automatically and let her phone drop unnoticed onto the passenger seat. She stared sightlessly through the windshield at the still-green pastures ahead, bordered with lichen-stained stone walls or sagging barbwire fences. She was over the dosage on the Dexedrine, she knew she was. She had been going to call Trip, let him know what she and Will and Eric had talked about at last night's meeting. Now . . . She bit her lip. She'd have to think of what to say. Maybe she could get him to postpone the test for twenty-four hours. Which completely obviated the purpose of the test, so she'd have to have a damn good reason. Which would be what, exactly?

The phone ringing again cut off her downward-spiraling thoughts. She opened it without checking the number. "Clare Fergusson here."

"Hey, Reverend Clare, it's Will."

Clare chucked her own issues into the backseat and focused on Will. "Hey. What's up?"

"I talked to Olivia last night. After our meeting. I told her it looked like her mom might have been involved with Tally McNabb and her husband."

Clare slowed for a truck lumbering toward her across the narrow span of Veterans Bridge. "How did she feel about that?"

"She was kind of upset. I mean, I tried to soft-pedal it and all, but there's no nice way to say your mom could have been on the take. Anyway, she gave me permission to look in her house for anything that might tell us more." He paused. "I mean, for you and Eric to look in the house." His voice faded. "I don't think the place is handicapped-accessible for me."

"How do we get in if she's away at college? Spare key?"

"She said you could call Roxanne Lunt, the Realtor. She'll let you in."

"The house is up for sale?" Her heart sank. Lord knows what had been tossed out to prepare the place to be shown.

"What's she going to do with a house? Even if her mom had lived, Olivia probably wasn't going to be living there anymore except for a few weeks in the summer."

"No, I understand. It's just . . ." She shook the explanation away. "I know Roxanne. I'll call her." *If her mom had lived.* "Will, it would have been an awkward question to ask, but were you able to get a sense of how well-off her mother left her? Was there an unexpected amount?"

"I thought of that," Will said. "There wasn't much. Some retirement stuff and the house. If she hadn't gotten the scholarship, she'd be carrying a ton of student loans right now."

"Mmm. Of course, that doesn't mean there wasn't payoff money. Just that it's somewhere Olivia and the estate executor couldn't find it."

"Or maybe it's like you and Eric said. Maybe she was set up to have an accident so nobody would have to pay her anything."

◆ ◆ ◆

Ellen and Olivia Bain's house was one of a string of 1920s workingmen's cottages along Meersham Street, small, pretty, with deep yards and spreading, now leafless, trees. Roxanne Lunt waved to Clare from a front porch decorated with corn shocks and pumpkins. Clare had offered to pick up the key from the Realtor's office, but Roxanne turned her down. Clare sensed a sales pitch in the making. Roxanne had been showing properties on and off to Russ since he had gotten rid of his house—*the house he shared with Linda,* her brain helpfully supplied. Clare and Russ were planning on living in the rectory for the time being, but he had to invest the money from the sale of his last home soon or pay taxes on it. A fact the Realtor was well aware of.

Roxanne held out her arms as Clare mounted the porch steps. "There you are! Only four more days to go, am I right?"

"Till what?"

Roxanne stared at her. "Until the wedding?"

"Oh. Yeah," Clare said. "Don't remind me. I've got—" An MKPD squad car turning onto Meersham caught her eye. It swooped down the street, scattering dry leaves in its wake, and tucked in behind her Jeep. She knew, before he got out of the cruiser, that Russ was the driver. He always parked in a way that suggested the vehicle in front of him was about to get ticketed.

"And here comes the groom," Roxanne caroled as Russ crossed the corner of the lawn and climbed the porch steps.

"What are you doing here?" Clare realized she could have sounded more gracious.

He cocked an eyebrow at her. "Good question. Roxanne called me. She said you wanted to look at a house?" The crunch of more tires against the curb made them all turn. Clare watched with a sinking heart as Eric McCrea got out of his SUV dressed in his Guard uniform for some reason. He stopped halfway around the hood of his truck, looking at the assembly on the porch.

"With . . . Eric? Gee, Clare, is there something you're not telling me?"

"Oh, for heaven's sake," Clare began.

Roxanne smiled brightly. "I'll just open up and turn the lights on, shall I?" She unlocked the front door and whisked out of sight.

Russ glanced up at the flawless blue sky. "Yeah, we'd better have the lights on."

"I'm sorry she called you," Clare said. "You can go on patrolling or whatever." She flapped her hand toward his squad car. "This has nothing to do with you."

He pinched the bridge of his nose beneath his glasses. "Why do I have the feeling that's not entirely true?"

Eric had squared his shoulders and walked up the driveway. He climbed the porch steps like a man climbing to the guillotine. "Chief." He cut his eyes toward Clare. "Will called. Said I should join you."

"Will?" Russ said.

"Will Ellis." Clare crossed her arms.

Russ frowned. "Will Ellis." He looked at her. Then at Eric. Then back at her. His face changed. "Oh, for God's sake. This isn't some sort of— this isn't about Tally McNabb, is it?"

"What if it is?" Clare knew she sounded like a five-year-old, but she couldn't help it.

"Whose house is this?"

"It belonged to Ellen Bain," Eric said to the floorboards.

Russ frowned. "Who?"

"Ellen Bain." Eric lifted his head. "She was the fatal auto accident back in July. Out at the juncture of Sacandaga and the resort road?"

"I remember. What's the connection?"

"She and Tally had the same job," Clare said. "Keeping books for the construction crews that went overseas."

"Tally was hired three days after Ellen Bain died," Eric said. "Because the job was so critical, the human resources director said."

Clare interrupted. "Her mother said she got the offer directly from the CEO."

"However, two weeks after Tally died, they still haven't replaced her. Despite the position being so important they were going to send her back to Iraq."

Russ held up a hand. "It didn't occur to you that they might have difficulty filling a position that involved living and working in a war zone?"

"Chief, you found the missing money at the resort, right? Doesn't that argue for another person on the inside? Wyler McNabb couldn't have been popping in and out of the Algonquin Waters all the time. He was part of the construction division."

"A bookkeeper," Clare said. "Somebody in a position to retrieve the cash and launder it."

Russ shook his head. "That was Tally McNabb's job."

"*After* the last bookkeeper conveniently died at the end of July," Eric said. "That money was stolen at least five months before then."

"I'm guessing you're the one who came up with some theory tying the two women together," Russ said to Clare. "What is it?"

"Ellen Bain was the third partner. She helped hide the money, and she greased the way for Tally to replace her."

"Why?" Russ said before she could continue.

"A big payoff," she said.

"Another job," Eric said. "She was long divorced, and her only kid was leaving for college. Nothing to keep her from moving somewhere bigger, with more opportunities."

"Do you know the Bain woman suggested Tally McNabb for her job?" Russ sounded skeptical.

Eric rubbed the back of his neck. "No."

"Did the HR director indicate Bain had anything to do with Tally McNabb getting the job? I mean, as opposed to her husband, who was a foreman on their overseas construction unit?"

Eric shook his head.

Clare jumped in. "Tally's mother says Wyler credited his wife with getting him his job."

"Uh-huh. And that fits in with your theory how?"

She opened her mouth. Shut it again. "I haven't had time to integrate all my facts yet."

"Did she rope you into this?" Russ asked Eric.

Two cars driving past the house slowed nearly to a crawl, their drivers rubbernecking at the Bains' porch. Clare realized they must look like the beginning of a shaggy dog story. *A cop, a soldier, and a priest walk into a bar* . . . Russ must have had the same thought, because he gestured toward the door. "Inside."

Roxanne, true to her word, had turned on every lamp and overhead in sight. The wide, wooden-floored living room and parlor were sparsely furnished, making the place look bigger than it must have when it housed mother and daughter.

The tap-tap-tap of heels announced Roxanne's descent from the second floor. "Well! Everything all straightened out?" Her smile wobbled a bit when she saw Eric was still with them, but she rallied. "What would you like to see first?"

"Personal papers," Eric said. "Checkbooks, tax records, bank and investment statements."

The Realtor's professionally groomed eyebrows went up. "I beg your pardon?"

"We have permission from Olivia Bain to look at any financial records her mother might have left behind," Clare explained.

Roxanne turned to Russ as if seeking a translation. "Don't look at me," he said. "I'm just a cop." He frowned and turned to the other officer in the room. "Do you want to explain why you're wearing your Guard uniform, Eric?"

Eric opened his mouth. He paused. Shook his head. "No."

Russ glanced up at the ceiling as if seeking divine patience. He took a deep breath. "Listen. Colonel Seelye has taken custody of the money on behalf of the army."

"You let her walk away with it?" Clare said.

"She was backed up by a platoon of MPs and a light bird from the judge advocate's office. I didn't have much say in the matter."

Eric sounded outraged. "But Lyle said you thought she was—"

Russ cut Eric off. "I thought wrong." He looked sidelong toward Clare. "I want you to note, I can admit when I'm wrong about something. Quentan Nichols was placed under arrest—"

"Oh, no!"

"—and I suspect Wyler McNabb will be in custody as soon as they can coordinate with the appropriate coalition authorities." Russ hooked his thumbs in his gun belt, a gesture that never failed to get Clare's back up. "The case, which was never ours to begin with, is closed. It's all up to the lawyers' wrangling now."

"Well!" Roxanne's voice was professionally upbeat. "If that's all settled, I'd love to show you the kitchen."

"Chief, you still have two women, both working in the same job, both dead within three months of each other." Eric's voice was heavy and low. "If Ellen Bain's death wasn't the accident we thought it was, that *will* be our case."

Russ looked at Eric steadily. "I'm going to overlook the fact that you're on suspension and have no business being here. For the moment. You were the investigating officer for the Bain death. Did you uncover anything that indicated her car wreck wasn't an accident?"

"No, but—"

"She tested positive for alcohol in her autopsy, and she wasn't wearing her seat belt."

"She was under the limit. Barely, but under." Eric sounded defensive. "And she was well known for not buckling up."

Russ's eyes unfocused slightly. "We never had the car checked for mechanical failure."

"There wasn't any need. The accident reconstruction backed up the witnesses' statements."

Russ frowned. Clare held her breath. She knew him. If there was one question to a story, one thread left dangling, he couldn't resist. He'd go after it.

Then why didn't you accept it when he said Tally's death was a suicide?

"Okay. Yeah." He rubbed his forehead. "It couldn't hurt to dig a little deeper."

"Wonderful!" Clare turned toward the Realtor. "Roxanne—"

He held up one hand. "For the *paid professionals* to dig a little deeper. Roxanne, do you know where Ms. Bain's financial records and personal papers might be?"

"Not here." She sounded as if she had finally accepted this wasn't going to be an open house for the future Mr. and Mrs. Van Alstyne. "We cleared the place out after her daughter went off to school. After the owner dies is the best time to show a property," she confided. "You don't have to find a spot for all the stuff people live with."

"Where did it go?" Russ asked.

"The furniture that wasn't sold is being stored in her mother-in-law's barn. Violet Bain. All the papers and the computer went to Ms. Bain's brother. He was the executor."

Russ nodded. "Does he live around here?" *Do I know him?*

"Oh, yes he does. He set that leg you broke so spectacularly a few winters back. He's Dr. George Stillman, the orthopedic surgeon."

◆ ◆ ◆

Will was stretched out on the weight bench in his bedroom, pumping iron, when he heard the doorbell's muffled chime. He ignored it, concentrating on his balance, his form, controlling the shaking of his too-weak muscles. Lifting without feet to brace against the floor was a challenge. Taking his body back after doing his damnedest to poison it was a challenge. Everything in his life was a frigging challenge.

He heard his father's footsteps in the hall. He quickly reset the bar into its cradle and used it to chin himself into a seated position. Dad would give him hell if he saw Will had been bench pressing without a spotter. His father knocked and entered. "Willem? You've got a visitor."

Will swabbed his face with the bottom of his T-shirt. "Reverend Clare?"

"Nope. Olivia Bain."

Will nearly fell off the bench. "What?" It was a six-hour drive from Geneseo. She must have set out before daybreak to be in Millers Kill now. "What's she doing here?"

"She wants to see you, evidently." Dad tossed him a towel. "Better mop off. You know what they say. Never let 'em see you sweat." He cocked his head. "Do you need any help?"

"Uh." Will's mind raced. "Toss me a clean tee and pants, will you?"

"You got it." His father pulled the clothes off the shelves and draped them over the weight bar. "I'll keep her company until you get out there."

Will lay back on the bench and wiggled his shorts off. He tugged on his baggy pants, curling his hips up, focusing on keeping his balance. He'd never gotten changed on the bench before, and he was damned if he was going to fall to the floor, to be rescued by his father.

His abs were aching by the time he snapped and zipped. He reversed his curl, sat up, and stripped off his sweaty shirt. He humped himself into the chair, grabbed the fresh tee, and was headed out the door before he had finished pulling it over his head. He rolled down the hallway, his flat pants legs flapping, and he had a moment to wish he had taken the time to fold and pin them, and then he was through the archway and there was Olivia, sitting across from his father, a backpack at her feet, looking—oh, man—even better than she had this past summer.

"Will!" She jumped up. "I'm sorry I—I wanted to—"

Dad stood. "You guys want something to eat? Maybe a soda?" Olivia shook her head.

"No, Dad, we're fine. Thanks." Will waited until his dad had strolled out of the living room before rolling closer to Olivia. "What are you doing here?"

"I had to see you. After we talked last night . . ." Her gaze went to his chest, his shoulders, his arms. "Wow."

"Wow?"

Her cheeks colored. "I mean, you're looking a lot better than I expected. After nearly killing yourself."

He loved the way Olivia just came out with what everybody else thought but wouldn't say. "Yeah, well. I figured as long as I was going to hang around in this body, I might as well keep it in shape. Aren't you missing classes?"

She sat cross-legged on the sofa. "I couldn't sleep after we talked last night. I kept thinking about my mom maybe being mixed up with this theft, and then I realized what you hadn't said." She looked him square in the face. "My mom's death might not have been an accident."

"We don't know that. It's a big jump—"

"You said you thought your friend's death was suspicious."

"Yeah . . ."

"Then my mom's death was suspicious, too." She picked up the backpack and rummaged inside. "I have a copy of the police report on her accident." She handed him several sheets of paper, stapled together.

"You kept a copy at school?"

"Yes." She paused. "You don't think that's weird, do you?" She shook her head, and her hair slid over her shoulders in interesting patterns. "Never mind. The point is, they never did an autopsy on her car."

"Her *car*? An autopsy?"

"Whatever you'd call it. I'm not good with mechanical stuff like that." She gave him that same direct look again. "But you are."

"Yeah, but—"

"It's at the MacVane brothers' junkyard. It's still there. I called them. You and I are going over there, and you're going to take a look at it."

"Me? Olivia, get real." He slapped his thighs. "I can't go waltzing through some junkyard, and I sure as hell can't tear into an engine while I'm sitting in this damn chair."

"So you get up on the edge of the hood. You're not a paraplegic. You told me everything still works." She blushed again, deeper than before, which made him color with embarrassment . . . and something else. She didn't see him as a cripple. When she said he looked good, she wasn't talking about his health, like everyone else was. She was talking about . . . him.

He let out a breath he didn't realize he was holding. "Okay."

"Really?" Her smile beamed like a laser. "You'll help me out?"

You'll help me out? He felt something twist in his chest, painful and pleasurable. Ever since he had woken up on a flight to Landstuhl, he had heard *Can I help you?* Now, for the first time in almost a year, he got to say it back. "Yeah." He smiled a little. "I'll help you."

◆ ◆ ◆

If he had been given free rein in the MacVane Brothers Garage and Junk-yard as a kid, Will thought, he might never have signed up for the marines. He'd have been hard-pressed to find anything more appealing than working between the piles of stripped and rusting auto bodies, the brilliant morning sun picking out a Ford Gran Torino, over there, or a cherry—except for the blown-out rear—'72 Dodge Charger. The beautiful girl with him only buffed up the fantasy.

The fact she was pushing his wheelchair did not.

"You're in luck." Buddy MacVane strode too quickly through the yard. "We sort out the wrecks into what we're gonna take care of first and what second, and so on."

"Triage," Will said. Was that an old T-Bird? Damn, it was. The chilly late October breeze carried the scent of steel and oil and mildewing leather.

"Triage, right. So like I was saying, you two are in luck. 'Cause the last ones we get to are the ones the county sends us that've been in a fatal accident. Used to do 'em the other way around, 'cause if it was bad enough to off somebody, they're usually no good for nothing but scrap."

Behind Will, Olivia made a noise. The big man slapped his head. "Aw, Gawd. I'm sorry, honey. I forgot."

"Why'd you change your policy?" Will asked.

"A couple years back we melted down something we got sent by the state police and then it turns out somebody'd been killed in the thing. You know, before the accident. Boy, didn't they scream blue murder. So now we just let 'em pile up in the back."

They rounded a squat industrial shed. "There's Sonny. My brother.

He's working on your car. We pulled it first thing this morning, soon as
you called." The crumpled Mini Cooper was on its back, beneath a heavy-
duty crane. The man digging in the undercarriage looked up at them. He
was Buddy's double, right down to the greasy flannel-lined jacket and
the oil-stained, drooping jeans.

"Hey, Sonny." Buddy thumbed toward Will and Olivia. "These here
are the kids who called. You got anything for them?"

"Maybe." Sonny wiped his hands on a rag. He stared at Will. "C'mere
and take a look."

Olivia raised her hands. "I don't . . . I don't know anything about cars."
Her voice shook.

Will squeezed her hand before rolling himself forward. "I do, but I
can't get to a good angle to see inside."

"Hell you can't." Sonny slapped the portable lift next to the crumpled
car. "Right here."

Will's face burned. "Look, I don't know if you didn't notice—"

"Sure did. What happened to you, kid?"

Will wanted to tell the old fart it was none of his damn business, but
they'd come here looking for a favor. "IED. In Fallujah."

Sonny looked at his brother. "What service were you in, kid?" Buddy
asked.

"Marine Corps."

Buddy grinned. He shucked off his stained jacket and rolled his thermal shirt all the way up his arm. An impressively large bulldog snarled
from his bicep.

"You used to be a marine?" Olivia said.

"No used to be about it, honey. Once a marine—"

"Always a marine," Sonny finished. He dragged his oil-spattered shirt
up to reveal an eagle-and-trident on his chest.

"Please tell me you don't have one of those," Olivia whispered.

"So drag your ass over here, marine, and tell me what you can figure out."

Cursing under his breath, Will maneuvered the chair next to the lift.
There was no way to get on it except flopping forward and then wiggling
around like a worm until he could wedge himself into a seated position.
With Olivia seeing every glorious second. God.

"You know, this'd all be a lot easier if you was wearing your prosthetics," Sonny said.

Will braced his hands on the undercarriage and peered into the Mini Cooper's guts. "Don't take this the wrong way, but what the hell would you know about it?"

A clang caught his attention. Sonny banged the crumpled sheet metal with a crutch. Two crutches. Forearm crutches—like Will had. They must have been leaning against the side of the car. Sonny grinned widely at Will, revealing less than perfect teeth, and shuffled back a few steps. He bent over and lifted the hems of his baggy jeans, looking like a shy girl inching her skirt up.

Will stared at the two black carbon prosthetics.

When the world reassembled itself inside his head, Will asked, "What happened?" He looked at Sonny, trying to guess where he might have seen combat. "Vietnam?"

Sonny shook his head. "Motorcycle accident."

"You wouldn't guess it, seeing as we're respectable business owners these days, but Sonny and me used to be a wild pair." Buddy hooted with laughter. Sonny joined him. Will tried to imagine how old he'd have to be, how many years he'd have to let go, before he could laugh like that at losing his legs.

"Did you have this business to fall back on, Mr. MacVane? After you got out of the service?" Olivia's clear voice startled Will. He had forgotten she was there.

"Naw, honey, we started this up after I lost m'legs. Nobody cares how pretty you look if'n you can fix up their cars."

"That's true," Buddy added. "We done real good. In fact, we got more work than we can handle. We been talking about bringing in a new guy to help out." He grinned at Will.

Will stared. His head was buzzing. "Are you—are you offering me a job?" He looked back at Sonny. "You don't know anything about me. You don't know if I know jack shit about cars."

"You tell me. On your honor as a marine. Do ya?"

Will started to laugh. He couldn't help it—it was like falling down the rabbit hole and getting interviewed by Tweedledum and Tweedledee. "I do, actually. I rebuilt a Charger and a Camaro. I've done work on my friends' cars. Including my priest's old kit-version Shelby."

"Sounds good to me," Buddy said. "Can you start next week?"

For some reason, Will looked at Olivia. She bounced up and down, nodding. "Yeah," he said. "I can."

"Good." Sonny pointed into the Mini Cooper. "Now tell me what's wrong here."

It took Will a minute to orient himself, seeing everything upside down. He felt like he might float off the lift if he didn't keep a tight grip on the edge of the car. He scanned the ball joints, the axle, the rotary—there it was. "One of the brake caliper pins is snapped off."

"Right."

"That can happen in an accident." Will lowered his voice. "Especially where the car was going downhill out of control."

"That's right, too. Metal stress. Or it was rusted out."

"Nobody washes their damn cars in the winter no more," Buddy put in. "Get their carriages eaten up with salt. Takes three, four years off the life of your car."

"My mother went to the car wash every Saturday, year-round." Olivia looked at the Mini Cooper with loathing. "She loved that thing."

"So what caused this caliper to break?" Will asked.

"Dunno," Sonny said. "Coulda been a stress fracture. Coulda been somebody who didn't like your girl's mama *made* a stress fracture."

"Takes five minutes with a metal saw," Buddy said.

"No way to tell," Sonny agreed.

Will sprawled across the car's undercarriage, careless of his dignity and clothes now. "You got a light?" Sonny put a flashlight in his hand.

"So you're saying the police report was right," Olivia said. "It was an accident."

This time, Will spotted the brake calipers easily. It helped that the pin was snapped clean off. Just like the brake on the other side.

"No." He pushed himself upright. "Two sheared-off brakes are no accident."

◆ ◆ ◆

"Ellen Bain's brother is Trip Stillman?" Russ stared at Roxanne Lunt for a moment before swinging toward Clare. "Isn't he in your group? Why the hell didn't you tell me this earlier?"

"I didn't know! He never said anything about his sister dying." Clare waved at the half-bare bookcases in Bain's living room. "It's not like there are pictures of him sitting around here."

"He did say there'd been a death in the family. Remember?" Eric was trying to be helpful. Russ wanted to tell him not to bother.

"Good Lord," Clare said. "I swear, this is the—" Her phone ringing cut her off. She snatched it out of her pocket. "Clare Fergusson here." She paused. "What? Oh, Will, that's wonderful! Your parents will be thrilled! Hang on." She clapped her hand over her phone. "The MacVane brothers offered Will a job at their garage."

"Why is he—" Russ began, but she was back on the phone. "Isn't MacVane's the junkyard the town uses?"

Eric nodded. "Yeah."

"What's Will Ellis doing over there?" He answered his own question. "Looking at the Bain woman's wrecked car." He pinched the bridge of his nose again. "Jesus, Eric, do you really think the kid's going to find something you didn't?"

Clare snapped her phone shut. "He did." Her voice surged with triumph. "Both brake calipers on Ellen Bain's car were sheared clean off. Sabotaged."

◆ ◆ ◆

They cleared out for Trip's office so fast poor Roxanne didn't have a chance to give away the house brochure. Clare sprinted for her Jeep, conveniently not hearing Russ's shouted suggestion that she go back to the rectory. *God.* In the driveway, Russ stopped Eric before he could get into his SUV.

"Ride with me. I'll bring you back here when we're done." Russ waited until they were both buckled up in his squad car before he said, "Your suspension's up on Friday."

"Yeah."

"What are you doing, running around like this?"

Eric shifted in his seat. "I haven't misrepresented myself, Chief. I'm unarmed, and I haven't done anything but ask a few questions. I haven't been collecting evidence."

"That you know of." Russ flicked on his turn signal and pulled away from the curb. "If Will Ellis and the MacVanes are right about that car, it changes everything." Russ bit back the sour taste in his mouth. They should have found this out back in August. They should have looked deeper. He should have pressed harder. Nothing could have saved Ellen Bain, but maybe—just maybe—they could have made a difference to Tally McNabb.

"I know. I swear, Chief, if it'd been just me and Clare at the house when she got that call, I would've let you know right away."

"Hmm." Russ slowed and stopped at the intersection. "Here's what I want to know now: Are you doing this because you got roped into it by Clare? Or have you decided you can't work within the limits of the police department anymore?"

Eric let out a noise. "No!"

"No what?"

"No. God. I don't know what I'd do if I couldn't be a cop anymore."

"You didn't file with your union representative. I've been waiting to hear from somebody."

"I didn't want to make a thing of it."

"You broke a man's cheekbone and fractured his skull, Eric. It's already a thing."

Eric stared at him. "I can't lose my job, Chief. You can't take it away from me."

God, Russ hated this. He accelerated down North Elm, fallen leaves scattering to either side of his tires. "Don't you think it's time to come clean about what happened in that kitchen?"

"You know what happened."

Russ sighed. "Here's my problem, Eric. You've never been anything except an asset to this department. You're the best investigator we have, excepting maybe Lyle. I want you on the streets. I need you on the streets. But I don't know if you're safe."

"It was just once!"

"Was it?" Russ looked away from the road for a second and pinned Eric with his gaze. "Was it just one incident?"

Eric dropped his head and hunched his shoulders.

"Listen to me, Eric. If you had come back from your deployment with your foot blown off, we'd make accommodations for you. If you had popped an eardrum or lost an eye, we'd make accommodations for you. It's no different if you've brought back something in your head. This department is ready to stand behind you and see that you get what you need to keep being the cop I know you can be, but you have got to come straight with me."

Eric stared out the window as they drove past a three-storied Victorian framed by tatter-leaved horse chestnuts. He mumbled something.

"What?"

"I lost it." Eric's voice was barely audible. "He swung at me and I lost it. I hit him. I hit him with my gun. When Knox tried to drag me off of him, I hit her, too."

Russ pressed his lips together tightly.

"I didn't mean to." Eric was louder now. "I swear, I didn't mean to. I feel like shit about it. It's like . . . it's like . . ." He raised his head. "Like this feeling, this mad, gets so big it squeezes everything else out. I can't think, I can't wait, I can't feel anything except . . ." He looked at his hands flexing, releasing. "I don't want to hurt anybody. I don't want to lose my family. I don't know what to do. All I've ever wanted to be is a husband and a dad and a good cop. What'll I do if I can't do that anymore? What'll I do?"

Russ slowed as he approached the curving loop of Church Street. The sight of St. Alban's settled him, so that his voice was even when he said, "Nobody's talking about you not being a cop anymore, but the first thing you need to do is get some professional help."

"I'm in counseling!"

"In addition to the veterans group. You need somebody who deals with anger management issues and who can prescribe, if necessary. Our heath plan covers—"

"Drugs? For God's sake. I can't be doped up on the job."

"Lyle has high blood pressure and high cholesterol. He takes drugs for both of 'em."

"That's different!"

"No, Eric, it's not." Russ stopped at the red light on Main. "He's getting medical treatment that enables him to show up for work every day without stroking out. You need to do the same thing. You can go through VA, or you can go through our HMO, but you're going to do it."

"It'll be on my record!"

"So is inappropriate use of force. I can guarantee you if I or your

Guard commander had to choose, we'd go for the Zoloft over assault and battery."

"Oh, God." Eric stared out the window. The downtown merchants association's Halloween window decorations—painted ghosts and cutout black cats—almost hid the fact that two of the stores on this corner had gone out of business at the end of the summer.

"Second, you're going out with a partner for the immediate future. I'd prefer to team you up with Knox, but obviously, that isn't going to work, so I'll put you with Kevin on day shift and Paul if you have to work nights."

"Not Paul. Jesus, all the guy does is eat junk food and talk about his porn collection."

"So you can show him what good policing looks like. Which brings me back to Knox. I'm going to have a talk with her. If she wants to press charges against you, I'm going to do it."

Eric didn't object to this one. He simply nodded.

"If she decides not to—and believe me, I'm going to leave it entirely up to her—then you have got to make things right with her." Russ turned onto Morningside Drive. "Have you spoken with her since the—since you hit her?"

Eric flushed a dull red. "No. I've been too . . . I couldn't. I couldn't face her."

"It's got to be done. We're a small force. We have to trust one another, without second-guessing, without hesitation. Something like this, between two people, starts to poison the atmosphere for all of us. Believe me, I know." He had carried a grudge against his deputy chief for months and months a couple years back, tending his bitterness and hurt like a hot-house plant. It had taken two .357 slugs in his chest and a near-death experience to snap him out of it.

Eric breathed out. "Okay."

"Okay." Russ eased the cruiser over the speed bump at the entrance of the Washington County Medical Offices. He spotted Clare's Jeep. "Bring me the name of an anger management specialist and the date for your first appointment when you come in Friday."

"You got it. I will!"

Russ found a space close to Clare. He threw the gear into park and turned toward Eric. "Lyle's throwing me a bachelor party Friday evening at the Full Moon in Glen Lake." He shook his head in disbelief. "I couldn't talk him out of it. Anyway, everybody except the night shift guys will be there. You come, too."

"Are you sure?"

"It'll be a good chance for you to reconnect. It might not be a bad time to talk to Knox. Less formal than at the station, and I'm sure she'll feel safer with a bar full of people around."

Eric dropped his head. "Okay," he said quietly.

"In the meantime, you can help me go though Ellen Bain's papers. It'll take some of the stress off the others—we're way overscheduled as it is right now. If the case is still open three days from now, you'll take lead."

Eric stared for a moment, as if trying to gauge Russ's sincerity. Finally, he said, "Thanks."

"Don't make me regret giving you a second chance." They got out of the squad car. Russ was halfway across the lot, headed for the squat cement building, when he realized he was alone.

"Eric?"

His sergeant held up a hand and half turned away. "Can you spare me for a minute, Chief?" His voice was clotted. "I gotta call my wife."

Russ found Clare at the Orthopedic Associates door. "Eric's having a moment," he said.

She bit her lip. "Is he all right? You didn't jump down his throat because of this, did you?"

"Yes, he is, and no, I didn't." He opened the door and let her precede him into the check-in area. The receptionist glanced up as they approached her. Her professional smile fell away and her eyes went wide. "Oh, my God." She clutched at her chest. "What's happened?"

"Nothing's happened." Russ realized they must look like some sort of death notification team: the cop and the minister. "I need to ask Dr. Stillman a few questions. Is he available?"

The receptionist pointed at Clare. "Then what's she doing here?"

"Good question," Russ said. The woman who had been sitting behind the SCHEDULING sign a few desks down wandered over to see what all the fuss was about.

Clare shot him a glare before giving the woman her most reassuring smile. "I'm Clare Fergusson. I know Dr. Stillman socially."

Socially? Clare's reverence for confidentiality was reaching new heights.

The scheduling secretary perked up. "Clare Fergusson? You're in the wrong building. Dr. Stillman's scheduled your blood test at the outpatient clinic at the hospital. You don't need a referral slip from us."

"Blood test?" Russ frowned. "Why is Trip Stillman sending you for a blood test?"

"I'm sorry," the scheduling secretary said. "Are you two together?"

"Ah," Clare said. "Um." She blinked several times. "We're engaged."

"You don't need a blood test to get married in New York," Russ snapped. "I know you don't like doctors and hospitals, Clare, but if something's wrong, you've got to *tell* me—" He faltered. He knew one reason she might need a blood test. His stomach sank. "You're pregnant."

"What? No! For God's sake, I'm not pregnant." Out of the corner of his eye, he saw interested faces turning toward them in the nearby waiting room.

"We don't do any pregnancy testing here." The receptionist sounded worried, as if this were a failing for an orthopedist. "If you think you might be pregnant, and you're due for X-rays, you should get confirmation first."

"I don't need a pregnancy test," Clare hissed.

"Would you please page Dr. Stillman for me?" Russ said. If he could just get these women out of his and Clare's faces for five seconds—

The scheduling clerk leaned against the counter. "Sir, engaged or no, you still don't have the right to patient information from one of our doctors."

"I'm here on police business," Russ said, at the same time Clare said, "I'm not a patient. Trip is just doing me a favor."

The receptionist put down her receiver. "He's on his way."

Russ wrapped a hand around Clare's arm and dragged her to the middle of the lobby entrance, as far from the waiting patients and the staring staff members as possible. "Okay. You're not pregnant. What's going on?" Every other reason he could think of for a blood test was worse than pregnancy. "Are you getting screened for cancer?"

"What? Why would you think that?"

"Because your sister died of colorectal cancer." Fear made his voice harsher than he intended. "That increases your risk of breast and ovarian cancer. And you hate seeing doctors. It would be just like you to hit up a friend for a favor if you were worried, instead of getting it checked out properly."

"No. Oh, love, no. Honestly."

"What is it, then?"

"Look." She bit her lip. "I don't want to get into it right now, but I promise you, I'm not going to die, I'm not pregnant, and I'm not—" She paused.

"Not what?"

She jerked her head. Trip Stillman was crossing the waiting room toward them. "Chief Van Alstyne." The doctor shook his hand. "Good to see you again. My receptionist said you have some questions for me?"

Russ gave Clare a look that said, *We're not done with this.* "Yeah. I'm afraid we're reopening the investigation into your sister's death. New evidence has come to light—" He broke off at the sight of Trip Stillman's face.

"My sister?"

Russ frowned. "Ellen Bain. I was told she was your sister." Oh, hell. If Roxanne Lunt was wrong, he was going to look a complete fool. "If there's been some mistake—"

"Yes. Yes. Ellen." Stillman took several shaky breaths. His skin looked waxy.

"Trip? Are you all right?" Clare glanced toward the reception desk. "Do you need help?"

"No." He cut her off with a sharp wave. "No. My sister is dead. She died this summer in a car accident."

"That's what we originally thought." *But we screwed up.* Russ gritted his teeth and went on. "Evidence has been uncovered that strongly suggests her death wasn't accidental, and there seems to be a tenuous connection to Tally McNabb's theft of army property."

"Wait—what?" Stillman lost his Madame Tussaud's look. "Tally McNabb? From my therapy group?"

"That's right." Russ glanced around. They were out of earshot, but well within everyone's line of vision. "Are you sure you don't want to move this to your office?"

Stillman made an impatient gesture. "Tell me what the connection is."

"Your sister's car was sabotaged," Clare said. "Both brake calipers were cut, which meant once she started down the mountain, she had no way to stop other than crashing her car."

Russ nodded. If the MacVanes were right, it must have been done by somebody at the resort. Somebody good with engines. He pictured Lyle complaining about Wyler McNabb. *Spent the afternoon working on his ATV. Kevin said he was trying to boost the performance so's he could drive it faster.*

Clare went on. "Three days after your sister died, Tally stepped into her job, giving her the ability to move or launder the large amounts of cash she and her husband stole in Iraq."

Stillman blinked several times but didn't comment.

"It's possible—in theory—that the McNabbs may have gotten your sister to help them before she died," Russ said. "Did Ms. Bain ever mention them?"

"I don't"—Stillman swallowed—"remember."

"Did she have any unaccounted-for funds when you settled her estate?"

Stillman spread his hands. "I don't remember."

Russ tried to tamp down his impatience. "I understand you're holding her paperwork and records. I'd like your permission to take a look at them."

"At Ellen's paperwork."

Russ glanced at Clare. "Yeah. Stuff Ellen Bain left behind that's stored at your house."

"All right. Let's go." Stillman dug into his pants pocket and came up with a business card and pen. He jotted down his address and handed it to Russ. "My address. I'll meet you at my house." Stillman pivoted and strode away without further farewell.

Russ pocketed the card. "Was that just me, or was he acting weird?"

"It's not just you," Clare said. She took her phone out of her skirt pocket and opened it.

"What are you doing?"

"Letting Will and Olivia know they should meet us at Trip's house."

"No. No, no, no. I'm grateful for their help, but this is police business now."

She gave him a look.

"I mean it, Clare. This isn't you and your buddies carrying Tally McNabb off the field anymore. We're talking homicide."

"I've been talking homicide the whole time. *You've* just started listening." She held the phone up to her ear. "Hey, Will. It's Reverend Clare."

God. For the rest of his life. What was he setting himself up for?

She walked to the office door, listening to something the kid was telling her, and pushed it open. Looked back at him. Clamped her hand over the phone. "Well? Are you coming with me?"

He sighed. "All the way, darlin'. All the way."

◆ ◆ ◆

The Stillmans' house was typical suburbiana, the sort of large and graceful home that fit in everywhere and was native to nowhere. The slim, leafless trees—some sort of ornamental fruit—were hung with tiny witches and black cats, and the entryway was festooned with cobwebs and orange lights. Two skeletons guarded the front door. Each of them had a large cast on one leg.

Clare parked behind a little green four-door with a SUNY GENESEO sticker in the rear window. As she was getting out of her Jeep, Russ's squad car rolled into the drive, followed a minute later by Eric McCrea's SUV.

"Do you need help?" she asked Will as he slid himself from the green car's passenger seat. The curvaceous auburn-haired girl bracing his wheelchair looked up. "We've got it, thanks."

"You must be Olivia." Clare walked up and shook the girl's hand. "I'm Clare Fergusson."

Russ and Eric joined them, and Will, panting, but in his chair, introduced everyone.

"I want to thank you two for what you've uncovered." Russ straightened, as if he were standing at attention. "And Miss Bain, I'd like to personally apologize, for myself and on behalf of my department, for not thoroughly investigating your mother's car earlier."

Behind them, a BMW nosed into the last available inch of the driveway. Trip Stillman got out, squinting in the sunlight.

"Sergeant McCrea and I can take it from here," Russ continued. "An officer is headed over to the junkyard right now to document the condition of the car and to take the MacVanes' statements. I'll be sure to let you know what we find after examining your mother's records."

"Sorry I'm late," Stillman said. "Olivia, what are you doing here?" He picked up his niece in a toe-dangling hug.

"Will and I want to look at Mom's papers along with the rest of you." She darted a glance toward Russ. "That's okay, isn't it?"

"Of course it is, sweetheart." The doctor frowned at Russ.

"This isn't a matter for civilians anymore. Sergeant McCrea and I will call in assistance from the department if we need any help in the investigation."

Clare could tell Russ was trying to keep his temper. She shouldn't feel so gleeful about that. "Russ?" She was a bad Christian. "Do you have a warrant to search Ellen Bain's documents?" A bad Christian, and a bad fiancée.

"I don't need one when I've got the permission of . . ." He trailed off. His eyes narrowed.

"Trip, Olivia, will you allow all of us to go through the papers?"

They nodded.

"Then let's all go in, shall we?" She shivered. "I'm getting chilled out here."

The detritus of Ellen Stillman Bain's life was in the Stillmans' finished basement, packed in a wall's worth of 18" by 22" moving boxes. Clare read the marker-scrawl on the ends and sides: LP's, WINTER COATS, WOODEN ITEMS, VANITY. She spotted some that would be of interest right away: PRIOR TAX RETURNS and BILLS and HEALTH/SS/INVESTMENT.

Russ bent over the boxes. "Are these in any order?"

Trip indicated the cardboard wall. "This is it. It's all labeled. What is it, exactly, that you're looking for?"

"A lead. Some sign of financial hanky-panky. Evidence of conspiracy."

Stillman looked offended. "My sister was the epitome of financial rectitude. Her living depended on her honesty and reliability. There's no way she would have been involved in any sort of *hanky-panky*."

Eric patted Trip's back. "Sorry, Doc, but the prospect of free money has a way of bending people's, uh, rectitude. Just look at what it did to Tally McNabb."

Clare figured now would be a good time to step in. "Trip, is there any-place upstairs where we can look at the contents? That way, Will can help, too."

Russ made a noise that sounded like a suppressed groan and picked up a box.

"The dining room table, upstairs." Stillman bent to pick up another box. "Plenty of room, and we won't have to stoop over."

The dining room had the elegant, unused air of a historic house ex-hibit kept pristine behind a velvet rope. Clare moved a porcelain bowl from the table to a sideboard for safekeeping. Russ was clearly reluctant to set his box on the snowy tablecloth until Trip thumped his down without ceremony. He hit a rheostat and the chandelier sprang to life. "You get started," he said. "We'll get the rest of it. But I can tell you already, you're not going to find anything."

"He may be right." Russ hauled one of the chairs out of the way to ac-commodate Will's wheelchair. "We're only guessing at the motive behind sabotaging her brakes. It could have been a jealous lover, or her ex-husband come back, or somebody she pissed off at work. Hell, it could be a family member, looking to inherit. Maybe the daughter."

"It was not!" Will's voice was vehement.

Russ looked at him. "No. You're right. I think we can take that one off the board."

They opened up the cartons on the table and got to work. They sorted the contents into two piles: the obviously irrelevant and documents that needed a closer look. Trip and Olivia and Eric brought up everything that might possibly be of interest, then stayed to open and sort. The piles grew higher and higher, then divided, then divided again. Eventually, they had the contents of eight boxes spread across the room, covering the table, piled in chairs, heaped on the sideboard.

"It looks like your office," Clare said.

"God. I hate paper trails." Russ polished his glasses on his shirtfront. "Give me ballistics and blood splatters any day."

There was a soft ringtone from the other end of the house. A door opening. "Hello?" They could hear a wary British voice from the kitchen. "Trip? Why is there a police car in the drive?"

"We're in here, darling." Stillman straightened from where he'd been hunched over a stack of old checkbooks.

Mrs. Stillman's eyes widened when she appeared in the dining room door. "Good Lord. What's going on? It looks like an office exploded in here." She spotted her niece. "Olivia, darling, why aren't you at University?" She looked at Russ. "Has there been some sort of trouble?"

"No trouble." Russ held his hand out to her. "I'm Russ Van Alstyne. Chief of police."

"Flora Stillman." She shook automatically, her face turning toward Clare. "You're the Episcopal priest, aren't you? At St. Alban's."

"Clare Fergusson." Clare waved from the other side of the table.

"We go sometimes. Well. Christmas and Easter, really. I've been meaning to try to attend more often, but you know how busy Sundays can get." Flora Stillman bit her lower lip. "Oh dear. I suppose you do."

Clare smiled. "You're welcome anytime. Come for Choral Evensong. It's less hectic."

Flora looked around her, as if trying to put a priest together with a soldier and a young man in a wheelchair. "What are you all *doing* here?"

"We have reason to believe your sister-in-law's death wasn't accidental," Russ said. "We think she may have been connected in some way with several people who stole a lot of money from the government." He indicated the papers stacked everywhere. "We're looking for a lead. Something to tell us why someone tampered with her brakes."

"Her brakes?"

Will spoke up for the first time. "They'd been engineered to snap the first time the calipers were engaged. It's not that hard, if you know what you're doing."

"That's . . . good Lord. I thought that only happened in old television shows."

Russ shifted his weight. "Did Ellen ever mention the name Wyler McNabb to you?"

"No." Flora looked at her husband.

"Never heard of him," Trip said. "Who is he?"

Clare and Eric and Will stared at him. Finally, Eric said, "He's Tally McNabb's husband. She talked about him in group. Several times."

"Ah." Trip got that waxy, stuffed look again, the same one he had had in his waiting room.

"How about finances? Did she ever say anything about coming into some money?"

"No, but she would have talked to Trip about that, not me." She turned toward her husband. "What about when we had her and Olivia for dinner? Just a few days before she died?"

"I remember," Olivia said. "Iola and I went swimming, and Uncle George made shish kebab."

"That's right." Flora looked at Russ. "Ellen must have spent an hour that evening closeted with Trip in his office."

"Huh." Russ frowned. "How about it, Dr. Stillman? Is there anything your sister said that in retrospect throws up a red flag?"

Trip looked blank. "I don't know."

"What did you talk about?"

Trip stood there, still, pale, his mouth slightly open. Only his eyes moved, darting from side to side as if trying to find an escape from his head.

"Dr. Stillman?"

Clare could hear the man's breath rasping in and out.

Flora Stillman's face pinched in worry. "Darling, you must remember. It was the last time we saw her alive." She glanced up at Russ. "I assumed they were talking about their mother. She's been getting a bit difficult, and he tries hard not to drag me into it."

"Was that what you were talking about, Dr. Stillman?" Russ's voice had sharpened, like a knife that was about to cut through to the truth. *It could be a family member, looking to inherit.* "Your mother?"

Silence. Clare heard a rattle in Trip's throat, like the harbinger of death. "I can't remember."

Flora faced Russ. "He's been under a lot of stress lately."

"I don't need word-for-word. The general gist is fine."

"I can't remember," Trip said.

Russ stepped toward him. "You can't remember what went on between you and your sister the last time you saw her alive? Even though you were alone together for an hour?" He dropped his voice. "Maybe that wasn't the last time you saw her. Maybe you were up at the resort the night of July twenty-ninth. Maybe you were watching as she drove away."

"For God's sake!" Flora threw her arms around her husband, as if to prevent Russ from dragging him away.

"I can't remember." Trip's face fell in on itself. "I can't remember anything." He disengaged from his wife. "I'm sorry, Flo. I'm so sorry. I've been lying to you. To you, to the partners, to everybody."

Clare had the stomach-dropping sensation of seeing her own life reenacted as a morality play.

"I'm not—I don't have PTSD. I'm not stressed, or getting older, or preoccupied. I have a traumatic brain injury to my frontal lobe. The effects include migraines, impaired judgment, and a pervasive loss of short-term memory."

Flora pressed her hand over her mouth. "Oh, dear Lord."

"I diagnosed myself back in . . ." He wiped his hand over his eyes. "I don't know. Back in the summer, I think. Not long after I got home."

Flora squeezed her eyes shut. "I knew something was wrong. I knew it. I thought maybe you were drinking or taking drugs or—" She hiccupped and started to cry. "I don't know what I thought."

Stillman folded his arms around his wife. "Oh, Flora. I'm so sorry."

"I should have said something," she sobbed. "I should have made you go to a neurologist instead of trying to ignore it and hoping you'd get better."

Trip shook his head. "No, sweetheart, no. I wouldn't have listened to you. I've been in carry-on mode since I figured it out." He bent down so he could peer up into her face. "You know. Stiff upper lip. Onward, the six hundred."

Flora gasped, a cross between a laugh and a sob.

"Your PalmPilot," Clare said, coming around the table toward him.

Trip pulled the PDA from his pocket and set it on the table. "I take notes." He smiled weakly. "I've always taken good notes. It's important for a clinician. I can keep things in my head for a day. Or two." Something blank and frightening drifted through his eyes. Clare involuntarily stepped back. "It's . . . disorienting, sometimes. Like going forward on a moving walkway. People and pictures flash by and then they're gone."

Flora yanked a chair from the table and collapsed into it. "Dear Lord.

Dear, dear Lord." Olivia sat next to her aunt and held out her hand. Flora took it, squeezing hard enough so that Clare could see her knuckles whitening. When she finally spoke, her voice was calmer. "Trip. You *cannot* practice medicine while you're suffering from this."

"I thought so, too, at first! But really, Flo, I can. I haven't forgotten any of my training." He pointed toward Russ. "Russell Van Alstyne. Fifty. Married. O positive, no drug allergies. Compound dissociative fracture of the right tibia. Two pins in a Stinowski conformation. No postoperative complications."

"That's good," Russ said, "except I'm fifty-two and widowed."

Trip's face went blank again.

"Trip," Clare said, "your sister could have told you everything that night. For all you know, she might have named her killer. Didn't you take any notes?"

The doctor looked at the PDA. "No," he finally said. "I reread her file after I spoke with you at the office. I don't have anything." He ran his hand over the top of his close-cropped gray hair. "You have to understand, I was still hoping then . . . I wasn't taking notes consistently."

Flora rocked forward in her chair. "Dear Lord."

Russ crossed his arms. "Mrs. Stillman, do you recall anything from that night?"

She took a deep breath. "Olivia spent the day here with Iola, swimming and biking. Ellen came over from work. She must have arrived around five thirty. No." Her brows knit together. "She was later than we expected. Six thirty."

"Go on," Russ said.

"We had drinks while Trip grilled. We ate. The girls were tired out and wanted to watch a movie. I joined them." She paused again. "We made sundaes right before that. I remember warning the girls not to drip on the sofa. It was then that Ellen asked Trip if they could talk. She went out to her car to get something, and right after she came back in they disappeared into his study. The girls and I were already in the family room."

"Did you see what she went to get from the car?"

Flora shook her head.

"Olivia?"

"I don't know," she said.

"Did either of you see her carry anything back to the car when she left?"

"Just her purse," Olivia said, "but that was small."

Clare looked at Russ. "What do you think it was?"

His face was grim. "The question is, *where* is it?"

"If she left anything, it's in Trip's study." Flora stood up. "Our cleaning service only dusts and vacuums in there, and the girls and I hardly ever go in."

Russ opened his hand in a you-first gesture. They trooped—or in Will's case rolled—down the hallway and through the foyer and squeezed into a small room at the front of the house. It was a true office; desk and file cabinets and bookcases and a whole shelf of tiny papier-mâché skeletons playing instruments, golfing, and otherwise enjoying the afterlife. Russ touched a skeletal police officer with a fingertip. "*Calacas.* From *El Día de los Muertos.*"

"The Feast of All Souls," Clare said. "Coming right up."

"We've been collecting them for years," Flora said. "Ever since we honeymooned in Mexico." She bit her lip again as she looked at her husband. "Do you remember?"

He took her hand. "Every minute. It's just the present I'm having trouble with."

Russ pushed to the center of the small room, scanning the contents. "Can you tell if anything here is out of the ordinary?"

Both the Stillmans shook their heads.

"It might have been papers," Russ went on. "If she was getting a payoff to look the other way—" He held up one hand at Trip's sound of protest. "*If* that's what happened, she might have documentation of a separate account. Something unconnected to her usual bank."

"You'd put any paperwork in the file cabinets, wouldn't you, darling?"

"Let's take a look," Russ said.

Trip retrieved a ring of small keys from his desk, squinted at their labels, and began unlocking the first file cabinet. Each drawer had its own key.

"That's a good system you've got." Eric rolled the top drawer open. "Most folks' file cabinets you can get into with a bent paper clip."

"They're fireproof as well. I've got patient information in here, and it's important to keep it safe."

"I noticed a keypad by your front door," Russ said. "Do you have a security system?"

"Yes." Flora stepped forward and took the handle of the bottommost drawer. "You can remove these entirely and put them on his desk if you don't want to work bent over."

Clare hadn't noticed any keypad, but she could tell what Russ was thinking. Tamper-resistant file cabinets in a wired and alarmed house must have been as close to a safety deposit box as Ellen Bain could come without actually going to a bank and leaving a paper trail.

As Trip unlocked his way through the cabinets, Eric and Clare pulled out the lowest drawers and set them side by side on the desk. They ran out of room well before Trip ran out of files. "I'll get the card table," Flora said.

Clare tugged on the next-to-last drawer. Something shifted inside, thudding against the metal front.

"Look at all this." Eric kept his voice low. "Do you think he'd have put it under her name? Or stuck it in anywhere?"

Clare drew the cabinet drawer out slowly. It didn't look any different than the others. Lots of manila folders, color tabbed, hanging on rails.

"Mom kept everything." Olivia looked up from where she was going through the top left drawer. "That's the reason there were so many boxes. Everything and copies of everything."

Clare unlatched the metal tab holding it in place and lifted it from the cabinet. She tilted the drawer one way, then another. *Thunk. Thunk.* "There's something in here."

Russ took the drawer from her. "See if you can get it out."

Clare shoved the folders back. A hefty envelope file had been wedged into the bottom of the drawer. She grabbed it and wiggled it free. It was more than an inch thick, its flap held in place by two thick rubber bands. She showed it to Trip.

"I've never seen it before." His mouth twisted. "That I can remember."

"What is it?" Will asked.

Russ let the drawer thunk onto the carpet. "Let's see." He removed the rubber bands and opened the flap. The folder was stuffed with papers.

"Here." Flora toted a card table through the door and kicked its legs into place. "You can put it here."

Russ dumped the documents onto the surface. Clare picked one up:

three sheets stapled together. The first two pages were an accounting, directed to the financial administration of the coalition, for thirty metric tons of steel rebar. It was detailed enough to make her eyes swim—cost of transport inter- and intracountry, cost of labor, percentage cost of insurance, interim and final disposition. The sheet stapled to it was much simpler: an invoice from Birmingham Steel to BWI Opperman for five metric tons of rebar. She flipped back to the second page. There was a string of signatures: one from the Secretary of Finance (Coalition), one from the Quartermaster General's Office, one from the Field Director of Operations (BWI Opperman), and one from the CID Compliance Officer attached to 10th Financial Support. That signature was neat, firm, and recognizable. *Lt. Col. Arlene Seelye.*

"Russ." Clare held the document out for him to see.

"I know." He read the signature. He showed her the papers in his own hand. "This one's for insulation. Five thousand square feet billed to the coalition, with an invoice for seven hundred and fifty square feet from a distributor in Kentucky."

"Are they all bills?" Eric asked.

"This isn't. This is a copy of a legal document." Will had parked his chair at the edge of the card table and was flipping through a hole-punched collation of thirty or more pages. "I think it's a contract for services between BWI Opperman and the coalition government."

Olivia looked over his shoulder, her forehead creased. "My mom didn't have anything to do with the legal department."

Clare picked up another paper. Rubberized tiles. She read another. Ductwork. And another. Sewage piping. All of them billing for five or six or seven times the attached invoices to BWI. All of them signed *Lt. Col. Arlene Seelye.*

"I just noticed this." Eric pointed to the bottom corner of one of the elaborate coalition accounting forms. There was a small slash, followed by *MM.*

"Mary McNabb." Clare handed the form to Russ. "That was Tally's real first name."

"She prepared these," Russ said, "and Arlene Seelye signed off on them. Every one."

Clare leaned against the paper-strewn card table. "There must be fifty of these paired-off invoices."

"More, I think," Will said.

Trip ran his fingers over one. "These are all copies, not originals. Ellen must have spotted the discrepancies early on and started keeping track."

"I don't understand," Flora said. "*Was* Ellen involved in some sort of criminal activity?"

"No. It looks like she was documenting someone else's fraud." Russ pointed to the legal document in Will's hand. "Can I see that?" Will handed it over. Russ scanned the first page. Flipped through a few more pages. Stopped and folded the sheet over. He held it out to Trip. "Double-check me. What's this contract worth?"

Trip pulled a pair of reading glasses on and examined the page. "Sixty million dollars."

Clare breathed in.

"BWI Opperman signed a contract in which it was paid sixty million for construction in occupied Iraq," Russ said. "Your sister was the accounts-payable bookkeeper for that part of the business. It was her job to keep track of and pay the bills BWI Opperman's special projects department generated."

Trip nodded.

"Somehow, she got hold of the invoices on the accounts-receivable side." Russ held up one of the coalition forms. "I doubt she was ever meant to see these. She put the two side by side and saw BWI Opperman was buying and shipping about a sixth of what they were billing the government for."

"You mean they were pocketing the difference?" Will said.

Eric took the copy of the contract from Stillman. "Holy shit. That's fifty million dollars." The sum seemed to hang in the air for a moment.

"Fifty million dollars," Will said, "and they just disappeared it into a bunch of papers."

"The company wouldn't even have needed to suborn the folks who hand out the contracts," Clare said. "All they needed to buy was the army clerk who created the invoices and the finance investigator who was there to prevent fraud."

"It sure explains Seelye's actions, doesn't it?" Russ's voice was dry. "No wonder she wasn't interested in splitting the million with Nichols. She was already on the BWI Opperman payroll."

"They must have promised to pay Tally off, too." Eric turned toward Russ. "Do you think they screwed her over after she did her part? Is that why she stole the cash?"

"No. She got paid. With Wyler McNabb's job." Clare looked at Eric. "Tally's mother said Wyler always felt he owed his job to Tally. *That* was her payoff. He went from being a high school dropout to having an income that bought them luxury SUVs and casino vacations."

Russ nodded. "He knew about the contract fraud. He didn't know Seelye, but he knew about the fraud. That's probably why he got named manager. One less person outside the fold. When she deployed a second time, her husband went over with the crew."

"Huh." Eric picked up the contract again. "And then he sees the money the DOD's flying in and starts thinking, *Why shouldn't I get mine?* If his wife can cover up the theft of fifty million, it's a cinch she can hide a single pallet of cash."

Russ chewed the inside of his cheek. "I'll bet you a million of my own Opperman and Seelye had no idea that money had been stolen. They must have been shitting bricks when Nichols started investigating." He tilted his head toward Flora and Olivia. "Excuse my French."

"Wait." Clare dropped the paper she had been holding. "Opperman?"

"*Mr.* Opperman?" Olivia's eyes were wide.

"Who do you think was behind this? The man is the CEO and controlling shareholder. He owns the company. The real theft here isn't shrink-wrapped cash. It's fifty million dollars, and it wasn't stolen by someone seducing an MP or sweating a pallet onto a cargo plane. It was stolen by people wearing suits and signing agreements in air-conditioned offices. It was stolen by someone who believes people can be bought and sold with gifts and jobs and, and"—he looked at Olivia—"four-year scholarships to SUNY Geneseo."

"No." The girl went pale. "Oh, no." Her aunt put an arm around her shoulder.

Russ leaned forward and braced himself on the rickety table, his large hands spread protectively over the documents there. "But Ellen Bain wouldn't be bought. She assembled this evidence, and she brought it to the one soldier she knew she could trust. Her brother."

Clare could picture it. Ellen Bain, picking her brother's brain for information on the military police and the financial affairs divisions, entrusting the package to him, swearing him to secrecy. Not knowing that within a day or two, he wouldn't be able to tell anyone even if he wanted to.

"Why didn't I warn her?" Trip's voice cracked. "If we talked about all this, why didn't I call the police and keep her here until the law took over?"

Clare ached for the self-accusation in his voice. She knew what it was like to ask *Why didn't I?* after it was all too late. "You couldn't have known, Trip. She probably thought she was risking her job and her benefits, not her life."

Russ nodded. "Opperman may not have known she smuggled this stuff out, anyway. He probably thought killing her and purging the original files would be enough to protect him."

"Wait a minute. Are you saying *John Opperman* killed Ellen?" Trip sounded torn between disbelief and fury.

"No." Russ shook his head. "I'm quite sure he was somewhere else surrounded by unimpeachable witnesses when your sister's brake calipers were cut. He delegates his dirty work. My bet's on Wyler McNabb. He was shipped over to the construction team in Iraq as soon as we started investigating."

"Can you get him back?" Will asked.

"Oh, yeah." Russ grinned, baring his eyeteeth. "And when we do, he's going to give us John Opperman on a silver platter."

◆ ◆ ◆

It seemed anticlimactic to Clare. They had uncovered evidence of a fifty-million-dollar scam. There ought to be screeching police cars and flashing lights and people led away in handcuffs. Instead, it was Russ, on the phone, first with his friend from the Judge Advocate General's Corps, then with an officer at the Department of Defense. He was talking with a Treasury agent when Lyle MacAuley and Kevin Flynn arrived, toting piles of plastic evidence envelopes, a laptop, and a portable scanner. He was debriefing someone from the Government Accountability Office when the FBI team from Albany pulled in. The Feds walked into Trip Stillman's office looking skeptical and came out with sharp, satisfied smiles.

Clare, who had been drinking cup after cup of hot, sweet coffee in the Stillmans' kitchen, snagged Russ before he had the chance to pick up his phone again. "When are they going to arrest Opperman?"

He looked startled. "I don't know. Another couple of weeks."

"A couple of weeks?" She lowered her voice. Olivia Bain sat disconsolate at the kitchen table, Will holding her hand. "Why so long? My God, Russ, you said it yourself. That man is responsible for Ellen Bain's death."

He put his phone in his pocket. "I know. Believe me, I'd love to drive up to the resort right now and haul his ass in." He took her hand, rubbing her knuckles with his thumb. "But this is going to be a very complicated case. I'm not even talking about all the agencies who are going to want a piece of the action. We need to have every piece of evidence lined up, every warrant signed, and every cop and agent in place, ready to drop the hammer on everyone involved. Until that moment, you"—he gestured toward the Stillmans with his head—"and they have to keep quiet about all of this."

"Justice delayed is justice denied."

"It won't be. I promise you, there will be justice for Ellen Bain."

"What about Tally? Will there be justice for her?"

"Clare." Russ's voice was gentle. "She knew from Nichols that an investigator was closing in. She didn't know it was Seelye. All she knew was that she was holding the bag for massive federal fraud and grand theft and she had nowhere to turn."

"She could have turned to Opperman."

"His solution was to send her back to Iraq. Maybe she would have had an 'accident' like Ellen Bain did. Maybe that's what she was afraid of."

Her voice rose. "So she killed herself?"

Russ steered her into the family room. "If she were alive right now, she'd be facing thirty years in Leavenworth and the loss of everything—family, home, money, reputation."

"If she were alive right now, none of this would ever have come to light!"

"I know." He didn't try to argue with her or persuade her. He just stood there, his grip warm and steady. Letting her hold the truth in her hands. Letting her raise it up and swallow it. It was cold, very cold, and no amount of sugar could sweeten its bitter taste.

"She killed herself," she finally said.

"Some people can't face the consequences of their crimes."

Clare pulled away from Russ. "She wasn't a criminal. She was a damaged soldier." She wrapped her arms around herself. "She was wounded over there, just as much as Will and Trip were."

"As much as you were?" Russ looked at her, looked *into* her, inviting her to lay down all her lies and deep-dive into the truth with him.

She couldn't face that bottomless well. "I'm afraid," she whispered.

"Oh, love. Of what?"

"Of what's in my head. What's in my heart. I'm afraid I'm not strong enough. That loving you and God won't be enough to keep me afloat. I'm afraid—"

He wrapped his arms around her. "That if Tally McNabb could choose to end it all, you might make the same choice someday?"

"I don't know if I'm dealing with it any better than she was," she said into his chest. "Or Eric, losing his temper, or Trip, pretending he hasn't lost a chunk out of his brain."

"I don't know how you're dealing with it. I don't know what you've been through, and I don't know where you've been hurt." He pushed her hair away from her face. "Tell me."

She wanted to. She was so tired of hiding and lying and going it alone. She opened her mouth—

It's the same reason Clare doesn't want to talk about drinking. Because she's afraid if she does, somebody will stop her from doing it. Tally had said that . . . and less than a week later, had killed herself.

—and shut it again. "Not now." She nodded toward the hallway, where a banging door and the sound of raised voices indicated some new investigator had arrived. "You're going to be here half the night. If Olivia and the Stillmans don't need me anymore, I'm going to"—*get my blood tested*—"go home."

"All right. Not now. Soon, though. I mean it, love. I'm waiting for you to tell me."

That was what she was afraid of.

The Full Moon Bar and Grill was packed by the time Eric got there, but he had no trouble spotting his party. Five helium balloons imprinted with handcuffs bobbed over their table in the corner. When he got closer, he could see they were weighted down with the real thing. MacAuley was being subtle. He had figured the deputy chief would've gone for a ball-and-chain motif.

He raised his hand. "Hi, everybody." A chorus of hellos greeted him. He dropped into a chair near one end, across from the chief. It was also as far away from Hadley Knox as he could get.

"Eric. Glad you could make it." The chief slid an empty glass and a pitcher of beer toward him. "You know Emil Dvorak, our medical examiner. This is his partner, Paul Foubert, who runs the Infirmary." The two men nodded at Eric. "And this is Wayne and Mindy Stoner. We went to high school together." The ruddy-faced farmer—he had to be a farmer—leaned forward and shook Eric's hand. His wife wiggled her fingers around a glass stein. "Eric's in the Guard," the chief said to the Stoners. "He got back from Iraq this past June."

"Really?" Mindy Stoner put her beer down. "Our son Ethan is in Afghanistan right now. He's with the marines."

Eric made some remark, and the ME chimed in, and pretty soon they were all talking about the wars, and Eric couldn't have recounted what he said two seconds after he said it. He was focused on the other end of the table, where Hadley Knox sat boxed in by Kevin and Harlene. She was smiling but quiet, following a rapid-fire back-and-forth between Harlene and the chief's sister, not noticing Kevin topping off her beer and filling her plate before passing the platter on to Noble.

Eric's attention was broken by Lyle dropping an identical platter on their end of the table. "Sausage hoagies and onion rings," the deputy chief announced. "Best in the state."

Mindy Stoner stared at the mountain of cholesterol. "He's trying to kill you before the wedding," she said to the chief.

MacAuley slapped the chief on the back. "Dig in. You gotta keep your strength up for tomorrow night."

"Lyle," the chief warned.

"Hey, where's the stripper?" Wayne Stoner asked. His wife glared at him.

"Aw, you know Russ. He's too much of a spoilsport to go for that." MacAuley grinned. "We'll play pin-the-whitetail-on-the-twelve-point-buck later on instead."

"When I got married the first time, I had a stripper at my bachelor party," Dr. Dvorak said. "All my friends at University chipped in and brought her down from Amsterdam."

Mindy Stoner looked from him to his burly, bearded partner and back again. "You had a stripper."

"Yes, indeed. Then she arrived, and she was fifty-five-years old and looked like my mother."

"Turned him gay," Paul Foubert said.

At the other end of the table, Hadley said something to Kevin and rose. Eric watched her disappear into the crowd, headed for the ladies'. He sipped his beer. Gave her a minute. Two. Women always took twice as long in the john as men did.

"'Scuse me." Eric stood up. The chief looked at him over the rim of his water glass but didn't say anything. Eric threaded his way through the tables and chairs as if he had all the time in the world. He wanted to catch her at the other end of the bar without having to lurk outside the bathrooms like some perv.

He timed it just right. She spotted him as she came out. He stopped where he was, close, but not in her way. "Can we talk?" He kept his back toward their table so she could face that way. Keeping her friends in sight. *She'll feel safer with a bar full of people around.*

"Okay." She shoved her hands into the pockets of her jeans. "Shoot."

He swallowed. "I, um, want to apologize." She looked at him with flinty eyes. "I, ah—" He rubbed the back of his neck. "I—"

Kevin Flynn walked past him, carrying a full glass of beer. "Hey." He handed it to Hadley. "Thought you might like your drink." He casually moved behind and to the side of her, right where he'd be most effective if Eric were to snap and attack her. Again. Eric felt a funny ache in his stomach. The kid used to look up to him. "I wanted to let you know I've started seeing somebody," he found himself saying. "Down in Saratoga. A doctor. He specializes in guys like me. Who need help holding on to their tempers. I've got—he gave me a prescription." He hadn't filled it yet. He was terrified of how it would feel, being drugged up.

"That's good," Hadley said. "I'm glad."

"Yeah, that's good, man." Kevin gave him the same smile Eric had used on six-year-old Jake when he was learning to ride a bike. *You can do it, buddy!*

"Hadley, I'm sorry. If there was some way I could go back and make it not have happened—"

She smiled a brittle smile. "It didn't *happen,* Eric. You assaulted me." Kevin dropped his hand on her shoulder. "You hit me and took my gun away from me, and then I had to lie to the chief about it. Which means, I guess, that I suck at being a cop but that I'm good at covering it up."

Kevin rumbled a disagreement.

Eric wiped his hand across his face. "Yeah. You're right. I mean, no, you don't suck at being a cop." He stopped before he could tangle himself further. "Oh, Christ. Look, I screwed things up. The chief knows it was all my fault. You don't have to forgive me—hell, if the shoe was on the other foot I don't know if *I* could forgive me—but I want you to know that I'm sorry, and that I'm doing everything I can to not screw up again, and that you will never, ever have to feel afraid of me." He paused. "That's all." His heart felt like he'd just sprinted a mile.

"The chief knows?"

"Yeah." His throat hurt. "If you want to lodge a complaint against me, he'll take it. Hell, I don't know." He looked down at his sneakers. "If you can't work beside me, you ought to go ahead and file. I got more experience. I can find another job easier than you can." He turned toward the bar before he could embarrass himself.

"Eric?"

He watched a pair of young guys trying for a tall redhead at the bar. "Yeah?"

She paused. "It'll be good to have you on the job again." She passed him, headed for their table, her drink in one hand. She didn't look back at him. Eric breathed in. It felt as if a strap around his chest had suddenly been loosened.

"You okay?" Kevin's voice was low.

He rubbed his gut. "Yeah. Thanks." He glanced to where Hadley was taking her seat. "She's a good person."

"Yeah. She is."

Eric looked at Kevin. "She know how you feel about her?"

Kevin flushed but kept his eyes on Hadley. "We work together. We're friends."

"Listen." Eric thought about Jennifer. He was going to have to go through all this again with her, and it was going to be harder, and take longer, and there was still no guarantee she'd ever forgive him and take him back. "A couple years ago I would've said good, keep it professional, but life's too damn uncertain, man. Hard and uncertain." He twisted his wedding ring. "You see something good, you go after it. Don't let it get away." At the table, MacAuley bent over Harlene and said something. The dispatcher shrieked with laughter. Noble Entwhistle looked puzzled. "'Cause in the end, that's all we have. Each other."

◆ ◆ ◆

Tell me. Tell me. Tell me.

Parked outside Margy Van Alstyne's driveway at midnight, Clare could still hear Russ's voice. His words had dogged her as she said goodbye to the Stillmans, surrounded by investigators in their own home. They throbbed with her pulse as her arm was tied off and her blood syringed into glass tubes. They kept time with her footsteps as she visited shut-ins, ran errands, cleaned house, walked down the still, silent nave of St. Alban's.

Tell me.

She kept promising herself later. After the communications committee meeting. After she took Morning Prayer. After her family arrived. After dinner at Margy's house. After the rehearsal. Then Russ was kissing her, smiling as their lips parted, murmuring, "I'll see you tomorrow," laughing as Lyle hauled him away to some hunters' bar.

She had run out of later. In her bedroom, she smoothed a hand over the white dress hanging from her closet door. From its velvet box, she took the ring she was supposed to give Russ tomorrow. She let it rest in her palm. Such a small thing to bind up so many promises. *With all that I have, and with all that I am, I honor you,* she would say. She closed her hand into a shaky fist. Some honor.

Her heart pounded. Her mouth was dry. She tried to slow her breathing down, name exactly what it was that scared her so.

If I tell him, he'll be furious with me.

No. He'd be upset, and worried, and overprotective, but he wouldn't be angry.

If I tell him, it will get out, and everybody will know what a failure I am as a priest.

That was closer to the bone. The thought of being exposed made her nauseous. She already had enough problems trying to live up to her position. Who wanted an addict for a priest?

Addict. She had never used that term before. She thought of all the ways she would describe herself. Priest. Pilot. Christian. Woman. Soldier. She wet her lips. "Hi, my name is Clare Fergusson and I'm a drug addict," she whispered. The words tasted like bottle dregs and the hard plastic coating on pills.

If I tell him, I'll have to stop.

That was the bottom of it. If she told him, she'd have to stop, and that scared her more than anything. Facing every day, every night without her chemical crutches—she didn't know if she could do it.

Tomorrow, Julie McPartlin would say, *I require and charge you both, here in the presence of God, that if either of you know any reason why you may not be united in marriage lawfully, and in accordance with God's Word, you do now confess it.*

So here she was, huddled in a dark, cold Jeep while her parents thought she was out on a pastoral emergency. She'd been waiting over an hour, expecting him back at his mother's well before now, praying that none of the neighbors called in a suspicious vehicle to the cops. Both her fear-fueled adrenaline and her amphetamines had given out long ago, so it took a beat, then two, before she realized the headlights coming down Old Route 100 were slowing down. The turn signal winked on, and Russ's truck bumped into his mother's wide dirt drive.

Clare tumbled out of the Jeep, shaking herself to get the cramps out of her legs. He was crossing to the kitchen door. "Russ." She kept her voice low, but he spun around like a gunslinger.

"What the—Clare?" He walked toward her, jamming his hands into his jacket pockets against the chill. "What are you doing here, you crazy woman?" He peered past her toward her car, tucked in beneath the dark hemlocks at the edge of his mother's property. He shook his head. "Waiting outside in the cold." He kissed her lightly. "It's Saturday, you know. I'm not supposed to see you."

"I need to talk to you."

His face shifted. "Okay." He glanced toward the house. An outdoor light cast a glow over the granite steps and green door. A single lamp lit one of the living room windows, but otherwise the place was dark. "Come inside. We can talk in the kitchen."

She shook her head. "Not here."

He looked at her closely. "My truck." He opened the door for her and then walked around to his side. When he got in, the pickup leaned beneath his weight for a moment. His door shut with a solid thunk. He turned on the engine and adjusted the heaters so they would blow on her. The air was still warm from his ride home. He reversed out of the driveway and headed west into the mountains. They rumbled over the stony Hudson River. "Okay. What is it?"

Face-to-face, in the moment, she panicked. Her throat closed. "I don't," she started. She pressed her fist against the ache in her chest. "I don't know—"

He held out one hand. "Hold on tight and tell me."

She grasped his hand and squeezed her eyes shut. "I have a problem. I haven't told you. I've been taking pills. Lots of pills. I'm addicted to amphetamines."

He breathed out. "Hang on." She heard the tick-tick-tick of the turn signal and then the pickup was turning, bumping along an unpaved road. Finally he stopped. The truck jerked as he hauled on the parking brake. "Love? Look at me."

She cracked open her eyelids. They were surrounded by hemlock and pine. Russ's face was outlined in the green-amber light of the dashboard. "Tell me," he said.

"I started taking sleeping pills and stimulants in Iraq. I came back with a, with a problem." Admitting it a second time wasn't much easier. "I also had antibiotics that I used to treat myself with. And Percocet. For a while I was taking a lot of Percocet."

Russ pressed his lips together and nodded.

"I was close to running out a couple weeks ago. I talked Trip into giving me a prescription for Ambien and Dexedrine. He told me I couldn't drink while I was on the pills, and he said he was going to spring a surprise blood test on me to make sure I wasn't mixing."

Russ closed his eyes. "The blood test you were supposed to get the day we found out about Ellen Bain."

"I told him I just needed to get through the wedding—" Russ made a noise, a kind of despairing discovery, and she grabbed his arms, digging her fingers into his jacket. "No. Not like that. It doesn't have anything to do with you, it never had anything to do with you."

"I pushed you." He winced, as if he were pulling a splinter out of his hand. "I should have taken it slow and given you time, but I was so goddamn fixed on getting us married—"

"No. Listen. I told Trip I needed the pills to keep my head on through the craziness of the past couple of weeks, but I was lying." She hadn't known that until she said it. "I was lying. I would've come up with some other excuse to keep the prescriptions going after the wedding, and if he wouldn't give them to me I'd find some other way. Oh, God." She could feel her eyes begin to fill. "I've been lying to everybody." Her voice broke. "I've been lying every time someone asked me how I'm doing. I said I was fine, and I'm not fine. I feel like there's something ugly inside me all the time, and I just want it to go away." Her tears spilled hot over her cheeks, and she covered her mouth, trying to keep the misery and shame inside where they belonged.

Russ tugged her toward him. "C'mere."

She leaned across the console and buried her face in his shoulder, awkward and ridiculous. She hiccupped and coughed, and a big blob of mucus splattered over his jacket. "Oh, God. I'm sorry." She pawed at her pockets, feeling for a tissue, but of course she came up empty. She started to cry again. "I'm sorry," she sobbed. "I'm sorry. Let's just call the wedding off. It's not too late."

"Whoa." He pulled a half-acre-sized handkerchief out of his jeans and mopped her face with it. "Because you got a little snot on my shirt?"

"Weren't you listening to me? I'm a wreck. I'm a wreck and an addict and a failure. I've killed people, Russ. I flew the ship and gave the orders and people *died* right in front of me and I don't know where to *put* that so I just keep drugging myself up until I don't feel anything anymore." She pushed her damp hair off her overheated face. "I'm not Linda. I'm not anything like her, and I never will be."

His mouth opened. He let out a huff that was almost a laugh. "Where did that come from?"

"You loved her. You never would have left her, and you loved her, and she died, and I can't replace her. I just keep coming up short."

"I don't want you to replace Linda."

"But you loved her."

"Yes. And now I love you." Russ framed her face in his hands, wiping her tears away with his thumbs. "You know, I could have resisted you if you had reminded me of Linda. I fell for you because you remind me of me. I was a wreck and an addict and a failure, Clare. I went to war, and I killed people, with these hands, and watched them die right in front of me. You and I, we're the same, love. We're the same."

"I'm afraid," she whispered.

"We'll get you help." He took one of her hands and interlaced his fingers through hers. "This is the thing I'm absolutely sure of: If we keep holding on to each other, if we don't let go, we can get through anything."

Her eyes burned. "I don't deserve you."

"This priest once told me we don't get what we deserve, thank God. We get what we're given."

She choked out a wet laugh. "A second chance."

"And a third, and a fourth." He smiled a little. "She convinced me, and I don't even believe in God."

She wiped her nose with her jacket sleeve. "I love you. It doesn't seem like enough, just to say it, but I do."

He kissed her. He got out of the truck and walked around the hood and popped her door open. "C'mon out here."

She took his hand, and let him lead her through the forest darkness to the back of the pickup. He hoisted her over the tailgate into the bed of the truck, then vaulted over the side and joined her. He unflapped a heavy cardboard box.

"Don't tell me you're still dragging those quilts around," she said.

"These are good quilts." He spread out first one, then another. "My grandmother Campbell made 'em." He patted the patchwork. "C'mere."

She sat on the thick fabric and tugged her sneakers off before leaning against the rear window of the cab. Russ shook out two more and sat down next to her. He untied his boots and set them against the side of the bed, then snugged the quilts around their shoulders. They were heavy and warm.

He took her in his arms. "Listen. As far as I'm concerned, we're already married." He pressed her hand against his chest. She could feel the steady beat of his heart. "In here, I'm your husband. You're my wife. Nothing we do or don't do in that circus your mother has planned will change that. So if you need more time, if you want to delay it or even call it off, we'll do it."

She kissed him. "That's my fourth premarital session."

"What is?"

She felt herself beginning to tear up again. "Marriage is a sacrament. An outward and visible sign of an inward and invisible grace. The only thing the church can do is recognize what we've already created between us."

He kissed her neck. "I know the religious part of it's important to you—"

"Do you want me as your wife?" she said.

Russ smiled against her skin. "I do."

"And I want you for my husband. Will you stay with me, sharing whatever life throws at us, good or bad?"

He laughed quietly. "I will. How about you?"

"I will." She kissed him again, slowly, and began unbuttoning his shirt. "And I promise before God to be true and faithful to you, to love you with my body and my heart and my mind." She pushed his shirt and jacket off. "Until we are parted by death."

"Yes." He pulled her sweater over her head. "I promise to be true and faithful to you, to love you with my body and my heart and my mind." His breath hitched as she wiggled out of her khakis. "Until we are parted by death."

He kicked his jeans away and pulled her against him, warm and solid, skin to skin. "I pronounce that we are husband and wife, in the name of the Father"—she kissed him—"and of the Son"—she kissed him again—"and of the Holy Spirit."

He framed her face in his hands. "We're married." His face was serious.

"Yes. All the rest of it's just tradition and show and law codes."

His fingers slid along her body. He cupped her breast and stroked her nipple with his thumb. She moaned. "A man and his wife become one flesh," he said, his voice low.

"Yes," she gasped.

"Yes." He rolled, pulling her atop him, and they sealed their vows beneath the stars and the pines and the thick old quilts his grandmother made.

SATURDAY, OCTOBER 22 Hadley was almost late to the wedding. Geneva insisted on putting on last year's Christmas outfit, which was too small, and then after Hadley had talked her into the new silk-and-chiffon dress—$1.99 from Goodwill—they had another go-round over what shoes to wear. When Hadley got downstairs, still struggling with her zipper and carrying her heels, she discovered Hudson had dribbled juice on his best pants while watching TV. Hadley tore apart his room for a replacement, finally settling on a clean pair of khakis she had set aside in the donation pile. When Hudson complained they were too short around the ankles, she gave him her best death-ray glare and herded them into the car.

St. Alban's was packed when they arrived. It looked like half the town and all the congregation had come. At the front of the church, Betsy Young was playing the organ and the full choir sat waiting. Walking up the aisle holding Genny's hand, she heard southern voices and saw lots of clerical collars. Rich Virginians and priests. It didn't bode well for a fun reception.

She spotted Kevin Flynn's red hair near the front of the church. At the same moment, he turned around and looked at her. He stood in his pew and beckoned to her.

"We saved you seats." He stepped into the aisle to let her and the children pass, and Hadley could see Harlene and her husband holding down the other end.

"Thanks," she said. "I didn't think we'd ever get out of the house." She looked him up and down. "Nice suit." She'd never seen him dressed up before. Kind of a shame, because he had the perfect build for it, long legs, wide shoulders, slim hips.

"Well, Genny Knox, aren't you just the prettiest girl here?" Harlene patted the pew next to her. "You slide on over and sit with me." Hadley followed her daughter, directing Hudson to the seat between herself and Flynn. She had discovered it was better to bracket them with adults during church services. Two to one was a good ratio.

"Did we miss anything?" Hadley asked, but before anyone could answer, the door by the sacristy opened and the priest came out, followed by the chief and Lyle MacAuley. The organ music stopped. A hush settled over the congregation.

"I don't think I've ever seen the dep looking nervous before," Hadley whispered.

"Hmph." The dispatcher spoke over Genny's head. "Probably waitin' to disappear into a puff of smoke and brimstone, being inside a church."

Flynn grinned.

The organ sang out, something loud and complicated, with lots of notes running up and down the scale. People started to stand up. At the back of the church, two men pulled the doors open. Flynn checked his watch. "I think this is it."

"I can't see! Mommy, I can't see!" Genny hopped up and down in frustration.

"Come here, Genny, stand in front of me." Flynn stepped back and let Geneva squeeze past him. She hung off the pew ends, leaning as far into the aisle as she could. Hudson twisted back and forth around Flynn, clearly wanting a better view, clearly unwilling to admit it. Flynn took him by the shoulders and maneuvered him into the space next to his sister.

Flynn turned to grin at Hadley, and she smiled ruefully back at him, and there was a moment—it must have been the soaring music or the dizzying smell of the flowers—when her smile ghosted away and she felt like she had a lump in her throat.

Then Reverend Clare's matron of honor walked past and Genny squealed and Hadley snapped her attention back to the aisle. "Oh, Mommy." Genny sounded close to swooning. "Reverend Clare looks like a *princess*." In truth, Reverend Clare's Christmas and Easter vestments were a lot more elaborate than her unadorned wedding dress. Her wreath of tiny cream and gold flowers was a little crownlike, though, and she did have a train, which upped the princess quotient. As she and her father walked past, Clare grinned and winked at Geneva. The little girl quivered with ecstasy. "And so it starts," Hadley said under her breath. She could foresee a lot of dress-up games involving tablecloth trains and half-slip veils in her future.

"Dearly beloved," Reverend Julie McPartlin began, "we have come together in the presence of God to witness and bless the joining together of this man and this woman in Holy Matrimony."

Hadley thought of her own wedding. Las Vegas, during an industry convention. What a cliché. When Dylan asked her, his eyes dark and soulful and a heartbreaker smile on his lips, it had seemed reckless and romantic.

". . . therefore, marriage is not to be entered into unadvisedly or lightly, but reverently, deliberately . . ."

She hadn't even been sober. They had smoked two joints beforehand and giggled through the whole thing. What did it say about your approach to marriage when you treated the start of it as an ironic joke?

"Into this holy union Russell Howard Van Alstyne and Clare Peyton Fergusson now come to be joined."

Beside her, Harlene honked into a tissue. Hadley watched as she reached out and grabbed her husband's hand. Mr. Lendrum was sixty-something and built as if he'd been stitched out of lumpy cotton batting, but Harlene looked at him, for a moment, in exactly the same way Clare Fergusson was looking at Russ Van Alstyne.

Was there some sort of secret everybody but Hadley knew? Or was it that some women had a clear-eyed view of the good guys, while all she had ever been able to see was users and bastards?

Then came the readings and the homily and the prayers and communion and finally it was almost over, thank heavens, because the kids were getting twitchy. The priest delivered a final prayer over the kneeling couple. "Is the chief going to become Episcopalian?" Hadley whispered to Flynn.

"I think he's going to stay Law-Enforcementarian," he said under his breath. She snickered.

The choir stood and the organ started up, a soft, rhythmic beat that sounded almost like the beginning of a sixties tune. "Ooo! I know this," Hudson said. "We're doing this with the adult choir at Christmas."

"Tomorrow will be my dancing day," the choir sang, and Reverend Clare and the chief walked back down the aisle, both of them looking as if they'd been lit up from inside. The music and voices soared, sharp and sweet. On every side of her, people's eyes were wet, and Harlene was honking, and Flynn turned to Hadley and smiled.

Weddings. It was like they put some sort of drug in with the flower arrangements.

"Do you think it'll last?" Hadley said, determined to break the spell.

Flynn looked at her as if she had asked if he thought the sun would rise in the east tomorrow. "Are you kidding?" He leaned in so his breath was warm in her ear. "It's true love."

"There's no such thing."

He thumbed toward Hudson. "Tell him that."

Her son was looking up at the choir, his hand keeping the irregular beat. "To call my true love to my dance," he sang in his piping soprano, "Sing O! my love, O! my love, my love, my love; This I have done for my true love."

Flynn smiled at her. "Let's go dance."

◆ ◆ ◆

The reception was a blast, despite—or maybe because of—the rich Virginians and the priests. There were other kids there, nieces and nephews and the children of friends, so after they had bolted down some dinner, Hadley let Hudson and Genny join the others playing flashlight tag in the field next to the tents.

The chief and Reverend Clare kicked off the dancing to the old Beach Boys tune "God Only Knows," and soon the floor was packed with everyone from Mrs. Marshall and Norm Madsen, sedately fox-trotting, to the youngest Ellis boy, popping and locking. Hadley danced with Nathan Andernach, the perpetual bachelor of St. Alban's, and with Nathan Bougeron, who had left the MKPD before she arrived for a job with the state police, and with a good-looking guy from Maryland who turned out to be a priest, which kind of freaked her out. She danced with Lyle Mac-Auley, and with Noble Entwhistle, and with Duane Adams, one of the part-time officers.

She didn't dance with Kevin Flynn. She had thought about it, driving over to the Stuyvesant Inn, and realized all those throat-closing, eyes-meeting moments were based on the fact that he was the only unattached guy remotely her age she saw on a regular basis. But, hey, at a wedding reception? Lots of possibilities. So she smiled at men she didn't know and said yes to anyone who asked her, and stayed away from Flynn.

After the cake cutting, Granddad announced he was taking Hudson and Genny home. "You stay put and have a good time," he said, when she protested she should leave, too. "'Tain't natural for a girl pretty as you to sit home all the time." He winked. "I'll leave a light on for ya."

So she stayed. She danced and chatted and laughed. She congratulated the newlyweds. "Are you Clare Van Alstyne now?" she asked the reverend.

"No, I'm Russ Fergusson," the chief said.

Reverend Clare elbowed him. "We're keeping our names just as they are."

"Good idea," Dr. Anne said, sipping a drink. "Professional identity and all that. How about you, Hadley? Is Knox your maiden name?"

Hadley shook her head. "No. It was Potts."

Reverend Clare frowned. "Didn't your grandfather tell me you changed your first name from Honey to Hadley?"

"Oh, yeah."

"Honey Potts," the chief said.

"My God, that sounds like a porn star name." Dr. Anne patted her shoulder. "You poor thing. What were your parents thinking of?"

"I suspect they were stoned when they came up with it," Hadley said. "When do we get to do the Chicken Dance?"

"Shortly after my mother is dead and buried in the family plot," Reverend Clare said.

Instead the guests twisted and jived and even swung to some country songs the chief had managed to sneak in past his mother-in-law. Eventually, steaming hot and out of breath, Hadley snuck out for some fresh air.

The open spaces between the inn and the tents were strung with small clear lights, giving a deceptively summerlike look to the autumn landscape. The near-freezing temperature was shocking on her bare skin, but it felt good. She tipped her head back and looked at the bright cold stars, like God's wedding decorations. A man came out of the dance tent. Long and lean, and for a moment she couldn't see him clearly. Then he walked toward her, and the soft light fell on his thick red hair, and she said, "Oh. Here you are."

Here you are. As if she'd been looking for him, not avoiding him.

Flynn held out a glass. "I thought you might like something cold."

"I'm driving, so I'm not—"

"It's ginger ale."

"Oh." She took the drink. "Thanks."

Here you are.

She was parched, she discovered. She drained the glass dry and handed it back to him.

"We haven't danced yet." His jacket was gone. He had loosened his tie and rolled his shirtsleeves up.

"No," she agreed. *No? Real swift.* She must have left her brains inside the tent.

"I figured it was because of the work thing." He took a step closer to her. "We're both young, we're both single, you don't want people to misinterpret what's going on."

That sounded reasonable to her. "That's right. Nobody ever believes you when you say you're just friends."

From the speaker near the tent flap, Bonnie Raitt sang, "People are talking . . ."

"So let's dance out here." He rested the empty glass against the canvas.

"Here?"

He held out his hand. "Okay. A little further away." Some force not under her conscious control lifted her hand and placed it in his. He walked backward, away from the door, away from the lights, until they were at the edge of the field, outlined in starlight and the glow from the inn.

"Could you be falling for me?" Bonnie sang.

Flynn put his hand at the small of her back and somehow her arms went around his neck and they were swaying together in time to the whisky voice and blues guitar. Dancing with Nathan Bougeron or the cute priest hadn't felt like this. She tried keeping *younger* and *work* and *bad idea* in the front of her mind, but he was so warm, and he smelled so good, and he was touching her, and all she could think of was the night they had spent together, the way his eyes had closed and he had cried out, turning his face into her shoulder.

Her body was tightening and loosening and she knew at any moment she was going to tip her face up and slide her fingers through his hair and pull him toward her—

Here you are.

—and then they were kissing, his lips soft and dry, sweet and tender, moving lightly over her cupid's bow, the swell of her lower lip, the corners of her mouth.

"Flynn," she gasped.

He pulled away slightly. "What?"

"Do you remember when we slept together?"

"Hadley." He let out a huff that was almost a laugh. "I'd have to be dead to forget that."

"Let's do it again."

He breathed in. He bent to her, kissed her forehead, her eyelids, her temples. "Why?"

Her eyes flew open. "Why?" She stared at him. She knew what she looked like. She wasn't vain, she was realistic. When she invited men into her bed, they said *Yes* or *I thought you'd never ask* or *Thank you Jesus.* Not *Why?* "Because we were good together, and it's been a long time since I've had sex, and here we both are."

"Because it's convenient, you mean?"

She could tell from his voice she had hurt his feelings. "Not just that. I like you. I'm not dating anybody else—I don't want to date, I don't do it anymore—" A thought stopped her. "Are you seeing someone?"

"No." He slid his hands along her jaw and tilted her face toward him.

He kissed her again, and this time there was nothing sweet about it. It was hot and hard and deep and wet. Hadley swayed against him, moaning, her knees buckling, her hands digging into his thick hair. If his arm hadn't been braced across her back, she would have fallen open on the ground right then and there, wedding party be damned.

When he pulled away, they were both heaving for breath. "See?" she said, when she found her voice. "Good. Together."

"I'm not seeing anyone—" He sucked in air. "Because I want to be with you."

"You can be with me." She deliberately misunderstood him. "Take me back to your place." She ran her hand up his chest. His shirt was damp with sweat.

He turned her around until her back was pressed against his chest. "I want to make love to you," he said in her ear. She shivered. "I want to go to the movies with you." He stroked her neck, her collarbone, her shoulders. "I want to take you and your kids skiing." He pushed her dress and strapless bra out of the way, exposing her to the cold night air. She breathed in sharply. "I want to have you over to meet my parents." His hands were doing unbearably erotic things to her breasts. "I vant to be," he said in an exaggerated German accent, "your boyfriend!"

She laughed, one sharp laugh that speared painfully through her. No one had ever tried to seduce her with *Young Frankenstein* before. Kevin Flynn was a dangerous, dangerous man. She stepped away from him, tugging her bodice back into place. She wiped beneath her eyes with her fingertips. Took a deep breath. Turned around. "I'm sorry, Flynn. This is a onetime offer."

He was very still. Finally, he said, "We are good together, Hadley. As partners. As friends. When we're with your children. When we're alone." He opened his hands. "Why won't you give us a chance?"

"You're too young."

"I'm twenty-six. My dad was married with two kids when he was my age."

"We work together."

"So we tell the chief. Get it out in the open."

"And when we break up? Then what happens? I have to leave the best job in town and what? Waitress? Commute an hour away from my kids every day?" The heat he had roused in her leached away. She twitched with cold.

Flynn bent down and retrieved her shawl from where it had fallen in the frost-touched grass. "Do you start every relationship with an exit plan? Or is it just me?"

She took the shawl and wrapped it around herself. "When I didn't have an escape plan, I wound up regretting it."

"Okay, then. *If* we break up, I'll resign. I could get a job with the staties or in the Albany force, no problem."

She laughed shortly. "You're crazy."

He took a step toward her. "No, I'm not. I'm just not going to assume it won't work out between us. Hadley—" He reached out, as if he were going to take her in his arms again, then curled his hands into fists instead. "I'm sick of trying to stuff my feelings for you into an acceptable box. I like you. I respect you. I admire you. But I also love you, and it's killing me to see you every day and not be able to be honest about that."

"You don't love me. You just loved the sex."

"Oh, Jesus, Hadley. Are you even listening to yourself? If all I wanted was a roll in the hay, we'd be headed for my apartment right now."

She felt brittle, exposed, like the fragile, half-frozen wildflowers around them. "You can't love me, Kevin. You don't even know me."

"I love what I do know." This time, he did wrap his arms around her. "Let me in, Hadley. Let me see the rest of you." He kissed her, lightly at first, then deeper, pulling her hard against his body. Oh, God. She wanted him. He was young and strong and ardent and more innocent than she had ever been. She wanted to crawl inside him and forget herself for a while.

He eased away from her just enough to speak. "Give me a try, Hadley."

She pictured letting him get to know her. To know her history, all the crappy things she'd done, all the terrible choices she'd made, all the shit she had dealt with. She pictured him backing away, not showing up, making excuses. She knew she wouldn't be able to stand it when that happened. "No." She pushed him to arm's length. "You were a good lay, Flynn." She marveled at how she sounded. So cool, so unemotional. "But I'm not interested in a relationship with you."

"No." He shook his head. "I don't believe you. Tell me you don't feel anything for me. Look me in the eyes and tell me all of this"—he pressed her hand to his chest—"is just one-sided."

God. He still thought lovers couldn't lie to him face-to-face. She looked into his eyes. "I don't feel anything for you. It's all one-sided." She thought she might throw up the ginger ale.

He dropped her hand. Stepped away. Turned his back to her. "God," he whispered. "God." He drew his forearm across his eyes. Finally he turned around again. "Okay. Okay." He rubbed his hands over his face. "I guess I really should've listened the first five or six times you slapped me down." He laughed without humor. It was a sound so foreign to him it made her heart twist.

"Look, Flynn, we can still be—"

"Friends?" His voice cracked. "With me slicing myself open every day and you waiting and dreading the next time I break down and beg you to love me? Is that what you really want?"

"No." Her throat was raw and tight. "I guess I don't."

"I didn't think so." He gestured toward the tent, glowing in the darkness. "Come on. I'll walk you back."

"You don't have to do that."

"Yes. I do."

She didn't argue. They walked through the field, side by side, separated by cold air and unspoken words. He left her at the entrance to the tent. "Aren't you coming in?" she said.

He shook his head. In the light, he looked like he had at Ellen Bain's fatal accident. Weary and sad and older than his years. "My coat's in the inn. I'm going to go home. Good night."

She watched him cross the plush yard. Mount the terrace. Disappear through the inn's French doors. She was strong. She could let him go.

She couldn't stop the voice in her head, though.

There you are.

THURSDAY, OCTOBER 27   When they went for Opperman, they let Russ
tag along. It wasn't his arrest—in the ten days since he had called in Ellen
Bain's evidence, the Army CID, the FBI, and the Treasury Department
and the GAO had all jumped on board. He was low man on that totem
pole. The army guys were respectful, and the Feds were polite, but every
investigator and agent he met let him know—subtly or baldly—that this
case and this collar were way out of his league. He just smiled and let his
Cossayuharie accent thicken until Tony Usher, who was on the prosecu-
tion team, said, "Cut it out, goddammit. You sound like you're audition-
ing for the lead in *Li'l Abner*."

Waiting in an unmarked government vehicle outside the Algonquin
Waters Spa and Resort, it was worth it. They could have called him a
traffic crossing guard and asked him to fetch the coffee, and it would
have been worth it.

"You ready?" Tony put on sunglasses against the early morning sunshine.

Russ checked his gun and reholstered it. "Oh, yeah."

Tony looked at his watch. "The MPs should be pulling Wyler McNabb
in just about now." He glanced over the seat to the CID investigator waiting with them. "And Arlene Seelye."

The radio crackled. "Hotel team, this is Square One." An anonymous
van held the FBI control team, which would be coordinating the raids on
BWI Opperman's Plattsburgh matériel depot as well as their offices in
Baltimore. "We are good to go."

Russ, Tony, and the CID investigator got out. Throughout the parking
lot, car doors slammed as agents and accountants and lawyers and evidence techs finally made their move. Bellhops stared and guests scrambled out of the way of the entrance and then the team was inside, barked

commands echoing off the paneled walls, a rumble of feet as they spread out to the offices, the computer room, the registration desk, locking down all communication, seizing every workstation, evidence-wrapping every file cabinet.

Russ caught a glimpse of the manager, her mouth open, as he led the arrest team toward the stairs. "Two flights up here, then stairs on either end the rest of the way up," he reminded them. "One elevator for the guests, one for the employees."

The FBI agent in charge, a short, curly-haired woman who looked way too young for her position, nodded. "You four, secure the elevators, Lofland and Born, with me." She gestured toward the stairs. "You can wait here if you want, Chief."

"I can manage it," he said dryly. They ran up the stairs, one flight, two, three, until they reached the top floor and Opperman's personal suite. They flanked the door, two on each side. Russ had just enough time to wonder who was bringing the battering ram when the teeny-bopper agent pulled out a magnetized card and sliced it through the keyslot. She swung the door open and she and her partner stormed in, shouting, "Federal agents! Stand up and place your hands on your head!" The other agent was right behind them, and then Russ. It wasn't his collar. It didn't matter. They would get the credit, but he got to watch John Opperman slowly rise to his feet, his face twisted in shock and fear. He got to watch Opperman's eyes darting from side to side, looking for a way out, looking for some flunky to make it all go away. He got to watch the moment when Opperman spotted him, his eyes narrowing, the fear on his face curdling into hatred.

"Gotcha," Russ mouthed.

◆ ◆ ◆

They held the CEO in his four-room apartment as the GAO and Defense accountants ransacked the place, loading banker's boxes with papers and external drives and a laptop. Downstairs, and in Plattsburgh and Baltimore, the same evidence hunt was going on.

Opperman lawyered up immediately, and the first suit arrived before they had even moved downstairs. The second and third got there while the first was still haranguing the agent in charge. Russ was impressed. BWI must have hot-and-cold running attorneys, to get them out to this remote corner of New York State so fast.

When the techs had wrung the rooms dry, the agent in charge announced they were taking Mr. Opperman to Albany to process him. The lawyers stopped their arguments and requests and comments, conferred in whispers with the CEO for half a minute, then disappeared through the suite's door.

"Rats leaving the ship?" Russ said under his breath.

The agent snorted. "I wish. By the time we get off the Northway, there'll be six of 'em waiting for us." She glanced up at Russ. "Would you like to help us escort the detainee to our transport, Chief?"

Russ guessed that was his reward for not stroking out during the run upstairs. "Yes, ma'am, I would."

All traces of Opperman's earlier rage and terror were gone. Walking to the elevator between Russ and the agent in charge, two FBI guys looming behind him, the CEO might have been strolling with some low-mid-management employees. He made the handcuffs look like a fashion accessory.

The three FBI agents packed the rear of the elevator, leaving Russ and Opperman staring at their own hazy reflections in the bronze doors. Opperman smiled at himself. "I'll be back here by tonight, you know."

Russ pasted a similar pleasant expression on his face. "I don't think so."

Opperman's smile thinned. "Do you seriously think you've taken me down, Chief Van Alstyne?"

Russ shook his head. "No. I think Ellen Bain and Tally McNabb took you down. I'm just here to witness it."

"Two tragic deaths, which have nothing to do with me."

"The CID's arrested Arlene Seelye, and Wyler McNabb is in army custody right now. I don't know about her, but he doesn't strike me as the kind of guy who's going to go down with the ship. My guess is, he's going to talk like a little girl at a slumber party."

"A disgruntled employee." Opperman's expression was bland. "I have access to the top legal talent in the country. They're going to tie these spurious charges into so many knots, you'll be retired to a trailer park in Gainesville before you see me inside a courtroom." The elevator chimed and the doors opened. They stepped out into the lobby. "You're a little man in a little town who has to go hat in hand before your aldermen to beg for the bullets in your gun and the paper in your copier. You have no idea of the power money can bring to bear, Chief Van Alstyne. None at all."

◆ ◆ ◆

He had to take a walk around the hotel to clear his head after depositing Opperman in the FBI's car. When he finally went back inside, he found Tony conferring with Amy Nguyen, the Washington County ADA, and a federal prosecutor up from the capital. They fell silent as he approached. The Fed excused himself to rejoin his colleagues.

"What?" Russ glanced from face to face. Tony was grim. Amy looked apologetic. "Okay, what's the bad news?"

"John Opperman's lawyers have already opened negotiations," Tony said.

"Christ. That's a land speed record."

Amy pursed her lips. "They want the state to drop the conspiracy to murder charge in exchange for full cooperation on the federal fraud and theft investigation."

"What?"

"It's a complicated case," Tony began.

"So what? It's theft. Murder beats theft."

"Conspiracy to murder." Amy massaged her temples. "Difficult to prove."

"Meanwhile, the Feds want to round up anyone involved with the fraud and hang them up as a bad example." Tony spread his hands. "Don't look at me like that. Do you have any idea how much money just disappears every damn day in Iraq and Afghanistan? If we can put a few heads on pikes to scare the other carrion-eaters away, we will."

"What's a head on a pike, Tony? Five years in a white-collar federal pen?" Russ had to turn away for a moment to control his temper.

"Russ." Amy Nguyen touched his sleeve. "Wyler McNabb will be punished."

"Jesus Christ. I can't believe this. Opperman has one woman killed and drives another one to suicide, and you guys want to take his deposition and send him to a goddamn country club."

"It's not what I want." Amy folded her arms and looked away. "It's what I can get."

"We have to work within the system, Chief." Tony shook his head. "You know how it is."

Russ pictured Tally McNabb floating sightlessly in her pool. He pictured Olivia Bain, pale and stricken. "Yeah," he said. "I know how it is."

◆ ◆ ◆

He knew Clare would be at St. Alban's, and he thought he might be interrupting something, but he didn't care. He needed to wrap his arms around her and smell her hair and remind himself that there were good things in the world. *The peace of God,* she said in the service. God didn't do it for him, but Clare could.

He was surprised to find her walking out of her office, car keys and coat in hand. He grabbed her and hugged her and she worked her arms free and hugged him fiercely back.

"You heard." Her voice was full of relief and sorrow. She pushed away to look him in the face. "Do you want to come with me?"

"Come with you where? Heard what?"

She blinked. "I thought they must have called you first. I mean, they got in touch with me because they need a minister and I'm the only one they know." She shifted her coat to her other arm and tugged him toward the door. "That's what the notification team suggests, you know. Before they leave. They want you to get a friend or a family member and your pastor."

"Clare, what are you talking about? Who called you?"

"The Stoners." Her face, above her white collar, was somber. "They've just received word their son Ethan was killed in Afghanistan."

IN THAT KINGDOM WHERE
THERE IS NO DEATH, NEITHER
SORROW NOR CRYING, BUT
THE FULLNESS OF JOY WITH
ALL THY SAINTS . . .

—*The Burial of the Dead: Rite One, The Book of Common Prayer*

He who raised Jesus Christ from the dead will also give new life to our mortal bodies through his indwelling Spirit. My heart, therefore, is glad, and my spirit rejoices; my body also shall rest in hope. You will show me the path of life; in your presence there is fullness of joy, and in your right hand are pleasures forevermore." The Reverend Clare Fergusson closed her prayer book and let the quiet spread. The sun, warm and bright as butterscotch, slanted across the graveyard, splashing over the markers of Ethan Stoner's forebears. Overhead, a V of geese split the flawless blue sky, silent, except for the thrumming of their wings. It seemed right, Sarah Dowling thought, for a country boy.

Fergusson nodded to the honor guard. The four marines fell in to their places. Two stepped to the ends of the coffin and grasped the flag. A tug, a snap, and they folded it, tightly, precisely, until it was transformed into a perfect triangle of blue field and white stars.

They turned on their heels. One step, two. They drew up and saluted. The white gloves of the guard flashed in the sunlight. One marine held the flag out.

Christy Stoner looked at her mother-in-law, standing behind her. Mindy Stoner placed her hands on the young woman's shoulders and said something in her ear. Christy accepted the flag. "Thank you," she said to the marine. She held it by its edges, looking, in her black dress and heels, like a little girl dressed up as Jackie Kennedy.

The honor guard fell back ten paces and presented arms. When the first volley rang out, the baby, in the care of some family friend, began to wail. The widow handed the flag to her mother-in-law and reached for her boy, clutching him close, kissing and soothing him.

Ethan Stoner's mother watched them, hugging the lifeless flag to her chest, and in her face was a grief so profound Sarah knew she would never reach the bottom of it.

Taps was played by a black-suited high schooler. Too many funerals, Fergusson had told Sarah. Not enough military musicians to go around. When the salute ended, Fergusson doubled over, as if she were bowing to the casket. Sarah was shocked to see her rise with a fistful of dirt. She held it over the now-bare coffin. "In sure and certain hope of the resurrection to eternal life through our Lord Jesus Christ, we commend to almighty God our brother Ethan." She opened her hand, and the dirt spattered across the satin wood. The bald assertion of what was going to happen to the dead man's body was a jarring contrast to the promises of life. Fergusson said something Sarah couldn't make out, and several of the family came forward and did the same thing, stooping and then scattering earth on the casket. "Earth to earth," Fergusson said, "ashes to ashes, dust to dust."

Sarah turned her head to see how the other mourners were taking the primitive ritual. She spotted Trip Stillman and a couple she recognized as the Ellises standing beside Will. The doctor's dress greens and Will's marine uniform stood out against the black and navy all around them.

"The Lord bless him and keep him; the Lord make his face to shine upon him and be gracious to him," Fergusson said.

Another flash of green caught Sarah's eye, and she watched as Eric McCrea made his way through the crowd toward the rest of the group. So. She had been right to come. When she had heard about the young marine's funeral—it was all they were talking about at the IGA—she knew, without a doubt, that her group would be here today. She thought of Tally McNabb, who lay just a hundred yards away, her grave as raw as the wound on Sarah's conscience.

All of her group would be here today.

"The Lord lift up his countenance upon him, and give him peace. Amen."

The mourners murmured their amens.

Fergusson dismissed them, and the crowd began to shift and split, some people departing for the line of cars parked on the access road, others huddling together to talk. The older Ellises said something to Will and headed over to where the Stoners were surrounded by well-wishers.

Sarah walked over to join her people. "So. Tell me how each of you knows Ethan Stoner."

"Broken ulna in seventh grade," Stillman said. "Plus I've set Wayne Stoner's metatarsals twice after his cows stepped on his foot."

"He was in my brother's class in high school," Will said.

"I picked him up a couple times for disorderly behavior." Eric looked back at their stares. "What? He was a wild kid before he straightened out and joined the marines. He did a year's community service for pulling a shotgun on the chief."

Eric thumbed toward the Stoners. Chief Van Alstyne was standing close by the bereaved father, one hand gripping his shoulder tightly. Stoner nodded at whatever it was the chief said; then they embraced in the half-hug of two fifty-something straight men uncomfortable with expressing emotion.

"Did someone forget to tell me we were having a meeting?" Clare Fergusson joined them, looking like an extra in a historical movie in her long white robe and ankle-length black cape.

Stillman nodded to her. "That was a beautiful service, Reverend."

"You usually call me Clare now."

"I do?" He frowned. "Thanks."

Sarah looked at the priest. "How are you doing, Clare?"

"Okay. I've got an appointment with an addiction counselor tomorrow. My husband"—at the words, her face lit up and she smiled an involuntary smile—"is helping me keep things under control."

"Enjoying marriage, are you?"

"It's wonderful." Fergusson glanced over her shoulder to watch her husband walk toward her. "I recommend it for everyone."

McCrea twisted the ring on his finger. "Any progress on that front?" Sarah asked him quietly.

"No."

He didn't say another word. Sarah couldn't tell if that was because things with his wife felt hopeless or because his boss was within earshot.

"Hi," Chief Van Alstyne said. He stood shoulder to shoulder with Fergusson. In his fitted dress jacket with its golden braids, he looked like a palace guardsman keeping watch over a particularly somber princess. "Hell of a thing."

Everyone nodded.

"I talked to him before he left for California for sniper training. Ethan, I mean. Told him to come back safe to us." He smiled a little. "Back in the day, Chief Liddle said the same thing to me, before I shipped out to Vietnam. And here I was, a lifetime later, wearing Chief Liddle's badge, and I remember wondering if Ethan—" His voice cracked. Fergusson took his hand and laced her fingers through his.

What a waste. Sarah could hear it in the air between them. Of course, no one could say it. The war dead are heroes. Their lives can't be counted as wasted.

"So," she said. "How do you all feel now? Here, today?"

They all looked toward the family in black. The girl and her orphaned baby. The mother's ravaged face. The coffin, waiting in front of the delicately concealed mound of soil. There was a long silence.

Finally, Will Ellis said, "Lucky."

Clare Fergusson laid her hand on his shoulder. "Yes," she said. "Lucky."

◆ ◆ ◆

The answering machine was blinking when they got home to the rectory. Clare cast a glance at it on her way through the kitchen. "Oh, God. That better not be a pastoral emergency. I don't think I've got anything left to give today." She headed for the stairs. "I'm going to change out of my clericals. Can you see who it is?"

Russ wrestled out of his close-fitting dress uniform jacket and tossed it over the back of a chair. He punched the button while loosening his tie.

"Hello, Ms. Fergusson, this is the Washington County Hospital Outpatient Clinic, calling about your blood test. I'm sorry about the delay— we're usually much more prompt than this, but Doctor Stillman's sudden retirement caused a bit of confusion over here. In any case, could you please call as soon as you get this? I have important information for you and your primary care physician."

Russ jotted down the number while his insides congealed into a frozen lump. That test was supposed to have been for Trip Stillman only, to determine whether he would write Clare another prescription for sleeping pills and Dexedrine.

"If it's my mother, *you* can call her back and tell her I'm writing the thank-you notes as fast as I can." She wandered into the kitchen in jeans and an old sweater. His wife.

His wife.

"Did you go ahead and ask Trip for another prescription?"

She glared at him, then settled. "No. I didn't. I ran out of sleeping pills two days ago, and I'm almost out of the uppers." She wrapped her arms around him. "I'm serious about kicking them, Russ. If I'm tempted to cheat, I'll tell you."

"You need to call the blood clinic. Now." He pushed her away and gave her the slip of paper.

She frowned as she read the number. "Why?"

"They called you. I don't know why. Just get back to them. Please." He walked into the living room while she dialed. Maybe she didn't think about cancer, but he did. He paced from the sofa to the desk to the teetering pile of gift boxes beneath the front window. Maybe she was happy to ignore the connection between her sister's cancer and her own increased risk of the disease, but he wasn't. He unhooked his parka from the coat tree and re-hung it on a different dowel. They hadn't even had time to move the rest of his stuff into the rectory. He wished he believed in God. It would be nice to have somebody to bargain with. *Let her be okay and I'll*—what? What did people offer an almighty being, anyway?

He forced himself to go back into the kitchen. Clare was standing with her back to him. She was very still. "Are you sure?"

He stopped in his tracks.

"Yes," she said. "Yes, I will." She paused. "No, but I can get a recommendation from my GP." She paused again. "Thank you." She hung up the phone. She didn't face him.

"What?" His voice came out more harshly than he intended. "For God's sake, just tell me."

She turned around. Bit her lower lip. "It's a good thing I was planning to quit the pills and booze." She started to laugh, a loose, helpless laugh that was very close to crying. She held out her hands.

He took them. "I'm holding on."

"Don't let go." She took a deep breath. "I'm pregnant."

For more on Clare and Russ, and the
other books in this series, please visit Julia at
www.juliaspencerfleming.com.

1. What actions of Clare's mark her as a priest? In what ways does she go "beyond the call of duty?" In what ways does she fail in her responsibilities? Is she truly suited for the ministry, or does she belong in the army?

2. What do you think of Tally and Kyle McNabb's troubled marriage? Did they love one another? Was Kyle taking advantage of Tally's position? Could he have saved her life?

3. Is Clare reasonable to feel so overshadowed by Russ's first wife? Is she comparing herself to Linda realistically? Or is she motivated by guilt?

4. Despite being an M.P., Quentan Nichols leads two MKPD squad cars on a dangerous high-speed chase. What was he afraid of? Why was it so important for him to avoid being taken at the hotel? Russ eventually accepts that Nichols was not guilty of embezzlement—do you agree?

5. Was Hadley right or wrong to lie about Eric McCrea's assault in the McNabb's kitchen? Would her expectation—that she would be frozen out by the other cops' "Code Blue"—have come true if she had blown the whistle on Eric? Do you think they'll ever be able to work together in the future?

6. The therapy sessions with Sarah Dowling allow us to see the characters from another, more impartial, point of view. How does Sarah's view of Clare, Dr. Stillman, and Will Ellis contrast with their own self-images?

7. Thousand of vets come home with physical, mental, and emotional problems, just like Will, Eric, Trip Stillman, Tally, and Clare. Are we, as a society, addressing those problems?

8. The story shows us different ways loved ones deal with their soldier's issues. Russ and Flora Stillman worry, but don't press hard for answers. The Ellises believe being cheerful is the right approach. Jenny McCrea prepares for the worst. Should the family members have handled things differently? How? What about the other characters who interact with the returned soldiers? Who has the most beneficial effect?

9. What do you think of Kevin Flynn and Hadley Knox? Is he naive, or genuinely in love? Is she unreasonable, or wisely protecting herself? Why do you think she's so reluctant to let him into her life? Should he have been more assertive in pursuing a relationship? What are the problems inherent in the two of them working on the same small police force?

10. Opperman tells Russ, "You have no idea of the power money brings to bear. None at all." Discuss the role of money in the novel. Is it realistic for the conspiracy to have so many layers? Why did the people who bought into the fraud agree to it? Why do you think Ellen Bain wasn't tempted by the money?

11. Clare is a helper who has a great deal of trouble admitting she needs help. How does this bode for the future of her marriage? Near the end of the book, she resolves to deal with her drug and alcohol addiction. Will she be successful?

12. *One Was A Soldier* ends with a bombshell, but doesn't tell us how Russ and Clare feel about it. What do you think happens next for them? Will pregnancy stress their relationship too much? Will they, in fact, be too old and too involved with work to be good parents?

13. Is *One Was A Soldier* an antiwar book?

For more reading group suggestions, visit
www.readinggroupgold.com.

Made in the USA
Middletown, DE
11 June 2020